FOGBOUND

ECHOES OF ONIRO

I

FOGBOUND

ECHOES OF ONIRO

I

N.J. ALEXANDER

Book Cover Illustration by Félix Ortiz

Book Cover Design by Fay Lane

Map and Chapter Header Illustrations by Dewi Hargreaves

Proofread by Scout Dawson

ISBN: 979-8-9888035-0-8

First Edition: 2023

CONTENT WARNINGS

Alcohol use
Coarse language
Blood and gore
Corpses and skeletal remains
Mind control
Psychological horror
Violence with knives, swords, axes, lances, bows, and magic.

To Mom,
For your support through all things,
this one's for you.

Map of
ONIRO

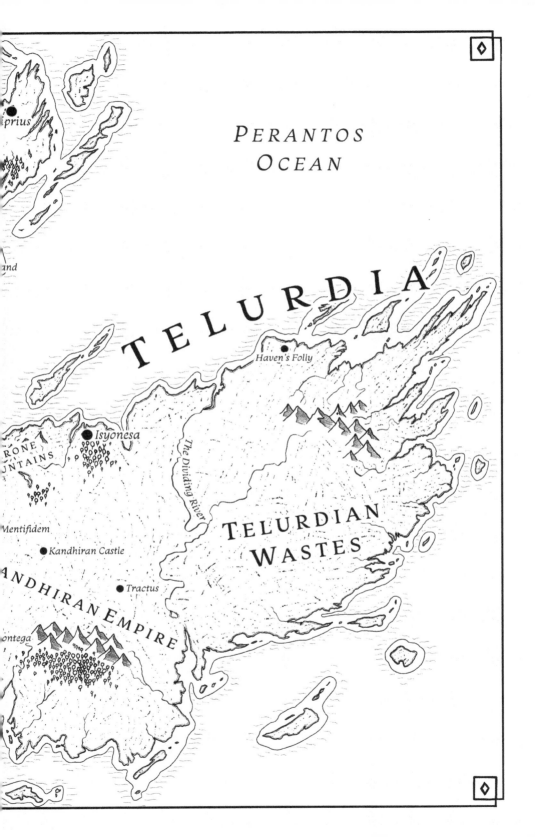

"If you do not run your subconscious mind yourself, someone else will run it for you."
Florence Scovel Shinn

"Saena tells me they're nightmares. I tell her she's right. But I'm lying.

My head shrieks as if lightning courses through my brain, and the fog that follows blurs my eyes like storm clouds in the sky.

I become someone I'm not. See things I shouldn't. Things occurring in the past—or perhaps not at all.

The man in the dark red hood that conceals his face. The beady, flaming eyes that pulsate within. He's not always there, but when he is, everything I've ever learned tells me I should be afraid. That I should tremble and beg for it to end.

But it is not danger I feel, nor fear. It's safety. Comfort. Warmth, like you feel when seeing an old friend after years apart.

I don't know why he's returned. I haven't seen him since I was a child. But with the beating of the drums of war marches my pain.

I can't tell Saena. I can't tell anyone. How could I explain nightmares happening when I'm awake?

All I know is everywhere I go, my shadow follows. With a knife."

-The Diary of Zercien Volnaire
Entry One

PROLOGUE

HOLUNT

Holunt gazed upon the battlefield where his allies fought against the horde, and thought of how he would soon betray them.

He wrapped both hands around the hilt of his broadsword amid the steel clashes pervading the sunset. Twisting his head about, he watched as each of the brave warriors he traveled with did battle against the horrid beings from the world below, whose shadowed bodies and faces swarming with maggots and humming locusts faded in the blood-red sky.

Holunt shuddered. Disgusting things.

But he feared not. Steel upon steel soon gave way to steel upon flesh, and masses of the disfigured shadows littered the dead grass. In time, the enemy would be eradicated. And at last, the plan would begin.

Holunt's ears perked at the thumping of approaching footsteps and spun his sword in unison with his head to turn away a serrated blade. Despite slaying countless numbers of such creatures, just a glimpse of his foe's pitch-black garb, that looked more the part of its misshapen form than armor, was enough to shoot a chilling spike throughout Holunt's body. Its shaded face, two eyes abuzz with flies and locusts, forced a wince. The earthy, decaying soil smell accompanying every movement invaded Holunt's nose and mouth with each breath, the horrid taste glancing off his tongue. He plunged his sword into the fell being's chest up to the hilt, and black blood oozed from the hole. A swift kick knocked the monstrosity from the blade's edge. The locusts buzzed in rhythm with its writhing body until the last of whatever life could possibly remain broke free, and the incessant whirring stopped. Though the stench remained.

It always did.

Holunt let out an exasperated sigh and shivered. "Goddamn dregs."

A light breeze lifted a strand of his brown hair, and he wiped a spot of black blood from his beige cheeks. Before he could turn, a hand plunged onto his shoulder. Holunt gasped and raised his blade, but soon lowered both it and his head when the hood of Voks's dark, bloodred robe met his eye. He groaned and freed his shoulder from his friend's grip.

"Announce yourself next time, will you?" Holunt said. "Nearly cut you in two."

Voks lowered his hood. His dark black eyes shone amid his pale ivory skin and the swirling red sky. A sly smile spread across his face.

"Soon, there will be no next time," he said. "My arrival marks the beginning. And yours—"

"The end." Holunt finished his friend's sentence with a sigh. "I know." He turned his gaze back to the battle. Just as he surmised, the foes from the world below dwindled, falling to the army he commanded.

Holunt threw his head back, looking behind at the mighty Haven's Folly fortress, where they had made their stand just one night prior, and drove the dregs into the open field. A raging battle resulting in the loss of half his fighting force, though he knew each life was a sacrifice for the greater good.

"Holunt." Voks' deep voice snapped him out of his thoughts.

"I know," Holunt said, inhaling a deep breath of stale air to try and quell his now-quivering heart, which he feared Voks may have heard. The primal screams of battle lessened, and even some shouts of victory flew overhead.

Holunt watched as his ally, the mighty Gunvald, slammed his black-bladed axe into a dreg on its hands and knees in an attempt to crawl to freedom, cracking its spine and scattering bone chips mixed with black blood onto his light brown face. When no more assailed him,

Gunvald raised the axe high into the air and whooped a booming battle-cry, and his green eyes met Holunt's.

"Holunt! The enemy flees!"

"At last," said Skjóturi, sheathing her blood-drenched sword with the dragon-head-tipped hilt. She tossed her long, single braid of black hair back over her shoulder. "We've won."

Behind, their army's Sanctum Knight allies stood fast, shields raised, preparing for an enemy assault never to come. Any retreating dregs wandering into their path met the crushing ends of battle-axes and the sharp blades of swords and halberds.

Holunt's lips curled into a smile, though short-lived. Voks' shadow cast over him, stretching in front.

They just won the war—he should be happy. But nothing could appease the dark shrouding his heart from what he was about to do.

Voks' hand gripped Holunt's shoulder, and he led him away, whispering. "It is time. Are you ready?"

Holunt gulped. "Yes. The Sanctum Knights are still in the vicinity, correct?" Though he knew the answer already.

"They will come running as soon as we act."

Holunt peered across the plains, watching as the companions he'd endured so much turmoil with joked and laughed among themselves. He turned back to Voks, closed his eyes and breathed deep.

"Are you sure you wish to go through with this?"

Voks nodded. "You still have doubts, do you?"

"Not *doubt*, per se." Holunt averted Voks' piercing gaze. "Our plan will work. But once we begin, our lives will forever change."

Voks sat still, listening and nodding. Somehow, just knowing his friend would grant an audience to his concerns quelled a bit of Holunt's heartbeat.

"It is because of us two, not them, that we stand here victorious," Voks said, angling his finger toward his circle of allies. "The world is forever indebted both of us. Do you not agree?"

Holunt cringed, and out of reflex he thought, and almost said, how wrong his friend was, but he knew. His companions scattered their weaponry at their feet and danced about. Weapons granting immunity from the accursed magic of the world below. If not for he and Voks retrieving the imbued armaments, none of them would be alive, able to prance about the battlefield, arm-in-arm, as they celebrated now.

"We deserve this, Holunt," Voks said.

Holunt couldn't disagree, nor find any fault in Voks' words. Instead, he nodded, eyes closed and a deep breath at his lips.

"We'll never meet again. Not as we are now, of course," Voks said, and extended his hand. "To our successful futures."

Holunt stared at Voks' hand, at the white and shriveled skin dyed a bloody red beneath the sunset.

The signal. Holunt inched his trembling hand closer. One last look at his companions, still merrily cheering and embracing, but then his eyes were on Voks, whose stare was unwavering.

"Come, Voks," Holunt said. "It is time we finish what we set out to do."

And Holunt grasped Voks' hand in a firm handshake.

Voks flipped his hood over his head, and his serene brown eyes erupted into fiery red jewels.

PART ONE
THE WAR IN THE NORTH

CHAPTER ONE
ZERCIEN

Zercien wrestled his arm free from the chair his baggy sleeve was caught on, careful not to drop the pile of old, crusty books occupying both hands.

"Confounded thing…" he said.

The chair fell over with an echoing thud amid the quiet hallway, but he freed his elbow at last. Heat rose to his beige cheeks, turning them rosy, but when he darted his head about, he saw no one but him occupied the hall. Because he was late for class.

Not a concern for most, but he was the teacher.

With his shoulder, he pushed the door to his classroom open. Children of nobles and other wealthy families of the city of Vellard chatted among themselves and snickered as their teacher, once again, wandered in a quarter of the way through their scheduled lecture.

"I told you Mister Volnaire would be late," he heard little Yua, daughter of a high-brow merchant family practicing more in gossip than trade, whisper.

"You could say that every day and almost be right!" whispered back young Shorli, a girl whom Zercien scolded more than others for speaking during class, followed by a few chuckles. Zercien pretended to ignore them, hiding his smile behind the wall of dusty books in his arms.

"Sorry I'm late," he said without a shred of sorriness in his voice, and not even lifting his head to meet his students' eyes. He knew they would be smiling and laughing at his several-times-employed 'apology.'

Saena often harped on him for it, too, and Zercien didn't have much rebuttal. His teenage and adult years revolved around history and his studies, so his beloved's accusations of squandering a "once-in-a-lifetime opportunity," as she put it, remained quite valid. Especially for someone in their twenty-fifth year. But he told her not to worry. As long as he finished the required coursework, the school was lenient.

Which, of course, was a lie.

While Zercien did consider the risk of one of his students someday telling a parent of their teacher's habitual lateness, he bought their silence with promises of no take-home work whenever he was tardy. A frequent-enough occurrence for the students to keep quiet.

He dropped the books onto his long wooden desk, their weight launching assorted quills and papers into the air. More laughter from the young scholars.

Today's lesson is proceeds swimmingly already, Zercien thought.

He took the top book from his pile—perhaps the oldest one, its cover torn at corners surrounding a faded, near-illegible title—and showed it to the class of well-dressed noble kids. *Legends of Oniro - Complete Edition.*

"Again?" groaned Shorli, before Zercien could even say to open their books.

"This was yesterday's lesson too!" said Yua, and complaint after complained pelted him across the face.

Zercien lowered his hands, palms out, quieting the masses. "We did not finish chapter six yesterday. We need to—"

"Because you were late!" Many voices at once.

Laughter and shouts echoed throughout the small classroom yet again, and soon Zercien placed both hands on his ears as a shield.

"Settle down, everyone. How about this?" he said, and raised one finger. "For the next three lessons I am on time for, there will be no take-home work."

The boy in the front row nearest to Zercien, Clyde, son of a noble family whose renown was bought through silver-tongued bribes instead of merit—though none would admit it—crossed his arms and scrunched his forehead.

"Four." His words soared through the air mixed with spittle.

Bargaining with seven-years, Zercien thought. *What has my life become?*

He went to speak, but his mouth hung agape. A stream of fog rolled under the door, spilling onto the floor and expanding until the classroom filled knee-high with grey. The students' faces twisted in wrinkled foreheads and lips, tilting their heads.

"No, no, no…" Zercien muttered under his breath and winced as a shot of pain pierced his head, like an arrow through the skull. It dissipated, and his back shot up straight without his mind telling it to. He stared with hard eyes at the young Clyde, who squirmed in his seat.

Zercien's words boomed in a powerful voice befitting a military leader. "There will be no negotiation on this topic, young man."

Forgetting the honey that coated his family's tongue, Clyde answered with short, rapid head-nods.

"Good," Zercien said. "Now, everyone, open your books."

Zercien's lightheadedness eased, and he shook his head to free himself from the trance. A brief "phew" exited his lips.

Pretending all was normal, Zercien fingered through the rough, crumpled and yellowed pages of the old book, but as soon as he flipped to his earmarked spot, the arrow again struck his head. He dropped the book, and it slammed onto the desk.

Zercien clutched his temple, his hands pushing at the throbs of his brain throwing itself against the bones in his skull.

His students' shouts of "Mister Volnaire! Are you okay?" came muffled, as if he were underwater. The dense fog rolled throughout the classroom, licking up the wood desks like flame, consuming the students and leaving only Zercien to stare into the dark grey. Below, on his desk, the book flipped itself back open to the spot he'd marked. Two men, side-by-side, covered the pages, each with a blank face. One in light armor, and the other, a set of dark, bloodred robes.

Within the cloaked man's hood, two fiery red eyes popped from the page. Staring, piercing, pulsing with dancing flame. Zercien reached for the book, but his arm would not listen.

"Let me go. Unhand me!" he screamed through clenched teeth as his arm pulled against his muscles, trembling each time he commanded movement.

From the fog, the robed man emerged, the gaze of his beady eyes lancing into Zercien. But the man didn't move, as if waiting for Zercien to act. And act he did—by breaking free of his stupor and slamming the book shut. He blinked hard, but his bleary vision caught the vacant stares of a classroom full of confused students, mouths open, looking at their teacher who was drenched in sweat.

Zercien swept his hands across his desk, scooping quills and books back into his arms and sprinted toward the exit, loose papers scattering in his wake. He opened the door and shot a quick look back at the students before stepping through.

"That will be all for today!" he said.

And he slammed the door behind him.

CHAPTER TWO
PERILOUS MIND

Zercien fumbled with his key, but his quivering fingertips at last allowed him entry into his own home. He stumbled on the way in, another quill and book falling to the floor. Bending to a knee, Zercien's shaky hands at last gave way, and his other supplies joined their brethren. Thankfully, *Legends of Oniro* landed cover side up, and no dastardly page-flipping took place.

With a deep breath, Zercien gathered his belongings and kicked the door shut, rattling the wall—but froze, back straight. Saena *hated* when did that, and she surely heard it. Zercien's eyes flitted about his home, though heard no yelling or angry footsteps.

She must be out, then, Zercien thought, and slouched against the door. Now that his nerves calmed—whether they were lingering from his vision in the classroom or fear of being chastised by Saena, he wasn't sure—Zercien brought his materials upstairs, laying them on his dark-wood desk. He ran a finger over *Legends of Oniro*'s cover and gripped the edge, preparing to turn back to that troublesome spot. He heard the gentle swing of his front door and pulled his fingers away.

"Zercien? Are you home?" came Saena's voice.

The sound of ruffling papers waded into Zercien's ears. He guessed he'd missed a few, and now Saena had to clean up after him.

"Yes, love!" he said. "Be down in a minute."

Zercien took one last glance at the book, inching his right hand toward the cover, but he shook his head and pulled back.

Saena was looking up at him from the bottom of the stairs, with her deep blue, ocean-like eyes capable of sinking him like a ship. She smiled, but tilted her head, as if waiting for an answer to a question she hadn't asked.

"Early day today?" she said.

There it is, Zercien thought.

"Ah, yes—" Zercien's brown eyes bulged as his robe's hem caught the lip of the bottom step. He stumbled but caught himself on the wood banister. He cleared his throat and pecked Saena quickly on the lips.

"I just walked in myself, see?" Zercien waved the silly long sleeves of his professor robes against Saena's face and hair, taking a few of the dark strands with them.

She smiled and pushed him away. "The boy in the front row give you a hard time again?"

Zercien shook his head and turned away to fidget with his robe, hiding his flush cheeks. "They were remarkably well-behaved today, if you can believe it. As a reward, I set them free a tad early."

Saena chuckled, placed both her hands behind his neck, and looked up. She pushed a strand of loose hair over his ear. "Early dismissal and little take-home work. Those kids must love you."

Zercien winced. "Love. Yes. That's the word for it."

She pulled her hands back and turned around to adjust her long, brown skirt. Zercien noticed she was dressed rather well, with an ironed white shirt cut below the neckline and a black belt between it and the skirt that connected the two.

"I've just come back from helping Mayla at the stall," she said, and removed her hair pin, letting the long black locks fall to her shoulders. "She gifted me a spot of the profits, too."

"You know you don't have to work." Zercien put a hand on her shoulder. "I earn more than enough."

She turned and smiled, placing her warm hand on Zercien's cheek, but tilted her head and shut one eye. "Until you forget to take your nose out of one of those books, miss a whole week's worth of lecture, and they tell you to never come back."

She joked, but the tone's not-so-subtle undertones weren't lost on him. Two years Zercien's junior, her wit and snark far surpassed his.

She ran a hand through his a-bit-lengthier-than-medium hair again. "You need a haircut."

"Fair point," Zercien said and cleared his throat, purposely ambiguous to what point he addressed.

She winked again and let go. "Now, what day is it—ah! It's my turn to prepare supper, isn't it?"

Zercien nodded as if he knew. It probably was. But he never could keep track.

Saena drew a few gold coins from a satchel across her waist and rubbed them together. "Let's take a walk back to the market and pick up something fresh, shall we?"

Zercien returned her smile. "If you're sure you want to spend those coins so quickly."

"Just follow me, already." She locked her arm around his and tugged.

He pulled back toward the stairs, planted a swift kiss on her cheek, waved the obnoxious sleeves about, and stepped up onto the first stair. "Let me change out of this ridiculous robe first."

"Be quick about it!" Zercien heard her call up to him as he jogged—carefully this time—up the stairs and turned into the bedroom. Quickly he disrobed, threw the annoying garment on the bed, and replaced it with trousers, a casual white shirt, and a brown vest. Nothing too heavy, as the spring months had rolled in.

He went to leave, but out of the corner of his eye, he caught the faded book cover on his desk. The old, waning letters of the title stared into Zercien like he'd wronged them. He gulped, and his heart thumped. With rapid breaths, he turned on his heels. Slow, nervous.

He wrapped three fingers along the edge of the cover, pushing into the tiny crease his earmark left, and the crumpling of the old paper rushed like a flood into his ears.

Zercien flipped it quick and shut his eyes.

No voices.

No fog.

When he was mostly certain of his safety, he opened just one eye, and the tattered whites of the pages in front revealed the words: *Chapter Six: Before the War*.

He breathed deep again. Even *he* was beginning to tire of his constant sighs. But then, he dropped the book. Little hairs on the back of his neck stood on end. Something was behind him.

Zercien craned his neck backward and caught a glimpse of robes. He darted his head forward, but before he could act, Saena's voice interrupted from downstairs.

"Zerc!" she called. "Are you ready?"

A cool wave of calmness bathed him. She only addressed him such when her annoyance about hit its maximum.

"Coming down now," he said.

He slammed the book shut, and turned and walked downstairs without looking back.

CHAPTER THREE
GENERAL BURGLAND

General Burgland raised his sword from the gut of an enemy soldier and watched as blood surged from the dead man's mouth onto the once-peaceful Entervian soil.

A quick scan of the body found nothing of note. No clues to help his cause. An overzealous scout, he surmised.

With a smirk, he wiped the edge of his blade along his dead foe's cloth shirt. Shaking his head at the notion of this enemy fodder slaying Entervia's greatest general, he continued his vigilance from his perch atop the hill. Though his reach waned with the setting of the late-afternoon sun.

General Burgland, a light brown-skinned man now in his forty-fifth year, had taken to mead a bit more often than in his twenties and thirties, though still possessed a towering stature and the gruff, grizzled features of a seasoned warrior.

But this decorated general was relegated to the back lines. "Too important to lose," he recalled King Durnan always saying to him. "Only take the offensive when necessary," his liege would nag.

Not what the general wanted. Not at all. He couldn't fathom what the issue was—Ankarth is hardly a country. They'd devolved into total anarchy since the wars of old, and most referred to the disgraced land as "The North." He often envisioned charging through the enemy's line and taking out as many of the bastards as he could before falling, his body surrounded by mangled corpses of the scum.

His thoughts were interrupted by an Entervian scout.

"General Burgland!"

"Eh? What?" He didn't bother to face the messenger. His gaze remained transfixed on the battlefield below, on the darkened silhouettes of his fearless soldiers wagering their lives at every second. The clanging of swords and hoarse battle shouts enchanted him as if it were music.

"Sir, the enemy defenses have suddenly doubled. We don't know where their reinforcements came from," said the scout. "His Majesty and Grandmaster General Urian have ordered us to pull back for now, until more soldiers take the field."

Now the general darted his eyes toward the scout. Just a boy—fresh-faced, wide-eyed, without a trace of hair between his top lip and nose. He knew nothing of the ebbs and flows of war.

But neither does Urian, he thought.

"Pull back?" General Burgland said. "We could crush them right here!"

"It's taken a negative turn, General." The young scout cleared his throat. "His Majesty thinks we could be overrun if we stay here."

The general unsheathed his steel longsword. "Then we'll take the fight to them. Kid, return to Vellard and tell that good-for-nothing Urian to send more soldiers, and to start recruiting for active service. We'll need all the help we can get."

"General Burgland, you're serious?" said the scout.

"Yes, but maybe leave out the 'good-for-nothing' part." The general smiled.

The scout gasped and turned to run back to the capital when General Burgland spoke again.

"Tell me this, soldier. Is Urian on the battlefield right now?"

"No, sir."

"What sort of general fails to even take the field during a war?"

"I don't—"

"Precisely."

The scout had nothing to say and remained as steadfast as he could in front of the towering General Burgland.

"Be off, soldier. And be safe," the general said.

"Yes, sir! You as well, General!"

"Good kid," General Burgland said to himself as he watched the scout run back. The boy would likely reach the castle by nightfall.

He groaned as he turned his head back to the battlefield. It seemed the scouting report was correct. More enemy soldiers poured from the darkened corners, the sheer number evident from his perch. General Burgland sheathed his longsword and eyed his valiant soldiers and knights, but then called for them to retreat.

"You bastard, Urian," he said as he turned away, Entervian soldiers climbing up the hill and flying past. "You better send more troops."

CHAPTER FOUR
WITHOUT A COMMANDER

Vellard—the picture-perfect capital city of Entervia. Accomplished in the arts and scholarly pursuits, Vellard paraded fair-sized homes and cottages fitting for the average citizen. People walked along the grassy fields and flower patches without a care in the world, for they knew King Durnan would provide all they would ever need.

While aware of the war, the citizens lived in blissful ignorance to its status, oblivious to their enemy now holding the advantage. With Ankarth's threat escalating, King Durnan sought to end it quickly.

"Urian," King Durnan said, as he sat with Entervia's Grandmaster General and the other members of his Ruling Council. All dressed in casual grey royal jerkins depicting the Entervian Coat of Arms—a crest bearing a sword on its left atop a bed of royal purple, a double-bladed battle-axe to the right bathed in a golden light, and centered atop them both, a triumphant monarch swimming in a deep, royal blue, clothed in white.

He had called a late-night meeting to his Council Chamber, dragging the leaders of Entervia from their soft beds to the hard seats. They sat in a semi-circle about a wood table with a splintered line through the middle from an angry fist at their last meeting. It caught the edge of the etched-on Entervian Coat of Arms, through the monarch's chest.

"What news do the scouts bring? Was our message to General Burgland delivered?" King Durnan said.

Grandmaster General Urian took his seat, ran a hand through his brushed back grey and white hair, and prepared the latest news. "A scout brought word from the field. Says Burgland requested more soldiers. While the scout safely delivered our message, it seems our reckless general interpreted it in his own way."

The king sighed, feeling at a spot on his head where black hair had once grown. Though not a young man any longer, talks with General Urian seemed to sprout greys with higher velocity than aging alone. "I see."

"Well, are we providing them?" Council Member Ellana blurted out. King Durnan cracked a slight smile at the oft-outspoken Council Member and motioned for Urian to respond.

Grandmaster General Urian lowered his black eyes into a fearsome scowl but answered anyway. "I did. They'll arrive in the morning." He paused and looked toward the gulping Council Member. "And do not to take such a tone with me again."

King Durnan shook his head and ignored it. "I trust General Burgland's judgment. Send additional soldiers to the already planned troop in the morning. All the scouts report the same. We're outnumbered."

Grandmaster General Urian stared into the grey ceiling. "We've no one else to send, Your Majesty."

King Durnan stood and placed his hands on the semi-circular table. He looked to each of his council members and nodded.

"You all are dismissed. Urian and myself will discuss our next steps in private."

The Grandmaster General gulped and avoided King Durnan's eye as the Ruling Council's chairs all screeched across the stone floor in unison. The king sat silent until the last of his council bowed and adjourned.

"Urian, we—"

"You're awfully concerned about the North, Your Majesty," Grandmaster General Urian interrupted. "I don't see the need in wasting so many soldiers on a country, and I use that term loosely, held together by ice, rotted wood, and rusty nails."

"Precisely my worry. The country may not be unified, but their attacks have been," said King Durnan. "That first night, if the border guards hadn't—"

"I know, Your Majesty, I know. 'If the border guards hadn't noticed, the initial attack would have reached the capital.' You've repeated this each night since."

King Durnan slammed his heavy fist on the table, knocking his mug of water off and onto the floor, its crash amplified by the room's silence.

"I repeat because you don't understand! This isn't the Ankarth we know." He ran his now-throbbing hand through his greying hair. "They have a leader. They must. How else could they orchestrate the tactical prowess we've seen?"

General Urian shut his eyes behind wrinkled eyelids. "I have been underestimating our enemy, Your Majesty. I could not fathom the North being a threat against us, let alone anyone."

King Durnan glared with his unwavering dark brown eyes into his Grandmaster General's. "We're losing. We've not seen a single enemy general, nor anyone giving orders. You better start *fathoming* pretty damn soon."

Grandmaster General Urian's craggy fingers quivered. "In his request, General Burgland urged the need for armed service recruitment. We can force conscription—"

"No, no, no." King Durnan waved his right hand. "I am not so desperate to send untrained soldiers to their deaths."

He drummed his fingers atop the wood table, their plodding echoes a soothing hymn in the dim chamber. "We will recruit willing participants. Send the Vellardian town guards to civilian homes. Set up posters, flyers, anything, saying all interested persons are to visit the barracks or find any guard on patrol."

"*All* interested persons, Your Majesty?"

King Durnan sighed and slid back onto his chair. "I may not be desperate enough to conscript every citizen in Vellard, but I will not turn down any able-bodied and willing persons."

"Understood, Your Majesty. Any orders for the main force?"

"Focus all efforts on locating an enemy commander."

His Grandmaster General nodded. "It shall be done, Your Majesty."

"Good. You are dismissed."

Grandmaster General Urian pushed his chair back and stood, bowed, and exited the Council Chamber, leaving his king alone in a dark room alit by wavering candlelight.

King Durnan reached for his mug, wishing it were wine instead, but remembered it was now smashed upon the floor, and he had nothing.

Chapter Five
A Foggy Obligation

Z ercien's walk to the schoolhouse led him through Vellard's center, a blooming spectacle of flowers in assorted blues, reds, greens, and whites, all brought together by a central fountain standing taller than he. He started the seventh chapter in the *Legends of Oniro* textbook last night, a summation of the Ancients' War's most renowned hero—Holunt. The topic of today's lecture.

Just a bit more, he thought. Once through today's lecture, he planned to return home and lock himself in his study.

But clogging his view of the scenery was a squad of Vellardian guards in light chainmail armor adorned with the Entervian Coat of Arms, hammering haphazardly scribbled papers and posters on any suitable post.

Zercien made the mistake of meeting one's gaze and sighed as the guard waved and approached. "You, there! You seem like a strong lad!"

Zercien rolled his eyes atop his fake grin but did glance at his arms and thin frame—though covered by stacks of papers and books and hidden by a baggy robe, he did spare some focus for his physique the past few months. Perhaps the guard had a point.

"Me? You must be mistaken. I'm a teacher," Zercien said. "No martial prowess to be found here, I'm afraid."

The guard looked Zercien up and down—which made him blush—and shrugged. "Those books don't look so light, friend."

Friend? Stop this nonsense, Zercien thought, trying his best to hide another eye roll but failed.

"If you'll excuse me, these books *are* quite heavy, and I've a lecture to attend—" Zercien turned to walk away, but the guard's heavy chainmail-covered hand slapped down on his shoulder. He shuddered. A quill dropped to the ground, followed by a floating paper.

"Indulge me, won't you?" the guard said to the back of Zercien's head.

He turned around, brandishing another phony smile. Who was he to brush off Vellardian authority?

"What can this humble schoolteacher do for you, sir?" He tried not to sound annoyed. Though the success was arguable at best.

"You are aware of the war in Ankarth, yes?" said the guard.

You'd have to be a real recluse to not know about it, Zercien thought.

"Yes, sir." He nodded, and the guard turned, pointing to the posters his fellows had placed, his other hand still gripping his shoulder.

"See those?"

Zercien squinted to read the lettering but couldn't quite make all of it out from this distance. "Something, Something, Soldiers Wanted."

He tapped his foot. *Would you get to the point?* he thought.

But the hairs on the back of his head stood on end. The point just became apparent.

"Name's Ardian. Ardian Calvus. Guard Captain here in Vellard," said the guard. "Yours, good sir?"

Zercien's stomach dropped, and he gulped. Nothing good ever came from a guard asking for your name, let alone a *captain* of the guard. "Zercien Volnaire."

"Well, Sir Zercien—" Nothing good ever came from a guard captain referring to a random man on the street as "sir," either—"We've a bit of a situation in Ankarth, I'm afraid." He loosened his grip on Zercien's shoulder, and his hardened white and bearded face contorted a grim, flat-lipped expression. Either this guard was well-rehearsed, or the situation with Ankarth was grimmer than King Durnan let on. Zercien wasn't a religious man, but he prayed for the former.

"A situation?" Zercien said, but immediately cursed under his breath.

Idiot. Don't engage with him. No questions. It'll only make this worse, he thought.

"I'll be frank," Ardian said, and removed his helmet, placing it at his side, revealing a head bereft of even a follicle of hair. It appeared to be shaved by choice, not necessity. Zercien conceded it was a good look for the gruff guard captain.

"Ankarth is stronger than we anticipated," Ardian said, taking Zercien's shoulder in his hand once more. "We need backup. More soldiers for the cause."

Zercien stepped back, pulling out from under Ardian's hand. The thought of being conscripted into Entervian military service was almost enough for him to soil his drawers.

Ardian raised his hands, a sign that Zercien should remain calm. He wasn't exactly sure how, but such was the guard captain's intention.

It didn't work.

"We're not forcing enlistment," Ardian said. "Just asking any able-bodied passersby."

A refreshing breeze flew through Zercien's body as he let his trapped breath escape. He thought he saw the air turn a bit grey but paid it no mind. "You're just… asking?"

The guard captain nodded. "Nothing more."

No harm in that, Zercien thought. Another speck of graying air appeared behind Ardian. His feet grew antsy, and he tapped the heel of his boot on the grass.

"Well, Sir Guardsman, you're making a generous offer, and while I do want to see my country succeed, I simply—" grey fog rolled through in sheets, and Zercien's mouth hung open, unable to finish. Though he urged the word "Cannot" to come to his lips, even lurching his head forward to force it through, his body was incapable of speech.

"Sir Zercien?" Ardian raised an eyebrow at Zercien's retch-like heaves.

A piercing pain lanced through Zercien's head, and he cried out, pressing two fingers against his temple and shutting his eyes. His lecture materials fell to the ground in a jumbled pile of loose books, papers, and quills.

"Sir Zercien? Are you all right?" repeated the guard captain's muffled voice. Zercien's head swirled with rapid punches of pain, but then his eyes shot open into a stern, bold stare right at Ardian.

"Guard Captain Ardian, I am well-trained in the blade," Zercien said, though his mind did not instruct his mouth to speak those words. "And I would be remiss in my duty if I did not offer my expertise to Entervia in her time of need. My country needs me, and you will have my aid."

What the fuck are you saying? Zercien's mind cried, but nothing came from his lips. So desperately he wanted to speak, to take it all back, but no amount of force could expel the words.

The fog obscured his gaze, but he felt the guard's outstretched hand take his in a firm shake. Somehow, his body reacted and returned it.

"Here. Take this," the guard captain said, and placed a quill in Zercien's hand. And in his other, a flat piece of paper. Ardian plucked a small inkwell from his bag and pointed to a dotted line at the bottom.

"If you'll just sign here, please. This is a contract legally binding you to the service of Entervia's military, only breakable by official discharge."

Zercien's hand moved on its own. He watched in horror, with a thunderous heartbeat, as his fingers dipped the quill into the ink and hovered over the dotted line.

His head sparked with the rampage of lightning as he tried in vain to stay his own hand. But nothing worked. He watched in abject horror as his fingers scrawled a signature, signing his life away into military service. Ardian took the contract, nodded and smiled.

"Thank you, Sir Zercien!" he said. "Truly, the Entervian army is grateful for your future service."

He extended his arm for another handshake. The fog lifted, fading as fast as it began, and Zercien's head soon returned to his own control. He absentmindedly shook the guard's hand until he pulled away, snapping back to reality with rapid blinks. The truth at last set in, and Zercien came to the realization that he'd somehow, both unwillingly *and* willingly, signed up for a war.

"What the fuck did I just do," he muttered under his breath, hoping Ardian couldn't hear and put a hand to his now-pain-free forehead.

"Please come to the barracks at this time two mornings from now to complete your Aptitude Exam," Ardian said. "Should you pass, of which I have no doubt that you will, you'll be admitted into Entervia's armed forces."

Zercien scrunched his forehead. His friend Euvard, who yearned to join the army, often spoke of this exam, and his difficulty in passing. "And if I do not?"

Ardian shrugged. "Entervia requires a passing grade for all armed service members, even now. Should you fail, you will be removed from the army."

Zercien's ears perked. "Then I will be ready."

The guard captain smiled. "The entire army—no, the entire country—thanks you, Sir Zercien." He looked down at his new recruit's spilled teaching materials. "Need a hand?"

Zercien raised both eyebrows but looked down to see the mess at his feet. "No, no. I'll handle this." He spoke between sighs.

Ardian nodded and bid Zercien farewell. Zercien watched as he and his fellow guards stuck the last of the posters about the city center.

I've made a right mess of things, he thought as he shook his head.

"Suppose I'd better alert the academy. They won't be pleased their new instructor needs to take a sabbatical so soon," Zercien whispered, and bent down to gather his quills and books. But he straightened his back, face flush with fear as the severity, and stupidity, of what he had just done set in. "What the hell do I tell Saena?"

He fidgeted with a handful of quills and watched as they fell from his weak grasp. "I am so fucked."

CHAPTER SIX
THE SWORD SLAYER

E uvard, enough!" Zercien dropped down to one knee. With his last spurt of strength, he stuck his wooden practice sword into the ground and looked at the gargantuan figure that was Euvard. His massive, muscular shadow loomed over him accompanied by an obnoxious grin. He laid his wooden battle-axe onto the grass and gripped Zercien's hand, helping him to his feet.

"You'll never make it into the army if you can't even go three rounds with me!" Euvard said.

That's the plan, Zercien thought as he caught his breath.

Euvard playfully punched Zercien's shoulder—except, coming from him, it was more like a rock falling from a long drop. "I'm still in disbelief you agreed to join, Zerc."

Me too, Zercien thought. He sighed. "I've had my fill for one day."

"So soon?"

Zercien ran a hand through his sweat-drenched hair and flicked the wet drops to the ground. There was a reason he preferred books.

"Considering your arms are as large as my thighs, I'd say I did quite well for myself," he said.

Euvard lifted his flexed arms into the air. "That's an insult to my muscles."

Zercien shifted his eyes from his legs to his friend's continued flexing. Maybe he had a point. "You are insufferable."

"That's why you love me, though!" And Euvard's hand came crashing down onto Zercien's other shoulder.

He grimaced and rubbed the impact zone where the metaphorical rock struck. "That's it, all right."

They both shared a brief laugh.

Zercien still hadn't a clue why he was so drawn to the muscular jokester, different as they were. But they remained as tight knit as any two friends could boast. Though Zercien *had* fainted upon their first meeting as seven-years, which Euvard reminded him about frequently enough to force an eye twitch.

Zercien had no love for swordplay, or sparring. Unfortunately, his oaf of a friend was correct—he should be able to protect Saena.

But Saena can probably handle herself, he thought.

Besides, it was Vellard. The perfect city of no crime.

Zercien wiped sweat from his brow and stacked his wooden practice sword atop the others on the grass in front of Euvard's home. How Mayla allowed this was beyond him.

"How fares your studying?" he said. "I can tutor you if you like."

Euvard huffed, and waved his hand. "I'm prepared."

Zercien smiled, but doubted that highly. His friend yearned to be a soldier since his fifteenth year. While his martial prowess was clear, passing the Aptitude Exam proved his greatest obstacle.

"I may have already failed it seven times, but I know it all now," Euvard said. "Soon enough, we'll both be off to the barracks to join the army!"

Hopefully just one of us, Zercien thought. *And that one isn't me.*

While Zercien wiped his hands on a cloth, out of the corner of his eye, he noticed a tall, lean figure wearing a black, cloth jerkin, and pants to match. With light steps hardly disturbing even the blades of grass lining the streets, the figure passed through like a shadow. They made brief eye contact, and Zercien couldn't help but stare into his deep, black eyes. A perfect match to his dark skin marred with small scars.

A hand came down on his shoulder, and he flinched.

"Jumpy, Zerc?" Euvard said.

Yes, I tend to jump when large people strike me, Zercien thought, and pointed in the stranger's direction. "Who's he?"

"I know him!" Euvard said far too loudly for Zercien's comfort.

"I'm concerned that this doesn't surprise me."

"Is that supposed to be an insult? That's Lloyd."

"Odd sounding name."

Lloyd turned away, his shoulder-length dark hair twisting in unison, though Zercien could still sense his gaze upon him. Over Lloyd's back rested a sheathed longsword, and attached to his belt, a serrated dagger hung loose. But the point of his jawline looked as sharp as any blade.

"How do you know him?" Zercien said.

Euvard shrugged. "He saw me training one day and said I was a 'worthy partner.' And now, we make a habit of it."

Zercien crossed his arms. "You don't think he looks dangerous?"

Euvard slapped both hands on his waist before erupting into a loud, boisterous laugh. "One of the scariest men I've ever seen in my life! Hardly says a word, just swings his sword around. But his technique?" Euvard whistled. "A thing of beauty. I think he's a Meistari."

The Meistari. Not surprising for Euvard to know about the elite warriors of Ariglioth, renowned for their combat prowess and unmatched sword-and-spear-play. Zercien never met one, though if he were to hazard a guess at the kind of person to look the part, it was Lloyd. But what would a Meistari be doing this far from Ariglioth?

"And you never thought he might use his technique on *you* some day?" Zercien said.

"He seems honest, actually," Euvard said.

"But didn't you say—" Zercien shook his head. "Just be careful, will you?"

Euvard didn't answer. Instead, he stared at three men in raggedy clothes, armed with swords, approaching Lloyd from behind.

"Zerc, over here," Euvard whispered and pointed.

"I see one dangerous-looking person," Zercien said. "Why would I move from this spot when three more join his company?"

Euvard was already walking. "Just follow me."

Zercien shrugged and did so. Once he caught up, Euvard beckoned him to crouch behind some bushes. Though Euvard's crouch wasn't much shorter than a normal person standing straight, Zercien obliged.

"People challenge Lloyd to swordfights in droves," Euvard said as the two watched the men approach Lloyd. "He told me that once. But I haven't seen it yet. One of these dolts might be wanting to try his luck."

"Euvard!" Zercien whispered, louder than he intended, but hushed himself. "We're to just sit here and watch?"

Euvard nodded.

"Of all the wretched ideas you've had, this may be at the top."

"Don't ruin the fun now, Zerc." Euvard flicked his hand in his general direction. "It's just a duel! Not a fight to the death."

"Did Lloyd *tell* you these were not fights to the death?"

"Well, no, but look! Someone's right behind Lloyd. We'll miss it if we stay here."

Zercien shook his head and sighed. "Fine. But we stay out of his sight."

The two crept further, jumping behind trees and bushes to stay hidden. Zercien's heart thumped with the strength of war drums, and a dull pain reverberated through his temple. *Not now,* he pleaded his mind. Fortunately, no fog. Yet.

Up ahead, one of the men shouted at Lloyd, gesturing the swordsman to turn. He didn't look especially muscular or battle-scarred, though he sported a few scrapes and bruises along one exposed arm. "Lloyd!"

Slowly turning to face him, Lloyd said nothing.

"Lloyd, I come seeking a challenge!" the man said again.

The swordsman didn't flinch, nor look this man in the eye.

"Scared of me already, Mister Almighty Swordsman?"

He was met with a piercing gaze capable of instilling terror into a seasoned general and silenced his laughter. Lloyd approached his challenger and looked him up and down.

"Your words are strong, but your sword arm says otherwise," he said. His voice was low and cold, slicing the air with icy wind.

The man gulped while his friends backed away.

"Tell me, is a challenge truly what you seek? You will not win," Lloyd said. "If you choose to flee now, I will not chase you."

"I don't run," his challenger said, and fumbled for the hilt of a sword on his side.

"Very well."

Lloyd reached over his back and pulled the longsword free, never losing eye-contact as he pointed the blade at his neck. "I trust you are prepared, for you've sentenced yourself to death."

"What did he just say?" Zercien whispered to Euvard from the bushes.

The man lunged toward Lloyd, but he nonchalantly stepped to the side and slashed across his body, the steel of both blades colliding. His opponent's sword flew from his grasp, and far out of reach. The challenger turned to flee but was cut short by Lloyd running his sword halfway through his chest.

"He killed him!" one of the others yelled as his friend fell. "After him!" The two drew swords and charged at Lloyd.

He parried both attacks, stunning one of the men. In an instant came the tip of Lloyd's sword, shoved deep into his throat. Pulling it free in a spurt of lost blood, Lloyd spun around, lunging into a stab that found the last assailant's midsection.

The man fell, clutching his wound to stop the oozing blood, and crawled with one hand pulling the grass. But soon he had a blade buried into his back.

Lloyd wiped his sword in the tall grass just as the heavy footsteps of a Vellardian guard rushed to the scene.

"What in blazes happened here?" The guard shot wide-eyed looks at the three dead men, and locked his gaze on the dark-garbed swordsman. "You, there! What have you done?"

Now turning to make eye contact, Lloyd's stare paralyzed the guard. He stood as still as a signpost.

"I have committed no wrongs," Lloyd said. "I was challenged."

The guard flinched. Zercien surmised the unfortunate patrolman realized whom he spoke to.

"I—yes, I'm sure," the guard said. "But you cannot just leave these bodies on the side of the road."

The swordsman said nothing as he sheathed his blade and turned in the opposite direction. "I believe it is your duty to maintain the cleanliness of the city." And Lloyd dashed away in a flash of shadow, leaving the bloody corpses.

Zercien's hands shook hard enough to cause the ground to rumble beneath his feet, or so he felt, as he and Euvard stood.

"Huh, maybe it *was* a duel to the death," Euvard said amid a long, troubled breath. "Zerc, are you—you're shivering!"

"Sorry," Zercien said, and gulped. He forced his eyelids shut, but his mind's eye turned into a mess of grey swirls. The mists reappeared, and in front of him a shadowed man, dressed in mail of pure black, eyes replaced by swarming locusts and maggots.

Stop, stop, STOP, Zercien yelled at his mind. *Make it stop...*

"Zerc!" Euvard's voice reverberated throughout his clouded thoughts.

Zercien crashed back-first onto the grass, vision blurring until all became black.

Chapter Seven
A Soft Side

Zercien's vision still swirled in haze as he reached out to both sides, his hands falling onto a hard wooden surface. A blurry waving hand interrupted his view, which he instinctively grabbed, and was helped to his knees.

"Where am I?" he said.

He expected Euvard, but it was a woman's voice. "Don't even know where you are? You okay?"

Zercien turned to face the voice, startled at hazel eyes and fair white skin, and medium-length blonde hair. His vision cleared—he was inside Euvard's house. "*Mayla*? This is embarrassing."

"Not at all." Mayla patted him on the head as if he were a pet. "Now where the hell is that oaf—Euvard! How long does it take to fetch water?"

"Here," came his friend's voice from another room. Euvard carried in a mug and bent down to hand it to Zercien. He gulped the icy water in large swigs.

"Sorry, Zerc, I didn't know what to do," Euvard said. "You look okay, though."

"I'm fine," Zercien said with a sigh. "I think."

"What happened out there?"

"I don't know. After he killed those people, I—"

Mayla scrunched her face at Euvard and punched him on the shoulder. "Start talking."

Euvard rubbed his shoulder. "I thought bringing Zerc back would be the most important—"

She needed no words to stop Euvard from tripping over his. Her hardened glare and impatient foot-taps hurried him along. Though Mayla's anger was palpable, Zercien couldn't help but let his lips curl into a faint smile. Only one person could reduce such a behemoth of a man to the size of a pebble.

"Remember Lloyd?" Euvard said. "Someone challenged him to a duel, and we watched. Well, Lloyd killed him. And his friends. But they looked to be bad people, so—"

"You were with *Lloyd?*" Mayla said. "What have I said about him?"

"Not *with*, but—"

Mayla shook her head and pulled Zercien to his feet with what looked like no difficulty whatsoever.

Has she been training with Euvard? Her arms look stronger than mine, he thought.

"It doesn't matter," Mayla said. "You two are unbelievable."

"I can't fathom how someone could slaughter three people within minutes and just walk away," Zercien said.

"To be blunt, Zerc, he probably didn't care," Euvard said with his arms raised. "I've hardly talked to the man, but I can already sense nothing bothers him. And from what we just saw, he doesn't give a damn about people he kills, too."

Zercien shuddered. "It's almost not human, don't you think?"

But Euvard had stopped paying attention to Zercien and proceeded to twirl his finger in Mayla's hair. Trying to get back on her good side, it seemed. She failed to hide her smile.

"I'll forgive you for being a dolt. *Again*," she said.

Zercien couldn't help but smile, too. It was amusing for him to see how gentle and sensitive his brute of a friend was when around her.

"Zerc, how about you have dinner with us?" Euvard said, wrapping his arm around Mayla's waist. Though everyone was short compared to him, Mayla still reached his shoulders.

A tempting offer. Euvard did most, if not all the cooking, and he'd grown quite skilled. Zercien could still smell and taste the slow-simmered beef and potato stew from several months ago. But what followed was a reluctant head nod.

"I shouldn't," he said. "Promised Saena I'd be back for dinner."

"She'd probably have your head if you were late," Euvard said, and Mayla punched his arm again.

"You should get home, then, if you're able," she said and exchanged glances with both he and Euvard. "You both have an important day tomorrow."

Zercien sighed. Despite his short lived, unintended unconsciousness, he appreciated the brief diversion from the next day's plans. "My invitation for a tutoring session is still valid, by the way."

Mayla crossed her arms in response, turning to face the blushing Euvard. "Might want to take him up on it this time."

He'd offered a lesson before each and every one of his friend's failures, but Euvard never obliged. Odd, but maybe it was a point of pride for him.

Though after seven tries, I'd think pride would be the last thing on someone's mind, Zercien thought.

"Maybe you're right," Euvard said. "Zerc, let me walk you out to the road and we'll talk about it."

Mayla nodded, and smiled at Zercien. "Tell Saena she's free to come back to the market stall anytime. She's quite skilled already."

"I'll be sure to." Zercien laughed, and Mayla headed toward the kitchen.

While walking from Euvard's front door to the main street, Zercien saw the flexed tension in his arms, a slight quiver in his step. Once far enough away from the house, Euvard broke the silence. "Mayla's birthday is soon. I need to tell you what I have planned for her."

Zercien raised his eyebrows. "You do?"

Euvard groaned. "Yes, I do. But first—laugh and I knock you out."

"After I *just* came back from being knocked out?"

"I'm not joking, Zerc."

Zercien blinked hard. Was he still in his fogged state? No. This was the real Euvard. Somehow.

"I apologize," he said. "I promise not to laugh."

"All right." Euvard huffed a deep breath and slowly let it free from his lips. "I hired a prominent artist from the castle to paint her portrait. Two portraits, to be specific. One for the wall, of course, but another for my pocket. I may be a soldier soon, and I need a way to keep her with me."

Zercien couldn't help it. His smile stretched from ear to ear, and a slight chuckle escaped. Euvard's face flushed bright red.

"Not laughing at you, friend," Zercien said, holding his hands up. "I'm amused at the change I see in you whenever Mayla is involved."

Euvard's blush subsided. "I've been saving a long time for this. It needs to be perfect."

"I imagine so. How did you learn of this painter? I didn't take you for a connoisseur of artistry."

Euvard raised his hands, palms facing the sky. "Dropped off some supplies to Mayla one day, and the idea struck me when I saw another stall lined with paintings of fields and trees. The vendor said they all came from Archibald, and he offers discounts for portraits."

"You certainly are good to her," Zercien said and patted his friend on the back. He wished he could be so thoughtful.

Toward the end of the road, the two said their goodbyes, and Zercien turned onto his street.

An out-of-the-ordinary number of guards patrolled—at least twice as many as normal. They all walked past him, said nothing, and continued in scattered directions.

Looking for more recruits, I'd wager, Zercien thought.

Vellardians didn't know much about Ankarth, and neither did he, despite his studies. All books he'd read said after the Ancients' War, Ankarth became a sparsely populated country of total isolation with no leadership to speak of, let alone an actual army. Nothing could thrive in their frigid clime. To require more soldiers for combatting such a nation, something else had to be afoot.

Although Zercien often listened to Euvard complain about Entervia's military force—they were "weak," soldiers were "soft" and "untrained," "Urian is the worst general"—he didn't pay much attention. He assumed the intense dislike stemmed from Euvard's inability to pass the Aptitude Exam, but now his words rang differently.

What if Entervia is weak? Zercien thought. *The only combat the army sees is against bandits on the borders. Are we prepared for war?*

CHAPTER EIGHT
UNDER THE TABLE DEALINGS

Zercien stood at his front door, heart beating fast. Saena was expecting him home for dinner, but nothing would prepare her for what he was about to admit.

He hadn't told her anything about his research. Or about what had occurred at Vellard's center yesterday morning. But with Euvard and himself set to take the Aptitude Exam tomorrow morning, he couldn't keep up the lie.

He thought to tell her his plan. Fail the exam on purpose and be discharged before even starting his enlistment. Foolproof.

She greeted him with a brief hug and a kiss, and he forced a smile. Dinner was already on the table. He sighed and sat down. Though the chicken and a side of fresh carrots and asparagus delivered a delicious scent that wafted throughout his body, his stomach refused to growl.

He forced it down, all while trying to hide the knife wobbling in his shaky fingers. Cutting through, he envisioned the white meat of the chicken as an enemy, ripe for the slaughter, and its juices ran red on his plate.

He dropped the knife. It clattered with an echo as it crashed and fell to the table and then the floor.

"Are you all right, dear?" said Saena.

Zercien shook his head. The chicken in front and its juices remained normal. No red, no visions of the murder he'd need to employ while on the field of battle.

Just think of the plan, Zercien, he thought. *Just think of the plan.*

"Fine, love." He flashed a quick smile and stretched his arm underneath the table to find his lost utensil, scraping his hand about the floor while maintaining awkward eye contact and a smile at his beloved. "My hands are just a bit shaky from today." He strained as he reached further, and bent his head beneath the table's lip up to his eyeballs. "You know how Euvard is!" He fake-laughed and she returned it with her own, albeit with curved lips and a tilted head.

"You're certain everything is okay?" she asked.

Soon Zercien lowered his head under the table, no longer able to see Saena, with the intention of finding his blasted knife, but mostly to stop himself from making this even more awkward. "Just fine! Nothing to worry about!"

Though Saena was concealed by the tabletop, Zercien knew she was making some sort of crooked face.

"What did Euvard teach you today?" Saena's strained voice came through while Zercien dropped to his hands and knees. He breathed a quick "Yes!" as he located the fallen knife between the table legs.

"It was fine." He winced when he realized the nonsense that was his answer.

Zercien shot up with an "Oh!" but smashed his head into the underside of the table, rattling the plates and silverware atop.

"That's enough!" Saena said, and Zercien heard a chair scrape against the floor as she slid out. Her upside-down face peered underneath the table, long brown hair falling to the sides. Zercien smiled while rubbing the lump on his head. But instead of anger, she just cocked her head. "Can I come in?"

Damn it, he thought. Try as he might, it would be impossible to resist.

Zercien tapped the floor next to him, and she sat. He hoped she too realized how silly this looked.

"Want to tell me the truth?" Saena nuzzled her head against his arm.

He breathed in enough air to make his stomach bulge. "Yesterday, while on the way to my lecture, I was approached by a captain of the Vellardian guard."

He stopped and looked down at her, but she just returned a narrow-eyed stare, prodding him to move along. Despite her eyes being half-concealed behind dark hair, a rush of heat flowed through his head.

Should he tell the truth? His mind wavered at the thought of un-weaving a host of other white lies about his condition, his episodes, his visions…

"And I was conscripted," Zercien said at last.

Saena raised her head from his shoulder, her eyes turning wide, the blues transforming from cheery to somber, and all color rushed from her face.

"Conscripted? For the army?" A nervous question, Zercien assumed. Saena knew what he meant, but didn't want to believe it. And of course, she had a right to *not* believe it considering it wasn't *exactly* how the events occurred, but close enough.

"The guard captain saw me and said I looked the part of a warrior." Zercien shrugged.

She took her time in responding, tilting her head to one side. Her face grew pale. "I thought those signs said they were looking for volunteers."

Zercien winced.

Should've known she'd see the posters, he thought. *Goddamn guards must have littered the city with the things.*

"That's what I told him," Zercien said. "But he said the Vellardian Guard had the authority to hand-pick recruits. Not much I could do."

But then came Saena's open palm, smacking him right across the arm. A stray tear formed in her eye.

"Nothing you could do? You could say no! You could have run away!" She rained a fury of light punches and kicks onto his side. "Were you even thinking?"

Zercien grabbed Saena's right arm as she landed another blow, and with a gentle tug, held it back. His other hand caught her left, and she was stuck watching him.

"You know they would have me arrested if I disobeyed the city guard," he said.

Saena let her hands down to the floor. "I know. But we've never left Vellard. No one does. I'm scared of what's out there."

Zercien raised his hand against her face.

She's right, he thought.

No Vellardians have reason to leave, and thus, no one did. Everything anyone could want was here. The thought of saying goodbye to their cozy city's walls did frighten him, too, and he shuddered.

"You have no reason to worry," he said. "I thought of a plan."

Some color returned to her cheeks. "Is there a way out of it?"

"The Aptitude Exam. All new army recruits need to pass. But if I were to fail—"

"Then they'd deny you!" Her smile at last returned as she spoke. "You will—"

"Purposely fail, yes."

She hugged him but couldn't stop a chuckle from slipping through. "A teacher failing the Aptitude Exam. Almost comical, if you think about it."

Zercien's mouth hung wide open as she buried her head into his chest, thankful of a way for him to evade his new armed services contract. But he hadn't thought of the aftermath. Would people know? A distinct possibility.

The shame, the humiliation. Would the schoolhouse no longer welcome him? He thought of the laughter he suffered on a near-daily basis for his habitual lateness, and how it wouldn't compare to the ridicule he'd meet should word of him failing a test make the rounds. Termination may be a more favorable outcome than facing his students.

And what if he told the truth that he purposely failed? Would the army find out and force him back?

He looked down at Saena, who still clutched him tight. Thinking he would be whisked off to war one second, then learning he'd found a loophole the next. But Saena's elation, those happy eyes, he couldn't disappoint those. He'd sooner endure a lifetime of embarrassment than see his life with her fall apart.

CHAPTER NINE
THE FAILED EXAMINATION

Z ercien and Saena's front door rattled under the weight of heavy fists. But Zercien didn't jump from his seat at the table, and neither did she. Only one person they knew was so blissfully unaware of how brutish their everyday actions were.

"It's still quite early," Zercien said as he opened the door to find Euvard, without his usual big, toothy grin. "Test isn't for another few hours."

"You're always late. Wanted to make sure you were up and ready." Euvard had his hands in his pockets.

Zercien shook his head and invited him in. "You are a terrible liar."

The corners of Euvard's fake smile stretched obnoxiously.

Zercien pulled out a chair and offered Euvard some of the last bits of their breakfast to calm him down—an apple, a slice of bread, a little cheese.

"What do you want to know?" he asked.

"What are you on about?" Euvard said with his mouth full of apple, its juices escaping down his chin. "Just here because I was annoying Mayla with my pacing all morning."

Zercien threw a quick glance at Saena as she raised her fist against her mouth, hiding a growing smile and laughter.

"Is it mathematics?" Zercien asked. "History? Grammar?"

Euvard set down his half-eaten apple and slouched. "Fine. *Fine*. I was trying to cram and thought maybe, if you'd want to give me a little—"

Zercien chuckled. "Some tutoring. Of course."

"I'm *elated* you're seeing the humor in all this, but I've failed this damned exam seven times already. The official rules say I can't even try again this year, but due to the urgency of recruitment, they're letting me have another go. This is my only chance."

Zercien said nothing and pulled a few books from under the table, stacking them on top of each other. Heavy, thickly bound volumes on history, math, sentence structure, even war tactics.

"Were you planning this?" Euvard thumbed over the books' covers.

"Call it a hunch," Zercien said, and took the top book—*The Ancients' War, Volume One*. "We've enough time to start here."

Euvard looked on, wide and hungry, as Zercien flipped open to the first page.

"The Ancients' War," Zercien cleared his throat and ran a finger along the text. "These horrid beings and beasts endangered all of humanity. Not just here on this continent, but on Telurdia, too." His fingertip brushed a humanoid draped in pitch black. Sockets of decay and maggots sat where its eyes should have been. Another depicted beside it was shaped more like a bipedal beast, with claws as long as knives. A chill coursed down his spine.

"Zerc!" Euvard said. "The Ancients' War, the Seven Legends— what is this, the first thing you teach those noble brats? I know this already."

"Well, do you know how it started? How it ended?"

Euvard raised his index finger and mouthed some words he wished to speak, but ended up just making random squeaks, ums, and ahs.

"Sorry. Bit of a trick question." Zercien turned Euvard's attention to the next page. "No one has ever *proven* how it all began, but there's some popular theories. The creatures arose from the world below, seemingly at random, and seven gallant heroes, led by the legendary Holunt, arrived just in time to drive them back—"

Euvard's laughter interrupted him. "You love your stories, don't you?" Euvard lowered his eyes and adopted a mock-serious tone. Unfortunately a quite adequate impression of Zercien, accompanied by exaggerated storytelling and hand motions. "Creatures from the world below! Heroes rising *just in time* to save us all!"

Zercien tried to hide his smirk but was unsuccessful, while Saena let a brief laugh free. "Do you want to fail?"

"You have to admit, the whole thing sounds farfetched," Euvard said.

"While you are correct that no one can prove the world below ours exists, this is the generally accepted theory, and you should know it. We *do* have evidence of the creatures that invaded. And I can think of no better place for them to reside than in the deepest and most depraved places in Oniro."

Meanwhile, Saena rose from her seat and chuckled. "I'd love to stay for this *enthralling* tutoring session, but I need to see your lady at her market stall."

Euvard grinned. "Mayla always says you're a welcome presence."

"It's quite fun," Saena said, fluffing her hair once or twice. Zercien didn't notice a difference. "And a way to supplement our income when my dear old Zercien oversleeps."

Thanks for saying it out loud, Zercien thought.

Saena kissed Zercien quickly on the cheek and patted Euvard on the shoulder before she made for the front door.

"Good luck today! Hope it all goes the way you want!" She stared right at Zercien, and left.

Zercien gasped—the plan. What would Euvard think?

He looked on at his friend as he read the next few passages, scribbling some notes. Despite his lack of formal education, he wasn't dumb. Not in the slightest. A total stranger could look upon this colossus of a man and still feel comfortable enough to indulge in long-kept family secrets. While it spent most of its time filled with red meat and bread, Euvard's gut more often than not was correct in its assessment of all people and situations he came across.

If Zercien *were* to fight in the army, having a man of Euvard's instincts by his side would do wonders to keep him sane, martial prowess aside.

Euvard will know something is wrong, he thought.

***

Zercien and Euvard arrived at the barracks just as folks queued for the exam. The army reserved and cleared one of its large training rooms in anticipation—not out of necessity, but the effort was apparent. Maybe fifty would-be recruits stood in line before the hall.

"Thought there'd be more," Euvard whispered.

Zercien did too, and his heart sank. He'd assumed many to enlist, and Entervia would recruit more than enough soldiers to compensate for his so-called honorable discharge. The country's scholarly identity couldn't have been more apparent today.

Euvard's fidgeting made his legs and hands occasionally brush by Zercien's. A brief "sorry" accompanied each occurrence.

Can't blame him, Zercien thought. *They say the third time's a charm, but I'm not sure what you call the eighth.*

A booming and powerful voice erupted over the small crowd's chatter. "Attention, all would-be soldiers of the illustrious Entervian Army!"

Euvard jabbed Zercien in the ribs with his elbow a few times. "Illustrious? I don't know about that. Maybe once we're there."

Zercien could only muster a wince as the voice came again.

"The Aptitude Exam will begin shortly," it said. "Please make your way inside and sit."

Euvard breathed deep, the loud exhale carrying over the crowd's footsteps.

They had their pick of desks, the look of them not dissimilar to those found in Zercien's classroom. Most of the hopefuls already eagerly sat themselves wherever they pleased. Many of the seats went unused.

The army can't be happy with this turnout, Zercien thought.

But the less people to witness him failing the exam, the better.

Zercien peered about the room, at the lances, swords, and battle-axes lining the walls, weapon and armor racks carelessly pushed against the sides.

"Okay, Zercien," Zercien whispered to himself. "First part of the plan begins now."

A crucial first step: Finding the right desk. It had to be uncrowded, but crowded *enough* so Euvard could not sit next to him.

"Zerc, are you—" Euvard said, but before he could finish, Zercien was plopped down at a desk in the back corner, against a rack of armor leaning on the wall. A woman sat at the desk to his left, and Euvard laid claim to the desk in front. Zercien chuckled as his large friend struggled to squeeze into the chair, and looked the part of a bear looming over a desk, instead. Other seats in the vicinity remained empty.

Good. Euvard can't see me, Zercien thought.

Euvard turned and placed an elbow atop the back of the chair. "Good luck, Zerc! I doubt you'll need it, though."

Zercien said the same. He tutored Euvard well, and he seemed to know the topics. His friend was sure enough as any to pass this time.

The same loud voice, without lowering its volume to accommodate the more enclosed space, turned all the chatter into whispers, murmurs and finally, silence.

"Thank you, all Entervian soldier hopefuls! Please, settle in."

As he spoke, four people walked about the room, putting the exam, a quill, and an inkwell on every desk, even the empty ones. Perhaps they envisioned some would arrive late.

"You will begin on my mark and have two hours to complete the exam. You may only indicate one answer per question. If you place a mark on multiple answers, we will void your exam and you must retake it. When finished, bring your exams up front, to my desk."

Good, Zercien thought. *Once I see Euvard finish, I'll walk up with him.*

A woman handed Zercien his materials, and he carefully placed them about his desk, though his hands trembled.

What if I drop the ink and it lands on the proctor? Would they banish me? Zercien thought, but shook his head. *Stop it. What would such antics get you? Probably a new inkwell and an angry proctor.*

Zercien glanced at the exam and flipped it over. Only one page, most questions asking for a best answer out of four. He scrunched his forehead.

They allow two hours for this? he thought. The entire exam was twenty questions, with the first being the only fill-in-the-blank. For the test-taker's name and address.

He wondered how Euvard managed to fail seven times. It seemed an easy exam to ensure only the most unread and ignorant lot are kept out.

An educated army would be stronger, Zercien agreed. But what of Entervia's, admittedly few, impoverished? For most, their situations were not their fault, and a military career could be a way for many destitute families to finally arise from squalor.

Perhaps this is not the way, Zercien thought.

But now was not the time to complain about ideology. Failing was his only way out, and today, Zercien was quite thankful for Entervia's high-brow military requirements.

"You may begin," said the man up front. "Good luck!"

Zercien's heart thumped as he read over the questions. He could finish this exam in seven minutes, with most of the time spent just making sure his quill had adequate ink. Each question he either covered in his lectures to seven-years, or he'd learned when he was but a seven-year himself. He expected it to be simple, but not *this* simple.

Failing this could ruin my career, he thought.

Saena popped into his head, wearing a long, black dress. Her pretty face covered by a black veil to hide her tears. She was placing her hand on a coffin, and others came by to comfort her. Mayla, Euvard, ambiguous faces on people his imagination conjured, offering hugs, giving speeches he couldn't hear.

Zercien gasped, but put a hand over his mouth and shifted his gaze to the nearby exam takers, hoping none had heard him. No reactions. He shook his head and rid himself of the frightful vision.

He couldn't see Euvard's face, but admired the confidence of his quill-strokes. The motions of a man who knew the right answers.

He'll be cross with me, there's no doubt, Zercien thought. *But Entervia's army will be fine.*

Zercien wrote his name and address for the first question in handwriting many could claim ill-fitting of a teacher and moved along.

Question Two: What is the name of the war that engulfed all of Oniro against legions from the world below?

Zercien smirked. *Told you,* he thought, and stared at his friend's back.

A: The Great War

B: The Ancients' War

C: The Battle of World's End

D: The God's War

Zercien sighed. He hovered his quill over *A: The Great War*, and froze.

From the corner of the large room, fog seeped under the door as if it were water.

No, no, no, not now, he thought. *Please. Not now.*

His hands shook. He couldn't grip his quill, and it fell onto his desk, a bit of ink splattering on the white space of the exam parchment. Breaths came and went in sporadic bursts, and the woman to his left glanced over. Zercien grinned, albeit faint, and she rolled her eyes, reverting her stare back to her own exam.

Grey waves lapped up her leg. Soon, she was gone, submerged underneath a sea of mist.

While Zercien still had control of his hands, he resisted their shakiness and grabbed his quill. He pushed hard, forcing it down, its tip a mere fraction of a fingertip away from Answer A.

His hand refused to move closer, no matter how hard he grit his teeth or pushed. Even bringing forth his other hand for reinforcement bore no fruit.

Instead, a pain rang through his head, and he yelped. Muffled scrapes of desks budging, and the turning of feet on the floor, filled his eardrums, though he couldn't see the sources.

His hand moved without permission from his brain.

"No, no, no!" When he realized he'd said it out loud, he went to move a hand to cover his mouth—but of course, it would not budge.

"Zerc? You okay?" Euvard's voice, in a whisper. He gathered his thoughts and managed to open his mouth through his own volition.

Of course now it lets me speak freely, he thought..

"I am fine." Zercien's voice was powerful, a near-boom. Though he did not command the spoken words. "Pay me no heed."

Or perhaps not.

"Excuse me!" said the proctor at the head of the faux classroom. "Quiet back there."

Zercien's head darted up, against his will, and his eyes fell upon the man sitting at the front desk, who no longer donned Entervian military attire, but a set of bloodred robes. The voice came from nowhere, as the space within the hood was all black.

Accept it, a voice pierced into his mind.

And Zercien snapped his head down, a sharp tingle running through his veins like an insect had burrowed underneath.

The muffled noises of shifting chairs and feet again echoed.

Zercien watched helplessly as his hand hovered over Answer B, filled it in, and moved on. To Question Three, Four, Five, and on, marking each question with the correct answer.

The fog lifted once Zercien answered Question Twenty against his will. Looking over the exam, he wished and prayed in vain to see a wrong answer, but his heart sunk as he realized he looked upon a perfect score.

He searched for a solution, any way he could change his answers, but there were none. Straining hard against the forces occupying his hand, his ill-fated attempts to stab his quill through other answers to invalidate his results failed. Nothing moved, and all looked pristine—save for the smudge from earlier.

"Bastard," he whispered to himself, though he hadn't a clue who it was aimed toward. Himself? Or—

Euvard slid his chair back and stood. Zercien's heart remained sunken, but somehow even lower. The signal of his sealed fate.

Zercien followed his friend to the front desk, and the two handed in their exams to the man together. He glanced at the two papers, raised both eyebrows at Euvard, and placed the exams in two different boxes. Euvard's was shoved into an empty box while Zercien's sat atop other completed exams.

"Results will be mailed to the address on your exams," he said. "Thank you."

Zercien and Euvard both nodded, but Zercien fell behind and followed his friend out of the exam room. Once outside range of any Entervian army personnel, Euvard let out a quick, "Woo!"

"I take it you did well?" Zercien said.

"I knew them all. I mean, I thought that last time too and I still failed, but I feel even *better* now! I'll give myself two wrong."

"I'm happy for you."

Zercien couldn't help but break his sullen state for one moment, and smile at his friend's elation.

"I probably don't need to ask you, so it looks like we'll be in the army together!" Euvard grabbed Zercien by the arm and wrapped him in a friendly headlock, running his closed fist over his head. "But what happened in there? We heard you yelp."

"Just one of my headaches."

Zercien's heart thumped the entire trip back home, and received no relent when approaching his front door. He stared at the wood, waiting for Euvard's heavy footsteps to travel out of earshot. His mind's eye conjured what he thought battle would be—the clash of steel on steel, bodies and severed limbs strewn about. Imminently he'd be embroiled within, and if the urgency for soldiers was as high as he assumed, he would be whisked off to his new life at the barracks within the week, depending on the swiftness of examination grading.

"How do I tell Saena?" He sniffled and went to unlock the door. But the handle turned and opened, his beloved on the other side.

"I heard Euvard's voice and couldn't wait. Did it work?" She was smiling, rubbing her hands together.

When he didn't return her smile, her lips flatlined, and a wayward tear slipped down Zercien's cheek.

"Zercien?" she said and reached out a hand. "What's wrong?"

Zercien fell forward onto Saena, pressing his face against her bosom, and said, "I'm going to die, Saena. I'm going to die in the bloody fucking North."

CHAPTER TEN
THE BOIL-FACED MAN

He picked at the boils atop his cheeks, ran his fingers along the scars marring his forehead. His hand stained red and yellow from wiping his pores overflowing with pus and blood.

One hand on his magnificent golden lance, using it as a walking stick, he trudged through the grasslands of the expansive Ariglioth Plains. The sky was dark, the late hours of the night, but he had no lantern.

He took a jar from his cloak, bulging eyes admiring the bloody contents, and licked its side, drool dripping from the jar to the grass. The blood spoke to him, goaded him along, honeyed words of power into his psyche. But he wouldn't open it. Not yet. His task remained incomplete. Instead, he returned it to his cloak to ease the temptation.

The large, steel gates of the Arigliothan capital city of Ciprius loomed. Nothing special came before, as the city seemed to sprout to life once he meandered over the hill.

Two guards, armed with sword and shield, stood watch, belt-high hanging lanterns conjuring small spheres of light at their hips. Though he couldn't hear the words, their murmurs, laughs, even the gentle pacing of bootsteps on grass, was like a grater on his brain. He winced, and hid behind the golden lance head, though increased his pace to try and outrun the noise.

"Shut up, shut up, shut up, shut up!" He ground his teeth in a whisper to himself. He was close now, and the shadows scattered by the two guards' lanterns illuminated their bare faces. Young men, well, younger than he. But their heads straightened, eyes darting about the increasing night.

He froze. They must have heard him. He cursed himself. Before the guards' watchful gazes fell upon him, he dropped to the ground, prone, laying his lance to his side, although its gold would no doubt be obvious in the dark.

Through the long grass blades, he watched one guard shrug. He said something inaudible to his partner, who nodded. The guard called out, "Who goes?" and put a hand to his ear.

The boil-faced man snarled. "A tithe. Just a tithe. All I need. It's close. Don't get in my way."

But the guard just put his hand down and pointed forward. Hand on his sword's hilt, he approached, darting his head left and right with each slow step.

"Get out of my way," said the boil-faced man. "Out of my way."

The guard jumped back upon seeing him on his stomach and yelled. "Who are you? State your business!"

The boil-faced man thrust both hands against his head, the guard's shouts pulsating in his skull. "No, no, no. Do as I say. No shouting. I will not hurt you. But no shouting."

"I said, state your business! Or I will be forced to—"

Using his lance as a lever, the boil-faced man leapt to his feet. His breaths sporadic and quick, he stood mere inches from the guard's face, the lantern illuminating his each and every bloody blemish and scar.

"What? Who are you?" the guard said and looked to his partner, waving him to follow. "We've got—"

"And I said, no shouting!" The boil-faced man lunged with his lance. It pierced the guard's chest, and he shoved deep, until the bloodied, golden tip protruded from his back, glimmering in the moonlight.

The other guard arrived, sword raised, wide-eyed at his partner's limp body hanging at the edge of the lance. With a kick, the boil-faced man slid the corpse from the lance shaft and swung across his body, slapping the sword from the other guard's hand. As the Arigliothan turned to run, he was skewered through the back.

He squirmed about, pulling at the sauroter to free himself, watching as his own blood coated the shaft and his hands.

Instead, the boil-faced man yanked the lance free, leaving the guard to fall to his knees and put both hands on the hole through his stomach in a vain attempt to block the surging blood.

But with one last stab downward, the lance pierced the guard's skull, the blade extending out of his mouth.

The boil-faced man dragged both bodies into a pile on the side of the road, throwing them on top of one another in a bloody mess. They'd likely be found by morning, but his mission should be complete before then. He jogged, using his now-bloodstained golden lance for balance, into the city.

Chapter Eleven
The Last Lecture

A nd thus we conclude the lesson on the heroes Holunt, Gunvald, and Skjóturi. Now, can anyone tell me why those heroes are important to Entervia?" Zercien said, looking upon his classroom of staring students. After a moment, thirty hands stretched high, each trying for an extra fingertip over the other.

Zercien chuckled. "How about we all try shouting it out? Ready—" and with instant regret, he slammed his hands on both ears as a discordant concert of a classroom full of high-pitched children screaming over one another assaulted him. The words "Royal," "Seal," "Coat," and "Arms" managed to slip through.

The students laughed as he held his crossed arms over his face and peeked out with one eye open accompanied by a smile.

"All right. Good enough," he said. "Yes, the Royal Seal, or Coat of Arms, of Entervia was inspired by those three heroes. On the bottom-left, the blade called Kyrios—Skjóturi's sword. The bottom-right, modeled after Symphora, the mighty axe of Gunvald. And on top, the—" He stopped short, and peered up, into the lecture hall's ceiling, staring at nothing in particular. "And the Regent, triumphant in victory, symbolizing the hero, Holunt."

He had their full attention. None said a word, and many strained their eyes to not blink. "Now, let's see who's been diligent. After the

Ancients' War, which one of the heroes spent the most time in Entervia?"

Clyde was the only one to raise his hand. Zercien tilted his head and called on him. "Holunt!" said the student.

Zercien narrowed his eyes, and his gaze returned to its absent-minded place amid the everyday ceiling. "Yes. Holunt…" He drummed his finger on his desk while other students were quick to shout at the boy.

"Not fair! How do you know?" said Yua.

Clyde shrugged. "I read ahead a long time ago."

"Now, now, hush, hush!" Zercien said and quieted down the students. He shot a quick smile at Clyde. Maybe the kid's future would bring actual merit to his family's name, after all. "This is a place of learning. And we *never* insult those who further it beyond this classroom."

"Yes, sir," came a quiet chorus of apologetic voices.

Zercien smiled at the class and set down the *Legends of Oniro* text. "We're out of time."

"That's it?" said Tafri, the daughter of Councilwoman Ellana. She never spoke up much in class. Until today.

Zercien chuckled. "I hadn't even prepared a lesson. I'd say this was a successful last lecture."

His voice croaked, and he cleared his throat. *What was that about? Am I really sad to leave these noble brats behind?* Zercien thought.

"But…" Tafri said, and she sniffled.

"Now, now, I'm sure your next lecturer will be just as good, if not better than me."

He had to cover his ears again as the uproar sliced through the open classroom air.

"Just one more! Please!"

"Please, Mister Volnaire!"

Zercien turned his back to the students, swiped his wrist over his face, and sniffled, hoping none could hear.

"I do wish I could." He met his students with glossy eyes. "I've already caved into your demands once, though, and we're over our allotted time now. You'll be late for your next instructor."

A hand raised in the back, and Zercien called on him. Jemad, a young boy and inheritor to his family's grandiose land and property. A quiet and unassuming kid, despite how his clothes depicted his wealth.

"Are you really leaving forever?" the boy said.

It was like Euvard punched him in the gut with all his strength. He nodded.

"I won't lie. It might be forever," Zercien said. "As you've seen in our studies, war is unforgiving. I will likely not—" He cleared his throat again. "Not return as your instructor. As sad as that would be for me."

"You can't!" Narla, daughter of the famed jeweler many visited for diamond rings, said. "You're our favorite!"

Zercien couldn't help but laugh. "Could have fooled me."

A huff from the front row. Clyde crossed his arms. "You should see what we do to our *least* favorite lecturers."

Moisture found its way to his cheek as Zercien shook his head. *Some mess I've made*, he thought.

"Well, if that is true, then—" Zercien caught himself sniffling again and had to wipe his nose with a handkerchief. He reached for his desk to gather his remaining supplies and books. The students' gaze followed as he walked to the door, his footsteps echoing about the classroom.

"If I do return from war, I will be sure to visit. And test to make sure your new instructor is following the curriculum, of course." He blinked to repel the imminent tears. "Farewell. Teaching you all has been the honor of my life."

"Thank you, Mister Volnaire!"

"Good luck, Mister Volnaire!"

The voices followed as he exited the classroom and shut the door behind.

***

It was a normal knock that rapped upon his and Saena's front door. A simple three taps, less than a second in between, and unremarkable in every way. But it was the worst knock he had ever heard.

Saena let go of his hand. He greeted and thanked the man with the letter, and upon closing the door, stared at the seal depicting Entervia's Coat of Arms. Zercien knew what the message would say, as did Saena. Just three days after the exam.

Mayla had visited earlier to bring news of Euvard's failure, and how the two wished to see Zercien off, should he pass. He knew long before the results that his plan failed, and now he would be off to war. Alone.

His heart sunk at the mention of his friend failing once again. He tutored Euvard himself. Those answers all appeared on the exam. He was sure of Euvard's ability to pass. A ping in his gut spread unease throughout his body, that something uncouth must have occurred.

But overpowering the thoughts of unsavory affairs were that of Euvard's mental state. Often he'd tell stories of his father, a renowned Entervian army leader that once led a campaign into the southern country of Duspen. He fell in that same battle, leaving Euvard and his mother alone. A younger Grandmaster General Urian delivered the news, and Zercien knew this was the beginning of Euvard's hatred for the man.

He cursed the ineffectual exam keeping his friend from his dreams.

Zercien stood, gulping hard, letter in hand. He never bothered to open it, for he knew what would be inside. He needed no words, but to only turn and stare with his small brown eyes at his beloved. Expecting Saena to rush at him with anger, bursting tears in a fit of rage, he raised his hands in defense.

But all Saena did was nod and wrap her arms about him, for tonight may be the last time she ever could.

Chapter Twelve
Never Much for Stealth

A riglioth Castle, in its splendor, emerged like a fortress in the night. The boil-faced man with the golden lance hid behind a small wall, watching as the nighttime guards paced about in their boring, predictable routines. The castle should have been quiet, but guards swarmed the place. Some solo, others in pairs. And he hadn't even reached the inside.

King Lennard was a generous man. Or so he had heard from rumor. He helped people. Came from nothing himself. Rose to power through election, not wealth or power.

The boil-faced man smirked, dry skin falling from the corners of his mouth. The king would surely help a man such as him, down on his luck, as he was. But how would he reach the benevolent monarch with all the blasted guards?

He peered over the wall. Two at the gate, and surely more would gather at the front of the castle. He debated killing them. It would be easy, much akin to the rabble outside the city. But he was too close to the streets. Others would hear. Could he eliminate every guard?

Perhaps. But not from his position. Too much commotion. Screaming. He shuddered at the thought of the noise. The grating, irritating babbling of squirming people. It sickened him, and he scratched the flaking dry skin on his neck.

From his crouch, he threw his lance over the wall. With a metallic thud, it landed on the road leading to the gate. The two guards jumped to attention and ran toward the sound.

The boil-faced man raked his jagged fingernails against his face, popping his boils and ripping scars, running his cheeks and forehead awash with blood and pus. He leapt from behind the wall, near where his lance had fallen, and rolled about the ground, whimpering.

"Sir?" a guard said, putting a hand on him. He straightened his back and almost jumped and wrung the fool's neck but forced his bloodied hands to the ground.

The other guard looked over the blood-covered lance lying nearby. "You find some trouble tonight?"

Behind his hands, the boil-faced man smirked. But he put on a fake pout before revealing his face. Both guards gasped at the fresh blood running down his cheeks, the yellow pus leaking from his punctured boils.

"I'm ... I'm sick. I'm bleeding."

The guard holding the boil-faced man's shoulder nodded at the other. "We've a medic inside. We'll get you examined."

"Oh, yes. Yes." The boil-faced man nodded so hard blood and dried skin flew from his face and onto the guard's chest.

"This your lance, too?" said the other, reaching his hand close but curling back his fingertips upon seeing the bloodstains.

The boil-faced man smirked. "Yes." He gulped air by the mouthful. "So much blood. Need help."

"We'll help you inside, then." The guard took him by the arm and helped him up. How he loathed the touch, but endured for the sake of his ruse.

The other guard reached down, wincing as his fingers grazed the blood-soaked lance. But he strained, grunting loud. The lance would not budge. "How heavy is this?"

"Perhaps you need to join me in the training grounds more often," said the first guard. "Just roll it, would you?"

The two guards led the boil-faced man down the winding road to the castle's front gates. Another pair stood on either side and were quick to question the approaching trio.

"Got an injured man here." The guard helping him move clutched the boil-faced man's arm. "Taking him inside."

Then, some asinine conversation. The boil-faced man didn't listen or care much about their pathetic words. Peering back for but a moment, all he could see was the pitch-black of night. No others in sight, and perhaps none even in hearing distance.

"All I'm saying is, he looks a bit—"

"He's injured. King Lennard wouldn't want us to turn him away."

But their voices. The agonizing song of gruff, hard-spoken men, twisting in his ears like a knife. He groaned. Loud. As if the knife was stabbed into his gut.

"Everything all right?" said the first guard. Instead of an answer, the boil-faced man just smiled wide, blood poking through the corners of his lips where the dried skin used to be.

He shoved the guard off him and dove to the ground, claiming his lance from the other's oppressive and annoying boot.

Leaping to his feet, he swung the blunt, golden lance shaft about his body, smashing two of the guard's heads, a spatter of blood combining with the pus on his face. His tongue moved about his lips, hoping to claim its sweet taste, but he resisted and bit down, retracting it back into his mouth.

The remaining two guards gasped at the sight of their fallen companions, dizzied from the blow, and unsheathed longswords. The boil-faced man met their charge with a forward thrust, puncturing one guard's arm and ripping the top layer of skin away. With a yelp, the guard dropped his blade.

Just as the boil-faced man was about to jab his victim through the head, the last guard jumped in front and deflected the blow. But with a quick uppercut swing, his lance knocked away the sword and slammed underneath the guard's chin, cracking bone and sending fragments of teeth about the darkened road.

He stabbed forward, lancing through the guard's midsection, and raised him into the air, his bloodied screams growing low and quiet. Blood trickled down, mixing with the stains on the lance. He raised the lance to his own mouth, lifting the guard higher into the air, and opened wide to welcome the sliding blood. As the guard's life slowly drained, the last thing he saw was his own blood lapped up by a ravenous man with a mangled face.

The boil-faced man lowered the lance, kicked the dead guard off, and spat out the blood, careful not to swallow. Now was not the time.

The three remaining men squirmed about the ground, pressing against the road, climbing onto all fours. One's arm was a bloodied mess, and he'd likely lose it, should he live.

The boil-faced man hovered over the struggling guard, his shadow causing him to look up, staring with wide, scared eyes into the head of the golden lance, knowing he was about to die.

"Cannot survive. Can't let you. Sorry," the boil-faced man said between heavy breaths, and drove his lance through the guard's back. The last of his air escaped his mouth.

And with two more downward stabs, he ended the others' miserable, annoying lives with little fanfare.

Drool leaked from his dried and flaked lips as he gazed about the corpses, blood oozing and pooling about their bodies like shadows. "Waste. Waste of time. Waste of blood."

Instead, he averted his gaze to the steel doors ahead. "Must get inside. Now. Not much time."

Pressing his ear against the doors, he feared others within heard the screams. The castle was sure to be filled with more hapless dolts, but he had no choice.

He pushed the heavy doors open, and with a bloodied smirk, entered Castle Ciprius.

Chapter Thirteen
The Star Recruit

N ew recruit?" said a loud, insufferable voice as Zercien entered the barracks with his one allowed bag. He dropped it next to what would become his bed—one of the many in a sea of identical, white-clothed blocks of wood.

No, just here for a pleasure trip, he thought, and extended his hand. "Zercien Volnaire. New recruit reporting for duty, sir."

"Another one of you fresh faces," the soldier said and shoved Zercien's hand away. "Thinking just because you're here, the war will turn tide?"

Zercien raised a finger, about to protest that the man—whose decorated casual clothes depicting the Entervian Coat of Arms made him look to be higher rank—hadn't quite used the phrase correctly, but opted for a less-combative answer. "You *are* right about the fresh part."

The soldier stepped right up into Zercien's face, less than a finger's length away. Cabbage and onions on his breath wafted straight into his nose, and he flared his nostrils and scrunched his lips in an attempt to stop the invasive force.

"You saying I'm wrong about everything else?"

So much for the less-combative part, Zercien thought, and paused. He opened his mouth,

but couldn't find the words.

"Huh, *recruit?*" said the higher ranked soldier.

If their faces were any closer, those cabbage-stained lips would be pressed against his cheek.

"I've been in the force for all of seven minutes," Zercien said. "Allow me to settle in, will you?"

While he turned, he grazed the superior soldier's chest with his elbow, and froze. The man's breaths assaulted him with sporadic, angry, onion-fused bursts.

"Did you just put your hands on me?" The words came in an angry grunt.

Other soldiers and new recruits gathered, whispers scattering throughout the barrack.

"He just arrived and already picked a fight with Benji?"

"Really? Doesn't he know who Benji is?"

"Suppose not."

Lovely, Zercien thought and raised both hands in an attempt at peace. "I think we've begun our friendship a bit awkwardly. Shall we start anew? My name is Zercien Volnaire, and I'm a new recruit."

Zercien held out his hand again, but Benji's eyes grew to the size of a shallot and slapped it away.

"You think you're clever, recruit?" he said. "How about you meet me in the training ground and we have ourselves a little spar?"

A loud cheer broke out among both new recruits and other more seasoned soldiers.

Not that Zercien expected unparalleled maturity from the army, but he'd witnessed scuffles between young children in the schoolyard that exhibited more diplomatic ends.

"An enticing offer, Sir Benji. But I've just arrived. Perhaps we can reschedule—"

"The recruit's scared!" came another voice from the growing crowd.

This is how the army acts? It's no small wonder that Entervia's losing to a country without one, Zercien thought.

Before he could react, Benji clutched his shirt and shoved him. If it weren't for the metal bedframe, Zercien would've been flat on his ass, drowning in the others' laughter.

"Sounds like a 'no,' then," he said.

"Practice swords are on the wall," said Benji, and tilted his head to the right, where a rack of wooden swords sat. "I'll be waiting, recruit."

He spat, but missed, and the goopy saliva landed on the floor next to Zercien's boot. Amid the cheers, Benji flexed as if it were the intended spot.

"You've made a terrible mess of this already, recruit," said another soldier passing by Zercien's bed. "Benji's in charge of all new recruits in this building. Reports right to Officer Kanivar. His experience squashes ours."

The crowd dispersed and Zercien was left alone to lie on his dirt-adorned bedsheet.

"Never been in a real fight in my life, and within the hour of joining the army, I manage to pick one with the strongest soldier here," he said, and sighed. "Just my luck."

Now that he could actually observe the barracks he would call home for the foreseeable future, he noticed racks of armaments and old armor sets pushed against the wall to make room, near the practice weapon rack, much akin to the room he'd taken the exam.

Not enough space for all of us, he thought.

Zercien squinted while inspecting the wooden swords, soon realizing he hadn't a clue which was most suitable. The one in the middle most resembled what he used with Euvard's training sessions, but what it was called, he had no idea. To him, anything longer than a dagger was a longsword.

Not that it mattered. This Benji, a trained soldier in charge of new recruits, had far more combat experience than he, a teacher who sometimes engaged in swordplay to please his friend. Though Euvard *had* called him a natural once.

Once.

The crowd already formed a circle around the dirt-covered training ground. Benji strutted, goading his onlookers and admirers into a roaring frenzy. They chanted his name over and over. Did the superior officers not care about this? Zercien just shook his head as he walked through. How anyone could see this raucous display and think it's acceptable behavior was beyond him.

"Excuse me, pardon me," Zercien said without any extra flavor to his speech as he wiggled through the riled crowd. He squeezed through the last two soldiers and entered the circle, with his wooden sword outstretched. The cheering and shouting pierced into his mind, reduced him to nausea, and he twisted and turned his head. For a moment, he thought he'd retch right there.

"Well, well!" Benji said, holding his arms high. "Our instigator decided to show!"

Was there another option? Zercien thought. He surely would have taken it, if so.

"Instigator?" he said, lowering his voice in an effort to sound tough. "Your attempts at provoking me won't work." But none could hear him over the howling of the crowd.

Zercien caught a faint grey lurking in the corner of the training ground, licking up the dirt. He raised his eyebrows as the fog grew, albeit slow.

"Huh." But he turned to face Benji, who stood with his own wooden sword out. He chose a standard longsword, much like Zercien. The two met in the middle, Benji staring, blinking at an off-putting slow pace, with his tongue out. He licked his lips like a starving wolf who'd finally found a meal. Zercien winced.

What a disgusting individual you are, he thought.

And then, quiet. Fog enveloped the training ground, blanketing the boisterous crowd and blunting their yells to faint whispers. Zercien focused on Benji, who retracted his tongue and looked prepared for a real skirmish.

He could almost predict it. A pain, deep inside his head, ripping through his skull and brain. He cried out and dropped to one knee, sword planted on the training grounds' dirt and one hand on his temple.

Benji's voice surged over the grey waves. "Surrendering?" His laughter broke through the fog, and he charged.

Zercien's mind exacerbated the clopping of Benji's heavy footsteps, each ringing louder and clearer with his advance. Just when the footsteps seemed on top of him, Zercien broke from his kneel and flicked his sword in front, deflecting Benji's strike and sending him recoiling backward.

"What?" Benji said and stepped back, blinking hard, like he'd dreamed it. He ran a hand over the wooden sword to ensure it was there.

Zercien sneered and pointed his blunt practice weapon at Benji's head. With his other hand, he gestured to the soldier to engage.

"Come, then, young soldier. Let us see if you've the swordsman-ship to match your tongue." Those were the strong, bellowing words spouting from Zercien's mouth, though he was not the one behind their command. The crowd's whispers soon turned to silence, and Benji quivered where he stood.

"You will not approach me?" said the voice impersonating Zercien, and he shrugged. "No matter. I shall bring the fight to you."

He sauntered forward, a smirk still spread upon his face, and met Benji's eyes—the once wide, hungry, and arrogant circles shrank into dried, shriveled onions in Zercien's shadow.

Zercien swung downward, and Benji met the wooden blade with a parry from his own. A quick follow-up strike sent Benji's sword sailing from his grasp. Now weaponless, the hapless soldier turned to flee, but Zercien's sword was faster. A strong blow across his body bashed Benji's back, and he was thrown from his feet, face-first onto the dirt.

"How?" said a hushed voice from the crowd, amid stunned silence.

A soldier dashed from the fog, breaking through the waves, hoping to catch Zercien unawares, but he spun around and slashed ahead, knocking the new opponent's practice sword free. Another charged, and Zercien met his blade, forcing his arm to the side. A strike across the ribs sent his opponent reeling.

One after another challenged Zercien, some in pairs and trios, oth-ers daring to try solo, but Zercien knocked them all down in quick suc-cession. And only a single bead of sweat dripped from his hair.

Soon, the crowd's cheers renewed, but it wasn't Benji's name they chanted. The waves of fog receded back through the door, and all was normal. Zercien's ears filled with the crowd's adoration, and his lips formed a slight, if not a little embarrassed, smile.

Now that? he thought, and tilted his eyes up, as if attempting to talk to his mind. *That is acceptable.*

A rush of footsteps, heavy boots, it sounded like, burst onto the training ground, and all the chants died quicker than when in the fog. A tall, well-built man in his forties with greying hair surveyed the practice carnage, focusing on the downed Benji and other recruits who still struggled to stand.

A hard stare lanced into Zercien. "What is the meaning of this, re-cruit?"

Zercien, to his dismay, saw he was the only soldier still wielding a practice sword. But dropped it as if this quite-important-looking man wouldn't notice.

"Shit," he muttered.

The man approached with one eye shut, whether it was on-purpose to look more intimidating or due to injury, Zercien couldn't tell. "Who the hell are you?"

"I am Zercien Volnaire. Sir." He gulped. "I am a new recruit. Arrived today."

But the man's eyes left Zercien's, again falling to the soldiers sprawled on the dirt. "You do this, boy?"

He didn't *sound* mad.

"Sergeant Kanivar," said a soldier. "Benji challenged this new recruit, and he lost."

Zercien glared in the direction of the voice. He didn't rightly care who said it. Sergeant Kanivar likely wouldn't be thrilled to find his direct report knocked on his ass with his face full of dirt because of a reckless recruit.

In your first day as a recruit, you successfully fought a superior, defeated a host of other soldiers, and angered a sergeant, he thought. *Excellent work, Zercien.*

If he wasn't in a heap of trouble, he'd be impressed with himself.

"Answer my question, recruit," Sergeant Kanivar said.

Zercien rubbed his hands together, tilted his head to avoid the sergeant's gaze, and pressed his index finger over his thumb. "I, well, I didn't do it myself."

He pulled back and held a hand up to brace himself for a stern talking to.

"The recruit has jests!" The sergeant's lips formed a hearty smile and he slapped him on the back. "Come, now. You're the only one with a sword, and you're surrounded by knocked out sparring partners. Including my hand-picked best fighter. You're quite modest."

Zercien opened his mouth to protest, but whatever he'd rehearsed in his head was worthless. "Excuse me?"

"Besting all these soldiers? This is the best display of swordsmanship I've seen from a recruit, maybe ever."

Warmth filled Zercien's face, turning his cheeks red. Embarrassment, yes, but it was a welcome change to his treatment thus far.

While he didn't know *exactly* what came over him, it still *was* him. Was it a lie? Zercien sure as hell didn't know, but he accepted the compliment regardless.

"Thank you, Sergeant," he said. "High praise, coming from someone of your stature."

Sergeant Kanivar took Zercien by the shoulder and walked him back to the area with all the beds, the crowd parting at the seam before the two.

"If this is what you can do against trained soldiers, it's a blessing to have your swordsmanship in the Entervian Army, son. We're glad to have you."

"I will continue to do my part for this army—"

"I'm pulling you out of these dumpy barracks."

Zercien tripped on the corner of his bed frame, grabbing the firm mattress to break his fall. He couldn't help but bring a smile to his face. Maybe he'd be awarded a paperwork or officer role, or—

"Your skill is far too great to be wasted here. I'm putting your name through immediately to join the battle with General Burgland on the front lines."

CHAPTER FOURTEEN
THE SHIFTER

The boil-faced man tip-toed into Castle Ciprius' dim hall, only kept alight by a scant few small torches and candles built into the stone walls. Countless wooden doors and paths branched from every which way. He opted to move forward, straight ahead.

Footsteps. Not his own. He stood up straight against the wall. Some ways down the hall, a light. Perhaps a candle, carried by a castle servant or attendant. No—too much light for one—at least two, maybe three.

The throne room must be there, he thought, and a crooked smile broke from his parched and dried lips.

Voices carried. Whispers, but he could make out the words.

"Probably a rat. Those two out front are scared of anything that moves."

The boil-faced man's smile stuck. A rat. Cunning creatures. And deadly if kept unchecked. He quite liked the word.

"Too loud for a rat," came another voice. "Let's have a look. I'm sure it will be nothing, though."

Two men, one an armed guard and the other, dressed in black attire carrying a candle. A woman in similar garb held the other light. Servants, more than likely. Good. Easier to take down.

The woman pointed ahead and gasped, keeping her finger aligned with the boil-faced man's eye. "Who are you?"

But he smirked and stepped underneath a hanging torch, the flickering flames illuminating his butchered face covered in vile pores and scars.

Before anyone could speak, he dashed forward, lance out front. The golden hue shined red in the torchlight as it speared through the armed guard. He dropped to the carpeted floor without as much as a scream, in a lump.

The male servant turned his back to run, but soon had the tip of the lance sticking through his chest. Ripping the golden lance out, the boil-faced man watched as the servant's body fell limp.

The woman dropped to the floor and scooted on her backside, trembling as all color left her face, and reached the wall. A dead end. She waved both hands in a frantic panic, breaths firing from her mouth in spurts while the boil-faced man sauntered toward her, his scarred visage awash with shadows of licking flames.

"Please, please don't hurt me," she said, the quivering of her head nods leaving a shakiness in her voice. "I'll look the other way. I'll let you go free. Please?"

The boil-faced man lurched forward and grabbed her by the collar of her blouse. With little effort, he raised her from the floor.

"Throne room. Show me the throne room," he said, his breaths small, rapid, and light. "Not much time. Don't scream. Don't shout. If you want to live, show me the throne room."

"The throne room? I can't—"

The boil-faced man raised his lance. "Show me, or you die here."

She held her hands out. "Yes, okay. Throne room." She pointed behind her. "Through the hall. Straight ahead. Up the stairs."

The boil-faced man released his grip, and she sighed as she slid back to the carpet. But he extended his arm to help her up. "You lead. Take me to King Lennard. Double-cross me, and you die here. Understand?"

She gulped. But nodded and allowed the boil-faced man to help her to her feet. Her cold hand shook, despite his grip.

"Yes," she said. "This way."

The servant led him through the hall, as she'd said, and they came to a set of stairs. Short, heading up. Good. She did not lie, though her every limb wobbled as she walked.

The two reached the end of the stairs, where more guards jumped to action, brandishing lances much shorter than the splendid golden one the boil-faced man wielded. But behind them, down a darkened red carpet alit by the same dull candlelight as the halls, sat the throne, and King Lennard atop. He squirmed in the iron seat.

"Miss, who—" one guard said, but the boil-faced man was not about to listen to more inane chatter between Arigliothans. His lance found the man's stomach, and jerked it up and away, guts spilling from the gaping wound. Another stab through the chest, and he was dead. Though he may have been dead before that, the boil-faced man would take no more risks with his goal in sight.

Quickly, to his right, he clubbed the other guard across the face with the golden lance, blood and broken teeth scattering about the carpet. With an upward jab, the tip of the lance bore through the guard's chin, piercing through his skull and through the top of his head.

The servant woman screamed, but her breath was cut short by the blade of the golden lance stabbing through her chest.

"No witnesses. No one can see," the boil-faced man said, and tugged at the lance to free it. To him, the slow pull was an act of respect for her help. The servant dropped dead to the carpet.

A thud caused him to turn around. Out of the corner of his eye, under the dim light, he saw King Lennard had abandoned his throne, and was running to the back. He'd leapt from the seat, and his crown fell from atop his head.

The boil-faced man's breaths came sporadic, legs wobbling with weakness. But with the last of his energy, he dashed ahead, sprinting on shaky knees toward the middle-aged King Lennard, who stood no hope of outrunning him. The boil-faced man dropped his lance and dove, tackling him to the carpeted floor.

He wrapped his hands about the king's, holding him down, though not without struggle. They both wheezed with hard breath.

The king went to scream, but the boil-faced man thrust his hands atop his mouth. Teeth sunk into his skin, but he did not relinquish his hold. "Quiet. Do not scream if you want to live. No shouting."

The boil-faced man released the king's mouth, but he just opened wide again. Back came the hands, along with an accompanying shaking of the head.

"No," the boil-faced man said. "You scream, you die. If you want to live, be quiet. I need you. And you need me."

The king nodded with muffled acceptance, and the boil-faced man freed his mouth to speak. "What is it you want from me? Gold?"

The boil-faced man shook his head in rapid beats, and blood, pus, and dried skin fell like rain atop the king's dark brown face. "No. The dungeon."

"You've a friend imprisoned? You are mistaken. Our dungeon is empty. We've no prisoners jailed here. Perhaps in the city jail—"

"No. You take me there, to the dungeon."

"You *want* me to take you to the dungeon?"

The boil-faced man smirked and jumped off the king. In one hand, he took his lance, and the other, he offered to help him to his feet. "As if I were your prisoner. Take me to the dungeon."

"But why?"

The boil-faced man shook, his smirk now a mess of dried skin. With his free hand, he scratched a scar and it burst, running blood down his cheek.

"No questions." He snarled. "The dungeon. Take me or you die here."

King Lennard nodded fast and stood. He pointed to his right, toward a doorway and another staircase, hidden in the shadow. "These stairs lead to the dungeon."

The boil-faced man jabbed the king with his outstretched hand. "Good. Take my hand. Lead me, as if I were your prisoner."

The king gulped and did as instructed. The warmth in his hand forced the boil-faced man to gag as he was escorted down the staircase and into the dungeon's depths.

"Guards?" said the boil-faced man.

"We've no prisoners captured here," said the king. "Little point in—"

"Good. Now, show your best cell."

The king furrowed his brow. "Best?"

"If you were to imprison me, where would I be?" The boil-faced man grinned, and his dried lips cracked and bled.

The king led him down another hall. Deep, and dark, with no candlelight. They reached a dead end, but the king ran his finger about the side wall, and his hand found the slightest out of place stone. Quivering, he pressed down and a *click* echoed in their small corridor.

Stones fell from the front wall, crumbling at the sound. Though the stones remained connected, telling the boil-faced man they could be put together in the same manner.

A small opening, preceding a larger room. Another cell.

"This is it," King Lennard said with a grimace. "A murderer such as yourself would be here. To rot."

The boil-faced man's grin returned. "Good. Perfect."

With the sauroter of his lance, he tapped the back of King Lennard's legs, urging him forward. "Go. I am behind you. If you want to live, go."

The king ducked on wobbling legs and entered the cell, the boil-faced man following.

As soon as they both stood inside, the boil-faced man threw his lance to the right, its clang ringing about the prison. He leapt before the king could turn and drove him to the stone floor. With one hand pressing down on the struggling King Lennard's chest, the other pulled a short bundle of rope from within his cloak. He flipped his prisoner onto his stomach and bound his hands taut behind his back.

King Lennard writhed against the rope to no avail. He propelled forward with only his legs, launching himself at the boil-faced man, but only managed a soft headbutt against his chest, and fell to the floor. Again, he opened his mouth to scream but was met by dry and bloody hands.

"Stay quiet. You will not die," the boil-faced man said, nodding. "If you want to live, do not shout."

One hand on the king's mouth, he used the other to bring out loose cloth from inside his cloak and stuffed it in between his teeth. King Lennard's attempts at screams soon became muffles.

The boil-faced man fished back within his cloak for a small knife, one used to slice vegetables or fruit, and his shadow hovered over the king. "Just a tithe, a little tithe is all. I will take care of you. You will not die. Just a tithe."

He sliced a bit of skin from King Lennard's arm.

Strained tears formed in both his eyes, but the gag blocked the king's muffled scream. The boil-faced man held a jar underneath the wound, letting blood trickle inside. A quarter of the small jar soon filled, and he stopped. A few gulps were all he needed.

The boil-faced man fashioned a bandage from another cloth and wrapped the king's wound. He smiled with crooked teeth at his prize, licking the edges of the jar.

Setting King Lennard against the wall, the boil-faced man ensured he was comfortable as could be and patted him on the head. He took his lance in hand and scurried through the hole in the wall, like the rat he was.

Finding the same spot the king had, he pressed down, and the fallen stones from the front wall formed again, repairing themselves. As the small opening closed, he poked his head through and said, "I will be back to give food, water. Each day you will live, as long as I receive the tithe."

And he pulled his head back, just as the stones had finished rebuilding, locking the shaking, wide-eyed king in complete darkness.

Too excited for subtlety, adrenaline overwhelmed his oncoming weakness and the boil-faced man ran back through the corridors and up the stairs, into the still-empty throne room. None had come to inspect the mess.

Good.

He approached King Lennard's throne and smiled. An iron seat with a hard, red cushion. Nothing out of the ordinary, though he cared not. The boil-faced man took his jar in hand and stared, licking his lips, at the king of Ariglioth's blood.

After unfastening the top, he tipped the cool glass edge onto his bottom lip and poured. Still warm, it tingled as he slurped, the blood inching down his throat. His eyes dimmed as he neared the end, saddened his tithe was soon to be complete, and lapped up the last few drops.

The boil-faced man envisioned the image of King Lennard in his majestic red robe and regal, Arigliothan blue attire. Soon, the searing heat he once knew so well and had longed for surged in his stomach and through his body. Pain burst and flew away, as if he were purged from a great evil.

First, his face. His skin darkened, and as if they never existed, the boils, scars, and blemishes vanished in favor of faint wrinkles. His eyes, next, turning to a gentle brown. And finally, a grey beard sprouted on his chin, accompanied by a thin mustache.

His cloak and clothes morphed. Soon, his dingy attire disappeared, replaced by the same robe as King Lennard, with his Arigliothan royal garb. To his right, on the floor like some cast away rubbish, sat the king's solid-gold crown adorned with emeralds along the sides and a great ruby at the front.

With his newly-wrinkled hands, the boil-faced man grasped the crown, and placed it atop his fresh head of greying hair. Taking his golden lance in hand, he slammed the sauroter onto the stone floor and sat upon his new throne.

CHAPTER FIFTEEN
A LESSON IN WAR

Dusk settled in the Entervian plains, not far from the makeshift border separating Entervia from the frigid Ankarth. And there Zercien marched on his first assignment, to meet the famous General Burgland and the Entervian standing army.

Though the walking bit tired him, he didn't mind the attire. Light chainmail, a bit of brown hard leather on the jerkin, the Entervian Coat of Arms depicted on the breast piece. Hardly the epitome of fashion, but he preferred it to his obnoxious long-sleeved teacher's robes. And it helped stave off the chill of the northern lands.

He traveled with the archery brigade, which Zercien thought odd, as he had no archery skill, though they did lend him a quiver filled to the brim with arrows. No bow, however.

But Sergeant Kanivar seemed hellbent on finding any excuse to send his "star recruit," as he referred to Zercien, to the front lines, and this was the first chance.

His first mission. His feet quivered with each step. If he didn't run the risk of being trampled by the soldiers at his sides and behind, he would have stopped.

He rubbed his hands together to relieve an oncoming chill, though not from the weather. He was told of this place, near Ankarthan territory. Further ahead would be a fortress, once used in the Ancients' War.

Many fortresses from the war days sat abandoned about the Entervian plains, but this was the largest. And their next target, according to the army debrief. For what purpose, Zercien wasn't sure. His guess was the army's scouts picked up Ankarthan activity nearby.

They marched upon a hill, where the Entervian Army arranged camp. Tents, doused campsites, swords, and lances all lay about, scattered on the hard ground. A stale smell of old meat wafted on the breeze.

This is how the army is organized? Zercien thought, stepping over a broken set of chainmail.

A man who filled out his heavy armor quite well, but popped a bit in the gut area, greeted the lot. Not old by any means, but a few grey hairs told Zercien he was a seasoned knight. When he spoke, he did in deep, gruff shouts, loud enough for all to hear.

This has to be him, Zercien thought. *Maybe I can just blend in—*

"Who's this star recruit I've heard so much about?" said General Burgland.

Zercien groaned. Some scout must have spoiled his arrival. Boots and armor shuffled about him, all turning in his direction.

He sighed as he stepped away from the crowd and faced the renowned General Burgland, who stood quite a bit taller than he. "Well met, General. I am Zercien Volnaire."

A scowl, accompanied by crossed arms was the reply. "You? You don't look like much. Hope those months of paperwork haven't made Kanivar soft."

Zercien winced—he knew he wasn't the picture of physique Euvard was, but that seemed overly harsh. He did wonder if that guard captain at the square had fed him a lie. A bit insulting, if so.

"I assure you, it is me." He stood straight, puffing out his chest.

"Sometimes the unassuming ones are the ones you have to watch out for, eh?" General Burgland said, and winked.

"I hope I will not need such babysitting, General. I believe my talents will help win us the day."

Despite how impressed he was with his speaking so far, Zercien dearly wished it would never come to that.

A swift, strong hand covered by a protective gauntlet pounded on his shoulder.

"I like you, lad. This way now," General Burgland said, and twisted Zercien around to face the brigade he'd traveled with. He winced under the growing pain of the general's grip.

Why do all these military types like me? Zercien thought. *I don't like them.*

"Archers!" General Burgland's voice carried above the chatter. "Stay here until I send word."

No verbal answer, but a chorus of slinking chainmail and iron from the bowing soldiers ensued. With a hand gesture downward, General Burgland led Zercien down the slope of the hill, where the army stood ready.

All tall and strong, armed with lances in their main hands and short blade side-arms, and the Entervian Coat of Arms embroidered at the center of mixed metal and hard leather armor. A few hundred maybe. Not the entirety of the main force, but a large number.

Zercien gulped when he looked out, toward the last of Entervian soil. The old fortress loomed like a darkened beacon in the night sky, in the cold air. But his heart leapt to his throat when his eyes caught the numerous small dots about the structure, patrolling.

The Ankarthan Army. Of this he possessed little doubt.

His hands went cold and numb, and he was glad his soldier's sword sat in the sheath on his side. Otherwise it would be on the ground.

"All right, soldiers! Listen up!" barked General Burgland. "Our long-ranged reinforcements are here. It's time!"

A raucous shout burst from the soldiers. Zercien wanted to cover his ears.

"Our scouts tell us swarms of those filthy Northerners file from the fortress," General Burgland said as he pointed behind. "If that waste of space of a country employs a commander, they will be inside."

A commander, Zercien gulped. *Perhaps I'll stay put—*

General Burgland's heavy hand crashed back down on Zercien's shoulder. "But we've got a new star recruit, who will help lead us into the heart of the fortress!"

Shit.

"You won't believe the stories I've heard! You all better be able to keep up."

Fuck.

The front lines of the Entervian Army stared, mouths agape, like he was some person of importance. They murmured among themselves, and Zercien caught wind of scattered compliments.

It was a good thing he wore a helmet, as the chill from before had been replaced by a heat in his cheeks.

At last, the general released his shoulder.

"The Northern bastards should be gathered near the front of the fortress. On my signal, the main force—you lot—" he said while pointing at them, "will strike the enemy in a furious, triumphant charge. The archers will cover our backs. Once through their line, a small squadron will infiltrate and seize the fortress."

General Burgland's grin fell to Zercien as he spoke. "Make ready. We depart on my order."

The soldiers split formation to tend to any battle preparations—weapon sharpening, a last bit of water and provisions, the like. Zercien thought to join them, perhaps meet and mingle with those he would soon call comrades-in-arms, when General Burgland, again, gripped his arm and twisted him around. Zercien's eye roll stopped as soon as he faced the general.

"Come with me, lad," General Burgland said, and gestured Zercien toward the outer embankments of their war camp, surrounded by spiked barricades. From here, Zercien saw the Ankarthans swarm, as if showing a formation themselves.

"Our enemy's onto us, it seems," General Burgland said as he dropped prone. Zercien followed.

"How would they know?"

"Just a hunch." The general shrugged. "We've only sent scouts and smaller forces the past few nights. I imagine the North's anticipating a full assault."

"And we're to give them exactly what they expect?" Zercien said, cocking his head to the right.

General Burgland said nothing, and the two watched as more Ankarthan soldiers poured from the fortress and stood with those already outside.

"What did you do before enlisting, lad?" he asked.

"I was a teacher at the schoolhouse," Zercien said, and furrowed his brow. "I lectured the nobles' children."

"A *teacher?*" General Burgland laughed. "Can't say I've seen a teacher join our ranks before. Usually, us army folk are born into it. I've been here since my seventeenth year. It's all I know."

Zercien could only stare, and no words came through.

A battlefield. The oddest place I've made small talk, he thought. Perhaps it was how soldiers kept calm before a battle. Or perhaps General Burgland was more than just some brute.

"Let's say you're teaching, and you come across something new. Maybe it goes against something you previously taught," the general said. His fiery, battle-hardened look turned soft. "What do you do?"

"I would tell them the new information, and to disregard the old," Zercien said, quick and confident.

"You would admit you were wrong?"

Wrinkles formed on Zercien's forehead. "Perhaps 'disregard the old' is incorrect. I would use it as a lesson. Even educators are always learning, and sometimes new research contradicts previously conceived notions."

A hard slap smacked his back, followed by another laugh. "You're too smart for this army business, lad. Hope you live through this to get back to those kids. Sounds like they're missing a good one."

Don't make me like you. Please, Zercien thought, though he did let a smile spread over his lips. "Are you saying you've learned some new information?"

The front door of the looming fortress shut, and no more enemy soldiers appeared from within.

"Every day, I see more and more Ankarthan soldiers," General Burgland said as he surveyed the field. "Our hit and run tactics won't be enough. We don't have the troops to outlast them, but we're trained. Despite whoever is commanding them from inside, they've never had an army, let alone a competent one. They're just like those barbarians from the South. And much like back then, we'll win today, too."

Zercien didn't know much about the South, but like Ankarth, not many did. To the common folk, the "South" and "Southerners" were interchangeable with the country and people of Duspen. Though all Vellardians know of Duspen's Arvaros—somewhat organized bandit clans who called Duspen home, and provided all matter of goods to its citizens through pillaging and theft. At times they mustered the bravery, or foolishness, to venture over Entervia's borders. Dangerous, but not problematic if Entervians remained inside their city's cozy walls, as was accustomed.

True to the moniker, the desolate country borders the south of both Entervia and Ariglioth, but Zercien always thought the name to be derogatory. Similar to his feelings on the nickname the "North" for Ankarth.

General Burgland groaned as he pushed himself to his feet and dusted his hands on his armored legs.

"On your feet, lad," he said, and tilted his head back to the war camp. "Looks like the enemy's prepared. It's time for us to do the same."

CHAPTER SIXTEEN
THE PARIAH

Zercien and General Burgland, with the rest of the Entervian standing army, stood within sight of the menace from Ankarth, both set in their formations, if one could call them such. A line of armored warriors with lances, shields, and side-arm swords, and a mishmash of brigades standing behind, of varying weapon types and armor quality. Further back, the Entervian archery squads lay in wait. As soon as the main force began their charge, they would let the arrows fly.

Perhaps the army hadn't the luxury of such diversity in its forces, Zercien thought, but there was a certain power in its simplicity. Much like General Burgland himself.

Zercien's hands trembled as he felt for his sheath, his breath cold and visible in the chill dusk. On General Burgland's order, they were to charge, and he, on his first mission as an Entervian soldier, would be side-by-side with the renowned general.

He tapped his shaking feet on the hard ground as he darted his head to the right and left, looking for any streaks of grey, or some fogged cloud. But the dusk-darkened sky remained clear, the torchlight from their war camp providing light in excess.

Come on. Please, Zercien thought and pressed against his temple with his leather-gloved hand as if to force a headache forth. Still nothing.

"Nervous for your first battle, lad?" said the general.

"A bit." Zercien nodded.

"Stick by me. If your swordsmanship is even half of what Sergeant Kanivar said, these Ankarthans won't stand a chance against you."

"Let's hope." Not the most confident choice of words. But without the benevolent interference of before, how could he be?

Perhaps my skill alone could be equal to half of what the sergeant spoke of, he thought.

But with a head shake, he disagreed with his own thoughts. Like Euvard said, he only lasted last three rounds of sparring. As he peered over his shoulder, he wished his friend would come sprinting through the encampment, shouting his name.

Who am I kidding? Zercien thought. *If I fight as I am, I'm fucked.*

General Burgland unsheathed a long, broad steel sword Zercien assumed would break his arm if it were in his hands instead, and raised it high. Zercien's heart leapt with it—the signal.

As soon as the general's sword sliced down—

And there it came. General Burgland swung and yelled, "Entervia! Charge!" A roaring crowd followed his shout, accompanied by stampeding armored boots sounding as if an earthquake.

A numbness filled Zercien's legs, but they were moving. Dashing about the cold-hardened ground, stride-for-stride with General Burgland. Then came Ankarth—none seemed to have ordered them to sortie, and yet they acted in strategic unison.

Shadows gathered overhead. Zercien glanced upward to see a hailstorm of arrows, faster than the army's legs could run. The arrows collided with the Ankarthan front line, littering those who dared to continue their charge.

Zercien raised his sword to his neck, in case the Ankarthans employed a similar strategy. Though he sincerely doubted he possessed the ability to block an arrow with just a longsword. When no arrows came, a breath alleviated the heat in his throat.

The surviving Ankarthan soldiers neared, their eyes meeting Zercien's. But a faint cloud of fog appeared at one of the soldier's feet.

A sharp pain pierced through Zercien's head. Not of a sword or a lance, but inside his skull.

Yes! Zercien's mind cried. He pushed through the stabbing ache and confronted the first Ankarthan soldier to cross his path.

With one slash, the enemy soldier's arm was gone, cleaved from their shoulder blade. A hearty "Ha ha ha!" appeared in his mind, though muffled. General Burgland stood at the border of where his vision met the fog, slamming his sword into a heavily armored Ankarthan soldier.

Zercien spun to his right and slashed across his body, slicing a red line across an Ankarthan's chest. With a jab, he shoved his Entervian longsword through the soldier's light armor. He kicked the dead man off the sword and jabbed it through the neck of another.

Though his sword arm acted on its own, Zercien's body allowed him to react to each enemy blow. Had his arm not dispatched the enemy first, he would've been stabbed, as his body's movements were just a second too late. Still, as he fought, he learned to predict and time his swings and dodges.

Amid a pile of dead Ankarthans, he delivered a quick kick to a charging enemy soldier, and leapt with his sword out, digging it into his chest. As the Ankarthan writhed, Zercien pulled his sword away and swung forward, lopping his enemy's head off his shoulders.

The corpse spurting blood from its neck slumped onto the ground, and Zercien felt nothing. He shook his head, questioning why he hadn't yet lost the pathetic excuse for food the army fed him.

"Forward!" General Burgland's muffled voice. Zercien's swift and hushed footsteps carried him to wherever General Burgland stood, somewhere within the fog.

They breached the Ankarthan front, and enemy soldiers fled. Some shouts of victory burst from the Entervian side. With no enemies left to engage, Zercien thought to do the same, but his mouth would not let him. The fog clouding his mind cleared somewhat, leaving the perimeter of the battlefield as a veiled wall of grey.

His lips opened and spouted something he had no control over. "No! Do not relent!"

"Think you're a general, now?" said a fellow Entervian. "They're running! It's over!"

No. It can't be, Zercien thought. *It was too quick. Too simple.*

Whispers of the Entervian soldiers wafted through his fog, as if they were bored.

But then, a low rumble.

General Burgland heard it too, and he and Zercien exchanged glances with scrunched foreheads.

Zercien's body lurched forward and onto the ground, an ear to the dirt. It bounced gently. He leapt from his prone position, spinning to his feet. Fast-moving figures upon outlines of animals charged from behind their ranks.

"General!" Zercien's mouth yelled for him. "Horses come from the rear!"

Before the general could turn, screams erupted from the Entervian army's back lines. Horses trampled through the archery brigade, their riders impaling soldiers with lances.

"Ambush! Ambush!" Entervian soldiers screamed as they ran in a frantic panic about the battlefield.

"No! Stand your ground!" General Burgland ordered while waving his sword over his head to rally his troops. But as soon as his army had turned to face the rampaging soldiers on horseback, Zercien's ears perked to the sound of a heavy set of doors swinging open.

A battalion of soldiers bearing lances and bows charged from the fortress doors with reckless abandon at what used to be the Entervian front line.

We're trapped in the middle, Zercien thought.

He rushed to meet their new enemy, joined by General Burgland and a scant few Entervian soldiers. A stray horseback rider readied his lance at Zercien, but with one flick of his blade, the rider's hand was separated from his arm, and he tumbled off his steed.

"Make for the fortress!" General Burgland's mighty voice carried above the carnage. "At all costs, get inside the damn fortress!" Zercien joined him in his charge, picking off the Ankarthans guarding the entrance.

The general pointed at Zercien and waved his finger around at a dozen other Entervian soldiers. "All of you, with me! The rest, guard the entrance with your lives."

General Burgland slapped Zercien on the shoulder as they flew through the fortress's front door and through the halls. "We're capturing this fortress. Now."

"Yes, General. It is a sound plan," said Zercien's mind-controlled voice. He watched as his legs and feet navigated the narrow corridors through his mind-induced fog, as if he'd already memorized their pattern. Sounds of battle deafened behind. No enemy soldiers barred their path. The possibility of Ankarthans escaping during the attack was low, but Zercien could think of no other explanation.

General Burgland then held out his hand before turning into the next hall. A faint torchlight danced upon Zercien's fog, morphing the rolling mists into orange waves. The rest of the general's handpicked squad followed.

Quiet now, Zercien heard each individual heartbeat thump within his chest. Sweat poured from his forehead. Through the fog, the faint outline of a man—tall, broad. Heavily armored.

He shook.

"Someone is ahead, General," Zercien said and lowered his voice to a whisper. "If this fortress does indeed hold a commander, we can assume it is them."

The general raised an eyebrow and nodded. "Let's have a talk with this commander, then."

He ordered Zercien and his squad to enter, and they stormed into the torchlit room. But their dash was short-lived, and Zercien's eyes widened to their maximum, while General Burgland skidded to a halt. The other Entervians bumped into each other's backs.

At the foot of the back wall leaned a man encased from neck to toe in black armor, adorned with red streaks as haphazard as blood smears. He straightened himself and drew a large, wide sword the size of General Burgland's. Perhaps larger.

"What in the…" the general whispered, and he pointed his sword out in front. "Is this the North's commander?"

Has to be at least Euvard's size, Zercien thought as the knight sauntered toward him, the general, and his squad, every step in his black armored boots sending a tremble through the stone floors. He bore no helmet or mask, but Zercien's gaze was drawn to his pale face, and the black, inhuman pupils stretched across his eyes.

The knight spoke, facing General Burgland. A deep, commanding, and powerful voice, but not frightening. "Do you lead these soldiers?"

What Zercien's brief time with General Burgland showed him was that he wasn't about to be scared off by an eerie scowl.

The general answered without a stutter or any semblance of fear in his voice. "I do. And you, the Ankarthan army?"

"Leave this place. By remaining here, you only prolong the inevitable."

"Like hell I will!"

The knight said nothing and raised his sword into the air.

A searing pain lanced into Zercien, and he fell to his knees. Two streams of black floated above the knight's head, the fires of the candlelight distinguishing them amid the dark. Waving his sword forward, the oozing streams struck two soldiers standing to the right and left of General Burgland, and their screams gave way to their bodies bursting into ash.

Zercien cried as if he'd been the one struck, placing both hands on his temple. He couldn't speak, his mind and body frozen. The blood running through his veins burned as if set aflame.

General Burgland's eyes now showed fear. "What in the name of... magic? How?"

"Pariah Arts were bestowed upon me from within my own mind since birth," the knight said. "I showed signs of their mastery in my youth."

"But magic is supposed to be—"

"Leave this fortress and I will allow you and your army to flee without harm."

General Burgland brandished his sword. "Never!"

The knight swung his sword downward again, and three more streams of black flew from his hand. One by one, General Burgland's squadron dwindled, reduced to ash and dust upon the stone floor amid blood-curdling screams. The general snarled and ran forward, sword out.

The enemy commander deflected General Burgland's swing with ease, and the blow sent his sword crashing into the stone wall. Other Entervian soldiers joined on the charge, but each met a sword through the chest.

General Burgland retrieved his blade, but the knight conjured yet another stream of black oozing magic, and threw his hand down, sending it into the air.

Zercien shouted and leapt to his feet. He watched as the magic lanced through his mind's fog, as if it were traveling underwater, and dove in front of the general. Swinging high, he clashed his sword against the enemy commander's, and held strong as the powerful knight bore down.

Just as the stream of magic appeared overhead, Zercien forced the knight's sword away and landed a heavy blow against his armor. The enemy commander recoiled and slammed against the back wall.

Zercien raised his hands outward, as if preparing to meet the black ooze with an embrace. But the fog about his mind soon dissipated, all becoming clear, and the magic darted straight for him. A searing heat burst within his veins, and he screamed as the magic absorbed into his skin, coursing through his body.

He fell onto the hard floor, blinking to keep the darkness away. The knight stood, wobbling, his black pupils shrinking. Zercien felt strong hands grip and lift him into the air, and soon he was flying back through the fortress.

PART TWO
OF BLOODLINES AND REVERENCE

Chapter Seventeen
Fynnian

18 YEARS AGO

A nother night, another visceral chorus of shouts and cries screeching into young Fynnian's head, piercing the barrier of blankets and pillows he forced against his ears. Even through the walls and closed bedroom door, his parents' words remained loud, clear, and hateful.

"Time and time again I've caught you! You must stop this heresy!" It was his father's voice.

"*No*! I refuse to let you control me anymore!" His mother's voice grew deeper with each word until her normal, serene tone was all but gone.

Fynnian's younger brothers awoke and sat up, holding blankets over their noses. In the darkness, he could see the bedsheets quivering atop anxious legs.

He flipped his hand over and rubbed the underside of his pale wrist, along the veins that shimmered silver and gold. Much to his brothers' objections and low whispers of "No! Stay under the covers!", Fynnian slid off the bed and tiptoed to the door, the padding of his small feet dwarfed by his parents' constant yells. With his heart in the midst of leaping into his throat, he cracked the door open just enough for one eye. He faced his father's back, watching as his mother paced about the room.

"I am going to master this power!" she said. "I will be the first to use it for good. I will protect our boys. I will protect everyone! I just need more."

"Garnet," his father said in a lower tone, with no more shouting, "I shall not, cannot, and will not sit idly while my own wife studies Pariah Arts. You know this."

Fynnian gasped as his mother raised her right hand. A brief flash of fire erupted from her fingertips. She released a small flame, and it bounced about the darkness, the fiery shadows dancing along the door-frame.

Fynnian couldn't move. His breaths turned sporadic. It was over in a second, but the ashen remains would persist in his mind forever.

His father's voice grew somber. "And my nightmares have been confirmed. Not only are you falling victim to the seduction of Pariah Arts, you can cast it as well."

Through the crack in the door, Fynnian saw his mother's eyes grow to fiery red circles.

"Can't you see? I am unharmed!" she said. "Your Seraph Arts drain your energy. But mine, I can use with impunity! With this power—"

"I see it plainly, and I have but one solution," his father said. "Your soul has already been corrupted. You are beyond redemption. I order you to leave our home."

Fynnian backed away from the door. His mother's cheeks formed into bloodred pools, a wide, eerie smile replacing the tender one he'd seen all his life.

"Heh." Her voice deepened, rose, and deepened again, as if unknowing which octave to sing. "Tyrrowan, you would simply throw me out? Your *beloved* wife?"

Fynnian watched as his father countered her with the raising of his right hand. A light, far brighter than those shining beneath his wrist, emerged from his father's hand.

"It has already devoured most of your heart." Tyrrowan stared down at the floor, and grasped the light in his fist. "I am sorry."

Another flash blinded the room and rushed against the door, the power throwing Fynnian onto his backside. The purest of holy light illuminated the dark house, serpentine beams of white and gold spreading to every corner. His mother flew across the room in a burst of red flame, her feet never touching the wooden floor. She crashed through the front door of their home, cracking and splintering the frame. Her fire dissipated as she vanished and disappeared into the night.

His father barged into Fynnian and his brothers' room, and they all rushed to his arms. "Where's Mother? What happened to Mother?" Fynnian cried. Tears streamed down all the boys' faces.

And their father could not help but shed one himself. "She's gone. Your mother is never coming back."

Chapter Eighteen
The Last of the Order

Now you know what happened the day before my father left us," Fynnian said, and swiped a mixture of sweat and tears from his cheek with his sleeve before leaning against the back of the pew. His gaze wandered between the altar in front and the large statue of a nondescript man behind. He'd spent more days in this church than his own home.

"This is what Tyrrowan did not tell me," said the wizened priest, Father Sarentus. He tugged at his white beard. "You witnessed magic, Fynnian. Both Seraph and Pariah. Poor child. None that young should ever have to experience what you have."

While relieved to at last tell his priest of the atrocities from his youth, it was not enough.

"I am not a child anymore," Fynnian said. "It's been eighteen years. But I have fulfilled my end of the bargain. What did my father say to you before he left?"

The priest drew a deep breath. "Tyrrowan had his secrets, and I swore to keep them. But now, it is clear you have your own plans." He exhaled. "Please do not be angry with me, Fynnian."

Fynnian narrowed his bright blue eyes. "Father Sarentus."

"Someone was hunting Tyrrowan."

"Hunting?" Fynnian jumped up from the pew and to his feet. "Someone wanted him dead?"

"Your father told me that if he stayed here in Vellard, he would attract some terrible evil. He instructed me to tell you, Jyrren, and Dyodore to keep praying for his safe return, but it is doubtful your father will ever come home."

A sinking feeling dropped from Fynnian's throat, slamming into his stomach—like he'd just swallowed a block of wood. "You mean to tell me my own father lied to us?"

Father Sarentus stood and returned his calming hand to Fynnian's shoulder. "Tyrrowan had his reasons. All he wanted was to protect his three boys."

"Yes, but,"—Fynnian wrested his shoulder away—"that's what my mother said, too. And now she's gone."

He paced. Back and forth between the altar and Father Sarentus, a hand to his chin. "A terrible evil?" Fynnian crossed his arms. "What could he have meant?"

The old priest inched closer. "Dear boy, my ears aren't what they used to—"

"Ankarth!"

And the priest jumped back, steadying himself on the arm of a pew.

"Could he mean Ankarth?" Fynnian said again while Father Sarentus recovered his balance.

"Fynnian." The priest rubbed his left ear, shaking his head. "How could Tyrrowan have known?"

"I don't know. But no matter what it is, all doubts in my mind have been stripped away. I need to find him."

Father Sarentus shut his eyes and drew a deep breath. "I knew this would be your answer. And you are old enough to choose your own path."

"Except I don't know where to begin. I can't just *leave*," Fynnian said, putting his right fist under his chin, and sighed as he ran the other hand through his short, dirty-blonde hair. "Year 728, two days into the Summer Moon. The date of Father's departure is burned into my mind, like a farmer would brand his cattle. I don't know what it is about this anniversary, but unease follows me no matter where I tread."

"You were very young when he left. Now you are beginning to understand and possibly wonder why."

"Perhaps it *used* to be mere wonder, but *now*, it is a feeling of wanting to act."

The priest gulped. "Your father has sent no word, no clue of his location. It pains me to say it, but his fate is in God's hands now."

Fynnian shook his head. "Not good enough. Not anymore." Though he winced when he spoke, and darted his gaze away from the old priest.

"I've many questions for him, unanswered by the texts and stories." Fynnian resumed his pacing between Father Sarentus and the church's altar. "I want to know the real reason for the founding of the Sanctum Order, where the World's Tower is, why the Order was never restored after the Ancients' War, why me and Father are the only ones left." His voice trailed off.

"The legend of the Sanctum Order is indeed an intriguing tale," Father Sarentus said. "'Tis a shame the ending was such a sad one."

Fynnian spun around and smiled big. "Precisely why I need to find my father! Together, me and him, father and son, we shall rebuild the Order and return it to its former glory!"

"Fynnian!" the priest half-shouted, holding out his hands, wrinkled palms out. "You mustn't jump too far ahead. While all the Lord's followers wish for the same, the reconstruction needs to start small."

Fynnian looked down and shook his head. "Forgive me. I let my desires come forth too strongly."

"I feel it is best for you to stay here and await your father's return, as you have continued to do," said the priest. "It has taken you eighteen years just to recount the day. Though traumatizing it may be, does this bode well for the courage to undertake such a grand adventure?"

Letting me down easy was never one of the priest's strong suits, Fynnian thought amid a wince. "You've just said you doubt he will ever return, and his fate is with God now."

"Should you wish it, you could join the priesthood, and serve God. You could become spiritually closer to your father."

He'd often considered becoming a priest even before this proposal. It was all he ever dreamed of in life, to live and speak with God and enforce his rule.

I've more to do before I dedicate my life to the church, he thought. "I am sorry. I cannot. Not now. Though I feel terrible for rejecting such a generous offer."

"I understand," Father Sarentus said, followed by a sigh. "You should feel no such obligations toward me. When Tyrrowan left, he put his faith in me to care for his three boys. I did without qualm."

The kindness in the priest's words exacerbated the sinking feeling in his stomach. Until he and his brothers were old enough to care for themselves, they lived here, in this church. Clothed, fed, and raised by the altruistic priest.

He opened his mouth to speak, but was interrupted by Father Sarentus's gentle words, followed by an outstretched hand. "Will you search for your father?"

Fynnian shrugged and nudged the priest's arm away. "I haven't slightest idea where to look. And the only strength I possess is my devotion. I've none in my sword arm. If the guards do not lie about Arvaros activity outside Vellard's walls, a simple trip past the gate would require more than faith."

"I loathe the idea, but you have mentioned an acquaintance of yours with a mind for martial training." The priest winced like a blade had struck him with the mere mention of swordplay. "You could dedicate the next long while to swordsmanship."

"Euvard?" Fynnian crossed his arms. "Perhaps he would take me on as a trainee, but if Ankarth is what my father spoke of, then I haven't the time to hone my skills."

"I suppose." Father Sarentus let a smile spread. "My boy, you are not the brusque, intimidating type. You will need a bodyguard. Perhaps your brothers will join you."

Fynnian grimaced, eyeing his slim, thin frame and arms. He'd never tried so much as swinging a sword. "I would rather not put Dyodore and Jyrren's lives in danger for a dream so out of reach."

Any roaming Arvaros would find us three easier pickings than an apple from a low-hanging branch, he thought.

The priest smiled and blew a bit of air from his nose. "You've grown into a caring young man, just as your father wished. Though I doubt he would ever expect this side of you. Perhaps your wanting to find your father stems from the sacred blood you inherited from him— maybe it calls, just waiting for an answer."

Fynnian looked down, at the underside of his wrist, into the deep swirls of the purest silver and gold. Just speaking of his father frightened him, and he feared the blood would burst free.

Father Sarentus spoke again, awakening Fynnian from his trance. "What will you do?"

"For now? Pray. Pray for some divine intervention, a special circumstance, anything to allow me to set foot on such a reckless quest."

Chapter Nineteen
A Profane Recollection

After his battle with the mysterious knight, Zercien recalled nothing of the night prior. And now he was to deliver a report to the castle, to King Durnan himself? How rude of them, he thought.

"Right this way, Sir Zercien," said the castle guard, gesturing him to follow through the hall at a brisk pace.

General Burgland detailed the encounter after he awoke—somehow, he'd absorbed the knight's magic into his body, saving the remaining soldiers and knocking the fiend back in the process.

He tried to hide his smile as he and the castle guard stepped atop the regal-red carpet through the poshly decorated Castle Vellard hallways, his every few steps met with either an ornate stone statue or painting. Each featured the same signature written in fancy, curved lettering on the bottom-right: "Archibald."

After countless hours on the cold ground near Ankarth, and then rushing back to the capital in less than a day, his legs wobbled as if he'd been at sea. More than once he side-stepped nobles jogging through the castle halls, faces awash with fear. While their expressions worried him, Zercien was more concerned with the state of his legs.

When he thought of soldiers much older than he handling such duties, like General Burgland, he winced. He could hardly manage the walk at perhaps half that age, and wasn't keen on returning to the bat-tlefield after the conclusion of this audience. But after last night, Gen-eral Burgland told Zercien he was likely to be honorably discharged for his service.

Another smile surfaced at the thought. Able to see Saena again, visit with Euvard and spar on his own accord, and perhaps return to a peaceful life with his students, should he be welcomed back.

To never have to walk such a distance again, he thought, his smile still stretching. *It will be glorious.*

Kicking back on his chair, wine in one hand, the other wrapped about Saena's—

"Sir Zercien?"

Zercien blinked thrice. He'd stopped walking, and the castle guard stood ten steps ahead, looking back. "Apologies. Still not quite right."

He jogged to catch up, grimacing to hide the pain from his burning legs.

The guard bowed and bid Zercien to enter the door ahead. Zercien returned the gesture, faced forward, but stopped. He stood straight, hairs on the back of his neck on end.

The open chamber he'd just entered was none other than the Castle Vellard throne room, with King Durnan sat upon a golden, regal chair, outfitted with some of the fanciest garb Zercien had ever seen. He glared back at the guard before resuming his walk.

Could've said something, he thought.

King Durnan's eyes glowed with curiosity, and Zercien shuddered as his gaze wandered, feeling as a test subject would.

His bow almost turned into a trip to the floor as he attempted to be formal, and his head spun, nausea rising to his throat. Zercien's mind ran amok, and a chill forced its way down his spine. He'd never spoken to a king, and was afforded no instruction on proper etiquette.

If you faint, you'll be the laughingstock of the country, he thought.

He straightened himself out and at last provided a serviceable bow. "Greetings, Your Majesty."

Good. Start simple. Innocuous, Zercien thought.

King Durnan took a moment to speak, continuing his stare. But his eyes didn't intimidate, as if Zercien and he were old friends. At last, he cleared his throat, though his words were not as powerful as Zercien expected. "Sir Zercien Volnaire, yes?"

"Yes, Your Majesty," Zercien said, trying to keep his eyebrows from raising at the king's nervous gulp.

King Durnan stood from his throne and approached, and Zercien's heart leapt with each footfall.

He blinked hard to prevent any wayward sweat from stinging his eyes, but upon opening, the king's hand was outstretched in front. A strong hand, befitting that of someone who'd spent their life working, not sitting on a throne. But it quivered, rocking with a slight back-and-forth.

With an equally shaky hand, he gripped King Durnan's in a firm shake.

"You are a hero, Sir Zercien.," the king said.

Zercien's heart leapt into his throat. He feared the sudden onset of heat would transfer to the king's hand.

"Your quick action saved the life of our finest general, and the remaining soldiers in your squad," King Durnan said. "Entervia thanks you, as do I."

"Your Majesty, I—" Zercien flushed red, and a quiver in his gut prevented him from finishing his thought. Was his deed *all* him? He couldn't say for sure.

"You are welcome, Your Majesty. I am glad to be of service to my country."

Good answer, he thought while nodding in approval. *Sounded heroic.*

The king released his grip and stepped back on shaking legs.

"Now." King Durnan cleared his throat again. "Please, your report."

A chill, like a cold breeze had conjured itself amid the throne room.

"We entered the fortress and encountered a knight—" Zercien said, but King Durnan raised his right hand. The chill was replaced by a heat wave.

Did I speak out of turn? Is he angry? Zercien's mind raced.

"I have been briefed on the altercation with the mysterious knight," King Durnan said.

Zercien's eyebrows at last broke free from their frozen state, and rose. *You dolt.* He furiously scratched above his eye in a poor attempt to hide it.

"Instead, I would rather you explain your encounter," King Durnan said, scratching at his black beard, accented with grey.

"How do you mean, Your Majesty?" Zercien asked.

"The knight can conjure Pariah Arts." King Durnan spoke as he paced about the chamber. "Oniro has not seen such magic since the Ancients' War. But you know that, I'm sure."

"Ah, well—" Zercien attempted to speak, but was too preoccupied by constant throat-clears. "It was awful, Your Majesty. My comrades, they were incinerated. Reduced to ashen remains on that cold, hard floor."

"And General Burgland would have joined them, had you not interfered." The king's footsteps grew louder as he approached Zercien again, eyes appearing stern, almost at a glare. "*You* should have, as well."

It was Zercien's turn to gulp. He jumped as King Durnan rested his hand on his shoulder. "Calm yourself, lad—erm, soldier. All I want to know is what happened. How you survived such an attack, when others could not."

His grip was warm, comforting. Not like Euvard's massive brick of a hand. But the nerves did jump, escaping their cages within his body.

"Truthfully, Your Majesty, my memory is foggy." Zercien smacked his lips. "I faintly recall jumping in front of General Burgland, and repelling the knight's sword stroke."

He caught the king smirking, but continued.

"Then the magic struck me. It burned. Like a flame erupting inside my body." With a brief eye roll targeted at himself, Zercien shook his head. *This sounds like a load of hogwash*, he thought.

"My skin, hair, blood. Everything felt as if I'd thrown myself into a fire pit," he said. "But then, nothing. The magic dissipated, and I was on the floor."

"Astonishing. Truly," King Durnan said. "And you're sure that was not the magic's intent? To cause such pain?"

"It seemed the same spell cast upon my allies. The knight's eyes may have been more shocked than mine."

The king removed his hand from Zercien's shoulder and returned to his throne, leaning his chin against his fist. "And you are fine? No ill effects?"

Now that the king said it, Zercien remembered he'd not been assailed by searing head pain yet today.

Best leave my headaches out of this, Zercien thought. Another interrogation was not something he looked forward to.

Instead, he nodded. "Yes, Your Majesty. I feel fine." His legs buckled, an ache traveling to his knee. "Perhaps a bit sore, but I'm fine. Truly."

King Durnan fidgeted in his golden seat, nodding to himself. "Your surviving comrades are understandably shaken. None of them will fight. You, along with all of them, are hereby granted honorable discharge from the Entervian Army."

Zercien couldn't stop it. His smile beamed, but only for a second in another terrible attempt to hide his true feelings. Though his heart did drop when King Durnan returned his smile.

"You need not hide such thoughts from me, Sir Zercien," the king said. "I am sure you've some loved ones who would be joyous to see you return unharmed. And with quite the tale to tell. However, I do ask that you not speak of magic. I fear our fellow Vellardians would not react to such news as calmly as you."

Heat rose to Zercien's cheeks. Before he could answer, the king raised one finger. "Once this war is over, I will arrange for you to receive a medal of honor for your actions against Ankarth, and for saving the life of General Burgland."

"You are too generous," Zercien said. "Thank you, Your Majesty."

"If only I could do more, my—erm, Sir Zercien. Now, you are excused. Return to those you hold dear."

Zercien bowed, and a guard escorted him from the throne room, all smiles for his return to a boring, everyday life.

CHAPTER TWENTY
A MODEST ACCOUNT OF WAR

Zercien skipped the whole walk home. Though his heart pinged with a slight uneasy heat. The thought of accepting the discharge and relinquishing his post lingered. This was all he wanted, but now that he finally *had* it, something prevented him from enjoying the moment. Perhaps he developed a sense of duty in such a short time, even if the encounter with the knight would likely haunt him for life.

Better than that robed man, he thought, and shuddered. He shook his hands in a strange attempt to rid himself of the feeling, for today should be reserved for happiness.

At last, he was to return to his beloved, and smiled upon reaching their house. The wooden exterior was unchanged, grass still the same height as when he left it.

Maybe I wasn't gone as long as I feel, he thought.

With a gentle knock, he tapped the door a few times. No answer. After a minute of anxious pacing, he knocked again.

"Have some patience, will you?" Saena's voice. Irritated. Despite her anger, it stirred a flutter in his heart.

"Now, what the hell do you—" she said while swinging the door open, but her mouth hung agape when Zercien met her annoyed stare with a goofy smile.

"Hi, love."

She dove headlong into his arms without another word, tackling him onto the grass. Rolling about their yard she assailed him with rapid kisses to his neck, cheeks, lips, wherever she wanted.

When she gave herself a moment to breathe, she rolled him over, laid on top of him and asked, "What are you doing home?"

Zercien smiled and brushed back her long hair, his hand lingering against her cheek. The sun's bright rays through the blue sky highlighted the already-stunning eyes he missed so dearly. Staring up at her right now, he'd give everything to remain in this moment, never to allow time to advance again.

"Honorable discharge. In my first mission. I may be in a textbook someday." He scrunched his face and shrugged.

Saena shook her head and planted another kiss on his cheek. But her smiling face then turned to surprise.

"Was it something heroic?" Saena gasped and jumped off him. "Or are you hurt?"

Zercien leapt up from the ground and onto his feet. He held his arms out like a performer would after a successful stunt. "Not at all."

Saena assumed her tackle pose. "Something heroic, then?"

Zercien smiled. "In a fashion, yes." He turned his head left and right, squinting, but then nodded.

"Secret military business. But I can tell you if you swear to never speak of it to anyone."

"Part of the army for less than a week and you're already indoctrinated, I see."

Zercien tilted his head.

"Fine," said Saena. "I won't tell."

He gestured to Saena to lean in closer and detailed his first mission—the full assault on the Ankarth-occupied fortress. She gasped and grabbed his arm during seemingly random intervals, or when Zercien embellished his deeds.

"We found the enemy commander. He slew most of my platoon, and was about to strike down General Burgland, but I stepped in and fought off the blow in his place."

Saena put both hands in front of her mouth to quiet the ensuing scream. "You saved General Burgland?"

Zercien nodded.

"What happened with the enemy commander?" she asked.

"Despite blocking his strike, I was forced to escape with the other soldiers. He could have slaughtered us all, given the chance."

Saena shivered—he could almost feel the chill and restrained himself from copying her.

"They discharged the surviving soldiers from that night for 'traumatic experience,'" he said. "I assume they feared us survivors would turn tail the next time the enemy commander appeared."

He wrestled with himself over whether to tell Saena of the magic. The Pariah Arts that turned his allies into piles of smoldering ash. While King Durnan requested he not, Saena was his exception to most policies. But he couldn't. He still didn't believe it himself. Magic, surfacing again, was not on his list of probable explanations for Ankarth's military might.

She wouldn't sleep a wink for the rest of her life, Zercien thought. *Best if she's kept unaware.*

"And they may not be wrong," he said alongside a shrug. "He's strong, Saena. I doubt many could defeat him in single combat. I surely could not. And he even withstood General Burgland's assault."

"Who was he?" Saena said. "Did he have a name?"

Zercien lowered his voice to a whisper. "He wouldn't state his name. He wore all black, with red streaks across his armor resembling blood, but showed his face. His eyes..." Zercien shuddered at the thought. "Black pupils, stretched to the corners. They didn't seem human."

"Soldiers tend to exaggerate."

"I couldn't be more serious."

"Then how will we win?"

"He is human. I think. He bleeds. Like you or me, a blade in the heart would kill him. Now the army knows of his existence and can refocus their efforts."

Saena nodded. "Thanks to you, they have hope. But for now, it's the army's problem." She beamed a wide smile. "And you are no longer part of it. Welcome home, my love."

They kissed again.

"If only we could tell Mayla and Euvard too," Saena said. "But Euvard told Mayla to take some time away from the stall for her birthday. Haven't seen either of them for a couple of days. They wouldn't answer their door, either."

Zercien chuckled. He remembered Euvard's plan. Hopefully it went smoother than the avoid military service plan.

"We can surprise them tomorrow," Zercien said. "But for now—"

Saena shushed him, grabbed his hand and pulled him inside.

CHAPTER TWENTY-ONE
AN UNEXPECTED MENACE

Zercien awoke to screams from outside his window. Jumping up
—but slow enough to not wake Saena—he raced to the glass and
peeked outside to see Vellard's early risers running about in a
frenzy. He rubbed the grogginess from his eyes and spotted a large
crowd toward the east exit. He couldn't make out who they were, but
they were facing another group, all men. A heated exchange, fists
raised, but the unknown group then drew swords.

Zercien massaged his temple in an attempt to assuage his rapidly
clouding mind. "Not now, please. It's been one fucking day."

His mind's fogginess was interrupted by a springing-awake Saena
stomping out of bed.

She pushed his head to the side while he played dumb, blinking
hard.

"Just a bit of commotion outside," Zercien said. "Looks like none
of our business."

"None of our business? You dolt!" She rammed her finger at the
glass. "Who are those people? They're armed!"

"Saena." He pressed his finger in circles along his forehead. "Keep
it down, would you? My head hurts."

Without another word, she changed into one of her comfortable
blouses and long skirts.

"What are you doing?" Zercien asked, though he knew full-well exactly what.

She threw him a shirt and fixed her bedhead in front of a standing mirror. "We're going down there."

Like hell we are, he thought. "This is a job for the guards."

"Do you see any guards?"

"I'm sure they'll be there soon—"

Before he could blink, Zercien was assailed by flying socks and pants in rapid succession. "Dress yourself. Now," Saena said.

Fuck.

Zercien grumbled, but his heart pinged as the fog in his head grew once more, like he knew this decision was the right one, and dressed fast. Arguing further was pointless. Though he did love her fiery stubbornness.

At times.

"Wait," Saena said, and put a hand on his shoulder. Unlike the others who made a habit of grabbing him by the arm, her touch was welcome. "I'm sorry. I'm being rash. You *just* returned. We shouldn't rush into anything."

Zercien stopped his arm mid-reach for his sword when the grey fog rolled through the windows and doors, curling like waves into the house.

Saena's words seeped into his ears as if he were underwater. "Maybe the guards will arrive soon."

Without his own mind's permission, his hand grasped the sheath and attached it to his belt.

"No. You were correct to alert me of the situation," he said, and Saena jumped back at the deep, commanding tone. With one hand, he opened the door and peered outside to see dozens of street-goers running past, through the fog. He nodded. "With me. Now."

Mouth agape, Saena obeyed, and followed him outside. "Zerc?"

He didn't answer, and instead caught the attention of an older man, out of breath.

"You'd be right to steer clear of that street," the man said. "It's dangerous. We're off to find any of the blasted guards supposedly patrolling."

"What's the situation?" Saena asked.

"Arvaros run amok. The fiends crashed through the gate, and no city guards are in sight."

"All guards must be preparing to sortie into Ankarth," Zercien said and took Saena by the hand. "Saena, behind me, now."

"You're scaring me. What's happening?"

"No time to explain."

She mouthed "What?" but followed.

The guard post at the east gate had already been destroyed, a scattering of hewn timber littering the grass. Men with scars along their exposed arms and faces, wearing assorted colors of ripped fabric sewn into something resembling clothing, ran roughshod over the nearby homes. Into their large sacks and boxes went stolen goods and food. As Zercien feared, the older man was correct—Duspenese Arvaros had attacked.

Zercien saw Euvard and Mayla crouched beside a house, opposite to where the Arvaros stood. His friend was armed with his trusty battleaxe over his back. A real one. Euvard furrowed his brow and pinched himself.

"*Zerc?* The hell are you doing here?"

"He was discharged. We'll explain later," Saena said before Zercien could. "You two look exhausted."

Mayla tried fixing her ruffled, fresh-out-of-bed hair. "A situation with a painter, is all. He—never-mind." She shook her head. "Another time."

Zercien bent down next to Euvard and nodded. "Report in."

Euvard shot him a side-eyed glance. "Since when do you talk like this?"

"I always have. Is that not apparent?"

"Not at all, but—" Euvard just shook his head. "Got a half-dozen Arvaros out there. No guards. We should step in."

Zercien surveyed the area, nodding. "I agree with your assessment. We are outnumbered. I will enter first and attempt to quell the situation before resorting to violence. However, if it does come to blows, I believe the odds to be in our favor based on fighting prowess alone."

Euvard blinked hard and pinched his own cheek. "Zerc, I mean no offense, but what the fuck are you on about?"

Zercien didn't answer, and instead turned back to Saena and Mayla, leaving Euvard to his dumbfounded expression. "Please do not follow us. A dangerous situation looms. Understood?"

"Uh, okay?" Mayla muttered. She mimicked Euvard's look.

Zercien glanced at his friend and pointed toward the Arvaros. "Come, Gunvald. Let us aid these fine citizens."

"*Excuse* me?" Euvard said.

As if nothing at all were occurring, Zercien sauntered through the middle of the chaos, ignoring any and all screams, fixed on one Arvaros standing still. Euvard walked behind him, and the two were harassed by course words and excess saliva.

"Hey, Muscles! And average-looking one!" said the Arvaros. "We're preoccupied. How about you leave?"

This Arvaros wasn't a muscular man himself, less in the bicep department than Zercien. Though he was thinner than thin, like he hadn't eaten in days.

Zercien felt his lips scrunch. Was it *he* who held onto some sympathy for this disgusting man? He had no idea.

"Won't be happening," Euvard answered.

"You looking to start trouble?" said the emaciated man.

"No, good sir. No trouble necessary," Zercien said, deadpanned and serious. "We merely wish for you to leave these fine folks alone. If you flee, we will not alert authorities, and you shall be spared."

The Arvaros laughed loud and obnoxious and called another over. A bit pudgier, but with brown splotches dotting his face, as if he had no home to shelter from Duspen's harshest days.

"Listen to these two!" He pointed at Zercien. "His speech is funny."

"Well, looks like talking to them won't help," Euvard said as he pulled his massive battle-axe from over his back.

"Ah, Gunvald. I suppose you may be correct," Zercien said and with a sigh, unsheathed his Entervian soldier's sword.

Euvard eyed him with a sideways glance, but shook his head and returned his gaze to the Arvaros. He brandished his battle-axe, gripping the handle with both hands. "Is this more your language?"

"That's what you're looking for, eh?" the pudgy Arvaros said.

Zercien wavered in between consciousness, everything in front of him unfolding at half the speed. His every breath was slow and pronounced, and all in his sight remained awash with grey.

The Arvaros came running, jagged sword out in front, his legs stuttering with every slow step. With one hand, Zercien grabbed the Arvaros' arm and forced his sword aside and shoved his own through his midsection.

The fog faded, and Zercien shook his head, bewildered and dazed. "What…what happened?"

But he had no time to think, as the skinny Arvaros accosted him. Time resumed its normal speed, and all the sparring he'd done with Euvard and his witness to combat on the battlefield melded together, exploded in his mind, and he matched sword strokes to the Arvaros'.

With a downward strike, Zercien sliced the fingertip of his enemy's main hand, and he recoiled in pain. Zercien finished off the Arvaros with a forward stab, and his hand sunk deeper into the skin and guts of the dead man. He nearly dropped his sword in disgust of the splattered blood.

Wait, he thought. *What's going on?*

He spun in circles on his feet, waiting for the fog to return. But it never did.

Zercien looked at Euvard and watched him cleave another Arvaros' head right off his shoulders, and shuddered. As he darted his gaze about the now-battlefield, he heard a yelp coming from his right, and his heart jumped. Another Arvaros, but ambling toward the house where he and Euvard urged Saena and Mayla to hide.

"Euvard!" he called to his friend. "With me. Now!"

Not waiting, Zercien dashed ahead, and before the Arvaros could turn around, he plunged his sword through his body and pulled, spraying blood upon the dirt and grass. Zercien shoved the dead man off the blade, and he fell with a thud at Mayla's feet.

She had a hand on her long skirt, as if reaching for something. But pulled it away as soon as she saw Zercien. He cocked his head, but before he could say anything, Euvard stomped into the middle, his bloodied axe over his back.

"About damn time, you two," Mayla said. "I was about to take them both on myself."

"Both?" Euvard said, looking around for the second Arvaros she spoke of. Though he was out of breath.

Zercien ignored her and instead put both hands on Saena's shoulders in a gentle hold to steady her shaking. "It's all right. The Arvaros are fleeing."

But he jumped at an unfamiliar voice. A pained shout. His nose found the grubby man on the ground before his eyes could. Euvard and Mayla already stood over him.

"This is the one, eh?" Euvard said as Zercien joined them, leading Saena gently with one hand. A line of dried, red blood formed between the Arvaros' nose and upper lip. A welt formed from under his chin.

Zercien looked over at Mayla, who was rubbing the palm of one hand over the other's clenched fist. Spots of blood dabbed on her knuckles. Not hers.

The Arvaros shifted on the ground, bending his legs to stand, but Mayla's honeyed voice kept him on his back. "Here, let *me* help you up."

The Arvaros gawked with a wide-open mouth and a stare to match, and reached for her hand. She pulled it away and kicked him—hard—in the side.

Euvard made a poor attempt at hiding a chuckle, overtaking the Arvaros' cries of pain.

"Just you wait!" said the Arvaros. "Once I get up, I'll run you all through, take over this city myself!"

A low rumble then trickled into Zercien's ears. Light footsteps, growing louder into an almost-stampede. Zercien's first thought was more Arvaros, and he turned in the sound's direction as a low scream emitted over the silent air.

His heart sunk as more men from Duspen ran down the side of the road, hands in the air. He couldn't make out what they looked like from here, save one wearing a black bandana, but as they approached, Zercien lifted his eyebrows. Were *they* being chased?

"Must be the city guard," Zercien said. But he was proven wrong when a streak of dark garb whooshed by.

Lloyd drove his sword into one of the Arvaros' backs, used it as a lever to fling himself forward, yanked it free, and leaped in front of the remaining foes. They skidded to a stop, slipping on the dirt road. The one wearing the bandana opened his mouth to speak but was cut short when Lloyd ran his blade through his throat. With his sword still sticking through the Arvaros' neck, Lloyd thrust his serrated dagger into the last one's stomach, all before the bandana landed on the blood-soaked ground.

A chill assailed Zercien's shoulders, sending a shiver throughout his body.

"Forget what I just said!" said the Arvaros on the ground between gulps, and Zercien's attention snapped back to him. "Let me go, and I'll leave! And, uh, I won't come back! I swear on my life!"

"I don't know." Euvard shrugged. "What do you think, Zerc?"

He replied to Euvard's shrug with crossed arms. "Let's have our friend here answer some questions before we decide that."

Euvard nodded. "We'll make him useful while he's here, then."

"Yes, yes!" The Arvaros agreed with rapid head bobs. "Anything you want, I'll do it!"

Zercien stepped closer, the entirety of his shadow stretching over the Arvaros. "Where in Duspen are you from?"

Duspen wasn't much for towns or cities, but the various clans founded their own mini states, or so the books said. Zercien had no urge to visit the cursed land to see for himself.

"My home? Denon-Hein. Right over the Castham River. Straight south from here," said the Arvaros.

"Why would you attack Vellard?"

"Not my idea." The Arvaros' thin strands of hair danced with his head shakes. "We were given orders to attack, steal as much as we could. The boss said it himself. 'Entervia's warring with the North. Ransack them while the army's busy.'"

"Really, now?" Euvard jumped in. "This wasn't just a random attack?"

"No, sir."

"Any more of your friends out there?"

The Arvaros gulped. "No. I swear."

Euvard turned to Zercien again. "Anything else?"

With one eye, Zercien pored his gaze into the Arvaros, stunning him with a mere look.

"One more and you're free." He resumed his cross-armed pose. Your leader, or your 'boss' as you called him. What's his name?"

The Arvaros' eyes grew wide, and blank white. His complexion paled. Perhaps just a natural reaction to such a question, but...

No, Zercien thought. *It's more.* Despite the seconds passing between them, the Arvaros never blinked. *He's terrified.*

"I can't tell," the Arvaros said, with more rapid head shakes. "Can I go now?"

Mayla readied her leg for another kick, and the Arvaros raised his arms over his face.

"Boss's name's Reaver. That's what he told us to call him, anyways. Don't know if it's his real name. Please don't tell anyone I told you—"

Zercien nodded. "You can leave. We won't hurt you."

Out of the corner of his eye, Zercien spotted Lloyd walking back up the dirt road he'd just chased the Arvaros down.

"But *he* might." Zercien winked.

The Arvaros jumped to his feet, yelped, and sprinted toward the city gates. Zercien watched as he fled out of sight. The vicinity's scent, though still of the aftermath of battle, grew much more pleasant.

Able to wrangle some information from him, at least, Zercien thought.

Wiping his hands on his shirt, he pretended to ignore the black-clad swordsman. He was prepared to let Lloyd just continue to walk on by, but Euvard *had* to call out. Zercien cursed under his breath as the swordsman turned around. He cast a glare upon all of them that oozed power—and annoyance.

Zercien felt Saena's hands grab his back, and she shuffled behind him, hiding half her body.

"I'd rather the Arvaros come back instead," she whispered.

"Don't worry about Lloyd, okay?" Zercien whispered back with a nod. At least that's what he *said.* He wasn't entirely confident in the answer.

"Thanks for the help, Lloyd," Euvard said.

"You put an end to this before it escalated further," Zercien added, though his voice quivered. Just standing in Lloyd's presence caused his muscles to tremble. "We may have been overrun without you."

Lloyd turned his back to them and just tilted his head. "My actions were not governed by such thoughts. The fools intruded upon my land."

"Did you at least warn them?" Saena blurted out and then went back into hiding behind Zercien.

"No."

And he was gone. Disappearing up the road in another rush of darkness.

"Uh, anyway," Euvard said, though his voice was not the usual confident, and boastful. A shaky undertone hung to his every word. "We did the city a service today, didn't we?"

Zercien looked upon the bodies of slain barbarians and cringed. But his friend's face looked far worse than his injuries, which were only a few scrapes. He could tell Euvard strained every bit of his strength for his movements to not match the fear in his voice.

A taste of real combat, Zercien thought, and the recent memories of his first battle flowed back into his mind. *Not even Euvard can be unaffected.* "We did. But the absence of the city guard concerns me," Zercien said.

"Not much we can do," Euvard said amid a shrug. "But now you're going to tell us what the hell that was all about."

Zercien's face turned a deep red. "What do you mean?" He played a fool and smiled.

"Don't try to wriggle your way out of telling us," Mayla said and crossed her arms. "After what happened the last time you and Euvard sparred, you think we wouldn't be worried?"

Saena shot a look at Mayla. "What happened?"

Fuck, Zercien thought, and pressed the tips of each finger and thumb into his forehead in a, frankly quite poor, massage. He'd have a lot of explaining to do once he and Saena returned home. His words came in rapid stutters as he tried to connect his web of lies.

"I don't believe I acted out of the ordinary—"

Euvard rolled his eyes and Zercien could have sworn he heard them turn.

"The fancy talk? The way you strutted around like some general?" Euvard spoke slow, enunciating each word. "And you called me *Gunvald*?"

"Oh, *that*." Zercien flicked his wrist away from him and fake-smiled with a forced laugh. "It's quite funny, actually. You see, I needed a little confidence. So, I roleplayed. Little trick the army taught me to overcome my nerves."

"You *roleplayed*?" Euvard just blinked a few times. "Because the *army* taught you."

"Just trying to muster up some strength from those old stories." Zercien hacked up another fake laugh. "You always said I paid too much attention to them."

He watched as Euvard, Saena, and Mayla just exchanged eyebrow raises.

"Well, there goes my question about why you got discharged. Because you lost your fucking mind." Euvard threw his arms up. "But it worked. I suppose."

Zercien exhaled.

Euvard stretched, looking like he was coming to a yawn. "We should be heading back now. Been a tough couple of days for us."

"Come by later, would you, Saena?" Mayla said. "I'll need some help opening the stall." Saena nodded and smiled.

Before they turned to walk away, Euvard pointed at Zercien. "Don't think I forgot! You're coming too and telling us what the hell happened up there in the North."

Zercien smiled. It sounded like his friend almost *did* forget. "I will."

As he nodded and went to walk home, Zercien expected Saena to be right behind him. But she stood still, glaring, tapping her foot. "That may have worked on them, but I know you're not telling me, or anyone, the truth."

Of course she knew. He should have known better than to think he'd outsmart her.

"I'm serious," Zercien said. "Have I ever lied to you?"

Except for right now. And those other times, he thought.

She groaned and stopped her fidgeting. "No."

And Zercien winced as she mouthed the word.

I'm so sorry.

CHAPTER TWENTY-TWO
SHADOWS RISE

King Durnan rested his chin on both hands, admiring the clippings from texts and scrolls he'd collected during his research. Upon his desk, writings and illustrations of the great hero Holunt, speaking of his ability to repel Pariah Arts with his mind. He placed his hand atop a hanging page, depicting an artist's interpretation of Holunt, and clutched it against his chest, which too bubbled with nerves that still lingered from his meeting with the young Zercien.

"Ankarth may have magic, but perhaps we, too, have a weapon none have seen in years," he whispered.

A hammering on his study door jolted him from his hunched position, and he dropped the paper. He arose from his chair with a gasp, but more annoyed at the disturbance of his research. Though his irritation dissipated when he heard, "Urgent report from the city, Your Majesty!"

"Enter," the king said.

A servant rushed through the door, breathless. "King Durnan!"

"Keep it down." King Durnan motioned downward with his hands.

"The city guard has just relayed us news of a Duspenese Arvaros attack upon the east gate. They infiltrated the walls."

"*What*?" King Durnan exclaimed even louder than the servant. "Alert the Ruling Council and Urian immediately. I don't care what they're doing. Tell them to meet in our council chamber. *Now*."

"Yes, Your Majesty!" The servant bowed and sprinted out of the king's quarters.

Without even changing in to his red gown, the crownless monarch rushed to the chamber, and in a few minutes was joined by Grandmaster General Urian and the rest of the Council.

The servant from before entered, a Vellardian town guard by their side, and spoke. "Your Majesty, Grandmaster General, council members, this is the guard with the report from the city." With a bow, the servant vacated the council chamber.

"Your Majesty, Grandmaster General Urian, esteemed Ruling Council. Earlier I was made privy to an attack on our east gate by Arvaros from Duspen."

"When was the attack?" said Grandmaster General Urian.

The guard gulped. "Early this morning, sir."

"And why were we not made aware? It's near midnight."

"I am afraid to report that the city guard did not mobilize until midday and spent the remainder of the daylight cleaning the mess. They could not spare a single messenger until now. Please understand."

King Durnan sighed. Something told him the guard didn't speak the full truth. While most of the city guards prepared to take positions on the front lines in Ankarth from the west gate, the forces remaining inside Vellard should have been enough for a prompt reaction to a breach of the city's walls.

"Civilian casualties? Property damage?" King Durnan asked.

"The guard post was destroyed, as were some items stolen. Thankfully, the only dead were the Duspenese."

King Durnan and Grandmaster General Urian exchanged looks.

"Dead Duspenese? Who fought them off if the city guard were absent?" said the general.

"He refused to give his name, but Guard Captain Ardian Calvus identified him. Zercien Volnaire."

The king regretted taking a swig from his cup while the guard spoke, and the remaining water ended up on the floor. "You are dismissed. Thank you."

Proceeding with a bow, the guard walked backward, and then turned to exit the chamber.

"It is as I feared," King Durnan addressed his council. "We now face attacks from both Ankarth and Duspen. We haven't the soldiers to defend both borders, and victory against Ankarth is eluding us. Continuing as we are, sheer survival, let alone winning the war, will be a daunting task."

No response, save for the tapping of nervous feet.

"We settle this matter tonight. Before the sun rises, Entervia needs a new course of action. Until then, none shall leave this room. Urian, my Ruling Council, I am open to suggestions. Spout them as you wish."

The late night turned to early morning. Idea after idea was brought up, discussed, and subsequently denied. It seemed Entervia was not going to win this war on the strength of the army alone.

"Urian, have we any new recruits to take our entrance exam?" said Council Member Dallonta. She winced, as if she knew the answer already, creating faint wrinkles in her forehead.

"No," was the brief reply with a sigh from their Grandmaster General. "We've exhausted our recruits. Every soldier enlisted in any sort of service is either on the field right now or in the barracks, preparing."

"Our only choice is conscription, then," said Council Member Ellana. "Anyone in a certain age range will be—"

"*No,*" King Durnan's voice barely carried over the slamming of his fist. "The damn Ankarthans are trained. Civilians will be massacred."

"Then I suppose the only way to go now is east." Council Member Ellana raised one hand, tapping a finger against her cheek. "We could petition Ariglioth for reinforcements."

Ariglioth, King Durnan thought. An ally by the virtue of being the only country on the continent they weren't at war with, but an ally nonetheless. A single Meistari could take on a squad of Entervian soldiers. Though he hadn't spoken to King Lennard in some time.

Grandmaster General Urian shifted in his seat. Even he would admit to the Arigliothan army being the stronger of the two.

"How do you intend to reach Ciprius? Our port's been shut down since the war began," Grandmaster General Urian said. "Can't even approach it without nearing the battlefield. And now Arvaros are afoot? Sending any sort of crew to prepare a ship would be slaughter. No ship has any hope of sailing."

Damn, the king thought. *He's right.*

"A search party by horseback should be able to outrun those barbarians," said Council Member Dallonta.

"We've no more horses. All have been sent to the battlefield," said Grandmaster General Urian.

"And not to mention the gossip about what sorts of creatures lie outside the city's walls," added Council Member Leeland, showing his hand, palm up. "We all know of the many proclaimed 'sightings'—"

"Don't tell me you believe those ghost stories. They're just wives' tales to prevent children from wandering outside the city at night."

"Nobody leaves the city. It seems they've worked."

A brief silence swept the room. King Durnan recognized foreign aid would be necessary, and any soldiers from Ariglioth could cross the land without fear of a Duspenese attack. Even Arvaros recognized their strength—they would flee from any banner so much as featuring the Arigliothan Crest. If only he had such a banner at his disposal.

"Hold. I've an idea," said Council Member Dallonta. "Zercien Volnaire could be our messenger."

King Durnan erupted in a coughing fit, and he rushed to cover his mouth with his hand while the other thumped in a fist over his chest.

"I quite like the idea, myself," said Grandmaster General Urian. "Albeit one of the shorter-lived military careers I've seen, he seems to have developed quite the reputation. Already proven he can take on those Southern scum, too. And as a former teacher, we know he's not just muscle."

Council Member Leeland shook his head. "Barbarians, yes, but what about the—"

"Quit it with the ghost talk, Leeland," said Council Member Dallonta, answered by the first shreds of laughter in many an hour. "Mister Volnaire could arrange some companions and—"

King Durnan, again, obnoxiously coughed. "Interesting proposal. Though we cannot just send citizens. They will need a proper escort from an Entervian officer. I'm afraid we cannot spare any of the guard—"

"We have a plan for reinforcements. I can afford to send one now." Grandmaster General Urian interrupted his king. "After his complete and utter botchery of the Arvaros attack, I'm keen to offer Captain Ardian Calvus to accompany Sir Zercien. Does His Majesty approve?"

Each Council Member's stare seared into King Durnan. Despite his hesitation, the council had come to a reasonable solution. To send young Zercien, a man capable of repelling the enemy commander, to

Ariglioth was not the solution he wanted, but he brought forth no counterarguments.

For my country, then, he thought. *I'll do it.*

"You are all dismissed. In the morning, I will arrange a messenger to deliver our request to Zercien Volnaire."

CHAPTER TWENTY-THREE
AMBITIONS ENTWINED

A heavy knock came on their front door. Zercien groaned.
Had Euvard arrived already? It was terrible enough he had to
spar the day after an actual life-threatening encounter, but to
start early was the true punishment.

"Did you really have to come all the way and—" Zercien stopped
mid-swing of the front door when it was not his hulking friend on the
other side. Instead stood a man in official recreational attire—it looked
a bit like pajamas, if Zercien was being honest—for Castle Vellard attendants.

"Sir Zercien, my apologies for disturbing you so early. But I've
come bearing a message of great importance. It is addressed from His
Majesty King Durnan himself."

Perhaps some army business. Or, maybe his medal delivery came
early. Saena already picked out a spot on the wall.

Zercien frowned as the castle attendant handed him a rolled-up
scroll. Unless this was the tiniest medal in the history of all wars, he'd
have to wait for his prize.

He expressed his gratitude and went to shut the door.

"Ah, Sir Zercien!" the attendant said and held a hand to prevent it
from shutting in his face. "It is of utmost urgency that you read it right
now."

Now? I'm already late, Zercien thought. *Euvard's crossness is growing by the second.*

But he humored the attendant and unrolled the scroll—his eyes bulged as it continued to unravel.

"Dear Sir Zercien Volnaire," it began, in subpar handwriting.

But he smiled. A hand-written note from King Durnan? Not something he would soon forget. Maybe he'd ask Saena to hang this instead.

> *I sincerely express my gratitude for your benevolent interference against Duspen's Arvaros. Much property, and possibly many lives, would have been taken if not for you and your allies' heroic actions. And for this, the city is in your debt. You have her thanks, on my behalf.*

Of course he found out it was me, Zercien thought as his smile turned into an uneasy line.

> *However, there are more pressing concerns than bandits. The following is a message for your eyes only. No one else may read below this line.*
>
> *You witnessed it firsthand. The war in Ankarth does not ebb in Entervia's favor. None outside the castle walls know of our struggles. Entervia has not the military force to win this war.*
>
> *We now look to our ally in the east: Ariglioth. Her army is strong, and her soldiers are needed. Hence, I, King Durnan, request that you, Sir Zercien Volnaire, in response to your righteous deeds of late, take up arms and lead a small group across the eastern lands to Ariglioth's capital city of Ciprius, and petition King Lennard for reinforcements.*

Oh, fuck. His heart thumped wildly. Was he about to be conscripted, even after an honorable discharge?

> *Should you accept, you will be joined by Captain Ardian Calvus of the Vellardian Guard. The rest of your companions may be chosen at your discretion.*

*I sincerely hope you accept my request and pray
you hurry in response. We fear that without aid from
Ariglioth, Entervia will lose this war.*

And at the bottom, King Durnan's signature above the stamped Entervian Coat of Arms. Below, a dotted line awaiting Zercien's name.

A sharp pain ran through his head, like a dagger shoved into his skull. He cried out, putting a hand to his forehead.

"Sir Zercien?" the attendant said, but all Zercien heard was a low mumble of gibberish. His mind's eye swirled about, encased in fog. All he saw was the greyed outline in the form of the attendant standing before him.

But instead of fighting, Zercien sighed and nodded. The fog, and the pain, both dissipated. He stared at the attendant, the contract in hand.

You already served, he thought. *Just say no.*

This time, when he opened his mouth to speak, he just clamped it shut.

Without aid from Ariglioth, Entervia will lose this war. His mind repeated King Durnan's written words.

"What will His Majesty's strategy be if I were to decline?" Zercien said. "Surely he has a backup plan."

The attendant fidgeted, picking his cuticles. "I am afraid this *is* his backup plan, Sir Zercien. To be specific, a backup to his backup's backup."

I'm it, Zercien thought. *Will I allow the future of Entervia to be placed in my somewhat capable hands?*

Of all the advice he expected to echo in his mind, he never thought it would be General Burgland's. To change course, to toss away the old and learn from any preconceived notions.

He *was* the Star Recruit, after all. For a couple of days.

The attendant reached out a hand, and Zercien watched as it trembled, awaiting a response. A signal. The pain in his head was a distant memory, and no fog formed. He was of his own mind, his own volition.

And Zercien thrust out his hand, grasping the attendant's in a firm grip. "King Durnan can count on me."

The attendant even looked surprised to see his hand shaking up and down. "When King Durnan requested this, I was sure you would say no—"

"I witnessed Ankarth's might firsthand. I won't shy away from this duty."

Zercien took a quill from the attendant's hand and set his decision in ink. The attendant smiled, but he soon formed an "oh!" with his mouth and held a finger up.

"I almost forgot," he said while removing a small stone from his pocket and handing it to Zercien. "Present this stone to whoever deems it necessary to allow passage. You will need it when you reach Ciprius."

A tiny thing, but etched immaculately with the Sword, Axe, and Regent of Entervia's Coat of Arms. Zercien thanked him, and the attendant was on his way, with a signed contract.

"Thank you again, Sir Zercien! His Majesty will send word within the next couple of days about your departure. Expect to leave in one week."

A flush of heat spread through his body, as if he'd come into contact with the knight's fell magic again. "A *week*?"

The attendant had long disappeared from sight, and Zercien's words fell to no one's ears.

Was it regret he felt? Nerves? He wasn't sure. Something about King Durnan afforded him strength, a feeling of trust. He thought of his question the other day, of the army managing to instill such values in him over such a short time. Perhaps the answer was yes.

Or this King Durnan exuded some hold over him.

"Zercien?" Saena's voice from upstairs. "Everything all right?"

"Yes, it's all fine," Zercien said. But not for long, he wagered. "Just a letter for me. I'm leaving now for Euvard's." Rushing out the door, he put the stone depicting Entervia's Coat of Arms in his pocket and neatly wrapped the scroll, vowing to tell Saena of what in the world he'd just done when he returned home. With hopefully less nerves.

***

"Look who decided to show!" Euvard said, already well into his stretches when Zercien arrived. "Sword out. It's time."

Zercien ignored him and took the rolled-up scroll from his pocket. He gulped and handed it to Euvard. "A Vellardian castle attendant delivered this to me earlier. Read it. Now."

"Weren't you discharged? Why's the castle sending you messages?"

Just as Euvard grasped the scroll did Zercien remember the note even said it forbade anyone else from seeing it.

Zercien noticed Euvard's changing expressions throughout his reading—raised eyebrows, frowns, more raised eyebrows, a grin, and then a straight-lined sort-of smile.

"You're not fucking with me, right? You think the war's as bad as the note says?"

"Unfortunately, it is."

"Did you accept?"

Zercien backed away a step and cringed, bracing himself with a held-out arm. "There's a reason I'm showing you this."

His response was met with a yell of joy, a mixture between "Yes!" and "Ha ha!" but he couldn't make it out.

"You're taking me, aren't you? You're not just showing me this to rub it in my face?" Euvard said. "I'll clobber you if it is—"

"Who else would I ask? And besides, this isn't some pleasure trip. You seem all too happy about Entervian soldiers marching to their deaths."

"Sorry. Caught up in the chance to be a part of the Entervian army. This wasn't *exactly* how I envisioned my heroic enlistment, but if Mom and Dad were around, they'd be proud all the same. So it's okay by me. When do we leave?"

He still seemed too chipper about the whole ordeal. Would Mayla not want to be consulted? Though Zercien winced at his lack of discussion with Saena, and chose not to open that conversation.

"One week. But best not get ahead of ourselves." Zercien pushed his two open palms ahead in a gesture to slow his friend down. Flush returned to his face. "I haven't quite absorbed it all yet."

"I'm shocked you said yes."

Zercien sighed. "After what I saw during battle, and the Arvaros attack, I feel like I couldn't say no."

Euvard smiled. "You've changed, Zerc."

Before, all he wanted was to be back in the classroom. Now, he hadn't even thought of a lesson plan since his discharge, nor a trip to the schoolhouse to announce his return.

"What now?" Euvard interrupted his thoughts.

Zercien brought his palm to his head, tugging at his still overgrown brown hair. "I haven't a clue. I was hoping you might know someone."

Euvard grinded his teeth. "Not many people here, well, move around a lot. Mayla will want to come, but I would never let her. What'd Saena say?"

Zercien cringed. "I haven't told her."

"I don't blame you. She already had to wait around for you hoping you didn't come back in a bag."

"I appreciate you reminding me of that possibility."

Amid an increasingly quick back-and-forth pace, Zercien racked his brain of anybody willing to join them—and what to say to Saena later. Thoughts of the latter kept interrupting those of the former.

Euvard tapped him on the shoulder. "Fynnian."

"Fynnian Lovell? You've introduced us, but did you not tell me he considered joining the priesthood? I cannot imagine that sort of person accompanying us."

"He visited while you were away. Said he's thinking about looking for his old man," Euvard said.

Zercien shrugged, and thought of his own father. Or lack thereof. He never knew the man, not even his name. The surname Volnaire was his mother's, and the only words she spoke of his father were usually accompanied by "cad." Most curiously, after her passing, he received a wealthy sum of gold from an anonymous benefactor.

While he didn't see the appeal of searching for a parent with no concern for meeting their own children, he sympathized with Fynnian's predicament.

"I see no better options," Zercien said. "But has he even lifted, let alone swung, a blade?"

"Oh, look at you, Sir 'Honorable Discharge!'" Euvard waved his arms over his head. "You think because you could defeat some lowly Arvaros you should be in one of those books you teach to the noble kids?"

Zercien about choked on his own saliva. "I suppose you're right."

Euvard took the lead, and the two were off to find someone who Zercien doubted would be of any help whatsoever.

***

Fynnian Lovell's home was far larger than Zercien imagined—bigger than his and Saena's. The green, bulging shrubbery alongside its walls was well-kept, and a few colorful flower beds of roses and hyacinths adorned the front yard.

The front door swung open at Euvard's knock, and a shorter man with frizzy, dirty-blonde hair answered. And Zercien thought *he* needed to work on his physique. He wondered if the scrawny man standing in front of him could even carry a sword.

"Fynn, we've got quite the proposition for you!" Euvard said.

Fynnian raised an eyebrow, and he squinted in suspicion. "Um…hello, for starters. Not sure I like your introduction."

"Read this," Euvard said and handed him the scroll.

"No, he can't—" Zercien thrust his hand ahead, but it was too late. Again, the scroll faced scrutiny from eyes that weren't his.

"Why are you disclosing this information to me?" Fynnian gulped as he scanned through King Durnan's words. "It seems confidential."

Not anymore, I suppose, Zercien thought, but then smiled. "We're offering to take you with us. That is, if you'd want to search for your father on the way."

Fynnian tripped over the front step into his home while backing up, and his ensuing stutters were interrupted by multiple throat clears. "This is a matter concerning the military, and my fighting skills are not exactly existent. But I would love to accompany you."

Nothing. Zercien's mind remained blank, his heart devoid of any sudden bumps. Having another to join them *was* cause for celebration, but what could Fynnian bring to their cause?"We're glad to have you," he said, "but our military objective comes first. Not finding your father."

He winced as he spoke—he didn't mean for it to sound so cruel.

"Of course." Fynnian's hair flapped and swooshed as he nodded his head no less than a dozen times. "May I train with you both? I loathe being a burden."

At least he's endearing enough, Zercien thought. Though he'd require protecting at all hours.

Euvard bellowed a hearty laugh and slapped Fynnian a couple times on the back, and the skinny-framed man cringed with each blow. "Knock on my door anytime!"

And with that, Zercien and Euvard bade him farewell.

CHAPTER TWENTY-FOUR
AMBITIONS UN-ENTWINED

E uvard?" Zercien asked. His friend hadn't uttered even a grunt throughout their walk back from Fynnian's home, but he continued with his hands folded upon themselves, fingers interlaced. He grinded his teeth.

"I have an idea of who we can ask," Euvard said.

"Why stay quiet, then?" Zercien said, his voice almost an annoyed groan.

"You won't approve."

Zercien planted his feet in front of his brute of a friend. "Just *tell* me."

"I assume we could use some extra…" Euvard gestured his hands as if juggling. "…Talent?"

"Talent would be ideal, yes."

"If we're in the market for skilled swordsmen, we should ask Lloyd."

Zercien backed away, shaking his head. An atrocious idea. His blood boiled at the thought. "Absolutely not. How can we trust him?"

"You barely even know him!" Euvard said.

Zercien could hardly force the words out, stuttering and stammering. "Were you not there when he killed those three people? Or those Arvaros who merely 'stepped onto his property?'"

Euvard waved a hand in front of his face, as if killing multiple people in a week was a normal way of life. "He did it out of self-defense."

"*Self-defense?*" Zercien shouted, and held a hand to his temple. A self-induced headache came on. "We've seen what he's done, what he's capable of. How do we know he won't turn his sword on us?"

"The three men charged him. And those bandits trespassed. See? He only kills when someone wrongs him!"

"What if I accidentally step on his foot?" Zercien motioned his hand across his neck. "Would he have probable cause to behead me?"

Another annoyed wave of Euvard's hand. "Now you're being absurd. Besides, if he is a Meistari, maybe he'll be interested in seeing his old friends again."

If he really is, or was, a Meistari, there was likely a reason for his departure. A reason Zercien did not care to think about at this moment, if he could help it.

"He's just not normal," he said amid a sigh.

"Maybe someone not normal is what we need."

Maybe if I push hard enough, I'll knock myself out, Zercien thought as he pressed the tip of his index finger against his forehead. "Fine. We'll speak to Lloyd."

"Knew you'd come around. Follow me!"

While he faked a smile and fell in behind Euvard again, Zercien surmised the probability of Lloyd *actually* joining them was about nil. But what if, by some chance, he smelled fresh blood and accepted?

Zercien's mind wandered. With the fearsome swordsman in their company, where would they even walk? Too far ahead of Lloyd, and he'd have a better angle for a backstab. Walk too far to the side, and he'd be out of sight. Right next to him was out of the question. What if they made eye contact? And forget about walking behind. He might step on Lloyd's foot.

He followed as Euvard took a turn on the street where they fought the Arvaros, leading to a secluded section of Vellard, usually where the lesser-off folks lived. Vellard wasn't home to many of poverty, though Zercien supposed any city as large could never be free of it. Some trash lay in the roads, and a bit of dead grass and flowers, but otherwise, not much different than the rest of the city. Lower-quality goods were sold at their market square, cheaper than in the typical Vellard stalls.

Zercien assumed Lloyd would live in a more comfortable spot, but perhaps wealth didn't accompany infamy.

Euvard stopped in front of a house—at its minimum definition of four walls and a roof. From its size, an interior of more than two rooms would've been a surprise.

Zercien stepped through the splotchy grass, examining the vines festering along the walls, some wooden practice swords laying in a neat pile beside. Zercien cringed at the hint of blood mixed with the dirt.

As they approached Lloyd's front steps, Zercien froze and whispered, "Would this be considered trespassing?"

Euvard didn't answer, instead choosing to knock on the door. A minute went by, and the door opened in what felt like just as much time, revealing a man in dark garb.

With a gaze that sent a chill down Zercien's spine, he spoke. "Tell me why you disturb me."

Euvard cleared his throat. Even though he'd spoken to the man before, his voice still quivered. "Hello, Lloyd!" He faked laughter and acted jovial. Lloyd's frown didn't change. "We, uh, Zercien and me, we have a request for you!"

"No."

"No?"

"You would make me repeat myself?"

Euvard waved again. "We have a mission, and we need you."

"And what sort of misguided quest has required you to seek me out?"

"A mission to gather reinforcements against Ankarth!" Euvard pointed to Zercien. "Show him the letter."

"I really shouldn't—" Lloyd's black eyes pierced into Zercien with the ferocity of any pointed weapon. "—Shouldn't keep you waiting any longer." He coughed.

While Zercien held the scroll out in front, Lloyd had already made his decision and pushed his hand away. So fast, Zercien stumbled backward.

"You believe such trifles concern me?" Lloyd said. "I've no need for nuisances."

"Why?" Euvard said.

"You have heard my answer. Leave."

"But—"

"Kindly move as I shut my door."

The door slammed an inch from their noses.

"Can't say that was effective," Euvard said.

Zercien nodded. "No, not in the slightest."

No complaints from me, he thought.

Cool relief washed over his face. But it was short-lived, soon giving way to nerves of flame. "I need to tell Saena."

Euvard huffed a deep breath. "Mayla won't like the news, either. Well, she'll be happy for me, and hate the part where she can't come. She always wants to help."

A part of Zercien wanted Mayla to join them, if he were being honest. She'd grown up an orphan, if Euvard's stories were to be believed, with constant housing changes. Even in Vellard, not an enviable environment for a child. If the skirmish with the Arvaros proved anything, she learned how to handle herself.

As a bonus, she'd keep Euvard in check. She'd be a welcome addition just for the latter.

Euvard stretched and looked in the direction of his house. "I'll see you tomorrow, eh?"

"Tomorrow?"

"You're a sly one." Euvard crossed his arms and squinted. "Think you can skip sparring one day and not make it up?"

What nonsense is this? Zercien thought.

"Maybe Fynn'll come too," Euvard said. "We can work on some early teamwork and synergy."

Synergy. Like this was some childish game.

Zercien laughed and the fires about his belly turned comforting. "I'll be by tomorrow morning, then."

And with a wave, Euvard was off. "Good luck with Saena!"

I'll need it, Zercien thought.

The entire way home, Zercien's comfort gave way to unease. Now alone with his thoughts—always a dangerous place for him—the worries of leaving on a journey settled in. Packing, training, the thought of being without Saena for a prolonged time…again.

The weights didn't dissipate as he walked through his front door.

"Where have you been?" Saena asked.

Zercien sighed, took her by the shoulders, and sat her down at the table. He told her everything.

Almost.

Chapter Twenty-Five
Left Unsaid

Y ou're going to Ariglioth for the *army*?" Saena said. Her voice
was quiet and soft. She scooted her chair closer to Zercien's and
laid an outstretched arm across the dinner table. "You were discharged. You owe them nothing."

"I was. But I received a request written and signed by King Durnan. I accepted," Zercien said, and braced for the almost assured swift
and terrifying reaction at his admission.

"I...Okay."

No shouting? Something wasn't right. Saena never missed an opportunity to speak her mind. Zercien scrunched his forehead. "What's
the matter?"

"You've changed," Saena said, her stare unwavering.

He slumped in his seat. "Euvard said as much."

She took his hand in hers, and tapped his palm with her other
hand's index finger. "If this happened a month ago, you wouldn't have
said yes. You'd probably have just thrown the thing away. But ever
since you joined the army, no matter how short the stint was, and how
much you poked fun at the soldiers, you've been different. And after the
Arvaros attack? It's almost like a totally different Zercien sitting in front
of me now."

"Saena."

She continued. "You've been getting those headaches more often, haven't you?"

Zercien gulped. "How did you—"

She smiled as she interrupted. "You can't expect me not to notice. Something happened the day you were conscripted. And again, right before you approached those bandits, didn't it?"

A big sigh escaped his lips. "Ever since King Durnan's announcement of the war with Ankarth, my headaches have grown more frequent and fierce. But I don't want to worry you with my problems."

Saena shook her head and moved a string of brown hair from in front of her face. "Your burdens are my burdens. Your pain is my pain. I don't want you to ever forget."

"Saena, I…" He moved his lips, but no words flew free. Instead, his eyes welled.

"I know there's something else," Saena said, now clasping both her hands around his. "Something you aren't telling me. Something you haven't told anyone. Am I right?"

Zercien darted his gaze away.

She grabbed his cheeks and turned him back to face her. "Don't tell me."

"I thought—"

"If it's going to bring you pain, then don't. But I want you to promise me something."

"Anything."

Her eyes mimicked Zercien's watery dark. "Focus on your mission, and focus on coming back to me."

They embraced, and the light drip of Saena's tears wet his shoulder. He couldn't help but shed one in response.

"I can't lose you," she cried, and buried her head into his chest. Zercien tried to pull away and comfort her, but her fingers pressed down on his back, keeping the two in a firm embrace. As his tears hit her hair, he thought of how badly he'd blundered. How awful it was of him to put her through this—not just once, but twice.

Am I being selfish? he thought. *Should I rescind my acceptance? Someone else could lead.*

She relaxed her grip and pulled back. Zercien looked her straight in the eye. He ran gentle fingers along hers and held tight. *No. I can't go back now*, he thought.

"You won't lose me. I swear it," he said, and nodded at the smile brimming from her frown. "This is no longer war, but a simple stroll. While I will be away for longer, I'll be in far less danger than a battle-field."

Saena wiped her eyes. "Tell me. Was that *my* Zercien, or the 'commander' that took his place?"

Zercien returned her smile. To tell her everything now... it would be natural, and allay her fears. But saying those words would change his life forever. He doubted it all. The games his mind played and the assailing fog may scare her more than any thoughts of adventure. And what if his assessment was incorrect?

He opened his mouth to speak, but soon shut it. *I can't. Not yet,* Zercien thought. *Not until I know for sure.*

"This one was all me," he said.

CHAPTER TWENTY-SIX
INTO THE WILDS

T his is the second time you've left me in two weeks," Saena said
as she handed Zercien an extra shirt for his pack.

Today marked the day of his departure, and he spent the early
morning gathering essential belongings. Something he knew he should
have allocated time for during the week, but he wasn't one for early
preparation.

"Must you be dramatic?" Zercien said as he left the bedroom and
proceeded down the stairs. Though he knew the answer.

Saena choked back a laugh. "Says the one who speaks like some
old-timey general caricature."

A sudden breath made him cough up his spit.

"It's not all bad!" Saena said. "When you come back, will it be you,
or the commander again? It's a surprise."

She'd made that joke every day since the incident.

It wasn't funny the first time, Zercien thought, but shrugged. *Maybe
a little.*

"You're not as nervous as when I left for the army," he said as he
looked up at her from the bottom of the stairs. "Or the night I told you
I accepted this task."

She stepped from the last stair and into his arms, wrapping herself
around him. "I thought about what you said. You're right." She traced

circles on his chest with her index finger. "You're not heading off to a battlefield. And..." She brought her lips to his. "You went toe-to-toe with an enemy general. I think you can handle a walk."

"Yes, my lady Saena Adaire. This seasoned general can handle a brisk walk through the woods," Zercien said, mocking his deep, commander voice, and Saena laughed.

"I love you," she said. "Please be careful."

"I love you too," Zercien answered, and brushed her long brown hair over her ear. "I will."

As soon as he shut his front door, his head pain returned. Rubbing his temple, he inched forward while the fog took over. His house, the dirt, and stone roads, all enveloped in a greyed outline. He came within feet of the not-quite-repaired east gate, and Euvard's loud, obnoxious greeting blasted the fog away.

"Zerc, you're late!"

No one ever had reason to leave Vellard. At a young age, children are told the outside world isn't safe, and his upbringing was no different. His mother spoke of bandits, beasts, and of course, monsters. Helldregs left over from the Ancients' War that roam the lands. People would claim to see them far from the city's outskirts, but never was one of those supposed sightings ever confirmed. Whether his mother believed the stories she told or not, he always returned home before dark.

He shivered. In his texts, Helldregs were described as being coated in all black, as if veiled in a permanent shadow or covered in ink, with misshapen faces made up of maggots. Occasionally, claws replaced hands. But they were all dead, destroyed at the hands of the Seven Legends after their final battle.

As he approached Euvard and Fynnian, he wondered what the other villages of Entervia and beyond believed, and if they bore similar distrustful views of the outside world.

"Sorry. Saena kept me a while," he said, and approached Euvard and Fynnian. "I don't see our guard companion, though. I suppose I'm not *that* late."

He diverted his attention to his soon-to-be ally. "How are you feeling, Fynnian?"

"A tad nervous," Fynnian answered with a stutter. "Well, a lot nervous, to tell the truth. I'm thankful for the training from Euvard, but I hope it's enough. Though I have spent many nights scouring over ancient Sanctum Order scrolls, too."

Zercien scrunched his forehead. The look in Fynnian's eyes told him those scrolls weren't just stories or writings of the Sanctum Order's accolades.

"Stay close to us and you'll be just fine," Euvard said with a wink. "Is that your real sword? Let me see it."

Fynnian fumbled with it as he attempted to yank the thing from its sheath.

"It's old," Euvard said as he examined the sword. "Still looks sharp, though."

"It belonged to my father," Fynnian said, and sheathed the blade. He fidgeted with its placement on his belt.

Not a promising start, Zercien thought.

Hard, heavy steps of tough leather boots clamored over the grass. In a moment, the bald and scruffy Captain Ardian Calvus stood before them.

A long lance and a metal kite shield bearing the Entervian Coat of Arms hung over his back, and he wore leather and chainmail tinted with Entervia's royal purple. Not the best for concealing one's identity.

Fynnian puffed out his chest and tried to make himself at least look bigger, compared to his tall and strong companions.

"Pleased to make your acquaintances!" the guard captain said. Zercien knew the voice. Some hint of authority, but otherwise, friendly, and jovial. Almost annoyingly so.

"Name's Ardian Calvus, a captain of the guard. I'll be accompanying you three to Ariglioth."

Zercien tried to look away, or in any other direction than their new companion's, but met his gaze.

"You already know who I am, though, eh? And I've heard *plenty* about you since our first meeting," Ardian said, and winked while shaking Zercien's hand. "The new recruits say you can fight like a trained warrior. Not bad for a teacher."

Zercien winced. "It was nothing—"

"I deserved a pay increase for recruiting you!"

His companions laughed, but Zercien just cringed.

I know you, all right, he thought. *The one responsible for all of this.*

"And these must be our *illustrious* allies!" Ardian said, as he shook hands and greeted Euvard and Fynnian. "Euvard Girant. And you are Fynnian Lovell, yes? It is a pleasure."

Euvard shot him a glance accompanied by crossed arms. "Been studying us?"

Ardian chuckled. "Grandmaster General Urian—who about threw a fit at the mention of your name, by the way—told me who you were, Euvard."

"Of course he did."

Seems the hatred between the two is mutual, Zercien thought. He held back a laugh.

"Nearly forgot," Ardian said and raised an index finger. He took his lance from over his back and brought its sauroter to the ground. Nothing exemplary, just your standard issue military-grade grey lance with some scratches and other wear, though its sharp and intimidating tip stood a foot above Ardian's head. "This here's *Spike*."

"You named your lance?" Euvard said, side-eyeing in Zercien's direction.

"Every good weapon needs a name, don't you think?" Ardian said.

"Can't say I do." Euvard covered his mouth to stymie an ensuing snort.

"You just haven't yet come upon the right circumstance. You'll understand someday."

"What's that one's name?" Euvard asked, pointing to the kite shield hanging over the guard captain's shoulder.

A near-inaudible "ah" whooshed from Ardian's mouth as he wrinkled his nose and brought forth his metal kite shield. Another unspectacular-looking armament, though its face bore no battle scars.

"Truth be told, we haven't spent enough time together to be on a first-name basis," Ardian said, and hung both Spike and his nameless kite shield over his back. "But that's enough of that, eh? Shall we debrief?"

"We know what we're here for," Euvard said.

The cheer in Ardian's face drained, giving way to wrinkles in his forehead. "You all need to be aware of the stakes, and what the army faces in Ankarth. Zercien, if you would?"

"Me?" he said, looking to see if someone else would speak instead. Perhaps it was too much to ask for everyone to forget he was their supposed leader.

"Tell them about the knight you faced," Ardian said, waving his hand at Euvard and Fynnian. "Your new companions should know the haste at which we must venture. Spare no detail. King Durnan has given permission to say everything. And I mean *everything*."

Zercien sighed and shut his eyes, beginning his tale of the knight encased in black and red armor. "He decimated our troop with Pariah Arts. I was lucky. I managed to pull General Burgland away, and we escaped."

Ardian sat straight, arms crossed and an eyebrow lifted. "What about where you—"

"Wait. Zerc," Euvard interrupted in a volume Ardian couldn't hope to compete with. "Why didn't you tell me about the magic? I thought magic was dead. You've told me as much."

Fynnian straightened his back like a plank. "You faced Pariah Arts?" He rubbed his sweaty palms together. "Oh, God."

Zercien watched as he fidgeted badly, as if overcoming a numbing chill.

Ardian lowered the palms of his hands to hush them both. "Let's not tell the whole city before the king makes an announcement, eh? Now you see why we're on a tight schedule. Time to depart, I say."

Euvard drummed his fingers on the handle of his battle-axe and smiled. "Off we go, then."

"Maybe the walk will help clear my head," Fynnian said, hesitation staining his words.

Zercien nodded, a fuzzy, warm heat bouncing about in his chest. "Lead the way, Ardian." He gestured toward the partially restored gate, though in its ruinous state it may as well have just not been repaired at all.

The guard captain kept his arms crossed and tapped his foot, one thumb rubbing the bottom of his chin. "That's my line."

"Excuse me?"

"King Durnan chose you for this mission, did he not?"

"Yes, but—"

"Then you are our leader." Ardian winked, and withdrew a folded map from his pack, handing it to Zercien. "I've marked a route to Ciprius."

Holding out the map, Zercien ran a finger down Ardian's small hand-drawn lines depicting a path, accompanied by scribbled notes. Even still, he recoiled at the sight of it. Ardian's firm hand slapped down on his shoulder.

"You needn't worry about a thing, Star Recruit!" Ardian said. "Should you lead us astray, I'll be the first to poke you with the sauroter of this lance."

"All right," Zercien said, and sighed. His heart pounded, and a slight pain returned to his head.

With his next steps, he led his companions through the gate, past a pair of guards on duty.

Placing guards at a guard outpost. What a novel concept, Zercien thought.

The two guards bid farewell to his party, and with a deep breath, he crossed the line into the Entervian countryside.

And with it, he knew his secret was as good as dead.

Chapter Twenty-Seven
A Legacy of Betrayal

Per Ardian's request, they alternated lookout duties while others slept, fearing Arvaros may be on the prowl. Tonight, their second night, was Zercien's first turn, and he spent his time kneeling by the campfire and looking at the map. He'd traced his fingers over Ardian's drawn trail enough times to worry he'd poke a hole through the thin parchment.

From the looks of things, Ardian didn't want to stop at many towns. He'd mentioned a village called Tiesel only a few finger-lengths away from their position.

There they would stock up on essentials and head for the Okoro Mountains, a mountain range splitting Dregnal in two, acting as a natural border between Entervia and Ariglioth. He noticed a path south, past Tiesel and around the Okoro Mountains, but everything below was marked as Duspen territory, with Ardian's handwriting spelling "A-V-O-I-D." A straightforward route, but Zercien agreed a climb through the mountains to be safer than risking a trek through Duspen.

A whoosh of wind, and the hairs on the back of Zercien's neck stood up. He dropped the map and jumped to his feet, knocking over a bag. A chill rushed his body, feeling eyes upon him. But darting his gaze all over their camp, he saw no one. No shadows in the shrubs, nothing moving behind the trees. Only the light breeze greeted his stare.

A tap on his shoulder. He jumped back.

"Something happen?" Ardian asked.

My first watch duty and you sneak up on me? Zercien thought.

"No," he said and shook his head. "Sorry to startle you. I thought—"

"First time and you're a little jittery, eh? I was there once too. Why don't you sit down? I'll take over for the last few hours."

"You're sure? You spent most of last night on lookout duty as well."

"Of course. Besides, I'm not the one leading us tomorrow." The guard captain capped it off with a wink and pushed Zercien away.

Though he loathed to sit on his makeshift cloth bed. Ardian had said the first night of sleeping on the ground was the worst, but Zercien disagreed—his back already ached, and now he had to do it a *second* time?

Eventually he fell into slumber, tossing and turning throughout the remainder of the night.

***

When morning arrived, the company shared a quick, un-appetizing breakfast of day-old bread and cheese. They prepared for their next leg, a half day's march to Tiesel. After ensuring everyone was packed and ready, they embarked. And all fell silent.

Zercien pushed his face close enough to the map, he could smell the dried ink from Ardian's notes.

"Get your nose out of there," Ardian said, and again, the guard captain's hand came down on Zercien's shoulder. "Your focus should be our surroundings. Try putting the map away for a spell."

Zercien thought it odd, but he put the map away and obliged. Now that his face was actually *up*, he noticed the beautiful scenery; the endless green, the tall trees. A peppering of flowers in the fields. Ardian's quickening footsteps rushed to his ear, and soon the guard captain positioned himself to Zercien's left.

"I remember you're a schoolteacher. Teach anything interesting?" Ardian said. "Subjects *we* would find interesting, I should say."

Some air blew from Euvard's nose.

"History, mostly," Zercien said. "Nothing you would want any lecturing about—"

"History?" Ardian said, accompanied by a grin. "Despite my rough and tumble appearance, I'm a bit of a scholar."

Euvard snorted out a laugh. "You? Sure. And I'm on the Ruling Council."

"I have access to the castle archives. When I'm off duty, I spend most of my time reading about the Seven Legends."

Zercien's eyes flashed. "The castle archives?" He just about screamed, and even Euvard jumped back. Ardian's belly-laugh was almost louder.

"A bit jealous, friend?"

"A *lot* jealous. Ardian, I *have* to know what's in those texts. The books available to the citizens hardly delve deeper than the surface."

Vellard Castle was home to one of the most expansive libraries in Dregnal—filled with books, texts, and scrolls all dating back to the Ancients' War. But access was limited to high-ranking Vellardian officials, and only a select few volumes were shared with the common people. Zercien loathed that he, a teacher, could not be granted exemption.

But a captain of the guard is allowed? he thought. *Ridiculous.*

"I read a fascinating excerpt, once," Ardian said. "The Seven Legends' weapons were bound by blood."

Zercien shivered just thinking about it. "Not something I've read."

"As if a part of their own body. Although the text did say that perhaps a descendant could wield their weaponry, akin to the Sanctum Order lineage." Ardian's stare grew stronger as he spoke. "Which does mean Holunt's bloodline could be passed down too. And we all know he had no weapon to his name, for his blood was enough to repel Pariah Arts."

Pretending to cough, Zercien darted his head away. "But no mention of where these weapons came from?"

"Not in the texts I've found, no."

"I've seen this one a few too many times to not know what's about to happen," Euvard said. "Hope you like boring history lessons, Fynn."

He doesn't even try to hide it, Zercien thought, but smiled and continued his talk with Ardian.

"Actually." Fynnian said and half-smiled. "I'd like to join them. Excuse me."

Zercien chuckled as Euvard threw his arms into the air and Fynnian inched closer, butting into the conversation.

"Um, hello." Fynnian waved his shaky hand. "You can't mention the Legends without also speaking of the Sanctum Order. And, um."

Fynnian rolled up his sleeve, revealing the veins on the underside of his wrist rippling with a light silver and gold, melding together in a harmonious knot. Zercien's sight twisted within its waves.

"The mark of a Sanctum Knight?" he said. "Fynnian, you—"

"Not quite," said Fynnian with a shake of the head, and a twinge of disappointment on his lips. "I'm not Anointed. But I bear the blood of the Sanctum Order."

A chuckle erupted from Ardian's mouth. "And here I thought the last of the Sanctum Order disappeared with Vellard's resident Sanctum Knight."

The blues in Fynnian's eyes seemed to deepen. "You knew of my father? I didn't realize he was well-known—"

"The *last* one?" Euvard said.

"Not many know." A small smile cracked through Fynnian's stoic lips. "But it seems this guard captain does."

Not even Zercien knew, and he cursed the blasted texts for not mentioning such a thing.

"How is it your family is the last?" Euvard said. "There *has* to be at least a few more somewhere in the world."

"Because they were wiped out by Voks?" Ardian said, as if the answer should have been obvious.

Voks, Zercien thought. Sweat poured from his brow, dripping between the hairs on his neck. He felt the trickle and tickle between each and every follicle.

Voks. His mind repeated without relent.

"This another one of those stories you teach the kids about, Zerc?" Euvard said.

Zercien cleared his throat. With every cough came a surge of spittle and phlegm.

"Seems you could use that lesson, too, Euvard," said Ardian.

"Fine." Euvard crossed his arms. "Nothing better to do around here."

With Zercien still coughing up spit, Ardian began the tale, but Fynnian's words came at the same time.

"Why don't you start this one, then," Ardian said to Fynnian.

Fynnian's eyes widened, but at last he nodded. "What I've read states it all occurred at the very end of the Ancients' War, though none know just how long, after the final battle in Telurdia."

After the final battle in Telurdia—Zercien's mind repeated, before a piercing pain ran across his temple. He managed to quell his yelp, but all about him exploded in a deep grey fog, inhaling all.

Something pulled at his hands, yanking them behind his back. A sea of flames sprouted in front, pouring from the clayed dirt, heat forcing gobs of sweat from his forehead.

Through the hissing flames, the rush of footsteps. Mighty warriors stood about the reddened field, each carrying blood-soaked weaponry, and shielded their eyes. Joining them, knights in shimmering armor, two carrying swords shining with radiant, golden light.

"We knew you could not be trusted!" a knight with one of the light-infused blades said.

A Sanctum Knight.

"Voks! Release him!" said a different warrior. One who carried a fearsome black battle-axe. Another holding a bow brought an arrow to nock.

Zercien stared at the gathering warriors. Familiar, and yet he could not speak their names. Looking to his side for only a moment, he glimpsed bloodred robe sleeves, and gasped. He writhed against Voks's grip, though it did not feel as if he tried with all his might. His body ignored his mind's commands to send strength to his arms and hands.

"You used Pariah Arts to drive away the fiends, but now you use it against us?" said the woman with the bow. "Release him, or this arrow will find your skull."

Zercien's head glanced backward, though he did not order it to. He locked eyes with the flaming rubies of Voks, and the robed sorcerer nodded. His mouth opened without his orders, and the words erupted, in unison with the crackling flames.

"Voks! Unhand me!"

CHAPTER TWENTY-EIGHT
DIVERSION

Zercien awoke to fire, but the crackles were light, welcoming, soothing. Looking to his left, his heartbeat quelled upon seeing a campfire, and his allies gathered about. All eyes were on Fynnian, sitting upon a stump and finishing his tale.

"What happened to Voks?" Euvard said.

"The Sanctum Knights imprisoned him in the World's Tower for interrogation." Fynnian shut his eyes, and breathed deep. "I am not proud to admit it, but they tortured him. It lasted years before they brought him to the pinnacle of the tower, where they would enact some divine power to make him speak."

"But he did not, I assume?" said Zercien, and he joined his allies in the circle, sitting next to Euvard. This was where his texts ended. None spoke much of the war's after-years.

"Ah! Our fearless leader awakens from his midday slumber!" Ardian said and winked. "Just when Fynnian's tale grew most interesting. Telurdia must fascinate you so."

Zercien scrunched his forehead. Those continuous winks—something remained veiled behind his gentle ribbing.

Euvard smacked Zercien on the arm, ruining his concentration. "You fainted again, and we made camp. You okay?"

Zercien rubbed the spot where Euvard's massive fist landed. The sky still bore some sun, but it'd be dusk in some hours. "I'm fine. Please, don't let me interrupt. As you were."

Fynnian nodded, accompanied by a shudder.

"Oh, but Voks did speak. And his voice..." He shivered. "My father told me Voks' voice just appeared in the minds of all members of the Order, taking over their thoughts. At least, that is the story passed down to him. But whatever the truth may be, one piece was certain. Voks' intention was never to answer questions."

Zercien faked a cough to cover his obnoxious gulp.

"Voks attacked," Fynnian continued. "With Pariah Arts none had ever seen. My father told tales of a black horse invading the Order members' minds, alongside Voks' demonic speech."

Fynnian's gaze turned to the roaring campfire, the shadows of flame dancing upon his face in the approaching dark. "Much of the Sanctum Order and its knights were slaughtered. Even those who wielded the Sanctus Dual Blades fell to Voks' terrible might. A scant few survived and escaped the tower, but would never dare to return and combat Voks again."

A deep breath, a lowering of the shoulders. Fynnian spoke again, but his voice grew somber with each passing word. "Soon, the divine blades were lost, and without the aid of the World's Tower, Anointing members into the Order was too slow to sustain the bloodline. Thus, the Sanctum Order dwindled. My father was anointed by the one surviving Elder of the Order and became the last of the Sanctum Knights."

Euvard drummed his fingers on the dirt, and Zercien furrowed his brow. His brute of a friend was scared.

"Voks is still there?" Euvard asked. The lowest, meekest voice he'd ever heard from the oaf. "He has to be dead by now, right?"

Fynnian winced. "That's the eerie part."

"You're saying that part before *wasn't* the eerie part?"

"The Sanctum Order survivors told of Voks splitting in two, near-identical replicas. One, a physical form, which fled during the massacre, leaving behind an ethereal, ever-present wraith inside the tower."

"You want me to believe that this man *split in two*? Just like that?" Euvard supplemented his skepticism with a snap of the fingers.

"Believe what you will," Ardian said. "But Pariah Arts are wholly unexplored. We're not quite sure the extent of their power."

"Fine, fine," Euvard said. "I'll play along. Ghost-Voks is sitting in the World's Tower, and human-Voks is where?"

"Anywhere," Fynnian said with a shrug.

Zercien shivered, hoping his crossed arms indicated the need of keeping warm.

"But what's more concerning is the form still within the World's Tower," Fynnian said. "My father never told me the specifics, but the World's Tower houses incredible power capable of altering the world itself. If it were to fall into the wrong hands—"

"Hogwash! All of it!" Euvard interrupted, and waved his hand as if throwing something.

Zercien's ears perked. A rustle in the shrubbery. He leapt from his seat on the ground and drew his Entervian soldier's sword. His companions followed, and Ardian took point. Lance out in front, he glanced back and held out his hand.

With each cautious step, Zercien peeked about their makeshift campsite for any shred of grey fog. But he wrinkled his brow—not even a drop in his periphery. Though his heart drummed, his head remained painless.

He watched as Ardian thrust Spike through the bush, and a clang of steel rang about. The guard captain jumped back and spun his lance in front.

"Arvaros!" he shouted as the barbarian leapt from his hiding spot. Crooked teeth accompanied a snide grin, dirt splattered about his face.

About the perimeter of their camp, four Arvaros emerged from behind the bushes and the trees. They bore ragged and tattered clothes and wielded old, rusty blades.

We're surrounded, Zercien thought, and slapped the side of his head. No pain, no fog.

Zercien watched as the Arvaros circled the group, and one spoke. Though looking no different, presumably this was their leader. His manner of speech was just as Zercien thought it'd be.

"What do we have here?" the Arvaros said, and stared at the Crest of Entervia stitched on Ardian's clothing. "Looks like some Vellardian birds escaped the cage!" His followers erupted in laughter. "What brings you all to the wilds, huh?"

"We are merely passing through," Ardian said. "Now, if you will, let us do so."

Looking around at his men, the leader said in a high-pitched, mocking voice, "Do we let them go?"

"Hell no!" "Kill them all here!" were the answering cries. A wide smile then spread on his face, showing years of questionable dental work.

"You heard them!" the Arvaros said, and he shrugged. "Sorry, but Reaver wants all Entervians dead."

While Zercien drew his weapon, he watched as Fynnian fumbled about with his, unsheathing it before the first Arvaros was upon him. He focused on stalling his opponents' blows and fought defensively, turning away strikes but never swinging on his own.

He blocked the jagged, rusty Arvaros blade and held strong, drool frothing and dribbling from the barbarian's mouth.

But it was enough time for Zercien to break through and run his sword through the Arvaros' back. Fynnian gasped as the bloodied tip stuck through his assailant's stomach, inches from his hand.

A booming crack echoed about the plains, forcing Zercien's neck to crane. Euvard had leveled his axe atop an Arvaros' head, splattering blood and shattered bone remnants about the field.

Zercien thought to aid Ardian, who went toe-to-toe with the Arvaros leader but found he didn't need the help—just as he arrived, the guard captain thrust Spike through the leader's chest, and he slumped to the ground.

"Run!" one of the remaining Arvaros screamed. "Run for your lives!"

They trampled the grass in their escape, leaving just as quickly as they arrived.

"Must've thought we'd be easy pickings," Euvard said as he raised his battle-axe over his back.

Fynnian struggled with shaking hands to put his clean sword back in its sheath. His face was paler than usual.

"This poses a new problem," Ardian said and instructed the party to sit and gather their bearings. "Those barbarians are probably running back to, who'd that ugly one say, Reaver? He's not going to like it when he learns a few of his goons were offed by Entervians."

"Not the first time we've heard the name," Zercien said.

"The ones that attacked Vellard said they were sent by Reaver, too." Euvard added.

"Let's consider this new problem a new *large* problem, instead," Ardian muttered. Zercien noticed a quiver in his voice, and a shiver in his hands.

Euvard stood and grabbed his bag. "If we leave now, they probably won't catch us. We should be safe."

"Not my concern," Ardian said. "They'll head for Vellard again. Not that I think bandits are *this* intelligent, but they could use what just happened here as an excuse to declare war on Entervia."

Zercien tapped his foot on the grass. "Is that not drastic?"

"Forget formal war declarations, then." Ardian waved off the idea. "You saw what happened when a few of them attacked the city. What if it was twenty? Or thirty?"

Shit, Zercien thought, and then muttered under his breath. He looked at the map, and at his surroundings. If his assumptions were correct, then the Duspen border was a few finger-lengths from their position. Just past the Castham River.

"Ardian, have we the time for a trip to Duspen?"

"Zerc," Euvard said and shook his head. "I know we can't let Reaver keep throwing his thugs at Vellard, but is it a smart idea to just walk into his territory?"

Ardian took the map from Zercien and ran his finger along it. "You know where this 'Reaver' fellow is?"

Zercien nodded, and pointed to 'Denon-Hein' on the map. "There."

"I see," the guard captain spoke quickly to himself. "We're not far from the border, and Denon-Hein is just over it. I think we've the supplies to last." His voice grew louder. "It would set us back about three days, but we could do it."

"What do you think, then?" Zercien asked.

"I *think* I should be the one asking you. You are our leader, after all."

Of course he would say that.

"Whatever you choose, I won't argue," Ardian went on. "If we don't go, we'll reach Ariglioth sooner, but risk an Arvaros uprising. If we do, we have a chance to stamp out these barbarians and prevent any retaliation against Vellard, but we will be late in sending reinforcements. And, of course, we take on much more risk."

While putting a closed fist to his chin, Zercien caught a streak of dark red out of the corner of his eye. Like the bottom half of a robe, flowing in the wind in the wake of someone flying across the field, in the direction of the Duspen border.

Accept it, a voice appeared in his mind. Not his own. In the distance, a figure in bloodred robes stood watch. A spot of fog whipped about its feet, curling about the red hem like a snake.

Accept it, came the voice once more.

A pain swelled in Zercien's head, and he slammed both hands to his ears. *Accept it, accept it, accept it,* prattled on the voice, growing louder with each repetition. With a quick yelp and a violent head shake, Zercien thrust the figure, and the fog, away, leaving only his bewildered companions in its wake.

"There's too much at stake if we leave these bandits be," Zercien said, ignoring his companions' confused stares. He turned to face Euvard. "I'm worried about Saena and Mayla, too. If the Arvaros were to attack again—"

Euvard put a hand on the heft of his axe and furrowed his brow. "Say no more, Zerc. I'm with you. We're going to the South. Just like my old man did."

Fynnian gulped. A chance for more fighting. "Well, if it is what the group decides, then—" his voice trailed off.

"It is settled. On your march, Zercien," Ardian said.

CHAPTER TWENTY-NINE
FROM THE DARK

G eneral Burgland, sir," a returning scout whispered. "The Northern army is just over the hill. They will be here shortly."

"Good. Merge with us, soldier," the general said. "Wait for my orders."

"Yes, Sir."

General Burgland looked out from his cover where he and a small regiment of Entervian forces stood. Across the field, more of his soldiers readied their arms, concealed by the trees and the cloudy, quickly darkening night sky.

But out in plain sight lay an even smaller squadron of Entervians— brave soldiers who volunteered to act as decoys for the approaching Ankarthan army.

General Burgland sighed. He'd received word from King Durnan that a resistance group had been formed and was marching on to Ariglioth for reinforcements, and he was to hold out as long as possible.

This, coupled with the humiliating defeat at the fortress, forced the general to, again, resort to guerilla tactics, setting traps and ambushes. Though he thought this type of warfare to be dishonorable, he had no choice. He was Entervian before he was a general. What he did was for the good of his country.

However, he did state to his troops that if the Ankarthan commander were to show, he would handle him *personally*.

Looking over the battlefield once more, he reassured himself of his strategy. The terrain befitted an ambush, with tree covering on both sides and wide-open space in the middle. Once the Ankarthans clashed with his soldiers sitting in the open, he would order the others to flank, giving Entervia an advantage.

He hoped.

The front lines of the Ankarthan army stepped over the hill. The small Entervian force stood with feet planted and still, unwavering.

"Don't budge," General Burgland whispered to his squad, his words as calm as his flowing breath. With a nod, he signaled an archer, who discretely loaded an arrow.

General Burgland repeated his gesture, and the archer fired, her shot piercing the neck of an Ankarthan soldier at the other end of the field. And the Ankarthan army retaliated, flying down the hill, colliding with General Burgland's decoys.

Watching his soldiers gallantly repelling the North, his hands twitched. He shook it off. But a moment later he felt for his sheath and could contain his urge for battle no longer. A bit earlier than he had intended, he jumped from his hiding spot and issued the attack.

Leading the charge, he was the first to crash into the Ankarthan army's right flank. In an instant he felled one with a swift strike through the chest, and another to his right. Once the enemy turned to face their new threat, General Burgland's reserves on the opposite side rushed the left flank.

With the Ankarthans surrounded, the general raised his hand, signaling the archers he had stationed within the trees and in the back to fire at will.

When it seemed he was gaining the upper hand, Ankarthan reinforcements surged from the hill, joining the main force. Each was better equipped than the last and were armored from head-to-toe with helmets hiding all but their eyes. Even still, they were shadowed, and none could see beyond the black. General Burgland ordered his soldiers to confront them head on, himself leading the pack. With a powerful slash he cut one down, but covered his mouth upon hearing the gurgling, oozing sound as the body hit the dirt. The stink of rotten flesh wafted into General Burgland's nostrils, and a light buzzing soared above his ears.

"What in the…" he muttered, but didn't have the chance to inspect the corpse before more enemy soldiers stormed onto the battlefield.

As Ankarthan fighters fell by way of the general's or any of his army's blades, the more the gurgling slurped into his mind. He lost focus moving from target to target, bleary and sweat-blinded. Before long he found himself surrounded, shouts sounding increasingly inhuman rushing into his brain.

His spinning vision managed to center on one, and a single cut brought it down. Amid foes swinging around him, he clawed at the dead one's helmet, ripping it off. And a darkness matching the night sky stared back as swirls of maggots crawled up and through its nose and mouth.

"No. My eyes, they must be—" the general murmured, but was interrupted by the clashing of steel right above his head. He shook himself back to reality and looked up to see an Entervian soldier's blade protecting him from the slash of an Ankarthan.

"General Burgland! Are you well?"

"I'm fine." The words flew from his mouth with speed, but not confidence. He stared at the slain being once more, trying in vain to assure himself it was all in his head, that the night and his tired mind were quite the trickster pair.

Once most of the Ankarthans were dispatched, General Burgland saw another surge appearing at the top of the hill, armed with longswords and lances.

"Entervia! Retreat! We've done enough for one day!"

Whether he was unsure they would win or just wanted to escape the gruesome beings attacking them, he himself had no idea.

Now leading a charge in the opposite direction, the general ordered his soldiers to disperse and travel in small groups. Looking over his shoulder, General Burgland noticed they were starting to pull away from the Ankarthans, and their enemy slowed to a walk, to which he smiled. He surveyed his own force, saw he'd not lost a considerable amount of soldiers, and they'd taken down twice or even three times as many Northerners. A successful gambit, he thought.

But he slammed his feet to a halt when he turned around, the Entervians at his back almost running into him. Not more than three feet in front, encased in ebon armor, its red streaks resembling dried blood, stood the enemy commander. Even in the dark, the knight's pupils pierced each soldier's gaze.

"I see you have not heeded my warning, still." The knight's words carried far across the battlefield. He conjured a small, black ball and heaved it over the Entervians' flinching heads, and it landed with a small burst behind the last soldier. The sound drew the wandering Ankarthan army closer.

In front of General Burgland stood the commander, and behind, the Northern army.

"Shit," he muttered underneath his quivering breath.

"What shall you choose, General?" The knight's eyes never blinked. "You either fall to my army, or to me. Your fate is yours to decide."

"Army? What kind of 'army' do you command?" General Burgland barked back, hoping to buy himself a bit of time, as the snarling of the inhuman shouts from the Ankarthans rang about his eardrums. "Those aren't people, let alone Northerners, are they?"

"It matters not what makes up an army, as long as they are loyal to a cause."

General Burgland laughed. "The North is too weak to battle Entervia on its own, then? And to think, I was worried they'd grown. Thank you for proving that they're still the same helpless fools as before."

The knight's expression didn't budge. "I do not have vested interest, nor do I care for Ankarth as a country. Its army is simply mine to control."

"These soldiers are expendable to you? You're a failure of a general."

And General Burgland and the Ankarthan commander stood silent for what felt like hours.

"...Enough," the enemy commander said as he raised his blade high, its steel shining in the moonlight. But before he could act, General Burgland yelled, "Entervians! Disperse!"

The Entervian army split and ran to the left and right sides, hidden by the trees and the dark, causing the Ankarthans to run in circles.

"We regroup at our fortress!" the general called before disappearing into the trees.

Chapter Thirty
Reaver

Caved-in wooden homes populated the path. Cracked wood scattered about the dirt. Lonely and forgotten gardens wasted away, and the tattered remnants of fences lay strewn. Zercien closed in on a lone sign, carved on with hasty, jagged letters to say 'Denon-Hein Lies Ahead.'

Zercien shivered as the chill grasp of being watched returned to his bones, and turned his head in all directions, pretending he was interested in the surroundings, but saw nothing. It throbbed as if a headache were incoming, but each time it dissipated.

"This is awful," Fynnian muttered as he tip-toed over strewn glass shards. "They may be barbarians, but I feel terrible for them."

"We have been told our whole lives Duspen was poor and degenerate, but I did not expect this," Ardian said.

Passing by the sign, the group came upon another dirt path, though this one actually bore signs of natural life—trees and bushes, though browned and dying, littered both sides. To the northwest was a small cliffside, maybe the height of three men, with wooden decorations atop, probably indicating it was used for announcements and the like. Tree branches blocked the view, and Zercien couldn't see above.

A loud voice then penetrated the silence.

"Outsiders? In Denon-Hein?" An unknown source, but the voice cued a dozen Arvaros to jump out from behind the rocky rubble and torn-down homes. They encroached upon the party, forcing them all to back up slowly and group back-to-back.

Zercien's head pounded—a loud rumble exploding in his mind, over and over. A small "Agh!" escaped his mouth, and soon he could only see fog and hazy outlines of his companions fumbling for their weapons, and the Arvaros. But to his left, for only a moment, a man on the cliffside appeared behind the brush.

The barbarians stopped and stared as a lone figure emerged from the tree branches.

"Greetings and salutations!" A man spread his arms wide in a large embrace, hands bringing the entire town into his bosom. Well-dressed, for someone from Duspen, he sported a loose-fitting white shirt revealing a bit of his chest, and brown pants with matching leather boots.

His gaze fell upon Ardian. "Entervians! Welcome, welcome, to Denon-Hein!"

Zercien raised both eyebrows at the man's speech— more intelligent than the others he'd met. Intelligent even for one not from Duspen.

His headache waned, and he stood tall. "You are Reaver, I assume?" Though all the bandits seemed to be in the open, he still couldn't shake the feeling of another gaze upon him.

The Arvaros leader smiled. "It seems the depth of Entervia's perception knows no bounds."

"You little—" Euvard started to say, grabbing the heft of his axe, but Fynnian put up a hand.

"Euvard, shh!" The shush sounded more like a whimper.

"Oh, how hasty," Reaver said, forming a circle with his lips, clasping his hands over his heart. "But we have only just met. I'd hate to end it so soon."

"Reaver!" Ardian called to him. "We would like to avoid bloodshed just as much as you. Let us speak. We've many questions for each other, I take it."

"You, at least, seem admirable enough." Reaver paced in and out of sight within the branches atop his cliffside perch. "You see, even though we thrive on banditry, Duspen is also home to children, families, workers, farmers, traders—those who do not steal or pillage. And while I've a hatred for Entervia, I begrudgingly admit that, as much as there are good people among barbarians, there are good people among Entervians. Might you be part of such a crowd?"

"Then why have we, twice, put a stop to attacks by Denon-Hein Arvaros in and around Vellard?" Ardian said.

Reaver tapped his fingers along a branch. All grew so quiet, Zercien could hear its light wooden echo. "You think Entervia does not deserve such? Then answer me this. After the Ancients' War, where was Entervia?"

Zercien looked at Ardian just as he did the same. The Arvaros leader spoke again, hardly allowing a moment for a reply.

"For years after the war, Duspenese leaders requested Entervia for supplies, for food, for shelter, for anything, but with no answer. All countries on this continent were allies during the war. Why did *our* letters go unanswered?" The taps turned into furious fist slams, shaking the branch and its scant remaining leaves. "I ask again. Where was Entervia?"

"You're expecting us to answer for an event taking place generations ago?" Ardian said. "Times change, Reaver. You should stop living in the past and forget what your forefathers told you of Entervia."

Reaver flared his nostrils. "Because of Entervia's inaction, our country turned into the barbaric lands the entire continent knows us for." He raised a finger in conjunction with a snide smile. "And, as for 'living in the past,' I'm willing to bet you didn't even know I *personally* wrote to King Durnan only five years ago. Ask me if I ever received a reply."

Zercien's heart sank, the confidence in his words all but dead. Not that he believed Reaver's, but the Arvaros leader didn't seem to be lying.

"Reaver, please listen," Zercien said. "I've spoken with King Durnan. His heart is true. Perhaps if we return to Entervia together, we can come to an amicable resolution."

Ardian bumped him lightly with his elbow and whispered. "You'd take this *Arvaros* with us?"

"I would sooner try than risk war with Duspen."

Reaver's gaze morphed from a piercing stare to narrowed eyes and a raised eyebrow. Like diplomacy from an Entervian was this abstract, unheard-of concept. But Zercien's heart sank again when the Arvaros leader waved him off.

"All Entervia does is hide," Reaver barked while half-hidden behind the branches. "Stuffed within Vellard's walls, uncaring of the outside world. Now, Entervia receives justice—a full-scale invasion from Ankarth while Duspen pillages its citizens! And Denon-Hein will be the first to recover. Soon after, all other Duspenese territories will join us, and we will prosper as we did eons ago. All while Entervia suffers, slowly whittled away by war, death, and hunger." A crooked smile spread across his lips. "Your country shall become the new Duspen."

Euvard groaned and scoffed at Reaver. "Your speech is glittery for an Arvaros, but glittery shit is still shit."

He readied his arm to hurl his axe straight into Reaver's wretched smile.

Reaver cocked his head. "Years ago, we were close. But those damned Entervians cut us down. Today is the day I begin Duspen's revenge!"

Euvard growled under his breath. "You son of a bitch! Why don't you come down here?"

The Arvaros leader walked out of sight, hidden among the branches behind him.

"An interesting proposal. I do intend to stay up here, however. And on my word, the men you see in front of you will kill you all. Sadly, I believe our chat was meaningless. I wish to be rid of you now."

"Ready yourselves," Ardian grunted as he grasped Spike and his shield. Even Euvard wielded his axe with fidgeting fingers. Zercien's heart raced, but the fog returned—and out of the corner of his eye was the outline of someone running through the trees behind Reaver.

"Good men of Denon-Hein," came Reaver's voice. "Dispose of these Entervians! Atta—"

A guttural gulp. A choking sound.

It was met not with raised swords, but by faint murmurs of "Boss?" and "Reaver?"

Reaver's limp body dropped down from the cliffside, flopping to the ground with a bloodied and severed neck. Before anyone could react, a lone man jumped from the cliff in a haze of darkness, and the figure parted Zercien's fog with a headfirst roll to catch his fall. Facing the barbarians, he drew a longsword from the sheath on his back, right over his shoulder-length black hair.

"He killed Reaver! Get him!" an Arvaros shouted, only to be answered with an uppercut slash from his belly to his neck. Three others then met the swordsman's blade before they could even swing, falling facedown to the dirt with severed necks.

Zercien shook his head as if trying to awaken from a dream, and Euvard grabbed his shoulder and rocked it back and forth.

"What the hell is Lloyd doing here?" he said, and then charged. Zercien followed, soon after by Ardian.

"Not a chance they capture me again!" shouted a familiar Arvaros. Zercien watched as he ran at Fynnian.

"I might be dying here, but not before I gut me an Entervian!"

"Fynn!" Zercien said and sprinted in Fynnian's direction, but not fast enough to jump between his ally and the Arvaros.

Fynnian again stayed on the defensive, parrying the blows with relative ease. On the next block, the Arvaros recoiled, and Fynnian ran the tip of his blade through his foe's chest, his sword arm pushing through every inch of cut flesh. Fynnian yelped and let his sword go as the Arvaros fell, the blade still lodged in his chest as he hit the ground. Zercien arrived and nodded.

Fynnian gulped, his breaths hard and fast. "Is he… Did I—"

Zercien rested a hand on his shoulder. "I learned not to think about it much. It helps."

No mercy was granted to the remaining barbarians. Even if Zercien had *wanted* to, Lloyd left none alive.

"Where the hell did you come from?" Euvard was the first to shout.

The swordsman sheathed his bloody sword. "I followed you here."

My senses were right, Zercien thought. *Or, whatever they are.*

"I assumed we were being watched by bandits, but—"

"My presence here has naught to do with you," Lloyd interrupted, but the gleam in his eye told Zercien he at least earned praise, if only a little.

"Then why did you come after us?" Fynnian said. His hands still shook.

"Vellard is home to no swordfighter worthy of my time," Lloyd said. "I seek opponents."

Euvard smiled. "You're joining us?"

"As I have already stated. Your mission means nothing to me. Your company provides a convenient method for travel about the continent."

"Pardon my interruption," Ardian said, raising his index finger. "You all know this man?"

"Not me," Fynnian said, his head shaking as he continued his rapid gulps.

"We watched as he dueled some ruffians, and later he slew Arvaros during their attack," Zercien said as he explained their history with Lloyd.

"For trespassing," Lloyd said.

"Though your motives are," Ardian juggled his hands, "*question-able* at best, I'm glad to have you with us." He offered a hand in greeting. "I am Ardian Calvus, a Vellardian Guard Captain. It is a pleasure to meet you."

Lloyd didn't even look down at Ardian's outstretched hand.

"Isn't it about time we leave?" Euvard said.

"What of the rest of the barbarians?" Fynnian said. "We may have rid them of Reaver, but they will be back."

Zercien took a quick look around and surveyed the area, at the carnage and dead littering the debris of broken homes. "None escaped. Others likely won't know what happened for some time, and without Reaver, they'll hesitate to attack."

He looked at Ardian. "Would you agree?"

"I do." The guard captain nodded. "Word will reach other Duspen territories eventually. I imagine the death of their ringleader will halt their advances, and for now, I think Entervia is safe. From bandits, at least."

But Zercien couldn't shake what Reaver said. First, the castle archives. Now, Entervia withheld supplies from an ailing border country.

Come off it, Zercien, he thought. *Don't believe that Arvaros. He talked nonsense. All lies.*

"Seems like it's settled then," Euvard butted in, interrupting Zercien's thoughts. "Take point, Zerc."

Carefully stepping through the paths of Denon-Hein, each, save for Lloyd, conveyed their pleasure at taking their leave of such a place.

***

Lloyd never expressed much. Less than much, really. More like nothing at all. He remained silent while the group walked. And despite his tall and imposing figure, his footfalls made no noise. He didn't pay any attention to the landscape or even to his companions. Until Fynnian approached him.

"Hello."

Lloyd made no effort to reply. Fynnian tried again, though his words came out as if interspersed by rocks. "We haven't had the pleasure of meeting. I'm Fynn. Fynnian."

"Your sword arm is weak," Lloyd said, and Fynnian stumbled at his words.

"I haven't had much instruction."

"When night falls, wait for the others to sleep. I will be training. Seek me out, and I shall hone your skills."

"You would teach me?"

Lloyd stared hard at the shorter man of thin arms. "I am not here to protect. There is potential in you, but it remains hindered. I seek to bring it forth."

Fynnian gulped. "Tonight? Any night?"

Lloyd resumed looking ahead and refused to make further eye contact.

"Perhaps I will take you up on your offer, then," Fynnian said.

"If you wish not to learn, I shall not be bothered," Lloyd said. "Your death is none of my concern."

CHAPTER THIRTY-ONE
ANCIENT SIGNS

The day was perfect. A gentle breeze provided relief from the warm sun, and evergreen trees twice as large as Euvard populated the grass. Bushes bearing berries filled the land where trees did not. No clouds in the sky. Nothing clogged the purest of blues.

Though the lack of any passersby did worry Zercien. Reaver's words kept crawling back.

Interrupting his negative thoughts, however, was a lighthearted conversation held by his companions. He heard his name mentioned once or twice and gave it no concern, but Euvard's easily distinguished laughter made him look back and listen in.

"Really, now, Euvard? You've been with just one woman your whole life?" Ardian said.

Euvard chuckled. "Don't sound too surprised, now."

"I won't lie, that's not the opinion I formed of you on first sight."

Euvard went to describe his beloved in all aspects, down to the last detail, and Zercien chuckled to himself.

He does love her, he thought. *Can't fault that.*

"You married?" Euvard asked the guard captain.

Ardian breathed a quick laugh, followed by a smile. "I contracted with the guard in my sixteenth year. Left me little time to seriously court. But I am not so…picky. Instead, I've met many a Vellardian for short times, so to speak."

"Whatever tickles your fancy."

"And many did!"

Zercien rubbed his forehead amid their hearty, insufferable laughter.

And here I thought a guard captain would bring some maturity to our travels.

"What about you, Fynn?" Euvard said.

"Huh? What about me?" Fynnian said, and the Sanctum Order descendant's face resembled a tomato.

Euvard nodded at Ardian, and ribbed him with a gentle elbow. "Ardian's curious about you."

"One person, and just once," Fynnian said, showing a brief smile, but then huffed. "She isn't around anymore. Truly, it is nothing you'd want to know about."

"Really?" Ardian said. "You're a handsome lad. I'm surprised."

Somehow, the tomato occupying his cheeks grew even more red. "A year ago, or so. A bit of time after our meeting, she told me it was best we went our separate ways. Never said why, only mentioning she felt ill. I don't know where she went, and I haven't heard from or seen her since."

Meanwhile, in the back, Zercien noticed Lloyd shrugging off the entire conversation. Shaking his head, he ignored every attempt at prodding him for information.

Am I truly agreeing with Lloyd on something? Zercien thought.

***

As soon as the sun set and the sky turned dark, they made camp. According to Ardian, if they awoke early the next morning, they could reach Tiesel before nightfall.

Lloyd stayed what looked to be as far as possible while remaining in sight, swinging his sword at nothing in particular. Zercien thought it odd, but was thankful a frightening, dark-garbed swordsman just slashing away in the night eliminated the need for a lookout.

I have to talk to him, Zercien thought. He watched as Lloyd continued his sword swings, slashing and stabbing with pinpoint accuracy. *Or do I?*

Though he felt he'd regret it, he stood from his makeshift bed and wandered toward the practicing swordsman.

The chill left behind in Lloyd's sword's wake blistered through Zercien's body. Or it was the nerves while staring in admiration at the swordsman's technique.

Speed, power, an unwavering glance. Zercien shuddered thinking about it. He still had his doubts about Lloyd's intentions, but if his plan *was* to kill them, he wouldn't have waited this long.

Probably.

"Lloyd?"

Lloyd didn't answer, but he turned to face him.

"I'm sorry to bother you," Zercien said and cleared his throat. "I have a few questions I'd like to ask you."

The swordsman's black eyes pierced through his head, as if he were looking at something behind him. But he sheathed his blade. "Speak."

Another cold wind blitzed through Zercien's spine. While he didn't expect the swordsman to make anything simple, his cooperation would save them both from what he expected to be a painful, awkward experience.

"We will be traveling together for some time," Zercien said. "I would like to learn more about you."

Lloyd turned his back to Zercien and said nothing. Standing in silence, a tingle crept up Zercien's spine.

"You wish for me to speak of myself?" said the swordsman as he faced Zercien again. "Unfortunate. You ask about a subject I know little of. My memory contains the last ten years. I know nothing of my early life."

"You have no memory of anything before the last ten years?"

Zercien then realized he hadn't the faintest clue how old Lloyd was, and by his answers, the swordsman likely had no idea either. Now that Zercien had a better look at his face, he saw traces of age—three faint lines underneath his eyes, a slight curled wrinkle emerging whenever he let his brow furrow.

"I awoke upon the deck of a ship docked at the port of Vellard. Its origin, I know not," Lloyd said. "A bag of gold etched with the name 'Lloyd' and a sword lay beside me. Such was all I required."

Being of other birth than Entervian wasn't a problem, but he was certainly not at an age to be experiencing such acute memory loss. Perhaps he unconsciously repressed a traumatic memory, causing a refusal to recall anything past a certain point. Or, this was an outright lie. Which Zercien leaned toward believing. But he shook his head—he was no medic and thought it best to not pry further.

I already disturbed him, Zercien thought. *Let's not anger him further.*

"And then you practiced swordsmanship for ten years?"

"My sword arm was immaculate. How is unknown to me. The way my blade swung was that of someone already taught."

"But you don't remember?"

"No."

And Lloyd went back to his training. Further conversation was pointless.

***

Their journey to Tiesel began early the next morning even though Zercien awoke with aches and pains. Euvard, Fynnian, and Ardian's slowness in preparing told him he wasn't the only one.

This was to be remedied in Tiesel, according to the guard captain, who had planned to stay at an inn for the night rather than sleep on the ground. He joked that if they could just find Lagana, they'd never need to rest.

"Lagana?" Euvard asked. "Who?"

Ardian squinted at Euvard. "You don't know of Lagana?"

Euvard just shrugged.

"One of the Legends," Zercien said. "The texts available to the common people don't speak of her much, though she is mentioned."

"I see. Most unfortunate," Ardian said. "If it weren't for the healing powers of Astrulux, the Seven Legends certainly wouldn't have stood a chance."

"I remember Holunt, Gunvald, and Skjóturi," Euvard said. "And I've seen drawings of Symphora and Kyrios." He whistled while tapping his axe handle. "Those weapons make mine look like a practice axe."

Probably because I taught you about those three and their armaments in the hour before our exam, Zercien thought.

"My texts briefly mention Abeo and Oculi, but nothing else," he said. "Though one book I teach from states not much is known about Abeo, or his lance, Einiquitar."

Zercien referred to the *Legends of Oniro – Complete Edition*, though now realized how much of a misnomer it was.

"Yes, that's true," Ardian said. "Though he is fascinating—a masterful lancer with the ability to disappear and reappear in battles. I can't say I'm not intrigued."

"Huh. Sounds like a coward to me." Euvard scoffed. "Just like that goddamned Oculi."

Ardian crossed his arms. "Is there a problem with Oculi, now?"

"Best not to get him started—" Zercien attempted to complain, but Euvard interrupted.

"I *despise* archers. Anyone who can't stand on the front lines isn't a worthy warrior."

Zercien excused himself from the conversation as soon as Ardian and Euvard began debating the effectiveness of archery. He knew his friend's bias and wasn't interested in hearing it for the hundredth—or was it two-hundredth? —time.

Off the grassy path, Zercien veered his gaze to four pillars in the distance. A monument of sorts. He saw Fynnian's gait turn sideways as he attempted, and failed, to crane his neck away from the ruins.

"Could we stop here?" Fynnian said, though his legs continued to move toward the pillars. As if he were only half in-control of his body movements.

Euvard shot Zercien a look accompanied by a shrug, and Zercien just answered with the same. He urged the remainder of his squad to follow and join Fynnian.

The four pillars stood taller than the lot of them—even Euvard—in a North, South, East, and West formation, each carved with symbols and runes. In the center, an ominous yet unassuming circular grey stone plate with no lettering. Zercien's breaths grew heavy and pained as he drew nearer, his throat scratchy with the dry air. At the same time, the ground was soft beneath his feet, light, as if one strong enough step would shatter the earth. Zercien's unease swelled as Ardian put a hand on the North monument and ran his finger over the letters.

"Is this the ancient language?" the guard captain said.

"The ancient language of the Sanctum Order!" Fynnian mumbled, just loud enough for Zercien to hear. "I've studied it some. Most of the Order's spells are written in it."

Ancient Sanctum Order writings. Here, of all places, Zercien thought.

Some mentions of this tongue appeared in his studies and lectures, but he never paid much attention, rather focusing his efforts on the Seven Legends.

He stood with a hand on his chin, looking up, but then turned to face Fynnian. "Can you read it?"

"Not all of it," Fynnian said. "I'll translate what I am able."

With his face almost pressing into the cold stone, he slowly started rattling off what sense he could make of it, skipping a symbol here and there, reading the ones he recalled. "When . . . four . . . power . . . released . . . tower . . . seal . . . unleash.'"

"What in the world could that mean?" Ardian said to nobody in particular, but Fynnian was too interested in pressing his entire face onto the North stone. Euvard poked him and he jumped.

"What about those big ones at the top?"

Fynnian stood as high as his toes would carry him to see the lettering.

"Entervia," he muttered, and moved to the East stone. "This one says Ariglioth."

"The names of different countries in Oniro? Fascinating," Ardian said.

Fynnian nodded as he approached the South stone, looked up, and squinted. "Telurdia." But he cocked his head at the West stone.

"Ruj? Rujh-mand? Looks like a jumbled mess of letters. But the symbols beneath these—each pillar carries the same pattern. 'When... four .... power ... released... tower... seal... unleash.'"

Zercien felt a rush of cold air and shivered.

"Shall we leave?" He shoved his hands in his pockets to hide their shaking. "I think we've seen everything we can here."

He could tell Lloyd had been ready to leave since they arrived. He hadn't moved any closer to the stones or attempt to uncover any mysteries, and just stood, waiting. However, when Zercien led Euvard and Ardian away, Fynnian didn't follow.

"Fynn?" Zercien called out to him. No answer. "Fynn?" Still no reply.

But Fynnian *was* listening. Just not to Zercien.

He watched Fynnian, as if he were in a trance, stumble toward the circular stone at the center, and throw himself onto it, embracing it with open arms.

"Fynn!" Zercien said and rushed back, Euvard and Ardian in tow.

His ally was still. Not even a shred of hair wafted in the breeze. Euvard grabbed him by his sides and flipped him over.

Fynnian's blue eyes disappeared, his pupils fully absorbed. Blank white spheres shivered as if freezing, and his mouth hung agape, drool escaping from the corners. His body convulsed, and a dull yellow glow emitted from his chest. The circular stone beneath him exuded a pure white light, encompassing both it and Fynnian.

Euvard let go and backed away. "What the hell's going on?"

"I don't know!" Ardian said. "Get Fynnian away from this place! Now!"

CHAPTER THIRTY-TWO
A MUCH-DESERVED RESPITE

Fynnian awoke to find himself lying on a soft, warm bed with white sheets. Stretching his arms out, he yawned, which garnered the attention of his companions.

"Well, it looks like you're finally coming around," Ardian said.

Euvard laughed. "Gave us a good scare, you did!"

Lloyd said nothing and remained in a corner of the room, by himself.

Coming around? Fynnian thought. Where exactly had he been? He just couldn't remember. "What are you talking about?"

"Those ruins knocked you out." Euvard snorted, going into detail about the mysterious lights and Fynnian's eyes.

"Oh, dear. Well, I feel fine. In fact, I feel rested. It was as if I'd been in a long, wondrous sleep." He jumped out of bed to show his company. But he darted his head about to see several wooden wardrobes, a bookshelf, and some other beds. "Where am I?"

"We're in Tiesel. Your slumber was four hours," Zercien said. "It's good to see you're all right, Fynn."

"I apologize. Something came over me, I suppose."

"What happened?"

Fynnian exhaled a long, winding breath.

"…A voice. It kept speaking to me in the ancient tongue. At first it said nothing. Nothing I could understand, anyway, but it pulled me closer. Then I just fell asleep."

"*It* pulled you closer? The hell does that mean?" Euvard said.

"My body was not under my control. It was drawn toward that voice. But before it put me to sleep," he said, and then gulped. "One word came through."

And he grew silent, leaving his companions waiting.

"Well?" Euvard urged.

Fynnian breathed deep. "*Release.*"

No one said a word for many long seconds.

Ardian broke the silence. "The innkeeper here saw Euvard carrying you and offered us a free night's stay. We've had a long few days. I'm thinking you all turn in and get a fresh start early tomorrow."

He caught himself and winked at Zercien. "Oh, my apologies. Is that agreeable, *Captain*?"

Zercien tilted his head. "Agreeable."

"All right, then!"

Ardian turned to leave, and was met with stares as he walked by.

"Where are *you* going?" Euvard crossed his arms.

"There's a pub downstairs. I figure I'll go and tip the ol' innkeeper for a bit." Ardian scratched at the side of his head. "I'd invite you all to join me, but I need a little *me* time."

"A little *mead* time is more like it," Euvard muttered under his breath, and Zercien choked back a laugh.

Stretching his legs, Fynnian wandered across the room, and then stopped in the corner. "Where's Lloyd?"

Zercien and Euvard darted their heads in all directions but couldn't find their dark-cloaked ally.

"Where the fuck—" Euvard groaned. "He was just here."

"Would he have just left us?" Zercien said in an almost-too-happy tone.

"It'd be odd," Euvard said. "He *did* say we were convenient for him."

Fynnian walked past Zercien and Euvard and grabbed his sword. "I shall look for him. He could not have gone far."

The two stared blankly at one another, and Euvard shrugged. "Sure you're feeling okay?"

"Mhm."

Zercien nodded. "But if he's left Tiesel, it might be best to let him go."

Without another word, Fynnian was off, exiting their room for all of thirty seconds. He poked his head back inside.

"Where are we?"

Zercien cracked a slight smile. "The *Legend* Inn."

A quick nod, and Fynnian was gone again.

***

Zercien passed a ripped and cracked wall, and picked out the bed next to a dresser with a fist-sized hole in the top drawer. Stains and tears marred the dirtied brown rug underneath.

He slipped the map from his pack as Euvard slid into the bed next to his, and started studying, muttering aloud. "Tomorrow, we'll be here." Zercien placed a finger on the Okoro Mountains. "Doesn't look *too* far—"

"Just going to ignore me?" Euvard's voice almost made him drop the map.

"Apologies. Lost in my own thoughts."

Euvard sat up on his bed and looked Zercien square in the eye. "What do you think of Ardian?"

"Now that I've spent time with him, he's nothing like I assumed," Zercien said. Albeit begrudgingly. This guard captain was more than he let on, and Zercien wouldn't soon forget that he was responsible for this mess, but couldn't deny his usefulness. "Which is a good thing, I would say."

"I wasn't thrilled when you told me the captain of the guard was coming with us," Euvard said. "I thought he was just going to be all stuck-up and speak in an 'I'm better than you because I'm the guard captain' voice."

Zercien chuckled. "I take it he has proven you wrong?"

"He's chummy with us, doesn't talk down, sounds like he actually cares about who we are. Not a lot of military folks are like that." Euvard cracked a smile. "And the man's down there drinking by himself just because he feels like it."

Zercien returned the smile. "As long as we don't have to drag him back upstairs tomorrow morning."

The two friends shared a brief laugh, and Euvard grabbed a mug of water sitting bedside.

"Fynn's grown a little bit too, eh?" He took a swig. "Going off to find Lloyd all by himself and all."

"He has, but I won't lie, I wasn't disappointed when we saw Lloyd had gone."

Euvard shook his head and inched to the edge of his bed. "Still don't trust him? Even after he saved us?"

Taking his own mug in hand, Zercien shook his head. "He told me he only came to Vellard ten years ago and doesn't remember anything before." After a quick swig, he said, "Can't say I've heard of anything like it."

"More than I've gotten out of him. But I think he's proven his loyalty."

"You've a talent for seeing the good in people," Zercien said.

Euvard snorted and turned to lie face-up. "Or I'm just gullible."

"It *is* thanks to you that we assembled any sort of force. Though we seem to have attracted some interesting personalities."

"You're right about that, Zerc," Euvard said as he held up three fingers. "A guard captain who's seen more bars than fights, a religious man looking for his long-lost dad that can't tell a sword's pommel from the blade, and a scary swordsman who probably sleeps with a sword in his hand, if he ever sleeps at all."

"And then there's us."

"Don't lump me in there with you!" Euvard's bellowing laughter filled the room, and he waved his hands about. "With your headaches and roleplaying, or whatever that was?"

Within Zercien's long cringe, a smile broke free. "You've got me there."

"By the looks of things, I'm the only normal person here!" Euvard said, a grin still pinned from his left to right ear.

"I'd drink to that, my friend. If Ardian had invited us downstairs."

***

Fynnian had walked through all manner of dirt roads and closed markets. With just a scant few lit torches along the main streets, not many townspeople wandered the night—both relieving and a tad unnerving.

Every second he was shifting his head in another direction, on the lookout for muggers and other assailants.

Coming to the town's front gate, he found Lloyd just on the outskirts.

Still practicing, he swung his sword in all directions, his focus never falling behind. Fynnian watched from a distance, staring with wide, curious eyes at the swordsman's concentration, the speed of his strokes.

With timid steps, he approached. "Hello?"

"Yes?" Came the reply after a moment's wait. He didn't turn to face Fynnian.

"We—" he gulped. "We were just wondering where you'd gone. Please return tonight."

Lloyd said nothing.

"Okay, then," Fynnian said, and he turned to walk away. But with his back toward Lloyd, he took a deep breath and called forth the strength needed to act on his true intentions.

"May I join you?" He moved his body to face the swordsman.

Lloyd did the same, and his piercing gaze shot lightning through Fynnian's spine. But the swordsman sheathed his longsword and picked a wooden sword from the dirt, holding it in a defensive posture. He seemed to have planned this, though Fynnian didn't see the swordsman carrying practice swords before. Either Lloyd was adept at hiding them, or—well, Fynnian didn't want to think about the methods employed for procuring the swords on such short notice.

"At your ready," Lloyd said.

Fynnian botched his mimicry of the master swordsman's stance and tripped as he unsheathed his sword. "I mean no disrespect, but shouldn't I have a practice sword as well?"

"I have witnessed your skills." Lloyd pointed the wooden blade at Fynnian. "That will not be necessary."

Chapter Thirty-Three
The Path to Life

Tyrrowan dug his calloused hands into the scorching sand of the Darutan Dunes, desperate for his search to end. Long had he spent cursing, digging, traipsing the wasteland, relying on the oasis folk for aid many a time. And yet, the Sanctum Order cache evaded him.

The oppressive heat roasted his back as he crawled about on all-fours, punching at the blasted sand.

They said it was here. It should be here. His mind wandered. He clawed with rapid abandon at the dune he stood upon but slammed down both fists when he could dig no further. Scattered sand whipped up into the air, the hot grains burning his cheeks like ashes.

Tyrrowan sat up and lifted his hands to his face. Singed and dried skin hung from his palms, leaving a layer of raw red behind. But his eyes remained unchanged, with no reaction to his desecrated hands. Instead, he shut them and breathed deep, focusing amid the rain of sand assaulting him from above.

A yellow-white glow appeared in his right hand, and he clasped it together with his left. The light traveled between the two palms, interweaved within his fingers, and then vanished. He cringed as if someone pinched him. When he unfurled his fingers, the callouses and burns dissolved, and his hands became blemish-free, ready to dig once again.

Instead, he reached into his satchel and unfurled a small scroll, holding it down against the sand. Wind threatened to yank it away, but nothing would keep him from his prize. Not after so many years of searching.

He read the same text again, in the ancient tongue of the Sanctum Order. He understood all except the most complex of passages, but this was one of them. Years spent studying the intricacy of the symbols, and he managed a scant few lines.

"Only land of death can bring life," he said, enunciating each word as he ran his fingers across. "Only light of death reveal path to life."

He'd checked every graveyard and old battlefield on the continent, spent years at sea, and found nothing. No other place could harbor death, though "Light death" was the troubling phrase. He guessed the sun, albeit without confidence.

Sweat dripped from his forehead onto the parchment, but he was quick to bundle it up before ruining the only clue he had left.

He leaned back against a palm tree and basked in the slightly scorching shade, repeating the words over and over in his mind.

"Only land of death can bring life. Only light of death reveal path to life. Only land of death can bring life. Only light of death reveal path to life…" Over, and over again.

A light *caw* echoed over the bright, cloudless sky. Tyrrowan looked up to see swirling carrion birds. He smiled and waved. They'd need to wait far longer for him than any desert creature.

"Only land of death can bring life," Tyrrowan mouthed. "Only light of death reveal path to life…" He gasped, but it was not nerves, nor fear. A smile stretched from ear to ear.

Tyrrowan stood away from the shade, basking in the brunt of the blistering rays bearing down with searing heat. His sweat dribbled and stained his clothes, and his mouth grew dry and sandy. But nothing happened.

Too simple, he thought. *Perhaps it is not the sun, but…*

He quieted his mind. He had it. It was not the sun, but another type of light.

Taking a deep breath, he concentrated his mind on the sand below. From his fingertips, a lance of golden, holy light escaped, jettisoning into the dune. The smoldering grains flew from their spot like a whirlwind, sending wave upon wave of ash-like dust onto Tyrrowan, burning his face and clothes.

He screamed through the pain shocking his body from continued use of his Seraph Arts, but held firm. His hands shook, desperate to release, but he would not let them. The strain in his muscles and arms burned far hotter than the desert sun.

Tyrrowan's arms and legs grew weary, shaking and faltering in the heat, and the carrion birds' cries snuck past the screeching of his light-infused javelin. He smiled through the noise, welcoming their sweet calls, shouting, goading them to circle lower.

"Come on. Come on!" He ground his teeth, crunching the hot sand sitting in his mouth.

A tear ripped through his abdomen, and blood trickled, sizzling as it landed atop the sands. Tyrrowan winced and covered the wound with one hand, propelling his surging light with the other.

Blood soaked his hand, burning and hot. The birds' calls sounded as if they buzzed just over his head. His vision grew bleary, and his legs wobbled. Breathing worsened, his lungs coughing up each gulp of desert air.

He collapsed, legs unable to carry his weight, and fell face-first onto the searing sand. Tyrrowan lifted his head, and moved a hand to wipe his face, though he felt he raked against hot coals.

The Sanctum Knight shut his eyes, and no matter how hard he forced his eyelids, he no longer possessed the strength to hold them open. Soon, his hand fell, unable to continue its constant spellcasting. His arms, too, trembled under his weight, and he dropped to the sand on his stomach.

Caws were drowned out by a crash, an earthquake hitting just once. Tyrrowan managed one eye, half-open, watching through blurred vision as the dune in front of him sprayed all its sand in a glorious explosion, forming a hole at the center.

The Sanctum Knight crawled, clawing up fistfuls of burning sand toward the hole, his own blood leaving a smoking trail in his wake. This was it. What he had been searching for, almost within his grasp. Teetering at the edge, he stared down into the dark, but his arms caved, and he fell forward, tumbling into the abyss.

Chapter Thirty-Four
The Dead Caste

The company bade farewell to the quiet town of Tiesel, and with extra supplies in hand, they embarked toward their next destination: the great Okoro Mountains—a range extending from the far north of Dregnal to Entervia's south border. Gates dating back hundreds of years marked entryways into the mountains, leading travelers from Entervia to Ariglioth or vice versa, but the path was treacherous. Many chose to forego the mountains in favor of ocean voyages. Soon, passage by sea became the only method of travel between the two countries, and the paths through the Okoro went ignored for many years.

Zercien's group didn't have that luxury, and with Duspen's banditry, Ardian thought to test the Okoro. And thus, the steep and rocky paths became their only choice.

Through the first ancient gate Zercien led his allies, its scarred and eroded grey stone shooting high into the sky, forming an arch above their heads. The soft ground then turned to solid rock.

Looking out ahead, Zercien saw no path, just as Ardian told them. Remnants of a past route existed, but now lay covered in rock and neglect. Zercien stumbled over messes of jagged stones and overgrown grass, hands grasping at anything for some sort of balance.

This makeshift trail led up, and a quick check at Ardian behind him resulted in a nod to keep pushing forward. With no map to help, Zercien somehow felt more at ease.

Zercien climbed up a ledge, grunting and using his entire upper body to pull his weight across, and found himself on flat land. The others joined him, though Euvard had to grab Fynnian by the arms and yank him up. Peering over the edge, Zercien could see Tiesel shrinking, but not as small as he hoped. He panted, wiping the sweat from his brow. They'd hardly progressed.

A body of water loomed ahead, and a skinny, winding mess of rocks at its outskirts served as the only way across. Pressing his back to the mountainside, he slid and shimmied his feet, the bottoms of his boots not an inch away from falling straight into the pond. Though it did look inviting. A perfect clear blue, Zercien swore he could see down into its depths with ease.

Or it was the exhaustion talking.

Nearing the end, he leapt the rest of the way and landed on both feet, watching, and trying to stifle his laughter, as Euvard stood on the edges of his heels, arching his back at an uncomfortable angle just to keep from slipping.

He mimicked Zercien's jump, but tumbled to the other side, landing on his hands and knees. Zercien nudged him and pointed up and stared at a wall of solid rock.

His friend's whistle echoed through the mountains. "Not ideal."

The wall lined with sharp rock and boulders stretched into the sky with no discernable path. For all Zercien knew, it carried for miles.

Ardian pressed a hand onto the wall and shook his head. "Must have been a rockslide. And Entervia never bothered to clear it. Or even noticed."

"And let me guess. You don't have any pickaxes in that pack of yours," Euvard said. Ardian showed Euvard a blank stare.

"Is there no other way?" Fynnian piped up, still trying to catch his breath, while Lloyd just stood behind them looking bored.

Ardian tugged at his stubby beard. "There must be."

Zercien wandered, but stumbled turning a corner as some of the mountain's rocks cracked and fell from underneath his footing.

"Zerc! Everything okay?" Euvard called as the rest of his company jogged over, except Lloyd, who sauntered in his usual apathetic stroll. Zercien dusted himself off.

"I'm fine. But look." He pointed down. A path ran along the side of the mountain.

Ardian smiled."Would you look at that! Nice find, Captain!"

Zercien rolled his eyes at Ardian, as he'd been accustomed to, and lowered himself down the ledge, one careful step at a time. He landed on the hard rock path, and lent a hand to Euvard, who followed right behind.

Zercien looked to his right and shuddered. He stood at the edge of the mountain, with nothing but freefall should he trip. At its end, the maw of a cave stretched its jaws wide to meet him. The outline appeared precise, as if it were man-made, but jagged edges gave the illusion it was torn from the mountain by force.

Staring inside, all Zercien saw was darkness, save for the sunlight shining into the entrance. The path sloped down, but he couldn't see much further than a few feet. His heart flew into a fury of beats as he inhaled the stale air.

"Curious," Ardian muttered, joining Zercien in looking down its throat. "I wonder…"

Euvard nudged Zercien for an answer, but he just shrugged.

"Shouldn't we go in?" Euvard said.

"Perhaps," Ardian said.

"*Perhaps?* Not sure if you've noticed, but we're strapped for options."

While Zercien, Euvard, and Ardian spoke, Fynnian tiptoed by them to peer into the cave. The sinister air met his face, and he coughed as it entered his throat. He shivered and stepped back on quivering boots.

"Something wrong?" Euvard said.

"Nothing!" Fynnian shook his head. "The air was a bit chilly."

Zercien darted his eyes to the cave entrance and then back to Ardian. "This may be our only way forward."

Ardian ran his fingers through his beard. "Yes, I suppose it is."

Pushing past Zercien, Euvard crossed his arms and stood right in front of the guard captain. "All right. Spill it."

Ardian groaned. "This passage. I've seen it before. In the castle archives."

Of course it was hidden in the archives, Zercien thought.

"When the Ancients' War was at its peak, not even cities and towns were safe from the Helldregs," Ardian said. "Only so many strongholds to safeguard citizens existed. When those met capacity, there was nothing Entervia and Ariglioth could do...above ground."

After a head tilt, Zercien shut one eye. Where the guard captain was leading with this, he hadn't a clue.

"The caverns beneath the Okoro already existed naturally, and thus the two countries constructed a miniature town to relocate many of their people underground," the guard captain said. "They connected the caverns to Entervia and Ariglioth, and citizens of both countries could enter with ease. Once inside, they were given months of supplies, and the entrances were concealed within the rock."

Zercien shook his head, mouthing "no, no, no." "They moved Entervians and Arigliothans underground? That cannot be true."

Ardian walked to the cave entrance and ran his hand along the jagged edge. "See these?" he pointed with his other. "These aren't natural."

Fynnian coughed. "You mean—"

Ardian nodded once. "Eventually, the Helldregs came upon the cave. After ripping apart the entrance, they slaughtered everything. I've read the Ariglioth side, too, was torn open by those monsters."

Zercien let out a stream of air from his closed lips.

"I doubt anyone's been near these caves since," Ardian continued, but was interrupted by Euvard's nervous laughter.

"Ah, *this* is what started those ghost stories in Vellard." He raised his hands and mocked Ardian's storytelling. "And no one's ever been into the caverns beneath the Okoro again!" An uneasy smile spread over his lips. "We all know the Helldregs are dead. Nothing will be in there. Just your run of the mill, uh, catacombs."

"Because calling it 'the *catacombs* beneath the Okoro' makes it *so* much better," Fynnian said.

"I suppose you're right, Euvard," Ardian said along a nod. "Maybe I let the old stories get the better of me."

"And this will lead us all the way to Ariglioth?" Zercien said.

Ardian shrugged. "If the old pathways haven't caved in, then, in theory, yes."

"We have no choice, it seems."

"Unless you believe heading through Duspen proper would be the smarter decision."

A bloodred hood caught Zercien's eye. It darted past, through the black entrance to the cave, and two flaming rubies shone in the dark. He gasped, though none of his companions reacted.

The rubies tilted down, as if nodding, and disappeared.

Accept it, appeared the words in Zercien's mind. A tiny lap of fog washed over his feet, but he shook it away.

Though it wasn't fear he felt, nor unease. It was elation, happiness, as if a guide was showing him the proper path. He gazed back at the distance they'd already covered, the tops of trees and Tiesel as small as his finger, dwarfed by the mountains.

We can't afford to trek back into Duspen, he thought.

They had already taken one detour and cost themselves precious days. And at least this far into the mountains, no Arvaros would be waiting in waylay.

"This is the shorter and safer route," Zercien said. "Unless we sprout wings and fly across, I see no better options."

The guard captain bent down and removed two torches he'd bought in Tiesel from his bag, handing both to Zercien. He soaked two pieces of cloth in some sort of thick liquid—Zercien hadn't a guess as to what it could be—and wrapped them around the torches, fastening them in place with metal wire. At last, he removed a steel loop he could fit his fingers between and a piece of flint, and struck the two together, creating momentary sparks.

Ardian was speaking of the caves as he did so, but Zercien found himself much more enthralled with this torch-lighting procedure, and stood in silent wonder as both torches grew fire before his eyes.

Fynnian flinched at the flame.

"We'll need to re-light them every so often," Ardian said, and winked. "Hope you were taking notes." Zercien went to hold the torch in front, but grimaced at the searing heat and inability to see.

"Like this," Ardian said as he grabbed and raised Zercien's forearm. The flame's blinding lessened. "Always hold it above your head or to the side."

So complicated, Zercien thought as he practiced holding his torch, seeing which position he preferred. And then thought of how ridiculous it was that he needed to "practice" such things.

"Seems we are prepared now," Ardian said. "But, steel yourselves. We will see the remains of the dead, or perhaps just their skeletons."

Zercien shivered.

I fail to see how that would be the preferred alternative, he thought.

"After you, Captain." Ardian smiled, and Zercien groaned. He stopped at the foot of the cave's mouth, and lifted his torch to reveal a set of stone steps leading further down. And with a deep breath, he ventured into the cave, plunging headlong into the heavy air of the twisting catacombs.

Zercien shined his torch in all directions, revealing an open space with plenty of room to walk. Though not even rats scurried about. And aside from his and his company's footsteps, no noises permeated the dark. Not that he minded.

Soon, the winding passage came to a three-way crossroad. One path to the east, west, and another straight ahead. Zercien looked to Ardian, but he shrugged.

I suppose none of us really know, he thought. *Straight it is, then.*

His torchlight revealed a rotted wooden door with a chunk ripped out of the side.

"A door?" Zercien said as he waved his hand around the cracked wood, and ran one finger as gently as he could, as he feared he'd knock it down with too hard of a breath.

Wet with decay, but the splintered, jagged edges remained sharp.

"How odd. These don't look like the marks around the cave's entrance," Ardian said as he stuck his head next to Zercien's.

"What do you mean?"

"Small cuts, like a human's hand would make." Ardian placed a hand on the edges, applying enough pressure to force a creak.

"Did the people try to escape through where we came in? Why would they—" Ardian's touch caused the door to fall backward, and it slammed down to the stone floor, the rotted wood cracking and breaking, splintering about the rock. Zercien cringed as the *crash* it made reverberated. Ardian mouthed "sorry" to everyone.

Zercien stepped over the smashed door, but jumped back. A rancid odor of decay wafted through his nostrils, and at the edge of his torchlight, he saw a centuries-old bed, fit with torn, tattered and bloodstained sheets.

And the lump in the middle told him someone was still in it.

He screamed as his torch revealed a skull with half its face hanging off the jaw, eyeless sockets staring with a forlorn sorrow. "Fuck!"

Fynnian gulped, walking forward but could only look for a second before shifting his gaze away. "How has it not decomposed?"

Ardian shook his head. "I don't know. Keep moving."

To the right lay an opening where another door had once stood. Zercien wasted no time in darting through, but now when he walked, he felt his boots sink further into the stone until a loud *crush* filled his eardrums.

A large circular room with four doors along the left and right loomed ahead—much like the last, each with a jagged gash ripped through. His path continued straight, past the smashed doors and through the middle, where his progress was stopped by a large stone door, cracked open just enough for him to sneak through.

"Gah!" he screamed again as he jumped back, his torchlight shining upon a half-decomposed skeleton from the waist down sprawled on the floor. Again, its eye sockets stared straight up, through Zercien's and into his mind.

Regaining his breath, Zercien stood over the body and stretched a hand to the door handle hoping to open it more, and not be forced to step across the bones beneath. But his torch caught deep, dark marks slashed upon the stone in random, haphazard designs.

"They look the same as the other door," Ardian said, shining his flame, running his finger along. "Lots of them. In all the confusion, they must've tried to run this way, while others toward the entrance." He looked to the floor. "It's tragic."

"*Tragic…*" came a whisper.

"We heard you," Euvard said to Ardian. "No need to—"

"Hush," Ardian interrupted him with a loud whisper and reached for Spike. "That wasn't me."

Gasping, Zercien spun around, a cold breath beating over his shoulder.

Nothing. Nothing stood behind him.

"*Yes, tragic…*" it rang again in a misty whisper all could hear. The company looked in all directions for the source but could find none.

The four wooden doors slammed against the walls on their own, revealing nothing in their stead.

"Trapped. They trapped us here," a voice came from the bottom right, and a transparent figure of a woman appeared.

"We thought we were saved, and yet..." uttered the top left, and the spirit of a young girl was revealed.

"When the monsters arrived, we received no aid," came from the bottom left. The ghost of a man this time.

"Some ran. Some huddled in their rooms. We awaited death," said the top right. A translucent old man in a dark brown tunic.

And right in front of them, a young boy.

"It's all so tragic!" came a shrill, piercing shout, the boy's jaw unhinging and showing rows of crooked, jagged teeth.

A gust coursed through the cave and Zercien held a hand in front of his face to guard against its chilling bite.

The fires atop both torches blew out like candles. He could see nothing in the foul air, save for the swirling silvers and golds from beneath Fynnian's wrist, shining so bright they burst through his sleeve. Zercien watched, mouth agape, as his friend fell and crashed onto the floor of bones and rock.

"Fynn? Are you—" Zercien said, but was interrupted by Fynnian's scream as he leapt to his knees, followed by a bolt of white light shooting from his wrist. It illuminated the cavern, revealing the ghosts yet again, who held arms in front to shield from the ray. Fynnian yelled another blood-curdling shout, and a thin, gold bolt rushed from each finger, homing toward a spirit. Upon contact they evaporated into mist, and Fynnian fell over, face-first onto the stone.

"Is it over?" Ardian breathed ragged, his quivering hands moving toward his torch to light it again. Zercien dropped his unlit torch, and he and Euvard rushed to their fallen ally.

"From our hellish deaths, we were not allowed to rest until now."

"Our spirits can leave."

"Thank you."

And the voices stopped.

"Fynn!" Euvard said. "What the hell just happened?"

"I—ugh!" Fynnian hacked up spurts of blood. Ardian helped him to his feet, and the coughing passed. He regained his senses and his breath.

"Fynnian, was that—" Ardian started to say.

"Yes," Fynnian said and nodded. "The Spirit Lord's Repose. A Seraph Art chanted during funeral rites to guide the dead."

"When the hell were you going to tell us you could do that?" Euvard said as he grabbed a piece of cloth for him to wipe his mouth.

"I can't. Or, I shouldn't have been. I've studied spells but was never taught how to spell-cast."

"Keep it up, then, eh?"

Fynnian clutched his stomach and lurched ahead, dropping the cloth and almost losing his balance. "No!" He heaved a surge of blood upon the cavern floor. "My stomach is on fire. Under my skin, it's burning. No more. No more…"

"Shit," Euvard said and stepped away from the seeping blood.

When it looked as if Fynnian had recovered again, Ardian asked, "Did your father ever cast Seraph Arts when you were around?"

Fynnian shook his head. "Not often. If anyone in the family fell ill, we were to be treated as usual." Heavy breaths. "But when I was three, I fell and broke my leg. My father uttered a spell, and it was healed. He cringed in pain afterward, though just for a second. The memory has always stuck with me."

Zercien noticed a wince, but didn't want to pry further.

"Even an Anointed member of the Order was affected?" Ardian said. "Curious."

"Yes, but since I am not," Fynnian said, "just one spell was enough to—well, you saw."

"Sanctum Order spells *hurt* the user? How does—" Euvard spoke up but was interrupted by an annoyed glare from Lloyd.

"We are wasting time. Cease your meaningless talk."

"Yes, as much as I'd love to keep talking and not advance any further, Lloyd's right," Ardian said, and re-lit Zercien's fallen torch.

But Zercien was too stunned to move, and he stayed stuck to his spot, watching as his companions gathered their bearings to continue. Ardian opened Zercien's hand for him, and closed his fingers around the torch.

"No texts have ever proved the existence of spirits," Zercien said. "Not that I've seen."

"Maybe mocking those ghost stories wasn't one of my better ideas." Euvard gave a half-smile and scratched the back of his neck, but no one laughed.

Zercien stepped through the following passage, delving deeper into the dark depths of stone. But once through, he faced a staircase leading up, a pitch of natural light shining down, and ran.

Chapter Thirty-Five
A Nightmare Reborn

Zercien stepped outside into the sunset and was surrounded by pine trees and dirt paths. To his left, a blue river stretching down the mountainside fed from a small waterfall above, and it shimmered in the receding sunlight. Below him, the tops of trees. And in the middle, a small clearing littered with stumps.

"We're outside?" he said as his companions joined him, leaning his torch against the rocky mountain wall. To his chagrin, though outside they were, it appeared to be atop one of the mountains.

"Looks like it, but…" Euvard pointed to his right. Through the thicket, another sky-high mountain wall with an entrance carved into the side.

Ardian rubbed at the stubble on his chin. "What in the world could this have been for?" A yawn escaped. "Oh, pardon me."

The sun finished its set and turned the sky to dusk. Ardian too leaned his torch against the mountainside and wandered to a tree stump.

Euvard joined him, and stretched, letting out a long yawn of his own. "I'm feeling a bit tired all of a sudden too."

Fynnian found a spot and laid out, spreading his arms on the soft ground.

"No shame in taking a little break," Ardian said. "We have been climbing mountains and trekking through caves all day, after all."

Euvard and Fynnian nodded their agreement with half-closed eyes, but Lloyd stood where he'd been since they climbed in, no change of expression.

At first, Zercien thought it odd they'd all just decided to rest at this very second. But when he gazed at the early moonlight reflecting upon the river, the gentle sounds of its parent waterfall filled his eardrums with the quiet, soothing music of a symphony of strings.

He gulped. "We shouldn't linger here." His breaths were long and deep, and his stomach warmed with nerves. No answer, save for Lloyd's footsteps advancing toward the mountain wall that housed their journey's next leg.

Zercien gripped Euvard's shoulder and shook. His gasp startled Ardian and Fynnian, who shot looks from bloodshot eyes.

From within the trees, Zercien gasped at the sight of a man in bloodred robes. But only for a second. Upon first blink, the man disappeared.

Accept your true self, appeared the words in his mind. Not of his voice. Lightning coursed his spine.

"Something is amiss here," Zercien said, his voice a whisper over his pounding heartbeat. "Please keep moving."

"Ach, fine. You are the captain, after all," Ardian said, and helped Fynnian to his feet before grabbing the torch. Euvard joined them, adding an annoyed groan to their complaints.

Zercien wasted no time plunging into the approaching cavern, illuminated only by the faint orange glow. A slender path ran along the foot of the cavern's winding walls, overlooking a lightless pit. Eyes up, with a hand on the rough wall, he averted the abyss's stare.

A half-decomposed corpse atop a ledge met Zercien's torchlight. With nothing more than a slight twinge in his step, he tiptoed past the boney hands of the dead scattered about, their arms outstretched, and empty eye sockets facing the encroaching dark.

With shaking hands, he pushed another door, and entered a large open chamber. A circular room, with neither door nor passage at the other side—another pit lay ahead.

A crude, rocky staircase of broken stones cut into the lip of the chasm, ramping downward in a spiral. Their hastened steps upon the slope akin to sliding down a hill. Zercien put a hand to his forehead and swallowed hard, shaking his head.

Descending in circles, the hole narrowed. Soon it had all but disappeared, leaving just the stairs behind and flattening into rock. The group broke their line to meet a large stone door, towering even above Euvard's head.

Zercien raised a hand to the cracked copper handle, pulling with a gentle tug. The heavy door grinded across the rock floor, opening just enough to squeeze through.

Before entering, Ardian rubbed his palm on the door, scattering a layer of ancient dust to unveil a message carved into the stone.

"'Here Lies Ariglioth, Nation of Might,'" he read aloud.

"Once we're through this door, we'll be in Ariglioth?" Euvard said and smiled.

"To the Arigliothan side of the caverns, I would assume," Ardian said. "Not quite out *yet*."

"We should waste no time, then," Zercien said.

When each man had stepped through, Euvard with great difficulty, Ardian stalled them for but a moment.

"I wonder," he said, holding his torch toward the door. "What does the message for entering Entervia say?"

He jumped back with a gasp as his companions turned around, and Zercien shined his torch on the back of the door. Dark blood splattered and clogged the insides of the carvings, and cutting through what would have been the message, a claw mark. Many times the size of Euvard's hand, its bloodstained nails ripped through the solid stone.

A chill shot through Zercien's spine.

"What in God's name could have done this?" Fynnian managed to stammer out. He shivered, boots jumping in rapid taps upon the floor.

Euvard shook his head in brisk jerks. "I don't know, and I really don't want to know. Zerc, can we expedite our little journey?"

Zercien's nods matched the pace of his companion's jitters.

The passage led to another open room littered with wooden doors along the sides. A clump of rocks sat in the middle, covered with a layer of ash. Decomposed bodies sat around, slumped over, toothless mouths facing the ceiling.

Zercien stumbled through as to not disturb their rest, and came upon a chamber mimicking what they descended to reach this place: a circular room bearing a hole in the middle with a staircase leading down.

A deep breath escaped his lips. Again he would have to endure a spiraling passage.

With each step, Zercien's mind spun with the twisting walls. Messages written in hardened blood flashed throughout.

Help.

Doom.

Shadow.

Demon.

Reaching the bottom, Zercien bent over and spewed his last meal at Tiesel upon the cavern floor.

"Zerc! Are you all right?" Euvard said.

"Yes," he said, and regained his posture. He wiped his mouth on his shirt sleeve in between large sighs. "I'm fine."

In every breath, Zercien inhaled the taste of flame. How could the Arigliothans stand this heat, let alone live in it?

As he approached the next chamber, a searing pain jolted through Zercien's head, and he fell to one knee. His allies surrounded him as fog spilled through even the dark cavern walls. A jagged outline stretched to the ceiling, surrounded by other lines that formed humanoids.

"What is it?" Euvard said, his voice seeping into his mind like water.

Zercien shushed him and stared up at his friend. "Something moves."

Shuffling. Footsteps. Armor clunking. Zercien jumped to his feet, and backed up, pushing his allies with him.

A roar erupted from the chamber, reverberating against each wall, raining dust and debris upon their heads. Each man put their hands to their ears to escape the noise, save Zercien, whose fog deafened the mighty howl.

From the other side of his fogged wall, the outlines moved, the large one approaching the chamber entrance. A massive, monstrous claw far greater than the size of a human hand with serrated nails erupted from the door, swiping side-to-side, knocking down the wall in a heap of dust and rock.

All Zercien and his companions could do was stare straight up at the monster that glared back down with its two heads.

The left, a black cyclops; the fat veins of its enormous eye pulsating in the dark. To the right, raising high above the other, the head of a black dragon with two mighty horns and red eyes. Along its back, a spiked carapace.

Its tail hissed as it curled around the long, shadowy lizard-like body—a misshapen human head, covered in insects and maggots, a bed of stringy, black hair oozing with pus atop.

Two giant claws reached into the dark and slammed down upon the cavern floor, sending another maelstrom of dust and old bone chips into the air.

"What the fuck is that," Euvard said, his quivering hands gripping his battle-axe.

"A Matriarch," said Zercien, strong and confident, his sword pointed in front.. "Commanders of legions of Helldregs."

The beast's many eyeballs pored over Zercien, and he never hesitated, never blinked.

Sizing me up, I wager.

But it stood, silent. As if confused, stunned.

Fynnian could hardly grip his sword in his sweat-covered hands. His words came in spurts. "A what?"

"A grotesque creature from the Ancients' War," Zercien said, gritting his teeth. "Conjured from failures, their body parts were fused together."

A jagged-tooth smile appeared on the human head, as if it could understand.

"Ever done a project at home where you need to cobble up something out of spare parts? This is similar," Ardian said. His words were followed by another mighty roar.

But through Zercien's fog, it was no roar he heard.

"Humans, here? This is my domain. Begone," said the dragon head.

"Your domain?" Zercien said back. "Humans built this place. It is ours."

"Why are you talking to it?" Euvard whispered loudly. "How do you even know what it's saying?"

"The humans are all dead!" shrieked the human head, swiveling about on the tip of its tail, which sounded like a shrill, ear-piercing shout to Zercien's company.

A claw pushed the human head aside.

"But humans return, nonetheless," said the dragon head. "And one who can speak and understand. Just as the one from long ago. I have been aware of your progress, human."

"You were watching us?" Zercien said, calm as could be.

"No. You made yourselves apparent. The light that freed the souls of those long dead carried through my cave. It was then I knew one of *them* walked among us. One of them which the master wishes eradicated."

The dragon's head spun on its neck; staring into Fynnian. "If this one remains, I shall allow you and the others to escape."

Zercien shook his head with slow turns. He brandished his blade in front. "I am afraid I cannot take your bargain. Fynnian is a dear friend."

Fynnian shrieked. "Why are you talking about *me?*"

Another bellowing roar from the dragon head and Zercien's fog was blown away, scattering into the dark. Humanoid beings veiled in black shadow, bearing crude axes, shields, swords, and armor, rushed through the hole the Matriarch created. Fewer in number were bipedal enormous cat-like monsters, whose claws sported daggers in place of nails.

Zercien squinted and looked into one's eyes—if one could even call them eyes—only to see swirling masses of black maggots and sludge where the rest of its face was supposed to be.

Euvard lowered his axe in disbelief.

"Helldregs," Fynnian murmured, his fingers quivering along his sword's hilt.

Zercien fell on his backside and tried to crawl, but the Matriarch approached and swung a mighty claw downward. Before Zercien could react, Lloyd jumped in and blocked the claw with his sword, pushing it away.

"I shall tend to this one," he said. "Leave."

Without waiting for Zercien's response, Lloyd yanked the torch from his hand and ripped through the closest Helldreg, closing in on the mighty Matriarch, leading it away from the group and further into the chamber. The rest surged forward at Zercien and his companions.

Ardian thrust his torch into Zercien's free hand and wielded both his lance and kite shield. The four stood together, within the torch's reach, the approaching Helldregs appearing as shadows dancing within its light.

Euvard hewed the head off one dreg, quickly swinging around his left to crash his axe through another's skull. A swift elbow to the chest sent the next to the stone, and a mighty downward spike crushed its innards, sending black blood and bone chips into the torchlit hall.

Fynnian was immediately swarmed, and held his sword horizontally in front, setting his feet to block. Parrying attack after attack, he couldn't land a strike himself, and even the new techniques taught by Lloyd were useless against a number this great. One smacked him on the side with a metal shield, sending him spiraling to the floor, and he rolled just in time to dodge a jagged sword.

He sliced at the Helldreg's bare legs, cutting into its raw flesh. It fell, and Fynnian closed his eyes and swung—he lobbed the head right off its shoulders, grimacing at the sight. From the darkness through slim light leapt a bipedal Helldreg, its dagger-like claws pointed for his neck.

"Fynnian!" Zercien yelled and rushed toward him. The tip of a Helldreg's blade just scraped his back as he charged. Ignoring the pain with just a grunt, he jumped into Fynnian's circle of foes, crashing to the floor and blocking the bipedal dreg's path. With a flurry of swings, Zercien slashed wildly at the monsters, slitting one halfway through its throat, black blood squirting from the line he cleaved. With an upward stab he shoved his sword through the bipedal dreg's chin until the tip jutted from its skull. He ripped it free and watched as the wretched thing writhed.

He urged Fynnian to grab his arm for balance, and he pulled himself to his feet. Soon they were joined by Ardian, using his kite shield as a weapon, and bashed one Helldreg against the wall, shattering its skull about the rocks. He lunged Spike forward, shoving the sharp tip through another's chest. But a blunt edge of a blade struck him on the back, and he recoiled, holding up his kite shield in time to block a jagged battle-axe, the scrape echoing about the hall. From behind, Euvard buried his axe into its brain before it could strike again.

***

Lloyd confronted the Matriarch, jumping and dodging its continuous claw swipes. The serpent tail with the human head lunged at the swordsman, but he wrapped his arm around the scaled appendage. Its eyes buzzed with locusts, and it opened its inhumanly wide jaws of jagged teeth.

But Lloyd was faster and rammed his sword through its forehead, splattering black blood on the blade. The head shrieked as blood and pus oozed from the wound. Lloyd yanked his sword free and shoved his torch where his sword had been, the flaming tip catching fire with the raggedy, stringy hair and erupting in a blaze illuminating the chamber.

With a booming roar, the Matriarch charged forward, its massive claws poised. Lloyd ducked from the first swipe and jumped over the second, slicing at the claw and cutting it off before it readied a third.

The cyclops head lurched forward on its long, bendy neck, its mouth agape with ragged teeth. A slash from Lloyd's sword connected with the jaw, but the blade just bounced off as if the teeth were a metal shield. Dropping his sword, Lloyd grabbed the head with his right arm, taking a powerful hold on its supple neck. As the cyclops struggled to break free, Lloyd reached for his dagger with his off-hand and pushed the serrated edge through its pulsating eye and piercing its bulging vein. The vein ruptured, gushing black blood, and the cyclops screamed, its terrible jaws pushing forward into Lloyd. The swordsman pulled and twisted the head, a ripping sound entering his eardrums until he tore it off the neck. With a nonchalant toss, he threw the mangled head to the floor, leaving a blood-gushing black hole.

Rising on its hind legs, the beast's dragon head towered over Lloyd, the blood from the severed cyclops and claw leaking about the floor. A red glow emitted from the beast's neck.

Lloyd sprinted ahead and leapt high, slamming the full force of his body into the Matriarch's chest, and dug his sword into the base of its neck. The monster roared in pain and shook, sending Lloyd flying off, but its slashed neck could no longer bear the weight of its head, and it flopped onto the stone.

Landing on his feet, Lloyd ran at the monster's limp head, and as soon as it opened its jaw for one last attack, he thrust his sword through, and slashed up, slicing its brain. As he yanked his sword free, the dragon head dropped down with a thud.

With two hands, Lloyd repeatedly chopped into its torn neck until nothing connected to its head. At last, the Matriarch stopped moving, blood gushing from all orifices amid a flaming heap of body parts.

The swordsman ran toward his companions, helping to gut the last of the Helldregs. No more appeared from the depths.

***

Zercien, Euvard, Fynnian, and Ardian fell to their knees.

"Lloyd, we—thank you." said a breathless Zercien.

"Hmph. As I have said before, your lives matter not," said the swordsman, peering off to nowhere in particular. "The beast appeared a worthy adversary."

Zercien allowed the rest of the company a moment to breathe and collect themselves before pushing onward.

"Helldregs. They're alive," Ardian said. "I still don't quite believe what my eyes showed us."

Fynnian shook his head. "I'm sorry. I would've used my power again, but I couldn't concentrate."

"And have you kill yourself with magic? I'm glad you couldn't," Euvard said. "But Zerc, you've something to tell us, I think."

Zercien gulped. "What do you mean?"

"You know *exactly* what I mean. You went up and faced that— whatever that was!" Euvard said and pointed at the pile of blood and severed skin. "And *talked* to it like you understood what it was saying!"

"Oh, I couldn't." He shook his head as he lied. "I wanted to distract it while you all could prepare."

"Don't give me the roleplay excuse again—"

"Euvard, please!"

Fynnian and Ardian exchanged raised eyebrows.

"We should continue this another time," Ardian spoke over the bickering Zercien and Euvard, but his gaze remained on Zercien an extra second.

Euvard scratched the side of his head. "Sorry, Zerc. My head's a bit foggy right now."

Would love to tell you how much I sympathize, Zercien thought, and nodded. "We are all a bit…dazed from what we've just witnessed."

Ardian at last threw his kite shield over his back. "How are your wounds, everyone? And Zercien, can you lead?"

Stretching a bit, Zercien felt the crack of hardened blood along his back. "I'll manage."

Zercien's head was pain-free, and no fog ailed him. He sure hoped that meant something now, as they stepped into the chamber the Matriarch had called home. They walked close, for only one torch remained.

But amid the crackling flames left from the Matriarch's fall, Zercien spotted a tall, foreboding black seat. Charred, or perhaps discolored with age. If he didn't know better, he'd say it was a throne.

His companions soon caught on to what he was seeing. And despite his incessance on leaving as soon as possible, Ardian cried out.

Zercien couldn't tell if it was sorrow or surprise—and the guard captain ran past him, to the throne illuminated by flame.

"I can't believe this," he said.

"Do we really have time for—" Euvard said, but Ardian's sharp stare interrupted him.

"The texts say the then-king of Ariglioth, Azamar, followed his people here. But the nobility begged him not to. He had no heir. When he never returned from underground, the royal bloodline was lost. Now, Arigliothan kings are chosen by the people."

"King Lennard's rule will eventually end, and a successor will be elected?" Zercien said.

More democratic than expected, he thought. Their mission may have been to attain the aid of the country's military might, but perhaps their allies possessed more than just brawn.

"Correct. They even have contingency plans to replace a monarch in an emergency, if need be," Ardian said. "Interesting stuff, eh? Ariglioth will want to hear about what we've found here."

"I've half a mind to just go right back to Entervia after all this," Euvard said. "Somehow, I don't feel so threatened by Ankarth anymore."

"It doesn't seem real," Fynnian said, shaking his head. His hands quivered still. "Helldregs, alive. My stomach… I could just—" and he dry-heaved.

While they spoke, Zercien spotted Lloyd staring at something on the cavern floor, and it wasn't a rock or bone. He watched as the swordsman bent down and grabbed it, whatever the item was. When Zercien opened his mouth to speak, the swordsman's eyes shut him up.

"In our report to King Lennard, we'll tell what we saw here," Zercien said as he turned to face his allies, pretending it was exactly what he had meant to say. "For now, we will continue the mission as normally as we can. I do not wish to risk becoming lost amid these caverns if we were to try and retreat."

Euvard shrugged. "You're in charge, Zerc." He gestured ahead and mocked him with a bow. "After you!"

Zercien nodded to his companions and began their march anew. Once past the beast's mangled body and the throne, a small hallway led into a room with a staircase winding upward, and wooden doors all along the sides.

Zercien winced as he climbed to the top, the stairs spinning in circles. Through the next room was another living area, and this time Zercien was uncaring of the bones he walked over. Crashing through wooden doors and entering passageway after passageway, he pushed ahead with no bearing of where his feet landed.

In the next room, he saw darkness, but not the type they were accustomed to in the cave. Rather, the darkness of the night sky. His walk turned into a jog and then to a sprint, but he tripped when the rocky cavern floor gave way to stone steps. Climbing fast on all-fours, Zercien breached the lingering foul air and plunged into the open fields of Ariglioth.

INTERLUDE
GENERAL RIKARD

5 YEARS AGO

Whenever Isyonesa crowned a legitimate monarch, the renowned General Rikard was seated in front. At today's coronation, he sat in the back.

A new ruler chosen to further Emperor Kandhiran's agenda, and to spur civil war again, no doubt. Such was the fate of all the continent of Telurdia's cities, to appoint a puppet ruler, with the title as a mere formality.

Representatives from each of the six cities across Telurdia served as witnesses. They all sat about the crowd gathering in front of the castle, now blanketed a bloodred hue below the Telurdian sky's red rays.

They murmured incoherently, though likely shared similar thoughts to the general. Telurdia's capital city was to be subdued under the fist of a hand-picked official bearing no governing experience.

All General Rikard knew about his new liege was her name. Kiara. A queen. Isyonesa had not been ruled by a queen in all its recorded history.

She stood upon the stage—too young, too inexperienced to rule. But perhaps the perfect candidate to mold into whatever woman the Emperor required her to be.

The impatient rumblings of the assembly soon faded, and General Rikard sighed and fidgeted in his chair. The ceremony was to begin now.

He craned his neck with the crowd. From the left, the man with the bloodred-robed hood, who always concealed his face, carried the Isyonesan crown. Emperor Kandhiran's Disciple, the one who poisoned the Emperor's mind with honeyed words many years before. Some had alleged him to be a sorcerer, and claimed sightings of flame and other Pariah Arts.

General Rikard shrugged. It was possible. He scratched at his beginning-to-grey beard and ran a hand down his dark brown cheek.

But the true question of the day: would the old emperor show his face, at the coronation for his own capital city? The general looked about in all directions, straining his eyes, and squinting at every corner for a sighting. He sighed when his searching came up empty.

He turned around in his chair, staring back in the direction of Emperor Kandhiran's Castle, where the continent's ruler resided and never left. He did no visits, took no counsel.

The general clutched the lush black wood bow over his back, careful not to tangle the bowstring and ran his fingers over the intricate patterns and designs in various squares, triangles, circles, and more. To have one shot at Kandhiran was all he desired—and all he needed—to end this senseless turmoil.

But Kandhiran's Disciple reached the stage. Though his long robe stretched down to his feet, General Rikard never saw legs lift.

The soon-to-be Queen Kiara bowed, no sense of fear anywhere upon her young face. General Rikard smirked—was she fearless, or too naïve?

He chuckled to himself. A general of a city but taking commands from a fake queen whose only tasks were the bidding of an emperor he desperately wanted dead.

Kandhiran's Disciple placed the crown upon the new Queen Kiara's head, and she stood, raising an arm to greet the crowd. A subdued clap spread about the audience—nervous, terrified of their future. General Rikard slapped his hands together thrice and placed them back atop his crossed legs.

And that was it. The new queen left the stage without a speech, as was designed, and the crowd scattered. No meetings with their capital's new ruler, no conversations among themselves.

General Rikard stood to do the same and stared into the red sky. A bit of a dark red now. He shrugged.

As he maneuvered the crowd, a hand tapped his shoulder. He spun around to meet eye-to-eye with an everyday castle guard.

"General Rikard, Sir," she said. "Newly crowned Queen Kiara desires your counsel immediately. Please come this way."

The general raised an eyebrow. "Does she not have other duties to attend to than meet with this timeworn general?"

"She requested your immediate attention at the castle. Please, General."

General Rikard nodded, and followed the guard to Castle Isyonesa, and was led into a remote corner room, devoid of any castle attendants.

Not meeting in the throne room or her quarters. What an odd new queen we have, he thought.

"Queen Kiara should be arriving shortly. Please wait here," the guard said, bowed and left General Rikard alone, closing the door behind.

Taking a seat on one of the plain wooden chairs lying about, the general crossed his legs and stared into a wall. No windows, only one door. While he knew Emperor Kandhiran employed spies in all of his cities, none of his eyes or ears would be here.

The door creaked open, and the general leapt to attention, on his feet.

Queen Kiara stood before him, already dressed in her red and gold regal coat, though torn and stained in spots. She had nary a line under her eyes, no wrinkles on her black skin. She was perhaps twenty-eight summers old.

"General Rikard. It is a pleasure to meet you," the queen said, and bowed.

The decorated general attempted to hide a smirk and crossed his arms. He then gasped and returned the bow. "I forget myself, Your Majesty."

Queen Kiara raised her right hand and shook her head. "Please. You know my royalty is merely a product of Kandhiran's procedure. You are as much of a monarch as I, as is the peasant peddling bread in the market. But such is unnecessary now. I've called this meeting to speak of pertinent matters to our futures here in Telurdia."

"Oh?" was all General Rikard could muster. Now he was intrigued. Was this not Kandhiran's lapdog, as he expected?

Queen Kiara peeked over the general's shoulder, and lowered her voice. "Under my leadership, we shall retake Telurdia, right under the nose of the hapless Kandhiran. And once again wave a common banner."

General Rikard shuddered. To speak such ill of Emperor Kandhiran would meet the guillotine, should any hear. This young woman exuded more political savvy than he realized—worming her way into a crown, all while plotting against the one that would be placing it atop her head.

Though the thought of his beloved continent once again flying a unified flag caused a tingle in his gut.

"I take it you have a plan, then, Your Majesty?" he said.

The young queen nodded. "I will be sending messages in secret to Dregnal. We've a direct route to Entervia's King Durnan."

The general frowned. Not the most complex plan. "Emperor Kandhiran has forbade all ships from entering and leaving the port, no? I cannot see how this will work."

Queen Kiara smirked and raised her index finger. "Ah, something even the great General Rikard is not privy to! Supplies and food have run scarce here in Isyonesa, and with no soil with which to replenish them, Emperor Kandhiran has allowed trade vessels to Entervia. Not often, mind. Maybe a dozen or two in a year."

"I see," said General Rikard, and he crossed his arms. "This is a surprisingly generous act from our warmongering emperor."

Queen Kiara shrugged. "Can't have a continent of people to rule if they're all dead of starvation."

"He would rather us live as ants to be crushed under his boot than allow us to slowly succumb to our own ruin. Such a gentleman. I presume the ports will be well-guarded by his lackeys. Have you another scheme?"

Queen Kiara winked, gestured behind her, and stepped to her right. From the shadows of the door, in walked a woman, shorter and perhaps younger than the queen. Stark black hair fell below her shoulders, with the ends of her bangs resting just above dark eyes. A perfect match with her brown skin. He met her eyes with the piercing black circles of his own, and couldn't help but feel heat rising in his chest.

Attached to a belt, lying against her hip, two daggers. Sharp, serrated.

"Allow me to introduce Faye," said Queen Kiara. "A spy."

General Rikard furrowed his brow. "A spy? You would trust her with your plot?"

"Emperor Kandhiran had my father executed for treason," the spy said before Queen Kiara could speak. "I would sooner see Kandhiran without a head than work for him."

General Rikard smirked again. Though the two were young enough to be his children, Faye sounded genuine, and dare he say, the young queen had already made quite the impression.

"This spy will lead the operation, I take it?"

Queen Kiara nodded. "She'll be infiltrating the network of guards about the port as an inspector. I've instructed her to leave rolled-up scrolls tucked away in barrels and piles of coin aboard as many ships as she is able. Without drawing suspicion, of course. If the ships reach Entervia, they will see my plea."

A smile spread on General Rikard's face as Faye nodded.

"'Tis a sound plan, Your Majesty. But…" As quick as it appeared, the general's smile faded. "Will Entervia send us aid?"

"I will not lie to you," Queen Kiara said, shaking her head. "Telurdia has not exactly kept up relations with Entervia. It is possible our messages will go unanswered. We can only hope King Durnan possesses a generous heart."

"It may be some time before aid is received, then. If at all," General Rikard said. His opinion of the once-promising plan soured by the minute.

"Yes, but we've other work to be done in the meantime."

"Is that so?" said General Rikard, tilting his head. This young queen knew how to keep his attention, if nothing else.

"It involves the bow on your back," Queen Kiara said with a wink. "Imperator is its name, no?"

The general's heart jumped to his throat. *She has done her research,* he thought.

"No sense lying, then, is there?" General Rikard brought forth the bow. Both the symbols upon the black wood and white bowstring glowed with a subtle red-and-yellow radiance.

"Imperator, the bow of Oculi, is mine, as it was my mother's. As my sworn liege, its use is within your right to command."

Queen Kiara's and Faye's eyes gravitated toward the bow, the latter running her hands about the symbols. Despite the carvings, the wood remained smooth to the touch.

"This is the fabled bow, then. I have heard stories," Faye said. Her gaze shifted to the general. "Your strength must be exemplary."

The general gulped. "I have done well for myself, lass."

Faye smirked, but Queen Kiara raised her right hand for silence.

"If our plan is to succeed, we will need this bow, along with the wisdom of Sage Draslean," the queen said. "It will be your responsibility to form an alliance with him."

"The eccentric old man who lives in the mountains?" said General Rikard. That may take longer than the ships."

"The very same," Queen Kiara said, with a nod. "It will require patience. But we will need to earn his trust. He bears the staff Astrulux."

"That kook wields Astrulux?" General Rikard stumbled, catching himself on the arm of his chair. "And you believe he'll help us?"

"Yes, but would he speak to a queen or a spy?" Queen Kiara answered for him with a shake of the head. "Not likely. But a fellow wielder of one of the Seven Legends' weapons? *That* he may go for."

General Rikard nodded, though slow and with a slight eye roll. Traveling back and forth to the recluse's enclave wasn't his vision of fighting back against Kandhiran, but it seemed a logical first step. "Let's say we succeed in befriending the sage. What then?"

Queen Kiara gestured to Faye, who dug into her satchel for a rolled-up, wrinkled map of Telurdia. General Rikard cringed at the site of each city's respective flag, with no unifying theme. His beloved continent had grown apart with the oppressive Kandhiran rule, and only drifted further with each passing year.

"Once we hear from King Durnan, we'll lay the groundwork for rebellion," the queen said.

"And if we do not?" said General Rikard.

She tipped her head toward Faye, and the young spy pushed her finger atop the closest city to Isyonesa on the map—Fidelien.

"Kandhiran has not appointed one of his lackeys to rule there," the spy said. "Not yet."

A small smile broke the crease on General Rikard's lips as he crossed his arms again. "Which means—"

"In our worst-case scenario, Fidelien is our target to infiltrate."

"But this is to be a last resort?" General Rikard couldn't hide a smile. He quite liked the bravado of the young queen and her spy.

"If we do not hear from King Durnan, then it may be our only choice," said Queen Kiara. "To accomplish our true goal—" The queen stopped, hesitating in her speech, and General Rikard rested his chin on a closed fist.

Queen Kiara took two quick looks about the room for any infiltrators, though no one was anywhere near earshot. She brought her voice to a whisper regardless. "The removal of Emperor Kandhiran."

A heat grew in the general's chest. Excitement? Nerves? He couldn't tell the difference, but his fingers clutched Imperator more taught than normal. "By force?"

"By any means necessary."

Faye's face remained stoic, as did Her Majesty's.

"As much as I would love to introduce the Emperor to Imperator, your plan will take many years, and much luck, to complete. What of the Emperor's Disciple? He's almost never away from his liege," the general said. "Even today, the slimy sorcerer vanished as soon as he stuck the crown upon your head, Your Majesty."

The queen gulped, her face red. Her hands shook. General Rikard furrowed both eyebrows. He wasn't sure how his comment could have been perceived as offensive or out of line, or anything to produce such a reaction.

"We have, well, something—" Queen Kiara said, but was cut off by Faye.

"We have an 'in' to Castle Kandhiran, she means."

The general cocked his head. The two had answers to everything he asked. He released his cross-armed pose and gestured Queen Kiara to continue.

"I have had my fair share of counsel with our contact," she said. "And he promises to help us. But slowly, methodically. It could very well take years to complete. Though he assures his pieces will be in place once the time to act arises."

Again with 'years,' thought the general. He admired the calculation, and wherewithal to not rush operations. But to wait years before the plan came to fruition, with no guarantee of success. Not the sort of gambit this general was used to employing.

"And if we fail?" He tugged at his greying beard. "After five years, I may not have many left in me to fight."

"Of course, we could fail," said Queen Kiara. "Though, our contact's tasks are far more slippery. In retrospect, sending messages and befriending old folk? A much easier ask than planting seeds of rebellion within the cities."

Again, with this mysterious contact. Another spy, perhaps? Not many spies would be comfortable outing themselves as anti-Kandhiran. He'd never met one until today, and he'd sooner not believe he'd find another within the span of an hour.

"This other spy, then," he said. "Can they be trusted?"

"I wouldn't quite say 'spy,'" said Faye, and she nudged the queen with her shoulder. Queen Kiara gulped again, craning her neck every which way.

"I suppose it cannot be stalled any longer," she said, and cleared her throat. "I shall introduce you to our—"

A brisk rush of wind howled through the room, pushing Queen Kiara's cape to flap upon it, and Faye's hair to stand straight. The general braced himself with Imperator blocking his face.

Through his squint, he saw bloodred robes, and General Rikard's heart jumped into his throat. To his right, against the wall, stood Emperor Kandhiran's Disciple, face hidden behind a hood, ruby-like eyes appearing as flame in a dark cave.

The general managed to find his quiver with a shaky hand, twitchy fingers grasping the feather of an arrow, but Queen Kiara reached in front.

"General Rikard, please meet...our insider."

And General Rikard's heartbeat escalated into rapid drum strikes as Kandhiran's sorcerer floated upon the air, approaching the three.

"He who holds the blood of Oculi in his veins," said the Disciple, only his voice did not traverse through General Rikard's ears. It appeared in his mind, as if he thought the words himself. He dropped Imperator and covered his ears, but it did nothing to stop the assault on his mind.

"My arrival marks the beginning."

Part Three
Under Martial Law

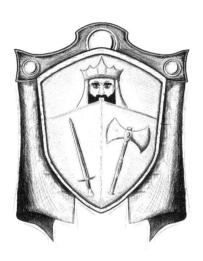

CHAPTER THIRTY-SIX
THE PRICE OF PRIDE

General Burgland looked upon the battlefield, the armies of Entervia and Ankarth standing ready to make their stand at an old fortress miles north of Vellard, just like the Ancients' War. Then, Entervia and Ankarth banded together against a common enemy, holding out for weeks against the Helldregs. Now, the two stared each other down as enemies.

General Burgland's soldiers had played a successful defensive battle from this fortress thus far, and tonight would be their test. Several lookouts spotted the Ankarthan standing army steadily marching to the fortress. Their force comprised of all foot soldiers, and General Burgland's scouts reported that the commander was nowhere to be seen.

He was outnumbered, but General Burgland's confidence remained as steady as his defensive strategy. From this fortress, his army had the utmost tactical advantage. As long as his archery division could volley blankets of arrows upon the North's infantry, they'd find great difficulty in reaching the walls. General Burgland's watch intensified, caring not for rank-and-file Northerners, but the enemy general that could turn the favor with just his presence.

"General Burgland," said a scout. "The North approaches."

With a swift nod, the general called to his archery brigade. "Line up atop the wall and wait for my signal."

Each archer nocked an arrow within their bows and aimed at the approaching Ankarthan foot soldiers. General Burgland held a hand high, its back facing his archers. "Fire on my order."

Squinted as he might, General Burgland could not see the eyes of his enemies hidden behind their helmets. The sightings from his prior battles replayed in his mind, the ooze pouring from the slain Northern soldiers, the maggots gnawing at their eye sockets.

But still, he rose his hand and slammed it down. "Fire!"

A volley of arrows answered his call. The opposing army scattered against the tidal wave, groups of varied sizes rushing at different parts of the fortress. The sheer randomness caused General Burgland to twist his head in all directions, trying to figure out what to hit and where to aim.

He hadn't expected this. A randomness he couldn't predict.

"Fire at will!" he ordered the archers. "Shoot them all down!"

The general charged down the stairs of the fortress, pulling a group of foot soldiers to hold against the enemy scattered about. Outside the walls, his legion stood their ground, fending off the mob of Northern soldiers while his archers rained down cover fire from above. General Burgland glanced at every foe slain but noticed nothing save the normality of a human cadaver.

A flash of darkness, a streak of red in the distance. The enemy commander stood at the back of his army, his black and red armor a stark contrast even within the growing night.

Though the knight did nothing but shout orders. No Pariah Arts, no swordplay. He neither engaged in combat, nor advanced on the fortress.

But now General Burgland saw a path devoid of enemy soldiers. A clear shot to the back line—where the enemy commander stood. It had to be an error, General Burgland thought. Though it mattered not. All he knew was if he could charge through the middle, he could take care of the blasted Ankarthan leader here and now.

General Burgland ordered his army to stand firm, to hold defense, and he did just that. Running past the enemy's soldiers, felling grunts along the way with his broadsword, General Burgland pushed to the back. He stared up at the massive Ankarthan commander, but he was soon surrounded by a host of personal bodyguards. Tougher looking than the soldiers he'd felled to reach here, more menacing and carrying jagged longswords. Through the eyeholes of their helmets, General Burgland could see nothing but darkness.

Before he could carve his way through, the enemy commander raised a hand over his retainers, an unwritten order to have them disperse. "I see you've continued to ignore my advice."

His heavy steps sent small tremors throughout the ground.

General Burgland gripped his sword's hilt tighter, tipping his head upward to meet the knight's ominous eyes. "A general does not turn tail and flee from what ails his country."

"Then what do you wish, seeking me out in the midst of this battle?"

The Entervian general pointed his broadsword at the Ankarthan commander. "To protect my people."

In response, the knight nodded and unsheathed his thick steel blade. "I see. Then I know my words cannot stay your hand. The outcome of this battle shall be decided on a duel between two commanders."

"No tricks," General Burgland said through grit teeth, and met the Ankarthan commander's sword with his. "This is to be mettle against mettle, steel versus steel."

"No matter your opinion of Ankarth, you forget not all enemies of Entervia are without honor," the hulking commander said, and nodded. "I accept your rules. We begin on your mark, General."

The two crossed blades.

General Burgland jumped toward the enemy commander, swinging a mighty forward slash met by a parry without a flinch. His enemy then cut sideways, the blunt end of his blade colliding with the general's, the pure strength behind the blow far surpassing what he anticipated, and his sword went flying from his grip.

He burst from his stance and ran toward the fallen weapon, just a steel gleam in the dark. His eyes enlarged as he glanced backward, watching as the enemy commander raced forward with impossible speed for one wearing such heavy armor. A metal boot connected with the back of his leg, and General Burgland was thrown to the ground.

He rolled away from a downward spike, scattering dirt just inches from his ear. With one hand on his sword he leapt to his feet and spat.

Unnatural, General Burgland thought as he readied another strike and charged. Just as he swung, the Ankarthan commander pulled his blade from the dirt and deflected three strokes in quick succession.

The general backstepped and wiped a hot bead of sweat from his brow. His enemy hadn't even stopped for a breath, but his came in rapid spurts.

Instead opting for a defensive stance with the sword outstretched across his body, General Burgland met the enemy commander's strike and turned the blade away. The edge of his sword just nicked the knight's chest armor, though he was met with a sweeping blow that, if not for a well-timed parry with both hands, would have knocked him onto his back.

The two locked swords, pushing against each other, both commanders gritting teeth and breathing hard. General Burgland used two hands to the knight's one, and his feet slid backward on the grass.

With a battle-cry, General Burgland put the rest of his strength into his next strike, pushing the Ankarthan commander. He watched the knight, for the first time since their initial meeting, recoil and stumble backward.

General Burgland dashed ahead, two-handing his sword and launched himself, lashing out with a quick stroke. But again he was met by the turning edge of his enemy's sword, the rumble of colliding steel reverberating through his hands.

A heavy gauntlet-covered hand then grasped General Burgland's sword arm, holding it in place. He writhed and struggled within the knight's grip, dropping his blade and clawing at the armored gauntlet. Nothing gave way.

He cried out as the knight squeezed tighter, the metal gauntlet pushing against his bone with such force he thought his arm would shatter.

But his cry turned to a whimper and a gasp, following a searing, burning pain into his midsection. The Ankarthan commander relinquished his grip.

General Burgland staggered backward and looked down to see the knight's blade, up to the hilt, lodged below his chest.

The Ankarthan commander pulled the sword free, and a splash of blood scattered from the wound, dripping onto the dark ground. He held a hand on General Burgland's shoulder, and eased him to his knees.

General Burgland clutched the hole in his chest, and the oozing blood coated his hands.

"Hear me, Knight." He gulped and stared with an unwavering gaze at the warrior, the red streaks along his metal plate armor growing blurry and faded. "This means nothing. My country will prevail."

And the great Entervian general fell, face-first onto the soil he swore to protect.

CHAPTER THIRTY-SEVEN
THE SERAPH HEIST

Tyrrowan sputtered for breath. Chills coursed through his body, despite being in a hole in a desert. Above, a small cone of light shone down from where he'd fallen.

Several rapid blinks later, he regained his vision, but only to see his own blood pooling about his outstretched body.

He raised his right hand and winced.

Employing Seraph Arts now brought forth great risk. How ironic, he thought, it was for a magic created for use near-death. As he envisioned a cascading chorus of yellow and white beams in his mind, his sight grew dark and hazy.

"I have to see this through..." he said, and clenched his right hand into a fist.

A small ball of yellowed light conjured in his fingertips, and he pushed it against his bloody wound. He shrieked at the pain lancing through his body, as the light crisscrossed through in alternating streaks. His skin sealed, and the bleeding stopped.

He crawled to the wall and leaned against it. But through his aches, pains and exhaustion, his lips turned into a gritty smile. Though bloodied and beaten, he sat within the secret Sanctum Order hideaway. At long last, he'd solved the riddle. Once his strength returned, he stood, holding his side.

Aside from the hole where the sun shined through, the cavern lay in pitch black. Tyrrowan invoked a small cloud of yellow light in his left hand to act as a light source and marched ahead.

He passed under the hole, and soon the sun disappeared. Sand had finished covering it, and now he stood in a pitch-black cavern, in between the subterrain and desert sands, illuminated by a small bit of magic. Curiously, no sand floated to the bottom. Perhaps it was some other Seraph Arts at work, though none he was familiar with.

Tyrrowan shuddered at the thought of this place becoming his prison. A never-ending corridor of darkness, entrances walled off by heavy sand. At least he was safe from the searing heat, though he'd likely be shaking sand out of his clothes for the rest of his life.

Toward the other end of the cavern, he spotted a wispy, white light. Despite his squints, he still had no guess as to what it could be. His heart leapt to his throat regardless. He knew it was his destination. It *had* to be.

Half-jogging, he slipped, tripped, and stumbled over rocks and other debris along the path. One sliced his pantleg, under his knee, but he paid it no mind and continued his charge, hardly giving a second glance to the trickle of blood forming in his footsteps.

As the wispy light came into view, the outline's shape materialized. Tyrrowan had no idea of the gender, but its light outline was a distinct humanoid shape.

And behind it, encircled by a ring of blue light that never flickered, an iron chest. It stood in front of a swirling mass of yellow light. His smile grew uncontained. The Sanctum Order cache, mere feet away.

His half-jog turned into a sprint until he at last reached the end, and the spirit. Tyrrowan forced himself to a skidding stop when it spoke.

"Lone warrior of the Sanctum Knights. Why do you disturb the last resting place of our Order?"

Tyrrowan jumped. He'd not expected speech, let alone a strong voice. But before he could muster a response, it boomed again.

"You should not be here. Our Order is finished." The spirit pointed behind, at the yellow swirling lights. "This light shall return you to the above world. Go back to your home and await your honorable death."

Tyrrowan shuddered. "I've not a clue who you are, but you are in my way. I have uncovered this place to retake what is truly ours, and to rebuild the Sanctum Order to its former glory."

"The World's Tower is taken. The Knight has returned."

With a gasp, what felt like a burst of flame erupted in Tyrrowan's chest. Not the news he expected. "He lives?"

"Go to him and accept your fate, Sanctum Knight."

I should have known he would return, Tyrrowan thought, and scratched the side of his head. *No matter. I must hurry, then.*

"I tire of your presence," he said. "With the power contained herein, I shall revive the Order."

The spirit's head shook from left to right. "You do not know the extent of the power within these walls. A forbidden incantation, conjured in secret, meant to be cast aside forever. Hence is why I stand guard, should any wayward Sanctum Knight trespass upon it."

Tyrrowan smirked. "And you shall bar me from my prize?"

"If it is needed, it will be done. A true knight of the Sanctum Order would have accepted their fated end. Why do you not? Do you fear death?"

Fear death? No, not quite. But Tyrrowan was not yet ready to accept that the Order would end with him.

"The Order *will* be restored!" Tyrrowan said. "I do not care what it takes."

"Then you are a fool. Begone from this place."

The spirit raised its right hand, readying a swirling globe of golden light, but Tyrrowan's voice rang throughout the cavern.

"It is *you* who shall take leave from this place, spirit," Tyrrowan said.

The Sanctum Knight chanted to himself, and the swirling globe above the spirit stopped. Its white, hollowed eyes bulged in fear, and an echoing yelp echoed throughout the passage.

"Sanctum Knight. You do not understand the gravity of what you are about to do," the spirit said. "If you respected the Order you call your birthright, you would stop this instant!"

Tyrrowan smirked again, and thrust his hand in front. From each fingertip, he released a ray of radiant light, all concentrated at the spirit. "I invoke the Spirit Lord's Repose. I pray you will enjoy your rest. I am sure yours was a long vigil."

"No! Sanctum Knight, you have committed an atrocity—" and the bolts engulfed the spirit, zapping it into the air, and releasing it from the mortal plane.

"There is nothing honorable in death. I *will* revive the Sanctum Order," Tyrrowan said, and lowered his hand.

He ascended the few stairs behind where the spirit stood guard, into the circle containing the iron chest. A strong push of the lid, his boots skidding on the rocky cavern floor, his arms bulged and tensed.

"I have no time for this," he snarled, and held his right hand up. Ignoring the pinch of pain on his side, he summoned a yellowed arrow and struck the cache, shattering the iron atop.

With twitching fingers, he held the side and peered within. First, his eyes drifted to a sword, tucked away in a sheath. He grasped the metal and raised it above the iron cache, into his bosom. He pulled the sword free, and it shone with a radiant gold light, illuminating the dark hall.

"The Right Half of the Sanctus Dual Blades," he whispered. The ancient swords, crafted by the founders of the Sanctum Order to combat Pariah Arts, he had thought lost to history. Though this was not the reward he sought, he licked his lips and sheathed the blade, and attached it to his belt.

Peeking back into the cache, his heart sank when he didn't see the sword's counterpart. But instead, he spotted the last item remaining: a rolled up parchment. His heart did somersaults within his chest. Etched on this yellowed paper would be the true prize.

He unfurled the scroll and shoved it against his face. And Tyrrowan squealed in glee at reading the words.

"Volumen Gentem" it read at the top, in the Sanctum Order language.

"The Scroll of Revival," he said. "Forbidden or not, with this spell, the Sanctum Order shall return to the world."

CHAPTER THIRTY-EIGHT
LIKE A KNIFE THROUGH...

S aena leapt from her chair, scurried into the kitchen and with quivering fingers, grabbed a knife she would otherwise use to chop vegetables. The knife's handle kept slipping from her grasp as sweat spread through her fingertips.

The knock came again. Three quick taps. Saena's heartbeat thumped with them. She dashed to the wall next to the front door and stood straight with her back against it. Knife in one hand, she put her other on the door handle.

Drawing a deep breath, she barked her fiercest, toughest voice. "Who goes?"

A second of silence, and then hysterical laughter from the other side.

"*Who goes!*" said the familiar voice. "Very funny, Saena. It's me."

It sure *sounded* like Mayla, but Saena wasn't about to take any chances. She shouted a mighty battle-cry, wrenched the handle and flung her front door open, jumping in front with the knife held high.

But her battle-cry was short-lived when she saw it was indeed Mayla. Her friend had a hand up to her mouth in a poor attempt to hide a smile, and a chuckle broke free.

"You invited me over, remember? Are you *that* paranoid?"

Saena lowered the knife and her light complexion turned red. She'd forgotten about her invitation, despite it coming three hours earlier at the market stall.

Mayla held a weaved basket of fresh carrots and potatoes and waved it around. "I brought the vegetables, like you wanted." Her eyes drifted to the large knife still in Saena's hand. "And it looks like you brought the knife!"

A smile at last found its way to Saena's lips, though her cheeks still matched the color. "Come in. I've got the fire on already," she said and stepped to the side, gesturing to Mayla to enter.

"A bit uneasy, huh?" Mayla said as she placed the basket on the table.

"Just trying to be vigilant, is all," Saena said, aiming the knife above a soon-to-be sliced potato.

"I don't think you have much to worry about. General Burgland is capable enough," Mayla leaned her elbow next to the basket. Even now, she towered over Saena.

"While true, I can't shake it," Saena said and sliced down. Her knife dug into the potato, gutting its insides and dropping specks onto the floor. "If lowly barbarians can infiltrate the city, then—" Saena interrupted herself to stare at her mangled attempt at peeling the annoying root vegetable. Traces of the brown skin stained the yellowed insides, with jagged holes strewn throughout. She shrugged and tossed it in the pot.

Mayla looked at her with pursed lips, nodding. Though her raised eyebrow indicated she wasn't pleased with Saena's potato peeling. "I won't lie, I've thought about it too. How I'd defend myself if someone were to attack."

Saena stopped chopping and left her knife on the cutting board. "I'm sure Euvard gave you some lessons."

Mayla shook her head. "He won't even let me practice with a wooden sword. He means well, though. Doesn't want me in danger. Thinks I'd go off to play hero."

"I wouldn't put it past you, either."

Mayla hiked up the hem of her skirt on her left leg. "I did sneak something by him, though."

A short, sharp knife hung from the side of one of her leather boots. Not a knife for cutting vegetables. Its edge gleamed with the fire from the pit.

"A dagger?" Saena asked, but Mayla shook her head.

"Close. A knife, but balanced for throwing."

"And how long have you been concealing throwing knives under your clothes?" Saena's forehead wrinkled with her furrowed brow.

"Some months now. Bought them from a shady arms dealer at the market. Almost found an Arvaros' face with one on that day." She took the throwing knife from her boot and spun it in her hand. "Would've ruined my secret, though."

Saena paced around Mayla, searching for other hidden knives. "You just bring the one?"

Mayla pulled the hem of her skirt above the other boot, revealing an exact copy of the knife in her hand. But her incoming smirk sent Saena's heart into a thumping tantrum. "How about I teach you?"

"Wait. To use those things?"

Mayla nodded with rapid bobs, her long blonde hair coming undone from her bun. "You said you wanted a way to defend yourself. And sorry, sweetie, you standing out there with that kitchen knife was not as intimidating as you may have thought."

Saena's cheeks grew so red they may as well have been a permanent color change. But she sighed and nodded. "Would you really teach me? I doubt I'd do well."

Mayla smiled and spun the knife in her hand again. "Why not? I have a few extra knives on me."

She stepped toward Saena, still maintaining the spin, the fire pit's flames reflecting in the steel. Saena backed up and winced when the back of her leg collided with the table.

"Aren't they sharp?" she said. "Much more dangerous than these kitchen knives?"

"Well, yes. They're made for slicing people. Not potatoes."

Another wince. "Mayla, maybe not—"

"I'll tell you what. We won't throw any today." With immaculate form, she stopped the spinning knife and clutched the handle. "I'll just teach you the basics of holding one."

Saena's gaze fell to the knife's tip. It seemed to shine, as if just sharpened. She wanted to say no. One wrong maneuver and she'd have nine fingers. Or less.

"Fine," she said, and huffed an annoyed breath.

Mayla's bright smile beamed. "Give me your hand."

CHAPTER THIRTY-NINE
THE CROSSROADS OF SAND AND MUD

An afternoon shower opened over Zercien and his company. He breathed deep and welcomed the tiny droplets with arms spread open, pointing into the sky. Anything that wasn't the air inside those dark halls was enough to make him smile.

He'd spoken at length with his group about the horrors beneath the mountains, and it was decided to pursue no further discussion until the end of their journey. With time on the mind, using more to debate matters outside their control served a poor use of their limited resources. Thus, despite the Helldregs' claws grasping within his mind, Zercien obliged, and focused on the mission.

"We'll stop here for today," Ardian said as he unloaded his pack of camping supplies. "Duspen fears Ariglioth. Doubt any Arvaros will come near these parts."

Zercien nodded and unbound his supplies, spreading his coat over the wet and soggy grass squishing and squelching with each movement. But he laid still, hands behind his head, without a care. They'd reached Ariglioth. The first major milestone of their journey, accomplished.

"Never thought I'd see another country, to be honest," Euvard said as he sat next to Zercien. "Not as exciting as I thought it would be, though."

A brief smile spread over Zercien's lips. Had his friend forgotten that Duspen was indeed a country? He decided not to poke fun. "Thought it would be like another world?"

"Very funny. Just thought—I don't know. Something special. Like I'd feel different, or—" Euvard shook his head and interrupted himself. "Nah, never-mind. It's foolish."

"No, I understand," Zercien said while sitting up. He removed the map from his pack and pushed his index finger just over the mountains, where he estimated their position. His elation deflated as he measured the maybe half-inch of map-space they'd covered since Tiesel.

***

That night the rain stopped, showcasing the sky's splendid stars for all to see. All could sleep to regain their strength—no lookout required. But that didn't stop Lloyd from his routine, and Fynnian watching his every move.

His flawless footwork. Swift sword strikes falling with precision upon his invisible target. Fynnian shot looks to his left and right, and listened as Zercien, Euvard, and Ardian's snores flew into the night. He rose to his feet and, with a deep breath, approached the swordsman.

"You wish to learn more?" Lloyd turned to face him this time and paused his practice.

Fynnian nodded, not leaving Lloyd's gaze. "Yes. I must train harder. Have I improved?"

"You still stand. If you had entered the caves with your skills of before, you would not have survived."

"But I need to be stronger still."

Lloyd picked up two practice blades, hanging on to one and handing the other to Fynnian, who tried and failed to hide a smile; did the swordsman fear he may actually hurt him with a real sword?

"You have progressed beyond the basics of swordplay quite fast," Lloyd said. "Let us advance to a maneuver of higher sophistication. The technique I shall present to you this night will be swift, and moderate in strength. A tactic allowing you to outwit your foe with rapid strikes."

This is a lot more complicated, Fynnian thought as Lloyd demonstrated the technique. The way Lloyd's feet moved in unison with his sword strokes, Fynnian felt like he was in the midst of a dancing lesson, not sword-fighting training.

Throughout the night, the blunt side of Lloyd's practice sword found Fynnian's chest, back, side, both arms and legs, and somehow even behind his knee.

"Again!" Lloyd would yell after all his attempts, all his falls. Every time he smacked Fynnian to the ground, he'd yell for him to stand.

Out of breath, Fynnian put his hands to his knees. "Lloyd, I need a break—"

"Stand up straight. Once more." Lloyd spun the wooden sword in hand.

Fynnian groaned and did as instructed, lifting his hands from his knees. Breathing out the last of his exhaustion, he forced the remainder of his energy into the smooth strokes. This time, he didn't fall, and matched everywhere Lloyd's sword swung.

With a nod, Lloyd swiped to his left and knocked Fynnian's sword clean out of his hands. "Good. That is enough for one night."

"But you—"

"I played the part of an average swordsman. You performed well."

"I did?"

"The next night we meet, we shall practice this technique once more."

Before Fynnian could reply and thank Lloyd for the lesson, the swordsman waved his hand as if he were backhanding the air and resumed practicing on his own. Even though he'd just been shooed away like a stray cat, Fynnian returned to his makeshift bed happy.

***

The following morning came quickly, and Ardian encouraged everyone to prepare as fast as possible. Zercien noticed a slight quiver in his step.

Is he nervous? Zercien thought as he enjoyed—as much as he could, anyway—a light breakfast of now-stale bread.

"Everyone, we've come to a route split," Ardian said. "Which means we must make a decision."

Euvard crossed his arms. "And by 'we,' you mean Zerc."

Ardian ignored him, and asked Zercien for the map. He spread it out over a tree stump and beckoned everyone to bend down and listen—all but Lloyd complied.

"We're *here*," he said, tapping around the exit of the Okoro Mountains, and after, traced his finger to the paths below. "Arvaros territory.

We'll continue to leave them be, eh?" He stopped and tapped on Ferronwood Forest to the East, and Darutan Dunes to the Northeast.

"Our first path is here—the Darutan Dunes. It spans most of Northeast Ariglioth and gives way to the route leading to Ciprius. Here." He circled it with his finger, and jumped back to their current location. "Our other route is traveling East to reach Ferronwood Forest. Smaller than the desert, but runs perpendicular to it. And as you can see, following Ferronwood is the town of Reland. After Reland, Ciprius is about a day's march."

"There's a town in the desert, too," Zercien said, tapping a finger on the map, right at the center of the Darutan.

"That too," Ardian said. "Thus, our choice is East to the forest or Northeast to the desert."

"Neither of them seem ideal, if I'm being honest," Euvard complained.

Zercien ignored him and looked to Ardian. "What else can you tell us?"

"Not much, I'm afraid." The guard captain shrugged. "Both paths should take the same amount of time."

"We'll at least know what to expect with a desert," Fynnian said.

"True. And the threat of attack is low." Ardian stuck his closed fist under his chin. "Though, heat, sand, more sand, and mirages would make the town difficult to find. The forest seems it'll be better on the ol' feet, and a more direct route to a warm bed. But snakes, bugs. Blech."

We just escaped a cave with monsters from the Ancients' War, and you're more concerned about flies? Zercien thought. He shuddered as his mind populated Helldregs hiding within the sea of trees.

"I know it's Zerc's choice, but I think it's obvious," Euvard interrupted. "Why would anyone *willingly* go to a desert? I *hate* hot places."

Ardian smirked. "If it helps, at night deserts turn from swelteringly hot to bitterly cold."

Euvard tossed his hands up as if they were scales trying to achieve the same weight. "Cold's fine. Hot? Never."

"Truthfully, I see no easy option," Zercien said, and was answered with a cringe from Euvard.

"I suppose you can just pick one randomly?" Euvard said, and then punched Zercien on the shoulder. "*Pssst.* Choose the forest." Ardian shot Euvard a glare.

"I'd like everyone's opinion on the matter first," Zercien said.

He looked to Euvard, who stood there smiling, ready to jump at any question, but waved him off and shook his head, knowing the obnoxious answer already.

Forest: One. Desert: Zero.

"Fynnian?"

Fynnian jumped back, as if he weren't expecting to be asked first. Which, in a different circumstance, he would have been correct. "After what we've just endured, we should avoid any surprises. We know what to expect in a desert. And, if I may, I feel drawn toward the Northeast."

Euvard threw his hands into the air. "If it's anything like those rocks before Tiesel, that's more than enough reason to stay the hell away."

"I have to agree with Fynnian," Ardian said, ignoring Euvard. Again. "Although the idea of a new town to drink in—erm, *visit*, is tempting, there's something whimsical about the desert. I feel those in the village would be fascinating to speak to."

Desert: Two. Forest: One.

Zercien nodded and looked to Lloyd, who stood far off from their circle, swinging his blade. His back was turned to them, and likely had been that way the whole time.

"Lloyd?" Zercien called out. No answer. "Lloyd!" Nothing.

Zercien shrugged and put a hand to his chin. His allies seemed split on the matter, but the desert *was* the popular answer. If he were to suggest the forest, they would be back to a gridlock. As he opened his mouth to speak his decision, a short burst of sharp pain pierced into his mind, and he clasped his temple. Euvard's faint cries of his name were deafened by the surrounding, all-engulfing fog.

One-by-one, his friends disappeared amid the grey. But one figure appeared from within its waves, and it stood, facing Zercien with eyes like flaming rubies, covered head-to-toe in a dark bloodred robe.

Accept it, the same words appeared in his mind.

Zercien slapped himself, and put his hands over his ears.

Without a word, the robed man turned. He raised a hand, as if beckoning Zercien to follow, and walked away, escaping the fog. Like shattered glass, the fog burst, sending an explosion of grey onto the field.

"You okay?" Euvard's voice.

East. He went East, Zercien thought. *Toward...*

Zercien removed his hand from his temple, now free of pain, and nodded.

Desert: Two. Forest: Two. And he makes three.

"We will brave the forest."

Chapter Forty
A Storm Upon the Branches

U gh, spiders." Ardian groaned and swatted at a web. Zercien chuckled but kept moving, not paying the guard captain any mind. Despite Ardian's claims that this place was the devil, Zercien's surroundings had him darting his gaze in all directions, admiring the towering green and leafy trees, and canopies stretching above. Though the dirt path they walked was overgrown, the plants and bushes clogging the way proved more pleasantries for the eyes. However, their sunlight waned. Rainclouds gathered above, looking as if they'd release at any time.

"What's that? A proud captain of the Vellardian guard is afraid of spiders?" Euvard said.

An incessant buzzing had found Ardian's ear, and with another groan and a slap, he at last vanquished the annoying mosquito that had plagued his eardrums for the past few minutes. Wiping its guts on his pantleg, he said, "I've a general dislike for bugs, but I wouldn't call it 'fear.' As soon as one of the ugly pests come anywhere near me, it's—
"

"Whatever you say, Captain!" Euvard said. "Vellard's finest, eh?"

Again, Zercien couldn't help but chuckle at the banter between his companions. Though he noticed Fynnian wasn't saying much; he walked with his head down, perking up occasionally to ensure he stayed on course. Lloyd followed close behind, and Zercien watched as he stared down the blonde-haired Sanctum Order descendant. Not a look of annoyance, but not complimentary, either. Just an expressionless gaze.

Zercien cocked his head as he looked forward once more. With a low "hmmm," he squeezed through two skinny tree trunks, catching a bit of bark on his shirt, and emerged into a clearing.

A few tree stumps surrounded a small hole filled with burned wood splinters and fragments of bones. To Zercien's relief, not large enough to be a human. His companions clambered through the same hole Zercien had—Euvard ended up taking some branches with him—and inspected the area.

"Curious," Ardian said, as he bent down and stuck a hand into the hole. "A campsite, I'd wager. Might've been used recently, too."

As Ardian spoke, droplets of rain pelted his head. He held out his hand, and they soon increased tenfold. "Blast."

Zercien stuffed the map back into his cloak. "We'll move quickly. Maybe we can reach Reland before the worst of it hits."

As Euvard and Fynnian covered their heads with their hands, Lloyd just stood there, unwavering, letting the cold drops drip off his long hair. Every few moments he'd shake his hair, splattering water in all directions—Zercien made sure to turn around and hide his smile.

Once ready, he beckoned his company to continue forward, through the clearing and into the trees. Above, all they could hear was the banging of heavy rain atop the canopy, and despite providing some relief, the growing storm still broke free to soak the tops of their heads.

Before long, the torrent of rain burst a hole into the cover above, pouring down buckets of rainwater. Zercien found his boots stuck in the now-wet path and at times he struggled to free them, mud caking around the soles and climbing above his ankles. With the brunt of the storm upon them, and the sun now blocked by dark purple rainclouds, they carried on in aggravated silence.

Zercien grabbed the right side of his head and let loose a shout through the wood. A throbbing burst echoed through his skull and knocked him off-balance into a large oak tree.

He heard Euvard's voice of concern, in what was becoming an all-too-common occurrence over the rapid firing of rain.

"I'm fine." Zercien shook his head side-to-side to try and force whatever it was out. He expected fog, but nothing clouded his vision.

Instead, his legs were weighty, difficult to move, and his companion's voices slow and hushed. Each raindrop crashed against the muddy ground with a satisfying *plop*, one after the next. While the storm hadn't subsided, the rain moved at half-speed—Zercien could see each individual drop fall. But above all, a low *whizz* mixed with the storm.

Zercien turned to the right only to see an arrow flying right at his head. He jumped back to avoid it, the projectile sticking into the tree he had been leaning against. And time resumed normalcy.

Ardian ripped his shield from over his back and stood in front of Zercien, holding it high. As if they coordinated with the pouring rain, Zercien couldn't tell if it was arrows or raindrops he'd heard bouncing off Ardian's shield. He leapt to his feet just as the satisfying *scrape* of Fynnian and Lloyd's swords rang out.

His ears perked to the sound of rushed, mud-hobbled footsteps to his right. A tall man in a light clothing and short pants ducked behind a tree. Zercien noticed the strange symbol painted onto his tan cloth shirt—four curved, white horizontal lines. The man nocked an arrow into his wood bow and fired, but Lloyd reached his sword in front and deflected it away. He charged ahead and lopped the head off the assailant, and then disappeared into the woods.

"Lloyd!" The onslaught of rain deadened Zercien's yell.

No answer.

More warriors in similar dress accosted them from the back, their own battle-cries drowning out all other noise.

Euvard reared his battle-axe backward and swung in unison with another, their axes colliding at the wooden hafts. He proved stronger and sent the warrior's axe spinning into the trees. With a shout, he drove his own axe head into the warrior's stomach and ripped it out, chunks of blood-smeared flesh mixing with muddy ground. A stream of red formed at Euvard's feet as Zercien rushed in to help.

"Euvard!" He stood straight against a tree, hiding his body from arrows.

"Zerc? Good, you're all right!" came his friend's rain-muffled shout.

"Where is everyone?" Zercien carried his voice over the storm as another arrow flew by his face.

Euvard darted his head in search of their companions, his hair launching water droplets in all directions. "I don't know. Can't see anything in this damn storm."

A synchronous battle cry made the two jump and turn. A rush of footsteps splashing in the puddles followed.

"Zerc, we need to go," Euvard said. "*Now*."

Zercien wiped a mixture of sweat and rain from his brow as he shook his head. "We can't leave everyone behind."

"If we don't get the hell out of here, *we're* going to be the ones left behind!"

Out of the corner of his eye, Zercien spotted more warriors rustling in the shrubbery. With a reluctant nod, he and Euvard dashed ahead, through the trees.

***

Ardian knelt behind his shield, blocking a flurry of arrows from the opposite side, their wielders hidden in the trees' darkened shadows. Inching ahead, Spike raised, he peeked over the shield to see the scurrying of feet fleeing further into cover. "Zercien, this way!"

No answer.

"Zercien?" Ardian turned his head to look behind, but an arrow clanked off his shield with a *ting*. He whirled his head back around to see a towering man in the same cloth-woven garb with the white lines staring down, a labrys held high.

Ardian jabbed ahead with Spike, stabbing clean through his attacker's left leg. The axe fell with a *thud* as Ardian ripped Spike from his flesh and stood. He swiped across his body and then stabbed through the enemy's chest.

Before he could fall back into his crouched stance, an arrow glanced off Ardian's knee and fell to the muddy forest floor. He grimaced with grit teeth and pushed further into the wood, stepping softly on his injured leg while stray arrows bounced off his shield. He heard the *whizz* of another flying to his right, and he turned the battered shield to block.

Three warriors jumped from behind the trees and stood mere feet away. Another group to his left, and then two more behind him and to the right.

He popped up from his kneeling stance and met each warrior's gaze—to his left, right and back, each carrying a bow, an arrow nocked. And to his front, three tall, intimidating, and muscular warriors reminding him of Euvard's physique.

"You have entered our lands without permission," one in front said, loud and clear above the storm. "Our Spiritual Leader will have your head on a pike, outsider."

"*Your* lands?" Ardian yelled back. "What are you talking about? This is Arig—"

"Silence! You shall be sacrificed to our gods, outsider!"

Gods? What other gods—Ardian's thoughts were interrupted by the faint *creak* of many bowstrings being drawn back.

Ardian raised his shield high and charged ahead, just as the *twang* of arrows erupted. Their whistles flew by his ears as he ran, and he slammed his shield into the middle warrior, knocking him onto the muddy forest floor. Ardian didn't stop—while he ran ahead, he thrust his shield behind him and ducked, protecting his head from arrows. Spike out in front, he swiped at any warriors who jumped out to block his advance.

An arrow grazed his lower leg, just catching the back of his calf. The guard captain snarled over grinding teeth, but kept moving, not slowing his sprint. More arrows aimed for his head then clanked off his propped-up shield and fell to the ground.

He grunted as the piercing pain of an arrow stuck into his lower back, and the blood trickled down onto his leg. Shooting a quick look behind, warriors flew through the mud, gaining steps on the hobbled guard captain. But ahead, he saw the end of the sea of trees.

Thirty feet. Twenty feet. Ten—he could almost feel the full force of the storm upon his head, unabated by tree cover. One last look back showed the warriors again gaining speed, nearly upon him.

The tree line approached, and his legs grew heavy. With each step, more breath, more force, to push himself forward. He didn't have any sprinting left within him, and he felt every inch of his warm blood seeping from his wound, running down his sides.

Ardian bent his legs and bit down to clench his teeth, quelling his pained scream to a grunt. And with a mighty leap, he launched himself over the wet ground, his cry like a gale ruffling through the leaves, and burst into the open field. He fell and rolled onto the mud, and peered behind to watch as the warriors halted their pursuit and disappeared back into the wood.

Chapter Forty-One
Secrets of the Spurned

Zercien and Euvard slid their backs against large oak trees, hiding away from their pursuers' muddied, sloppy footsteps. Pointing at his friend, Zercien motioned for him to drop to the ground, behind the trunk of a fallen tree.

They both dove onto the wet grass and held their breath as more footsteps rushed by. One pair remained, the squishes against the ground growing louder. Zercien's heart rushed into his throat when they stopped.

But he exhaled slowly as the footsteps walked away, soon becoming too faint to hear alongside the pouring rain. He peeked his head up, just able to see over the tree trunk. Ahead, a dozen warriors with torches. Their voices could be heard, but too muffled to make out the words. When they dispersed, Zercien nodded to Euvard and they both pushed up on the ground, rising to their feet.

Only to come face-to-face with a warrior bearing the cloth garb with the white line pattern and his drawn bow. "The outsiders are over here!"

Euvard went for his axe, but Zercien put a hand up. As a dozen warriors surrounded them, Zercien placed his sword on the muddy ground and nodded to Euvard to do the same with his axe.

The one who'd spotted them aimed his arrow at Zercien's head. The others followed.

Why? Why would he lead me here? Zercien thought, cursing the robed man.

He saw a hand then come down on one of the warrior's shoulders.

"Lower your weapons." A woman's voice. Somehow both soft and commanding. "They have surrendered."

Zercien watched as every warrior removed the arrows from their bows, and a fleeting joy warmed his heart beneath soaked, heavy clothes. The warriors all fell to one knee as the woman approached. She was clad in a long-flowing tan robe with the curved, horizontal white line design painted multiple times from top to bottom. Long, white hair flowed past her shoulders, a complement to her beige skin. She eyed him and Euvard up and down.

"Outsiders in our home. Something I have not seen for many years," she said, her frown emphasizing the wrinkles and creases across her cheeks and forehead. "Why do you intrude upon the wood?"

Zercien caught Euvard's gaze. It wasn't often he saw fear in his friend's eyes, but now he'd seen it twice within days. He gulped but managed to stand tall.

"If we have done any wrong, I apologize," Zercien said. "We are traveling to Ciprius from Vellard and did not know the proper route."

"For those without malicious purpose, you seem to have killed a great many of my people," the woman said. Her voice stung as if it were one of her warrior's arrows.

Zercien cringed and froze. Partly as a natural reaction, but also in an attempt to stall and wait for a head pain that never came.

Looks like I'm on my own, he thought.

"We did not come into your forest with the intent to harm. We were attacked and did as anyone would do in response."

Footsteps rustled at his words, but the woman in front put a hand up to stop it.

"We have things we must discuss. But Caelum is angry this day. Let us take shelter."

Zercien glanced at Euvard and he shrugged. Not a name he'd ever heard, nor read in any texts.

The woman marched forward, her warriors following in pairs. Two grabbed Zercien and Euvard's weapons from the forest floor, and with nods, beckoned them to follow. They walked within inches, almost shoulder-to-shoulder, and Zercien couldn't see over their heads.

Soon, their leads turned and descended into a cave illuminated by standing torches, the flames casting shadows over the white, curved line pattern painted upon the wall, and helping to dry their rain-soaked clothes. How they remained lit, Zercien hadn't a clue.

Zercien noticed the odd structure of the place—almost perfectly circular, it seemed manmade rather than natural. In the middle sat a feather-cushioned seat sewed with patterns matching the woman's dress, and surrounding it, eight pillows embroidered the same.

She sat in the middle and pointed at the two cushions in front of her, gesturing Zercien and Euvard to sit. On shaky legs, Zercien obeyed while warriors gathered around and watched, expressions as fiery as the torches. The woman put a hand to her chin as she spoke. "Your names. Tell me."

Zercien cleared his throat. "I am—" the woman waved a hand and shook her head. "You speak too much." She looked to Euvard. "I would like this one to talk now."

"Okay," Euvard stammered, straightening his back. He fidgeted, drumming his fingers against the solid ground. "I'm Euvard Girant. This here's Zerc. Erm, Zercien. Zercien Volnaire. We're from Vellard, in Entervia."

The woman nodded, a small smile breaking through her stern face. "You *can* speak. Though you have not asked my name."

Euvard's cheeks flushed red. "Sorry. And you are?"

"You may call me the Spiritual Leader."

So much for transparency, Zercien thought.

"You lead these people?" he then asked, though he had assumed as much.

"You are correct."

"We have told you where we hail. I have not heard, nor read about, a people led by a Spiritual Leader. Are you from Ariglioth?"

She burst into a short, loud laugh. "Ariglioth-born? No, no. We have been here for generations, but we came from the far northeast, in a land of beauty beyond this place you call 'Dregnal,' to escape those from below."

"In the far northeast of the world?" Zercien was now the one putting a hand under his chin. "Outside of Dregnal, there is only Telurdia, to the southeast. Is that your home?"

The Spiritual Leader shook her head but was not angry. "I am not surprised. My people have observed much knowledge of Oniro willingly buried and hidden from the commoners. Our ancestors comprise of people from the world over, but our beliefs labeled us as outcasts. Upon our journey here, we were forced to make this wood our home." She pointed around the cavern. "This structure is but an escape from the forest elements. Our homes lie deeper in the wood, in a town you would see as similar to any in Ariglioth or Entervia. And yet, we are shunned. Our efforts to keep outsiders away may be harsh, but I believe it necessary in order to maintain our peaceful lives."

Zercien blinked twice, sucking on his bottom lip. "I'm sorry. I don't follow."

"You would not. You are typical outsiders. But it is not your fault. It is your home's desire to make people equal to gods."

"Do you mean the Seven Legends?" Euvard squeaked out, which drew another loud laugh from the Spiritual Leader.

"Ah, *that* word. Legends. I refuse to call them such, but you are correct. '*Heroes*' that saved the land. Preposterous. They are conquerors, and nothing more."

Not something Zercien had heard of, though that was becoming a theme of late. His forehead felt akin to a roaring flame.

"Conquerors?" he said, intending for more, but no words came.

"Are you unaware?" She tapped a finger onto the hard floor, a faint echo emitting with each tap. "I am surprised an Entervia-born does not know the tainted history of the fellows depicted on her very Coat of Arms."

"Miss Spiritual Leader, they did not remain on the continent," Zercien said, though he knew Holunt remained in Entervia for quite some time after the war. "This is fact, is it not?"

"A half-truth, at most," she said, a smirk brimming. "They did indeed leave Dregnal, but I assume you do not know that Gunvald fathered children in Entervia and fled with the very axe he used to liberate the land? And this is just one of likely many such tales. Instead of obeying the true gods of Oniro, Entervia chooses to worship flawed mortals." She fixed her gaze on Euvard. "I assume Entervia is still ruled by a king?"

"It is," Euvard said and nodded.

"Held back by old traditions and nepotism. One family retains power through no means other than birthright." The Spiritual Leader clicked her tongue with the words. "While Ariglioth has shown some advancement, it is not enough to maintain true strength or order."

Zercien's forehead dripped sweat, hands shaking as he tried to wipe it away. Despite his urge to, he could not disagree.

"I understand," Euvard said in his stead. "Those in power hold it indefinitely through generations, and the old stories about the Seven Legends and the Sanctum Order never made sense to me." He looked at Zercien. "And what was his name... Voks? He betrayed them all in the end anyway."

Again, Zercien shuddered.

The Spiritual Leader leaned forward in her seat, staring with a deep, penetrating gaze into Euvard. "Hm. Your eyes tell me you are not lying." Another brief smile escaped. "I knew I was right to hear this one speak."

"My words aren't going to mean anything, but I'm sorry for how everyone here's treated you and your people," Euvard said.

The Spiritual Leader nodded. "You are correct. Your words do mean nothing." She faced Zercien. "This one, I am unsure of. But you?" And her gaze shifted back to Euvard. "You, at least, speak from the heart, with none influencing your beliefs."

Zercien gulped, words still unable to flow.

The Spiritual Leader stood and looked to her warriors. "I have heard enough. These outsiders are free to go. This time."

A chill of relief ran from Zercien's head to his stomach and he at last managed to spit an answer. "Thank you, Miss Spiritual Leader."

He and Euvard stood.

"My warriors will escort you to the outskirts of the forest. And they will bestow upon you a gift for listening, and showing sincerity, to an old woman's ramblings," the Spiritual Leader said. "And to ensure you stay far, far away from this wood."

"Truly?" Euvard said. "You don't have to if—"

"Hush. Your honesty is refreshing, but I think it best to stop talking. Lest I retract my offer."

Euvard's back shot straight up, and he went to speak, but instead mouthed "yes" and nodded. The warriors led Zercien and Euvard out of the cave, grouped together as close as they had been upon entering, and back into the forest.

The torrential storm shrunk, its fleeting remnants of gentle drops dripping from leaves. Before long, Zercien, Euvard, and their escorts came to the last wave of green, and stepped outside the trees. The warriors returned Zercien's sword and Euvard's axe, and pointed at two large, brown horses with short and well-trimmed black manes.

Euvard reached out to pat one on the neck, and it welcomed his hand. "Is this the gift?"

"Our Spiritual Leader may have said gift," one of the warriors said, "but it is temporary. These steeds came with us from the old land, ancestors of a race of equine imbued with ancient strength. Stronger, faster, smarter, these are not the horses of your homeland. They will listen to your commands now, but will return to us. Our Spiritual Leader sees them as a means to have you outsiders leave us as fast as possible."

Zercien inched toward the horse, and would have said out loud that he felt power and energy cascading from the beast, but he thought otherwise. He'd never read of a horse species imbued with anything, but after all that's happened since leaving Vellard, he learned not to question a damn thing.

He clambered—with the grace of a man who spent longer than intended at the pub—onto the horse's back but managed to steady himself. The horse didn't even flinch under his weight, or awkwardness. It took one step forward, and the energy emanating from its legs made Zercien feel he would soon have the means of flight.

Saena and Mayla had arranged a horseback riding lesson some years back, though Zercien wanted nothing to do with it then. Now he hoped he at least remembered the basics. Before he could say a well-intended thank you, the men had already disappeared into the woods.

"Know where we're going?" Euvard said as Zercien managed to convince the steed to walk forward.

He reached for the map, though it was waterlogged and ripping, Ankarth hanging on by a thin string. "If I were to guess, we're on the path to Ciprius. The exact spot I don't know, but we are in the right direction."

"Lead the way, then." Euvard nodded and waited for a reply, but Zercien never granted him the honor.

The Spiritual Leader did have a point, Zercien thought. *The Seven Legends' hero worship is extreme, but is it not valid?*

No, it was her beliefs that were extreme. Yes, the Seven Legends fled, but they disappeared into obscurity to live normal lives. A direct contradiction to their supposed plans of conquest. How could power-hungry monsters be such when they removed themselves from Oniro's affairs immediately after liberating it? Despite this, doubt continued its descent into his mind. Gunvald's story was not one he knew, and now he desperately wished to learn the fates of the others.

An increasingly loud clopping carried into Zercien's ears, and he turned back.

"Zerc, that's enough," Euvard said.

Euvard rode right next to him now. Zercien's back shot up in surprise, and he pulled on the reins to make sure his horse didn't start a gallop or throw him off.

"Hm?"

"*Hm?*" Euvard sneered. "Talk to me."

"I'm a bit tired, is all. Worried, too. We don't know where everyone is—"

"Nice try. Something else is bothering you, too. Has been the whole time. And now? It's even worse. You better start talking. Because I'm not going to stop asking until you do."

Fuck, Zercien thought amid a sigh.

But his friend was right.

"What the Spiritual Leader said about the Seven Legends reminded me of the castle archives, and how texts there are unavailable to the public," Zercien said. "Are they hiding knowledge from us?"

Euvard shook his head. "That may be annoying, but I know there's more to how you're feeling. The headaches, what happened with the bandits, in the mountains... Oh, and Helldregs were never truly eradicated, which we are expressly forbidden from discussing now. Am I the only one who cares?"

Zercien breathed a deep sigh, his head drooping, coming within an inch of hitting his horse's. To him, he felt he'd encountered the monstrous beings from the below world before.

"I haven't been completely honest with you. To anyone," he said. And for the first time in hours, Zercien at last looked Euvard in the eye. Light scratches marred his face, and his beard had grown far longer than he'd ever seen it.

Tears formed in Zercien's eyes. "Those headaches, they cloud my vision. My thoughts. Everything. The world walks at half-speed. I see fog. Everyone is a thin, grey line. It changes me into someone I'm not—"

Euvard interrupted before he could finish. "That's what happens when you get one of your headaches? I shouldn't have brought it up."

Zercien coughed. "Before, my head pain was so infrequent I never had a problem. But since we've been on this journey, they're a constant worry. I'm sorry for not telling you. But not even Saena knows to such an extent."

"No, I understand. But I'm starting to worry about those two. Mayla and Saena."

Zercien huffed out a quick breath, praising his fortune for the change in subject. "As do I. We have no idea how the situation is unfolding, and no way to know. The uncertainty of it all…"

"Not to be unfaithful to our little band here," Euvard said, "but if we were to receive word that Entervia was about to lose the war, I'd drop everything and run to be by Mayla's side."

"No need to explain. I would do the same."

A big, goofy grin spread over Euvard's face. "Given any more thought on asking her to be your wife?"

"I did, but then…" Zercien laughed, and raised both hands from the horse's reins, into the air. "All this. After the war, after this is all over, then I will."

"Makes sense. Not the best timing for a proposal, huh?"

"I just hope she doesn't find the ring while I'm gone. I hid it well enough, but could you imagine?"

The two shared a brief laugh, and Euvard leaned over to reach for Zercien's shoulder. Though it seemed he forgot he was atop a horse, and he teetered for a moment before pulling himself back. He cracked a slight smile, like he was proud of himself.

"I'm envious, I won't lie. Not like I can do the same for Mayla anytime soon."

"I've told you before," Zercien said. "If you are in need of gold, I'm more than willing to lend you—"

"I know. It's just… I want it all to be from me." Euvard shook his head and huffed. "It's a personal self-esteem sort of thing. Her market stall earns enough, but we don't have much luxury. I may take care of the cooking and the house, but she's the one who makes sure we have a home."

This time, it was Zercien's turn to put a hand on his friend's shoulder. He doubted the reliability of his reflexes, and his was a slower, more cautious act of kindness.

"Even if you can't afford the most extravagant ring ever crafted, she would accept and wear whatever it is you could," Zercien said.

With a hearty laugh that even caused their steeds to stumble in surprise, Euvard said, "What a pair of hopeless romantics we are."

Zercien returned his laugh and agreed while repositioning his reins.

"Well, I'm glad you're back to your old self, Zerc. *I* had to talk us out of that situation in the woods. You know shit's bad when *that* happens."

"You're not wrong. But I do feel better," Zercien said. "Thank you, Euvard. Truly."

And the two spent the remainder of the day speaking jovially of memories from their youths, laughing like the old friends they were.

CHAPTER FORTY-TWO
DIVINE INHERITANCE

Fynnian at last stopped running and put his hands on both knees. His breaths came out in coughs. He heard no other footsteps nor sounds of combat. He slid down the base of a tree, landing with a slushy *plop*.

"You coward," he cried, slamming a hand onto the puddle-filled dirt, splattering mud onto his shirt. "You left them all…"

His eyes grew puffy, and he waved his dirty hand to wipe away whatever drops slid underneath. "You, an Order descendant? You're nothing like them."

With a long sniffle and a deep breath, he stood, mud sliding off the back of his legs. Looking around, all he saw was grass and trees darkened by the storm.

"Where am I?" he muttered, turning his head, and spinning in all directions. He crossed his arms to stop a chill from climbing through his body, and moved forward, opposite of the way he came.

Not far from where he'd rested came a break in the trees and greens. Inching through, he slid his body sideways to not scrape against the sharp, thorny bushes, and appeared outside the forest into a large, open area with little foliage. A smile broke through his tear-covered face as he looked around. It wasn't familiar. At least he knew he hadn't gone backwards.

The chill seizing his body left as fast as it had set in, and sweat formed atop his forehead.

"Phew," Fynnian said, breathing deep as he wiped his brow.

While he had escaped the forest, now he was alone in the open—at least what he thought to be—Arigliothan plains. A salty mix of sweat and trapped rainwater continually dripped from his blonde hair and seeped into his mouth. He shook his head and trudged forward, into the blazing heat.

He stared at the sky-high beige dunes carrying far across the land, and cacti as tall as people populated the land. Fynnian released a pained breath, angry with himself that he'd wandered so far off their path, his question of where he'd ended up answered by the scorching sands beneath his boots.

Hoping for a brief respite, he sat down and placed his hands by his feet. The hot sand burned his fingertips and he gasped, burying them into his shirt. He looked up at the cloudless sky.

"Zercien!" His shout collided with the nearby dune, dissipating into the air like the grains of sand swirling about. No reply. He called out for each of his companions, voice straining and growing hoarse with each yell. Even for Lloyd, for which he was certain the black-haired swordsman would fly down the dunes to his aid. But none came.

"How did I end up in this mess?" Fynnian whispered, and he lowered his head between his knees. Sweat poured down his forehead and dripped onto the hot sand. "Why did I run? Why?"

Every muscle in his body refused to move, and his brain repeated, "Sleep." Fynnian let his eyelids touch, a brief calming pitch-black soothing his burning eyes. But he jolted awake, and shook his head in quick, snapping motions. "No, no, no. If I fall asleep here—" He shuddered at the thought.

Fynnian shoved himself to his feet and stretched his arms across his body. The silver and gold veins in his wrist glowed brighter than normal. When he stretched his arm to the left, the light faded, but upon bringing it back in front, the brightness returned. As he moved, his wrist flickered.

He scrunched his forehead. With no other leads to go on, he held his arm out in front and followed his veins, changing directions to suit the light.

He passed in between a set of mountainous dunes, a steady wind throwing sand into his face. Though he attempted to shield himself with his outstretched arm, the wind carried burning sand over and under.

A howling echoed through the dunes. Within Fynnian's sights, a tornado formed—taller than him and was growing larger with every grain it scooped. "No, no, no, no—!" Fynnian covered his face and dove into the hot sand. The tornado soared by and pelted his body with a mixture of sand and pebbles. It passed as quick as it set in, and Fynnian opened his eyes, but the stinging pain forced them shut. His tears only created tiny mud piles in his eyelids. Rubbing them until they burned, their blues turned bloodred.

He forced himself to stand and wiped the sand from his clothes with both hands. His wrist told him to move straight ahead, and as he walked, the sweltering mid-afternoon sky gave way to the bone chilling night.

The path in front of his every step glistened within his wrist's dull light, and the mix of accompanying starlight illuminated his way. He couldn't help but stare at the sparkling sand marking his failure, though it was a beautiful melancholy.

Fynnian shivered and shook out his boots of the hard, bitter-cold grains. The chattering of his teeth brought forth a shiver throughout his whole body. He crossed his arms to provide some modicum of warmth and looked up at the shimmering sky—no clouds hindered his view of the stars.

The glowing silvers and golds in his wrist pulsated, shining a dim light into the dark. Further ahead, Fynnian squinted to see the faint outline of a man's back taking slow footsteps deeper into the desert.

Fynnian's heart thumped, bashing against his chest. It couldn't be. His pace quickened to a jog, his careless steps kicking up the desert sand in his wake, and his wrist's lights burst into a sphere of radiant white.

The man turned to face him, his hard blue eyes staring through Fynnian's. His pale face was pained, cheeks thin and scarred. Scruffy stubble that glowed within Fynnian's light covered his chin.

"Father?" was all Fynnian's dried lips could muster.

"Fynnian?" came the hoarse reply, as if he hadn't had a drop to drink in days. He mimicked Fynnian's jog.

The two met in the middle, and all Fynnian could do was stare up with the smile of a little boy who'd just been given the toy he wanted. Wrinkles covered his father's face, and his golden-blonde hair was now interspersed with white sprouts.

"This is not some fell desert mirage, is it?" A stray tear leaked through Fynnian's welled right eye, past the streaks of brown sand. "Father…"

"No, Fynnian, it is I." A matching tear slid down his father's cheek.

Fynnian raised his hands and leaned forward, and the embrace they then shared felt everlasting.

When the two released, the cold, the wind, everything ailing him seemed to dissipate.

"Father, I don't know what to say," he said.

Tyrrowan smiled as he looked down at his now full-grown son. "You have become a fine young man, Fynnian."

"I have been studious, Father. But the questions keep me awake—"

"I can only imagine," his father said. "But I must ask, my dear boy, what in Oniro are you doing in the Darutan? In Ariglioth, for that matter?"

Fynnian shook his head and craned his neck as he spoke of the war with Ankarth. "I was separated from my allies, and now I am here. But Father, I saw them. In the Okoro Mountains. Helldregs lived and attacked us. We hardly escaped unscathed."

His father raised an eyebrow at the Helldregs, but that was all. Fynnian mouthed a few words to try and continue, but he'd expected his father to have a stronger reaction.

"I had suspected the Helldregs remained," Tyrrowan said, "But the war in Entervia is what I have feared."

Those words caused the desert chill to shoot back into Fynnian's spine. "What does that mean?"

"Whatever you know about the Ankarthan army, you must tell me."

Fynnian cringed and grit his teeth, remembering Zercien and Ardian's warning to keep all knowledge of the war a secret. But surely the last Sanctum Knight could be told such things with impunity.

"I don't know much, Father. But I do know Ankarth's army is led by a figure in jet-black and red armor, with the ability to cast Pariah Arts."

It was Tyrrowan's turn to wince. He lowered his head into his hands.

"A knight in black and red armor. Pariah Arts…" He repeated Fynnian's words again and again.

"Father?"

Tyrrowan exhaled a deep breath and looked his son stern in the eye. "What do you know of Efaltis?"

"E-what now?"

"Efaltis. The world below ours."

The name of the accursed land beneath the soil. Never mentioned in any of the scrolls, which Fynnian thought curious. He tapped the sand with the heel of his boot, and his father continued.

"I shall spare you the cumbersome details," Tyrrowan said, though he stumbled and stuttered as he spoke. "A knight in such armor is a servant to the one who rules below. They are capable of minor incantations of Pariah Arts. Spells created in the infernal place beneath the world, Efaltis."

"Father, if they are such a menace, why have I not heard or read of these knights?"

His father coughed, clearing his throat, as if buying time. "They are fearsome but thought long dead. However, Fynnian, there are more pressing matters. The existence of one here means the lord of Efaltis aims for Entervia, using Ankarth as a supplemental, easily manipulated force."

"But why?" Fynnian shook his head in rapid jerks. "Father, did you know this would happen?"

Another long pause between replies. Tyrrowan furrowed his brow and ran his hands through his hair. "It is the reason I left, Fynnian. I feared my presence would attract Efaltis and claim my life, all while Vellard burned. To disappear and prevent any harm from befalling our home seemed the wisest choice."

Fynnian had his question answered, but unease drifted through his stomach. He breathed through his pursed lips, shrugging. "But you've been away for almost twenty years. Why would Ankarth attack now?"

Again his father froze, stalling his answer with repeated throat clears. They grated on Fynnian's nerves.

"It baffles me, too, Fynnian. Truly," Tyrrowan said, and gulped. "Perhaps they knew of my location, and it took many years to respond. Or maybe there is something else they seek in Vellard."

Fynnian nodded, strait-laced and strong. "Father! Come back with me!"

And Tyrrowan about lost his balance.

"You are a full-fledged, Anointed Sanctum Knight," Fynnian said, his face awash with glee, a smile brimming. "You could slay this knight, Father!"

Tyrrowan shut his eyes and opened them slowly, taking a deep breath. "I cannot. I'm sorry."

The color drained from his cheeks, and Fynnian shook his head and pulled at his hair. "If not you, then—"

"The years have taken a toll. I do not have the martial prowess I had in my youth," Tyrrowan said. "I fear I could not defeat such a foe, not now."

Fynnian didn't reply and just stood, his shoulders drooping. While his father looked older, he didn't seem frail. He would have a lifetime's worth of advanced Seraph Arts. Before he could answer, Tyrrowan continued his speech.

"And much like you, I am on a quest of extreme importance. My duty is to explore the deepest corners of Dregnal, seeking clues on how to rebuild the Order. There is nothing left for me in Vellard. I'm sorry."

Fynnian opened his mouth, meaning to say "But what about me? Jyrren? Dyodore?" but nothing came out. "What have you found?"

"Nothing immediately actionable, but clues aplenty. For the Sanctum Order to return to its former glory, we must retake the World's Tower."

Fynnian shuddered as he spoke. "How? It is in the hands of Voks, if the stories are to be believed."

"Do you recall the keys?"

Fynnian put a hand to his chin. "I have read the World's Tower's floors are locked by four keys."

Tyrrowan smiled. "Those keys were distributed to non-Order members, only to be used in dire times. Sanctum Order Elders could pass through without the need of keys, but they are all dead, and their knowledge of the keys' locations, with them."

Fynnian mouthed "What?" before speaking. "And they never wrote it down?"

Tyrrowan shook his head. "It appears our ancestors wanted to keep these keys a closely guarded secret."

"I suppose I understand," Fynnian said, biting his bottom lip. "For us to restore the Order, we must reclaim the lost keys?"

"Yes, though my search has not determined their whereabouts."

"What shall we do until then?"

"While I must continue my mission, you, Fynnian, must continue to Ciprius." His father then pointed over Fynnian's head. "The people of this desert have taught me much of its geography. Walk straight and you will arrive in the Arigliothan plains, away from this accursed sand. It is not far."

Fynnian smiled and breathed out a long sigh. "But what of Ankarth? How do we win if they've that knight leading them?"

To his surprise, his father unsheathed his sword. It glowed with a radiant golden bright light, piercing the surrounding darkness.

"Father! That sword—" Fynnian said.

"The Right Half of the Sanctus Dual Blades." Tyrrowan held the sword in front of his son. "And now, I pass it on to you, Fynnian."

Fynnian jumped as those words crossed his mind. He stared down at the sword's dazzling blade, at the diamond-encrusted gold and white hilt. "I couldn't possibly—"

"Our paths have not crossed on sheer coincidence. This is surely a sign from God," Tyrrowan said, and nodded. "Take it in your hands and feel its power."

Fynnian reached a hand out but pulled it back and looked up to his father for reinforcement. He smiled. With quivering fingers, Fynnian grasped the sword's hilt, and held it in his shaky hands. The light dwindled to a low glow.

"Only those of the Sanctum Order bloodline may wield it, and the aura's strength depends on the Seraphic power within the bearer," Tyrrowan said. "In contrary to the Left Half, which eludes me still. Its strength is determined by the world's faith in the Order, not the wielder's." Fynnian couldn't help but sigh and drop his shoulders as he examined the sword and its puny light.

"You are not yet Anointed," Tyrrowan said. "So its light is faint. However, merely holding the sword will grant you immunity to Pariah Arts."

"Father, what do you—"

"My son, you are the only other person on Oniro with the power to wield this blade. Take it and strike down that accursed knight."

Fynnian jumped back and almost dropped the sword. "Father! I-I am not yet skilled enough to take on one of such power. I…"

"You must, Fynnian. He *may* be felled by normal means, but many more will die if you do not face him."

Taking the sword's sheath from his father, he put the Sanctus Right Half away and attached it to his belt. He detached his other sword and handed it to Tyrrowan.

"Do you understand your mission, Fynnian?" his father said.

"I do, Father," Fynnian said, and gulped. "On behalf of the Order, I will take on this knight."

"Good, Fynnian. I am trusting you to save me—" his words were interrupted by a quick, forced cough. "To save the *Order*. And now, we must part."

Fynnian cried out as if that little boy's toy were then crushed by a wagon wheel. Tears brimmed at his eyelids, and the cold desert air creeped underneath his shirt. "But we've only just reunited! There are so many questions I've yet to ask, so many times we've yet to share."

Tyrrowan placed his warm hands on Fynnian's shoulders. "It pains me, but I must. I cannot tarry here much longer."

His father then gripped him in one last warm embrace, a final shield against the cold.

"I am so glad," Tyrrowan said, and relinquished his grasp. "And I am proud. So very proud."

Without another word, Fynnian watched his father disappear into the darkness, the sounds of his footsteps negated by the sands.

CHAPTER FORTY-THREE
THE WAR HERO

On his hands and knees, Ardian dragged his bruised and beaten body through the gates of the approaching village, Reland. He was met with gasps and mouths agape as the villagers surrounded him, their whispers and murmurs gurgling into his fugue-state of mind.

"What in the world?" A woman's voice. "How did you get here?"

Ardian stared blankly as she stepped into his shaky sight, her leather boots shifting left and right. From his position, she appeared taller than he, with medium-length white hair and faint wrinkles across her pale skin. A scar ran down her cheek.

"Never mind." She held out her hand. "Come with me. I'll get you cleaned up."

"I—all right," Ardian said and allowed the stranger's kindness. With unexpected strength, the older woman pulled him to his feet and motioned him to lean on her shoulder.

Despite him needing rapid blinks to see anything, Ardian admired the homes they passed—all constructed of bricks or logs, and similarly sized. Rustic, cozy, homey. Trees and gardens scattered throughout, with colorful flowers interspersed. Reminded him of home, of the Vellardian gardens.

They approached another log-built home with a small flower garden in front. His leader pushed the front door open, and guided him onto a wooden seat at a large oak table. On the placemat already was a cup of water and a small plate of chopped vegetables and chicken, with a similar spread at the other side of the table.

"Thank you. This is much appreciated," Ardian said, and swigged the cold water to soothe his ailing throat. From a drawer, the woman produced a handful of bandages and cloths.

"Nothing to worry about, my good man." His timely savior smiled as she bent to wrap the wound on Ardian's knee. "What's your story? Oh, my manners." She tied off the cloth and pulled a chair in close. Before sitting, she stretched a wrinkled, rough hand for Ardian to shake. "Name's Aoife Dílis, former captain of the Reland militia."

Captain of a militia? Ardian thought. *What luck.*

"Well met, Aoife. And thank you. I'm Ardian Calvus, a guard captain of Vellard." Ardian noticed a flash and a gleam in her eye.

"Vellard, eh?" she said. "And you choose *this* backwater town to visit? Why don't you tell me why you're *really* here?"

Backwater? From what Ardian saw, though rustic it seemed, Reland was quite populous. "Could take a while to explain that."

With a smirk, Aoife put her feet up on the table and crossed her legs. "I'm retired. The rest of my life is free time."

Ardian shrugged. "I'm part of a group traveling to Ciprius, initiated by King Durnan of Entervia. We journeyed over the border, through the Okoro Mountains, and into Ferronwood, where I was separated from my companions."

"Well, it was obvious you braved the wood, but the Okoro Mountains, too? I didn't even think the path still existed. What in the world could Entervia want from Ariglioth so badly that you'd make such a ridiculous trek? Without voyaging by sea, no less."

Ardian chose not to divulge what happened inside the Okoro caverns. "We seek reinforcements."

Aoife shifted her crossed legs off the table and leaned forward in her seat, a strand of white hair covering one eye. She sported a scar there too, though not as pronounced as the one on her cheek. "Eh? Why?"

"Entervia's at war with Ankarth," Ardian said, "but they're more formidable than expected. We need Ariglioth's help."

Aoife breathed deep and let it loose slowly. "Haven't caught wind of the war. But I assume you didn't risk your life in the Ferronwood just to lie to us."

"You'd assume right."

"Friend, if that's what you're after, Entervia would have a better chance at winning the war with you leaving Ariglioth and never coming back."

It was Ardian's turn to leave his relaxed position, crossing his arms and cocking his head. Not the news he wanted to hear. "What are you on about?"

"You said you're looking to meet with King Lennard?"

Ardian nodded with pronounced head bobs. "That seems the proper route, yes." He winced. Sounding like a smartass wasn't his intention.

Aoife beckoned him to move his chair a bit closer, saying "C'mere," in a soft voice. Ardian leaned in as she looked from side-to-side.

"Listen, Ardian," she whispered. "King Lennard isn't who he used to be."

Ardian's stomach dropped. "I've always been told King Lennard is a kind man and ruler."

"*Was* a kind man and ruler. He's just declared martial law upon Ariglioth."

Ardian shot back up into his chair. "*What*? Martial law? When?"

"Keep your voice down." Aoife put a finger to her lips. "We're housing a few Ciprian runaways here in Reland. They're the ones who told us. The announcement hasn't reached us here. *Yet*. But we fear it won't be long. It's probably next to impossible to enter Ciprius now."

"We've official documentation from Entervia, signed by King Durnan himself," Ardian said. "Entering Ciprius should be the least of our concerns."

"The runaways also tell of forced labor on an enormous moat around the city." She took a long drink of water and crossed her legs. "So let's assume your paperwork is accepted. You find yourselves allowed entry into Ciprius. But now you've got a shovel in hand, and a high-and-mighty city guard is barking at you to dig." With a smirk, she placed the cup on the table. "Congratulations."

Ardian raised an eyebrow. *A moat? For a coastal city?* he thought.

"What is King Lennard's plan?"

"I don't know," Aoife said as she shrugged. "I fear we have a dictator on our hands, Ardian."

"Shit," Ardian whispered. "Zercien…"

"Hmm? What'd you say, lad?"

Ardian sprang up in his seat and exclaimed, "Aoife!" to which the older woman jumped back, sending the chair to rock back and forth. "You can help us."

"What could this retired military woman have that you need?" she said, eyebrows raised.

Footsteps echoed from the other side of the room, and another woman who looked about Aoife's age, pale-faced with faint wrinkles and short, black hair adorned with white streaks, entered. She carried with her a small child huddled in her arms.

"Aoife, who is this?" the woman said. "Another one of those—"

"Oh, my manners!" Aoife shook her head, but then smiled and stood. "Ardian, this is my wife, Larilyn, and daughter, Eimelia. Larilyn, meet Ardian. He's come from Vellard."

She smiled a half-smile, tilting her head. "Vellard? Truly? Well, it's a pleasure, but I'm sure Aoife has told you of the goings on here in Ariglioth."

"The pleasure is all mine," Ardian said. "And she has."

Aoife took Eimelia from her arms. "Ardian, when I retired, I quit the force for good and devoted my life to Larilyn. I didn't have time for a family when I led the militia, but now I have Eimelia." The child looked up at her with a smile.

"She was an orphan. Parents died some years ago," Aoife said, and tickled Eimelia's tiny chin. "Your cause is worthy, but I've a daughter to take care of. I can't help you. I'm sorry."

Larilyn shot her a wide-eyed look. "What is this about?"

Ardian stood again, though he grimaced putting weight on his injured leg. "All I ask is you request the militia to aid us. You needn't take up arms yourself."

"If the situation is truly dire, would our militia be enough to do much of anything?"

Ardian's gaze fell to the floor. "If I may be honest, I've no way of knowing. But we are desperate. Even some hundred strong fighters would be worth our time."

Aoife returned Eimelia to her wife and ran a hand through her short strands of hair.

"And my companions are still out there. Captained by a man named Zercien. I imagine they're bound for the capital as we speak," Ardian said before Aoife could reply. Again, she shook her head. Though this time with eyes closed and lips in a straight line.

"If your allies have made it to Ciprius, their mission is already doomed," she said.

"I don't care!" Ardian shouted as his heavy boot slammed the floor, shaking the dining table and a painting hanging on the wall.

Eimelia's ensuing cry deafened the room. Larilyn turned around to hush her child, but not before lowering her eyes at the rude visitor.

Ardian mouthed "Sorry," and stepped back, beginning to pace about the dining room. "Not long before we embarked, Vellard was assaulted by Arvaros. Something you Arigliothans would know nothing about."

Aoife huffed. "I'm not sure where you're leading me with this, but I'll oblige just one more story."

"They ransacked a whole sector of the city," Ardian continued. "Stealing goods, brandishing blades at Vellardian citizens who were doing nothing other than trying to maintain normalcy amid a war." With one hand leaning against a wall, Ardian turned away and sighed. "Care to guess where I was?"

Aoife and Larilyn exchanged glances, and the two shrugged. Their confusion was met with Ardian's quivering eyelids.

"The goddamn barracks, still awake from the night before, a mug of mead in my hand as the early-morning sun burned my eyes. Trying to forget the fear of my imminent sortie into Ankarth." He lifted his hand from the wall and stepped closer.

"We were lucky Zercien and his allies came to the citizens' rescue. But because of me, the Vellardian guards were absent." A sigh came to his lips as he grabbed his cup from the table, and tilted it in his hand. "Pings and pangs of regret flare into my gut every time my hand grips the cool glass of another drink, but damn does the forgetfulness feel good when it hits my lips."

Aoife stood, her careful footsteps echoing in soft bursts. "I'm sorry, lad. The pain of leadership consumes us all, at times."

With a deep breath, Ardian said, "I regret it every damn day. If I cannot meet Zercien in Ciprius, then I will bring some semblance of reinforcements to Vellard. Even if Reland spurns us. Hell, I'd sooner ask the denizens of Ferronwood than return home with nothing."

A soft hand hit his shoulder, though with the force to make him wince. "Don't be cruel to yourself, lad. Your dedication is inspiring."

"And what of yours, Aoife?"

"Pardon?"

Ardian turned his shoulder to free himself from her grip. "Would you do as I did, and sit back while others are fighting and dying? Or would you act, and prevent more senseless death?"

The older woman let a stream of air through her lips and sighed. "How could you ask such a thing?" She looked back at Larilyn. "What do you think?"

Ardian watched as a slight smile broke through Larilyn's locked lips, and she too walked to join them. Balancing Eimelia in her arms, she placed a hand on Aoife's cheek. "I know you want to help. Go."

Aoife responded with a heavy sigh.

"I can take care of Eimelia," Larilyn said.

"But—"

"Don't give me time to change my mind."

Aoife turned to face Ardian and nodded, a smile sprouting. "You win, lad. It'll take a week or two to prepare, but I'll contact the new militia leader and have them gather. I've still got a little pull." She winked. "And this old war dog will accompany you to Vellard, too."

Ardian's smile stretched far, and an exasperated sigh escaped. "Thank you, Aoife. From the bottom of my heart, I—"

"One condition," the old militia leader said and held up one finger. "We are to go nowhere near Ciprius."

Ardian's stomach dropped, and he waved a hand and shook his head. "What of my companions, then?"

"We will almost certainly be caught and jailed for marching near Ciprius armed."

Fuck, Ardian thought and then mouthed. Leaving them all behind forced a shudder to course his spine.

"Fine. We won't," he said, and the weight of his words dropped down his throat like medicine.

Aoife nodded. "Good. We'll take the route through Duspen. If we wave our Arigliothan banner high, we'll have no problems with Arvaros. It'll be a long journey to Vellard by foot, but we'll make it."

"A sound plan," Ardian said, but now realized he had nothing but the clothes on his back and a lance and shield to his name. All his supplies and coin lay scattered on the forest floor.

"Would you be able to put a good word in for me at the inn?" he said. "I would say the pub, too, but for the first time in months, I've no desire to drink."

Aoife chuckled and slapped the young guard captain on the shoulder. "Learned nothing, have you? Say, Larilyn, could Ardian stay in our guest room until we depart?"

"Of course," she said. "You'll be helping us around the house, though."

"I cannot thank you both enough. Is there any way I can repay you?"

"Why don't you ask me that once we beat Ankarth out of Entervia?" Aoife smiled. "Come now, I'll show you to your room. We'll take good care of you, but only if you indulge in an old woman's war stories."

Ardian laughed. "Of course."

He followed Aoife on stiff and bruised legs, wanting to collapse on the tidy bed beside the wall. Once he was alone in his room, he drew a deep breath. "I'm sorry, Zercien. Would you want me to do this?"

Ardian leaned Spike against the wall and brought his kite shield over his head. Before setting it down, he ran a hand over its metal, pressing his finger into the newfound welts and scratches left by arrows that would've otherwise pierced his neck.

"I have you to thank, too—" He put his index finger on his lips, interrupting himself "—*Arrowsbane*." He brought his hand to his chin, and he nodded thrice. "Arrowsbane. Yes, that'll do."

CHAPTER FORTY-FOUR
THE DUTIFUL AND THE DESPOT

King Lennard sauntered toward his throne and leaned his golden lance against the seat. He stared at the four men awaiting his discipline, all of whom were arrested for various crimes relating to his new moat construction. The first victims of his newly decreed martial law.

A royal guard in chainmail armor bowed and spoke. "Your Majesty, I have brought you the ones who have caused us ill at the moat."

"You may stand down," King Lennard said with a strong and booming voice echoing throughout the hall and concentrated his stare on the first man. "Why have you deliberately chosen to hinder Ariglioth's progress? Do you wish to cause our beloved country to plummet into obscurity?"

"No!" cried the prisoner, a grizzled man in his forties. His crime was taking a sip of water outside the designated drinking hour. "I hadn't even a morsel to eat since—"

King Lennard slammed the sauroter of his lance against the tile floor like a gavel, its echo silencing the man's hoarse screams. "You dare raise your voice to your sworn liege?"

"I haven't—I didn't mean to—"

"Silence!"

King Lennard leaned forward on his throne, pointed to one of his guards, and then to the prisoner. "Behead him."

The guard slouched, his head drooping as he unsheathed his sword. The prisoner was headless in one slash across the neck. His body slammed onto the stone floor in unison with his head.

The other prisoners' screams rang about the hall, and if they were not shackled, would have run for the door. King Lennard smiled.

"Now, for the rest of you," he said. "You are sentenced to after-hours of labor upon the moat. From sunup to midnight, you will work without breaks. You will sleep outdoors. And should your family come to see you, they will be executed on the spot."

"Your Majesty!" said a prisoner whose crime was fainting during work hours. His cheeks still hadn't regained their color. "I've a new-born at home—"

"If not for your own weakness, then you would be returning to your home tonight," said King Lennard.

The guards nodded for the remaining prisoners to follow. But King Lennard tapped his finger atop the arm of his throne and beckoned the man he'd just spoken to. "You. To me."

The man gulped but turned to comply. Before he could bow, King Lennard was on his feet, golden lance in hand. He thrust it forward, jabbing the spiked end through the prisoner's chest, and pushed until he could see the bloodshot eyes of a man whose life was about to end.

"You are too weak to be Arigliothan," King Lennard said. "Worthless to me and my kingdom." He pulled the lance, and the squirming man fell to the tiled floor, blood gushing from the hole in his chest.

"Clean the floors," King Lennard said to no one in particular, but his words spurred one of the guards to rush off for a bucket of water. "The first prisoner. Has he left behind any family?"

"Yes, My Liege," said the other guard. She cleared her throat thrice. "His son contributes to the moat as well."

King Lennard smirked. Terror was shining through her face, much like every guard that spoke to him. Their hands, always wavering close to their swords, and the halls abuzz with murmurs, suspicion. And they didn't think their dear old King Lennard would notice?

He knew they performed his bidding through fear alone, but it worried him not. Had he simply steered the same course as the man previously in his seat, no progress would be made.

They wouldn't dare cross me. My ways will better Ariglioth, he thought. *I am benevolent.*

King Lennard pointed to the severed head on the floor, now drained of all color. "Leave the head upon his family's doorstep. Show them what it means to defy their lord and king."

The guard stumbled forward, but caught herself before falling. "Yes, Your Majesty."

***

King Durnan, his Grandmaster General and the Ruling Council sat in silence, their heavy gulps permeating the still air. Their finest general was dead, and the Entervian army ran in circles. All avoided King Durnan's gaze.

"Rulers of Entervia, we need a solution," he said. "Fast. What shall we do?"

Not a word from either the Ruling Council or Grandmaster General Urian. After a long minute, however, Council Member Ellana spoke up.

"Your Majesty. This war is pointless. To eliminate more meaningless death, Entervia must surrender."

All but King Durnan shouted in every direction. With the slam of his fist upon their meeting table, which he worried any more of his slams would at last break the blasted thing, he held everyone's attention once more.

"Cease this foolishness. Bickering at one another leads us nowhere. Urian, your thoughts on surrender?" The words left a sour taste on King Durnan's tongue.

"General Burgland was one of our best," Grandmaster General Urian said. "But we are not surrendering."

"And we still await Sir Zercien's return," said Council Member Leeland. "Reinforcements from Ariglioth could very well sway the battle in our favor."

"But what if the reinforcements are too late?" said Council Member Dallonta. "Our army surely can't last much longer without Burgland."

King Durnan put a fist to his cheek, and elbow onto the table in front. "What is the status of the army? Spare no detail."

Grandmaster General Urian pursed his lips and breathed slow. "Our latest report spoke of horrifying losses. The enemy commander captured Entervia's last remaining stronghold, but allowed the fleeing soldiers to escape. And he delivered General Burgland's body to one of our encampments. Fully intact, I may add, and sponged of blood."

A kindness? From one who controls Pariah Arts? King Durnan thought.

"Will he use the fortress against us?" said Council Member Dallonta.

"Not likely." Grandmaster General Urian answered with a slow shrug. "The fort is far from Vellard. And if it's Vellard he wants, he will launch a full-scale assault."

"Then we must survive as long as possible," King Durnan said. "The army will be told to hold positions outside of Vellard and not budge. They must defend the city at all costs."

"Your Majesty, that is a dangerous move," Grandmaster General Urian said. "We have the soldiers to do so for some time, but the enemy has proven shrewd. Should they surprise us and breach the walls—"

"Then we are lost. I am aware."

Silence abounded.

"We now know our strategy," King Durnan said. "Urian, I trust you will lead our army well from the front lines?"

The Grandmaster General lurched in his chair. "Pardon, Your Majesty?" Spittle flew with his words.

"As Grandmaster General, I expect you to take the field in our time of need."

"I protest, Your Majesty. What if something should befall you? I must be here as a precaution."

King Durnan jumped to his feet and slammed his fist on the table. "I tire of your excuses, Urian. My orders are final. Understood?"

"Yes, Your Majesty. Come tomorrow, I shall embark for the battle-field—"

"You leave as soon as our meeting adjourns." King Durnan nodded at his Council. "And this meeting is now adjourned."

Grandmaster General Urian's head drooped, but he soon nodded.

"Urian," King Durnan said, putting a hand on his shoulder before he left the chamber. "When you've the chance, send a messenger to deliver word of General Burgland's death to his family. I knew them well. Tell them that when Entervia has finally found peace, we shall honor his name."

"I will, Your Majesty. Posthaste."

"It's a tragedy, Urian. His boy just turned twelve last week."

"In his stead, Your Majesty, I will not fail. The North will pay."

And the two shook hands.

Chapter Forty-Five
An Old Friend

Zercien tapped his horse's thigh with his foot on accident, and with a mighty *neigh* it rose to its hind legs. He gripped the reins until his knuckles pulsated, and the horse galloped ahead.

"Zerc!" Euvard half-laughed as he and the horse rushed by. "The hell did you do?"

The words blew faintly by his ear, drowned in the rampaging clomps of Zercien's horse as he disappeared over the plains' green hills.

Zercien sat straight, and the blood that had shot into his head dispersed. He rode through the tall grass, and a breeze ran through his hair, its satisfying chill blasting against his face. Out of the corner of his eye, he noticed Euvard's steed gradually coming up from behind.

"Wait," Zercien whispered, shooting a quick look back at the gaining Euvard. "So he wishes to pass me, does he?"

Now neck and neck, Euvard waved at his friend and, with a smile, shot past. Zercien blew some air from his nose. He tapped his horse on the side again to urge rapidity, its hooves now trampling over the grass.

They rode over another hill, and the mighty city of Ciprius appeared on the horizon—its tall buildings towering into the sky, and its castle seated among the clouds, just before the sea. Zercien's heart jumped to his throat and butterflies tingled in his stomach. Memories of leaving Vellard, their confrontation with Reaver, the Okoro Mountains,

Ferronwood Forest, everything rushed back. He felt like they left Vellard years ago…and soon, it would all be over.

Zercien managed to bring his horse to a lazy trot. Euvard pulled up next to him and rattled off excuses as to how Zercien had won their 'race,' which Zercien just learned they were having.

The appearance of a dark-haired man practicing his sword swings ahead interrupted him.

"*Lloyd*? How the hell did you get here?" Euvard said, and Lloyd peered over his shoulder but didn't bother to pause his training.

"Hmph. You're late," said the swordsman.

"*Late?* Didn't you see what happened? You just ran off!"

"Many warriors challenged me. I carved a path that none of you used. A shameful display."

Zercien put a hand up in front of Euvard, who was shaking his head. "It's good to see you unharmed, regardless." Though he wasn't sure himself whether he was glad or not. Lloyd *had* saved them on two occasions, but Zercien still couldn't bring himself to trust this wayward swordsman.

Would it have killed him to shout? he thought.

Lloyd said nothing and continued to swing his sword.

"Hope Fynn and Ardian are all right," Euvard said. "Don't see them anywhere."

"We should camp and wait a while. In case they arrive," Zercien said.

Euvard groaned and his shoulders drooped. "You're serious?" He pointed to his right, and grabbed and yanked Zercien's shoulder to face it. "Right there. Literally our goal."

The mighty Ciprius, with an unusual amount of activity by the front gates, Zercien now noticed. People meandered in and out, past what he assumed were guards.

"If we walk now, we'll be at the gates before we run out of daylight," Euvard said. "Know what happens then? Beds and real, hot food. Not cave floors and stale bread. And you want to *wait*?"

Zercien pushed Euvard's hand away. "Aren't you worried about them?"

"I am, but—"

"If we enter Ciprius, they'll have no official documentation. We risk leaving them behind—"

"Fine, I understand. You win, Zerc. We'll camp here for a while, all right?"

The two spent the remainder of the afternoon setting up a makeshift camp—with no help from Lloyd. Zercien watched him swing his sword about and wondered how someone could stand that much training. And he had no clue how long Lloyd had even been there for. But the brooding swordsman, credentials be damned, likely could have attempted to enter Ciprius without them.

Did he wait for us? Zercien thought. A kindness he didn't think existed.

But in an instant, Lloyd vanished. Mid-sword stroke—gone. Zercien jumped up and stood, scouring the plains for Euvard, but he too was nowhere to be found. With arms raised to protect his face, thick fog crested and struck like a tidal wave, covering his camp, rising past his knees, and over his head. He could see nothing through the mists.

What the— Zercien's mind cried out, but no words would flow to his lips.

A man clad in a bloodred robe materialized in the fog, his back facing Zercien. He turned his shoulder, and Zercien's eyes met the empty darkness inside the hood. Running a hand over his chest, he expected a heavy heartbeat, but instead found the normal, rhythmic beat.

"You." Zercien's voice carried into the fog. "You again."

The robed man turned to face him and spoke. "Old friend, you finally speak to me. After all these years." His voice was calming. Wispy, it too echoed throughout the mists.

"Do I know you?" Zercien ran a hand through his hair.

The man in the bloodred robes inched closer, though his footsteps made no noise, as if he floated above the fog-covered ground. "It is rude to not recognize an old friend, Holunt."

Chapter Forty-Six
Union

You have not yet accepted it, have you?" said the robed man.
"I don't know what you're—" Zercien said but stopped as the
figure he'd come to recognize waved a hand around the area, as
if pointing out something he should have more easily seen.

"This fog. You choose to hide yourself within it. You refuse to let
any in—even your beloved."

Zercien looked at his feet, like he'd just been scolded by a parent. "You are right. Ever since I—"

"I know, Holunt. I know. I have been watching."

"You've been watching me?"

"Is that not what old friends do?"

Zercien clenched both fists by his sides. "I want it to stop." Though
he couldn't see into the robed man's hooded face, Zercien sensed confusion.

"What to stop?" the robed man said.

"All of this!" Zercien waved his hands in circles, pushing the mists
apart, watching as they bent and twisted in his fingers. "I want the
headaches to stop. The fog to disperse. And to cease changing into
someone I'm not."

"Do you not agree that the interference has helped you? I am afraid
it is not something within my control, Holunt."

Zercien hated that this ominous figure made an excellent point. "Then who? Who do I ask? I will do whatever it takes to make it stop."

The robed man pointed at Zercien's head. "It is he we must ask."

Despite his squints and rapid darting, Zercien's gaze met none whom this man could have meant. He and the figure stood alone in this prison of fog.

"Help me," Zercien said. "I don't understand."

"Very well." The robed man sauntered further ahead, again his footsteps, if they could be called as such, making no noise, one hand in front. "He says you have grown quite strong, and have learned much from his intrusions. You will be relieved of your head pain, and he will no longer control your mind. You will not see me in this form again. But your glimpses into a life that once was, those I cannot reverse."

What are you talking about? Zercien thought.

"However," the robed man spoke before Zercien could. "In return, you will accept your other self. Your other blood. Your other mind."

Zercien clasped his head between both hands. "This is nonsensical. Am I Holunt? Am I Zercien? Am I even human? Who am I?"

The robed man's hood shook, as if laughing. "Whatever do you mean? You are you. As I am I."

An exasperated groan left Zercien. Almost a growl. "If that is to be believed, then I do not know who I am."

"You are Fogbound, young schoolteacher. An inheritor of this gift of mine."

As Zercien thought of how absurd that sounded, the fogged walls around him darkened like dusk. Grey waves of fog rippled amid the black, pushing, pulling, and then darting away.

The robed man raised both hands into the air, and ankle-high grey stones popped in over the dark green grass. Innumerable, but in organized rows and lines. Upon each, runes and lettering Zercien wasn't familiar with, let alone able to read.

One stone emerged, as if from nothing, in front of Zercien. When he bent down, he gasped upon seeing no lettering adorn its smooth grey face.

"Many Fogbound have come before you." The robed man floated next to Zercien. "But none successful. Most do not even realize they possess the gift before their passing."

"You mean to tell me this is some common occurrence?" Zercien said, lifting his head. "Ridiculous." Though he still ran his hand along the stone, hoping to wipe away some invisible layer of dust to reveal an unintelligible name.

The fire in the robed man's eyes flared, and Zercien fell on his backside atop the hard ground. "My words are no jest." A wave of energy dripped from his speech. "You are not special. You have merely survived."

Perhaps this was the answer the mysterious figure desired. Though Zercien cursed himself for not coming to such a conclusion before being fed the solution.

"Then I am Zercien Volnaire. A Fogbound," Zercien said. "That is who I am."

"You forget one piece," said the robed man. In a flash of grey light, the stones dissipated, fading into the ether. The darkness flung through the ripples of fog like arrows. Zercien clamored to his feet and dusted off.

"While you are Zercien Volnaire, the warrior Holunt is within your mind, your blood," the robed man said. "But you are not Holunt. Not yet."

Zercien loosed a held breath, hard against the roof of his mouth as it escaped his lips. "Please, help me understand." Creaks in his voice forced a throat clear. "If I am not Holunt, then why address me so? Cease these riddles."

"I speak to your mind. To the power that lives dormant in your veins. You have felt it. I sense it so. For each time you experience interference, some of the hero of legend remains. Albeit only a sliver."

A tremble. Zercien's foot shook upon what he assumed was the quaking ground, but was just his own nerves. "You mean to say I'm slowly losing myself." A stern stare matched his tone, but as much as he attempted to remain firm, his legs shook.

The hood turned left and right, as if disagreeing.

"You cannot lose what you already are," came the words from the faceless head. "However, your method is inefficient. Unbecoming of one with such potential."

"You speak as if I want this 'potential.'"

"Is regaining full control of your mind not what you seek? Perhaps I was mistaken." The robed man turned away, his heels not touching the grey ground. "You may carry on as you like."

Zercien opened his mouth and watched as the mysterious figure drifted away. The fog surrounding him skewed and started a gradual fade. He gulped, and clenched his trembling fists.

"Stop," he called. Commanding and strong, no hint of worry in his voice. The fog grew dense, as did the grey darken. And the robed man did indeed obey.

"Yes, old friend?"

"Is this truly the way to regaining my mind?"

In moments, the robed man was turning and floating toward Zercien. He stood close, and Zercien could see the depths of the pitch-black hood. An outline of a face, though its features remained obscured.

"Only when the schoolteacher and the warrior of legend form as one."

Zercien motioned his arms, gesturing the enigmatic figure to continue. "Will you not tell me how?"

The hood shook the same as before, befitting laughter. "By merely accepting who you are. You will be bound to your inner fog. You will follow your own vision, no longer having need of my presence as you know me, nor the aid of the other who occupies your mind. But from it, you will gain strength, more than you know. If you wish, we will grant you this bargain, or treaty, of sorts. And you shall embark on the path of your true self."

"I only need say the words, and you will grant me this?"

The hooded robe bobbed up and down.

"And I will no longer lose control of my own mind?" Zercien knew the question was answered numerous times already. "Forgive me, but I need to be certain."

"Do you not trust me, old friend?" The hooded man sounded wounded. "After the many occasions my silent supervision guided you to the correct path?"

Duspen. The caves. The woods. While controversial in the moment, this path directed them to their goal.

"It is not an easy decision to make," Zercien said.

"Is that so? I would imagine becoming the master of one's own mind to be a boon," the hooded man said. "In conjunction with what you may face in the coming days, you would do well to assume your newfound strength."

"Hold, this is different." Zercien tapped his foot, the ensuing sound fading away within the fog. "What do you know?"

"I cannot foresee what is to pass. However, you have seen myriad atrocities that those without power cannot hope to combat. Accepting your true self will stabilize your mind, yes, but will too help prevent your home from becoming ash."

Zercien's mind filled with images of flame. Of buildings burning. Innocents screaming, running in panicked crowds through streets awash with fire. Saena's face burst through the red, coating her face in dark bloodstains, a silent scream rushing from her mouth. An unseen force yanked her away, back into the ocean of flame.

A gasp. His own. Zercien shook his head back to whatever reality it was he faced. The robed man, unmoving, still stood close, awaiting his answer.

To be free of him. To never be questioned again of his demeanor. Zercien held his closed fist against his chin. He would miss the benevolent interference, for it had saved him. But to be granted a power so strong, he could save his home. A tantalizing prospect.

"I accept," Zercien said. No hint of fear, no remnants of doubt. "I will become my true self."

The bloodred-robed man raised a hand toward Zercien, and a warm energy filled his body and mind. Not unlike the sensation of the Ankarthan commander's Pariah Arts, but instead of pain, power coursed through his veins like lightning. His blood pumped and flowed through his arms and legs to the tune of a furious drumming heart.

All around him, the fog shattered into thousands of pieces. Pointed, jagged edges fell to the ground, though no noise accompanied. The man in the bloodred robe turned translucent before his hand at last faded into the night, and from Zercien's mind.

Holunt, there is still much you must do to fully embrace who you are. But this will help you begin to understand, the bloodred-robed man's voice echoed in Zercien's head, his words just appearing in his mind. *And when you do, I will be by your side. As I always have, old friend.*

Zercien blinked four times, and the land returned. He stood upon the open, grassy plains of Ariglioth once more, with Euvard lying face-up on his makeshift bed, Lloyd in the distance swinging his sword, and the roar of their campfire crackling into the night.

CHAPTER FORTY-SEVEN
BLUNTED AIM

S aena held her knife in hand, concentrating on an oak tree. She imagined the branches as arms, the small bushel of leaves atop as a helmet, and the entirety of the wood as openings for her knives. She focused her gaze upon the center burl, which would soon be her target.

"Now, raise your hand like I told you," Mayla said, her voice a whisper, close enough for her breath to tickle Saena's ear. "Pretend the wood is an enemy's flesh. You want your spin to end at the moment the knife's tip sticks right in and burrows itself within your enemy. Drawing blood is the quickest way to induce panic."

Mayla positioned Saena's hand above her head. "This is your release point. If you release when the knife's tip is directly at the target, you'll miss. Also, don't flick your wrist. Oh, and you want to make sure the knife can spin multiple times—"

"Mayla!" Saena said. Her head throbbed. "Can you slow down?"

"Sorry," her friend said and backed away. "Try a throw now."

Saena readied her knife and cocked back her arm. Tilting her arm down, up, and down again, she envisioned the knife soaring through the air, and the blade sticking into the oak tree's knot. She frowned. Not good enough. Her mind's eye warped the tree into one of those ugly, rotten Duspen barbarians, with a toothy grin. The branches, its arms, carrying two jagged swords.

Saena released the knife. It spun and flew through the stale morning air—and the handle clanked harmlessly off the imaginary Arvaros' side.

"Damn," she muttered under her breath.

"Great work!" Mayla said, clapping a few times.

Saena tilted her head. "Was it? I wouldn't have drawn blood—"

"Expecting such on your *first* throw? I'm impressed you hit the target at all."

Such high hopes. Saena reclaimed her knife and prepared for another throw. Again, she pictured a brutish Arvaros, his face and broken teeth awash with slobber, and threw.

The handle bounced off the wood yet again, but this time it smacked the illusory Arvaros on the head.

"Damn it!" Saena snarled.

"Good!" said Mayla. "If that were a real enemy, he'd have a miserable headache right about now."

Perhaps this was good enough. She picked up her knife, and her and Mayla packed for the day.

"Be honest. How was my first lesson?" Saena asked.

"Much better than mine," Mayla said.

Saena smiled and some heat flushed her cheeks red. "You mean it?"

Her friend nodded, gathering her own supplies and throwing the small bag over her back. "Your aim is excellent. Even if you don't land the blade, better to hit your enemy with the handle than not at all. Knocking someone on the head may allow you the extra second you need to escape."

Saena winked. "Or disorient them enough and have your more skilled friend do the dirty work for you?"

Mayla smiled and punched her on the shoulder, but it hurt like a real punch. "Let's get to the market and buy you your own set. You have potential."

And Saena smirked. She was beginning to enjoy this.

CHAPTER FORTY-EIGHT
RELIEF REBUFFED

Zercien's right eye twitched as he stared down into the ground. After such a peaceful sleep, too.

He rolled himself onto his back and looked up at Euvard's big grin. The backdrop of early-morning sunrise behind his friend's obnoxious smile served only to further his annoyance.

"It's early," Zercien said as he pushed himself to his feet and wiped the dirt off.

"Look," Euvard said and pointed behind Zercien. A lone figure approached, slow, and clutching his right arm.

Is that Fynn? Zercien thought.

He breathed a heavy sigh as a cool breeze found his heart. Euvard called over to their lost companion, and the three jogged to meet in the middle.

"Fynn!" Euvard laughed as he grabbed Fynnian in a bear hug, smacking his back with his strong hand.

"Hi, Euvard, Zercien. Good to see you again." He flinched and coughed. Euvard released him from his trap, and Fynnian could at last breathe freely.

"We thought we lost you," Euvard said, rubbing his hand on his shirt. "Is that sand?"

Fynnian gulped and cleared his throat. "I… I lost sight of you all in the woods. But managed to escape into the Darutan Dunes. Not on purpose, mind you."

"The Dunes? You must've had a tough time of it, eh?" Euvard nodded to Zercien and led them both back to their camp. "We have a bit of food and water left."

"Oh, yes, I am quite famished," Fynnian said as he sat on ripped cloth. Lloyd was sitting far away from everyone, sharpening his sword's blade on a whetstone. Zercien caught him glancing over, but only for a moment before returning to his work.

"Where is Ardian?" Fynnian said as he looked around, fixating on the mighty brown steeds roaming and eating the long grass. He tilted his head. "Are those yours?"

"We were separated from Ardian in the woods," said Zercien. "The horses are a longer story."

Fynnian sighed. "I hope he's okay. We need him."

"How did you find us?" Euvard said. "No map, wandering through a desert. Sounds like you've some luck on your side."

With a deep breath, Fynnian announced, "I found my father in the desert."

"You did not!" Laughing heartily, Euvard grabbed hold of Fynnian and gave him a slap on the back.

Fynnian rubbed the ensuing bruise. "Thanks."

"I'm happy for you," Zercien said and smiled. He truly *was* happy for his companion, though his heart panged for the father he never knew. "But he's left?"

"He did leave again." Fynnian sighed and winced at the words. "His mission is very important, you see." He shook his head back and forth. "But more importantly, my father told me many things about our mission. And Ankarth."

Zercien and Euvard exchanged looks, each raising an eyebrow.

"What could your father know about them?" Zercien rebuked. "We were ordered to not speak of this to anyone outside our group, save for Entervian authority."

"I apologize," Fynnian said, and looked down at his feet. "But when it related to Pariah Arts, I assumed a living member of the Sanctum Order to know more. And he did."

Zercien forgot his annoyance, and instead tilted his head. Perhaps he'd ignore his companion's error in judgement.

"My father said the knight you faced is an envoy of Efaltis—the world below ours," Fynnian said. "He's manipulating Ankarth for the sake of his master."

Efaltis. So that is its true name, Zercien thought, and raised his fist to his chin. The stories that told of such a world were true.

"An envoy of the world below ours?" he said under his breath, while Euvard just sat with his mouth agape. "The people of Ankarth are his pawns, then. But what could he want from Entervia?"

"Even my father did not know. But..." Fynnian breathed deep. "He bestowed this upon me."

Fynnian drew the Sanctus Right Half from its sheath, and Zercien and Euvard stared at the aura of pure light reflecting in the early morning sun.

"Fynnian, that's..." Zercien started, but his voice trailed off.

Staring at its benevolence, Fynnian explained the sword of divine light. "The Right Half of the Sanctus Dual Blades. Only those of the Sanctum Order bloodline may remove it from its sheath."

Euvard continued to stare. "Now *that's* a pretty sword."

"It is, but in my hands, the light is faint. Perhaps one day, I—" Again, Fynnian shook off his rambling and sheathed the holy blade. "Zercien. I know you probably want to wait for Ardian, but somehow this is even more dire than we all thought."

Euvard nodded. "Not that I want to, but I agree."

"You're both right. We need to enter Ciprius as fast as we can," Zercien said, and bit his chapped lip. "Ardian wears official Entervian attire. Perhaps he'll be allowed entrance."

The three approached the horses, and Fynnian sat on the back of Zercien's.

"Lloyd?" called Zercien, looking for the swordsman, but he was already far ahead, well on his way to Ciprius.

The three began their ride—a casual trot through the grassy plains—carrying on in stalwart silence. Over a hill, Zercien saw the towering Castle Ciprius breaching into the bright blue skies, and the bustling city in front, the same gathering of people entering and exiting the city. They each carried shovels, hammers, saws, all manner of tools. He thought it odd, but breathed a heavy sigh and stared, his heart jumping to his throat.

At long last, through all the hardships they'd faced, he had successfully led them to Ciprius.

Zercien halted his group some feet from the entrance—a towering wrought iron gate. All around him knelt workers with shovels clearing dirt and rocks.

Two guards stood on either side of the gate, alternating stares between Zercien's group and the workers.

"Well, here we are," Zercien said, and Fynnian peered out from over his shoulder. Euvard rode up next to them, stopped his horse and looked at Zercien.

"Just one more thing left to do, huh?" he said.

The three dismounted and approached the guards on duty. Lloyd joined the group, standing behind Fynnian. How he outran the two horses, Zercien didn't want to waste the energy attempting to guess.

"Who the hell are you? What are you doing here?" the left guard barked.

"Erm, uh," Zercien stammered.

Not a particularly warm welcome from an ally, he thought.

"Greetings," he then said, and cleared his throat. "My name is Zercien, and we are from Entervia."

"Entervia, eh?" the right guard said. "What're you here for?"

"We are on business for King Durnan."

"Sure you are. We can't let you through. Buzz off." The guard shooed him away.

Euvard gave Zercien a side-eye, mouthing "What the hell?"

Instead, Zercien took the Entervian Coat of Arms and King Durnan's letter from his garb and showed them to the guards.

"Humph. From Durnan himself? Fine. You have legitimacy to be here," the left guard grumbled, and returned Zercien's possessions. "You may pass, but know the mighty city of Ciprius is now under martial law, as declared by His Majesty, King Lennard. Any commotion and you'll be jailed, no matter what your paper says."

Zercien's eyes widened, as did Euvard's and Fynnian's. "Martial law? Has something happened?"

"Move along, sirs."

Zercien shrugged and went to walk past, but before leaving, asked, "Have you seen another Entervian around here?"

"No." Was the flat answer.

Despite looking like Vellard in structure, the city reeked of sweat, metal, and stone, and a constant ringing of hammer to rock never left Zercien's eardrums. Lines of soldiers in heavy armor, carrying longswords, halberds, and lances patrolled the streets, each eyeing Zercien with piercing looks, as if they knew he was foreign.

"Are you slacking off on my watch?" Zercien overheard one soldier yell at a laborer.

"I was taking a break."

The guard smacked him with his sword's sheath, drawing blood. "Tire on your own time, not King Lennard's!"

"Yes, sir." A voice of defeat.

Zercien shuddered, but his thoughts were interrupted by a woman clothed in rags, holding a child in her arms. "Please, humble sirs, can you spare some coin?"

Zercien looked at Euvard, and his friend just shrugged.

"I'd be happy to give you a bit of gold," Zercien said to her. "But, between us, we're outsiders to Ciprius. In return for gold, tell us what's happened here."

She beckoned for his group to come closer, keeping an eye on Zercien's coin purse. "King Lennard's declared martial law. We didn't argue. He's always been good to us, so we trusted he was right. But our once-wonderful king has become a devil. He's got every able-bodied person digging this moat in front of the city, all day, every day, with no pay. My poor husband, he works at the moat now. We have no money."

Why Ciprius, a coastal city, would have need for a moat, Zercien couldn't quite grasp.

"For what purpose is this moat?" Fynnian asked.

"Well, what do moats do? Keep people in, and others out! You're lucky you came when you did."

"Sounds like this king's fixing to keep his city secluded," Euvard said.

A patrol of soldiers walked by, and the woman darted her head around. "We've talked enough. You should go."

Zercien handed the woman six coins and they bid their farewells. When she walked away, Euvard said, "Not exactly how I envisioned our grand entrance."

"It might be the last thing I wanted to hear," said Zercien. "But the mission remains unchanged. We meet with King Lennard."

A deep sigh escaped his lips. What once was a sure success had soured all in a manner of minutes. The brief elation he felt upon reaching Ciprius had all but faded.

Through the city they walked, past lines of guards and soldiers keeping watch on everything and everyone that moved. Zercien followed the stone road to the castle entrance, and the stretch leading up was teeming with Arigliothan authority. Before approaching, he was stopped by two guards straightening their lances to block the path.

"Halt! You dare trespass upon the great castle of Ciprius?"

"Sir, I mean no offense," Zercien said, surprising even himself in his formality, while bowing. "We are messengers from Entervia and come seeking counsel with King Lennard."

Before being asked, he took King Durnan's letter and Entervia's Coat of Arms from his pocket and handed them to the guard. He thrust the items back into Zercien's hands without looking down.

"His Majesty King Lennard is not accepting meetings for the remainder of the day. We ask you return tomorrow."

"We came all the way from Vellard for this!" Euvard said over Zercien's head. "Can't you just—"

"I don't care where you came from! Get out of my sight."

Zercien motioned for Euvard to be silent and thanked the guard for his time. Without an answer, he led Euvard, Fynnian, and Lloyd back into the bustling center of Ciprius, away from the castle.

Damn it… his mind cursed their misfortune. Or perhaps it was fortuitous they now had a night to prepare.

"All we have left to do is find an inn," Zercien said.

"I don't like it, but you're right," Euvard said.

"Hmph," Lloyd muttered. As usual, he had nothing constructive to say.

Scattered about the market were merchants working stalls. Some with trinkets and toys, others with rings and earrings so cheap looking it would take skill to purposely craft. But none with any customers. Nothing like the Vellardian market.

Must be some of the only people not sent to the moat, Zercien thought.

The merchants paced about, speaking to each other, waving cloths and rags in front of their faces to keep cool.

Zercien saw an inn on the left—loud voices, clanking mugs, and annoying drunken shouts pierced through the wooden door and into his ears.

"Go on ahead," Euvard said. He was already halfway to one of the stalls by the time Zercien looked back. "I'll see you inside."

Zercien called after Euvard, but his friend disappeared into the market. He and Fynnian shared a shrug.

Nonetheless, he led his two remaining companions into the rowdy inn, with every seat taken by off-duty soldiers and guards drinking, shouting, laughing, some even climbing onto tables. As he squeezed through the sweaty, drunken masses to the front, Zercien stepped carefully over shards of broken mugs and spilled drinks.

"Oh, thank god," the barkeep said as he approached, and took a cloth to her brow to wipe the sweat. "An actual paying customer?"

"Is that so strange?" Zercien said, accompanied by a furrowed brow, though he had to lean in to hear her over the inebriated guards' buzzing, obnoxious voices.

"Damn guards come in here whenever they want. Drink and eat anything they can get their hands on. Without paying, of course."

"Martial law allows them to do this?" Fynnian piped up.

"No, but who am I to tell a person with a sword pointed at my throat that they need to pay for a drink?" She took Zercien's gold. "Your room's upstairs and to the left. Not the nicest place, but beats the streets."

The noisiness of the bar below dimmed to a low hum beneath the floorboards as Zercien traipsed the battered steps, hands gliding over the ripped wooden railings. Torn wallpaper lined the halls, and carpet stained by stray mead covered the floor. Five small beds with filthy sheets and pillowcases sat against the back. All much too close together for comfort.

Zercien sat on the edge of the right-most edge. He rustled against the cloth—hardly any softness sat between his back and the bedframe's wood. Easily the worst bed he'd ever sat on.

"I question if we should still wait for Ardian," Zercien said to no one in particular.

Lloyd groaned. "We cannot waste more time. We are here, he is not. There is no telling what opportunities we shall miss should we wait."

Not only did Lloyd *speak*, he actually offered advice? A foreign concept to Zercien. "I understand. It's—"

"You have been chosen to lead. You cannot hesitate in your judgment."

A twinge. A light poke on his shoulder, though no one touched him. Was it unease? Guilt? He knew Lloyd was right, but perhaps he would have welcomed a headache if it meant a decision. Unfortunately, those were no longer a crutch in his times of need.

The bangs of heavy footsteps punched at the back of his head. Accompanied by a heavy sigh, Euvard entered. "Ridiculous down there, huh? Did I miss anything?"

"Where did you disappear to in such a hurry?" Fynnian asked.

"I felt bad for those people down at the market. Wanted to at least give them the time of day." Euvard scratched his ear. "I didn't buy anything, nope, I didn't. Just browsed a bit. Made them happier at least."

"I sometimes forget your inability to tell a believable lie," Zercien said. He did know from experience.

"Fine."

Euvard reached into his cloak and unfolded a long piece of cloth with the Arigliothan Coat of Arms stitched on it. Unlike Entervia's, Ariglioth's Coat of Arms was a plain square design with a fist bearing spiked knuckles. To them, strength was simple, and their crest depicted it so.

"One of the merchants convinced me to buy this thing. Looks like a placemat. Real cheap work."

Zercien raised an eyebrow but didn't question further—he had more pressing matters to ponder.

"Never mind. I've come to a decision. Although I would like to, we cannot afford to wait for Ardian." His stomach dropped as the words rang about in his ears. "First thing tomorrow, we visit the castle, whether Ardian has arrived or not."

"Whatever you decide, I'm with you," Euvard said, but then gulped. "Tomorrow it is, then."

And they spent the rest of the day and into the night speaking of how they'd talk to a king, proper etiquette, and the like.

**

When nightfall came, Fynnian noticed Lloyd remained with them and even chose a bed.

"Lloyd?" Fynnian said as he sat on the edge of the one next to the swordsman.

"Why do you disturb me?" Lloyd didn't bother turning around.

"It's not usual for you to spend your nights, well, sleeping."

An awkward pause.

"Training here is problematic," the swordsman said.

"Why?"

"If the guard were to see me swinging a blade, they would attack en masse."

Fynnian raised an eyebrow and hesitated, attempting to mouth a response. "And it is unwise to take on so many—"

"No. I speak of how counterproductive it would be to kill those we wish to sway to our cause." Lloyd then sat up, turning to face Fynnian, making him recoil. "You have a new sword.

Amid a gulp, Fynnian's mind swirled. "Yes. My father—"

"Show it to me."

Fynnian unsheathed the Sanctus Right Half, its dim, but pure light shining about the darkened room. Lloyd fixated on the gem-studded hilt, staring for what Fynnian felt like hours. Without blinking, the swordsman's gaze wandered from tip to hilt.

"A fine sword. Now, leave me be."

And Fynnian sheathed the sword, bothering Lloyd no more, though watched as the swordsman gazed blankly at the dirty ceiling.

CHAPTER FORTY-NINE
THE KING'S JUDGMENT

K ing Durnan sat at his round table, eyeing the rest of the Ruling Council while muffled shouts and the crashing of stones upon the castle's walls rang into their eardrums.

"The Council has come to a decision, Your Majesty," Council Member Dallonta said. "We implore you. Do not yield to their demands."

King Durnan tilted his head toward the doors leading to the balcony. But he shuddered as a series of small rumbles rang about the room, the sounds of tumbling dirt and rocks sliding down the outer wall. However, it wasn't Ankarth or Duspen awaiting him on the other side. Today, he faced his own citizens, clamoring about the castle grounds, demanding answers.

With a deep sigh, King Durnan turned his gaze back to his advisors. "If this council is to be believed, then I should either lie or simply let them tire themselves out?"

"They will cease eventually, Your Majesty," said Council Member Leeland. "The people will panic if made aware of General Burgland's death."

Leeland had a point. The ruckus endured for hours. They would return to their homes by dark. But King Durnan knew this wasn't how he wanted to rule. Not how he would want to be remembered.

Over and over again, incessant shouts of how he should ignore his subjects interrupted his thoughts. He scratched at the sides of his head, at the hairs that, since the war's onset, had turned far more grey.

The voices of his Ruling Council and the citizenry outside soon melded together, and all King Durnan could muster was to put his hand against his forehead and massage his temple. Soon, the shouts attacked his eardrums in a cacophony of piercing shrieks.

He slammed his fist onto the table, silencing all save the stifled noises from outside. "Vellard's citizens will be told of what has occurred."

"This is an outrage, Your Majesty!" "My king, please reconsider!" "King Durnan, this is ludicrous!" were the barks from his council.

"I'm not a mere figurehead," King Durnan said as he pushed his chair out and stood. "And I am not here to serve just you." He pointed to each council member individually. No more words of protest.

Before the Ruling Council shook off their stunned state, King Durnan flung the doors to the balcony open, stepped outside and raised his right hand. The shouts from below thinned and dissipated, leaving behind stray coughs.

While anger seemed the cause from behind closed doors, King Durnan at last saw the truth. Amid his scanning of Vellardians standing before the castle, their arms lowered.

Powerless. I cannot say I feel different than they, King Durnan thought, and cleared his throat. His voice boomed over the crowd.

"Citizens of Entervia. I understand your anger. If I were fed half-truths for as long as you all have, I too would take to the streets in rage."

In the back of his mind, all he could think of was how cross his Ruling Council would be. Though he rather the bunch of stuffed up nobles be angry than his subjects.

"Since this war began, I have failed in my duty as your monarch," he said to the crowd. "From this moment forward, I vow to no longer harbor secrets. I will now detail the occurrences in Ankarth, and the truth of the war that plagues our beloved country."

Nary a throat clear or whisper pierced the all-consuming silence. Even the very wind stood still.

"The great General Burgland has fallen. Defeated in combat by the Ankarthan commander." King Durnan shuddered at his own words, and murmurs and gasps leapt from the crowd to his balcony. The general's popularity exceeded even what King Durnan assumed of his reputation. "The effects of his loss have rippled through our ranks, and even now, Grandmaster General Urian takes to the front lines in his stead. But even still—"

A light breeze bristled through his hair. Not ordinarily cold enough to force a shiver, but King Durnan rubbed his now-shaking hands together for warmth. "While our defenses remain stalwart, the enemy grows stronger and draws nearer with each passing day. Ankarth's might is nothing we could have predicted."

More gasps. Voices grew louder from below. King Durnan raised his hand to attempt some modicum of silence.

"We've tasked a Vellardian messenger by the name of Zercien Volnaire to reach Ariglioth and request reinforcements. Her army is mighty, and we will need her strength as ours wanes. Our resources run thin, and time quickens. I ask you continue to pray for his success, for he and the Arigliothan reinforcements are our only hope."

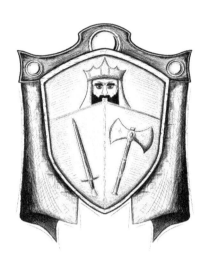

Chapter Fifty
The Valiant

A knock interrupted Mayla's late-night reading. She groaned, put the book down, and forced herself out of bed. Before reaching the stairs, the knock came again.

"This better be important," she muttered, and opened the door.

Outside stood Saena sporting an awkward smile, holding both her hands together at her chest. Mayla shook her head, smiling, and invited her in.

"Sorry I'm here late. I couldn't sleep," Saena said. She sat at the kitchen table. "I hope I'm not disturbing you."

"Come off it. You know me better than that!" Mayla said. "Can I get you something?"

"Oh, no. Well, maybe some water?"

Mayla stepped through her spotless—from lack of use, not thorough cleaning—kitchen.

"I don't think you walked all the way here to have a glass of water," Mayla said as she handed Saena the glass, but she could already guess.

"After King Durnan's speech today, do you not feel unwell?" Saena said. "I do."

Mayla cringed. The riots, protests, the people demanding answers from King Durnan. His words re-entered her mind. "General Burgland is dead. We're losing the war."

"Killed by the enemy general," Saena said. "The same man Zercien told me he faced." Just thinking about it sent a chill down Mayla's spine.

"They didn't spend much time together, but Zercien spoke highly of General Burgland. Of how he led his troops, carried himself. It's sad. Not just him, but all this death."

Mayla put a hand on Saena's shoulder and rubbed until her frown flipped. "Entervia's got way more fight in her than this. Don't lose hope, okay?"

A crash rocked the foundations of Mayla's home, silverware on the table jumping with the sound. The screams of Vellardian citizens from outside rang about. Saena dropped her glass and it shattered upon the floor.

Mayla ran to a window, Saena following behind. Flame burst into the skies, black smoke clogging the night. A rush of townspeople ran past, toward the fire.

Mayla turned to Saena and grabbed her hand. "Knives at the ready."

Saena lifted her long skirt's hem, revealing a set of throwing knives attached to her boot, just as Mayla had shown. With a somber smile, Mayla nodded.

Through the black smoke-ridden streets they ran, Mayla not letting go of Saena's hand. They were passed by hordes of Vellardian citizens, all in search of the same answers. As they neared the fire, the red-orange light illuminated the area around the northern gate, revealing a line of heavy armored guards forming a barrier to block Vellard's entrance. In front of them lay a man bloodied and bruised, leaning on his sword for balance. And standing over him was a tall, foreboding man encased in black armor with red streaks.

"Is that—" Saena said.

"We need to hide," Mayla said, and shot her gaze at some bushes and shrubbery. Tugging at Saena's arm, she urged her to follow. "This way. And keep your hands on your knives." And the two hid among the bushes, watching as everything unfolded.

"I must commend you for your bravery, Grandmaster General Urian," the Ankarthan commander said. "But your battle prowess is not deserving of the title 'Grandmaster.'"

His voice boomed so far that Mayla and Saena heard him, even over the crackling fire. The Grandmaster General couldn't even muster the strength to look him in his eerie eyes, and his breaths came hard and sporadic.

"What do you want?" He managed to spit out.

"Whatever my lord and master desires."

Like wind, a silhouette of a man with a sword blitzed by. Through the smoke, Mayla couldn't tell who.

She reached down to her leg, gripping one of her knives, and could do nothing as the Ankarthan commander raised his blade high above Grandmaster General Urian's head, and swung down.

But the knight's sword was met with the gasps of every soldier and the crashing of steel. Another man stood in front of the Grandmaster General, pushing the sword away with his own.

"King Durnan," the enemy commander said while pulling his blade back. "How unexpected."

Mayla grabbed Saena's arm and gasped. The two exchanged blank looks.

But King Durnan still stood with his sword out, chest rising from hard breaths. No crown to be seen, nor a regal robe, he donned leather armor with loose rings of chainmail, in the Entervian army's royal purple.

"You will never win. Not while I still stand," said their king.

"Convenient," said the Ankarthan commander.

King Durnan lowered his sword and cocked his head.

The enemy commander raised a hand into the air and a small ball of black energy formed, the flames below sending it aglow within the night sky.

"Your Majesty!" Grandmaster General Urian shouted, and jumped to his feet. "Protect King Durnan!"

The line of soldiers rushed forward, behind the Grandmaster General, but King Durnan pushed his general back. "No! Stay behind me!"

Before it could even reach King Durnan, the spell dissipated into the air with a splash resembling waves.

"It is as I thought," the Ankarthan commander said, no change in his tone, and lowered his hand. "This is why my master wishes for your death."

"Answer me this," said King Durnan. "If I am slain, will this war end?"

"Yes. There is more I must do, but your country need not fall."

"Do not listen to him, Your Majesty!" Grandmaster General Urian said. "The North cannot be trusted."

King Durnan tossed his sword to the side, striking the dead grass with a low hum that hardly carried over the crackling flame. "Shut up, Urian." And he stood with his arms outstretched, open palms facing the knight. "Then do it."

Grandmaster General Urian and his subordinates flew to their feet, but King Durnan silenced them with the raising of his right hand.

"You would willingly allow me to strike you down?" the Ankarthan commander said.

"To end my people's suffering, I will do whatever it takes," said King Durnan.

Drawing his sword, the knight raised it high and prepared to swing.

"Archers!" King Durnan then commanded and ducked and dove to the side. Dozens of archers hiding on the tops of buildings popped up and fired at will, scattering arrows over the field.

"Now!" Mayla said and jumped from the bushes, a throwing knife in hand. Saena joined her, stumbling as she stood, but too raised a knife. They joined in with the archers' volley, uncaring if they actually hit their target.

The knight was forced to hold his blade sideways to protect his head from fire, blocking arrows and one stray throwing knife.

He turned and retreated as arrows harmlessly clanked off his heavy armor. Once he'd withdrawn far enough away, Vellard's archers halted their assault, and King Durnan could stand.

"Your Majesty. That was incredibly reckless—" Grandmaster General Urian began to say.

"Focus on the battle, Urian," King Durnan said. "I imagine he'll bide his time before striking at us again, but he will. And when it comes, Vellard's defenses cannot be breached."

CHAPTER FIFTY-ONE
AN IMPROBABLE PHENOMENON

W
ho goes?" a guard yelled at the same spot in front of the castle as the day prior.

Zercien drew a deep breath amid his thundering heart and
spoke loud, clear, and powerful, as if in one of his trances. Even he was
surprised at his own tone. "I am Zercien of Entervia. We inquired yesterday about requesting counsel with His Majesty, King Lennard." He
unfurled King Durnan's missive.

The guard read the letter and his tone turned from harsh to somber.
"I will alert His Majesty of your arrival. He will relay a message stating
when he wishes to meet."

"Thank you, sir," Zercien said, and the guard retreated into Castle
Ciprius' mammoth doors.

The four paced about, and Zercien couldn't stop his legs from quivering, his breaths coming in erratic bursts. But footsteps approached,
and he turned to see the same guard returning, his face red.

The guard's breaths came in rapid spurts. "His Majesty, King
Lennard, has requested you see him now."

"Are you certain? We need no appointment?" Zercien said.

"No." An uneasy gulp followed. "Please do not keep His Majesty
waiting."

With a quick nod, Zercien led his group through the entry gates and approached the doors leading into the castle. Entervia's sister country may not have been as wealthy, but her castle was far superior—turrets, towers, and battlements jetted into the sky, high above where they stood, all armed with ballistae. Not one stone out of place. Every window shimmered in the sunlight.

The two guards out front bowed and pushed the heavy doors open, creaking with each inch. But before Zercien could step inside the dimly lit castle, one guard put a hand in front to stop him.

"You are armed. Surrender your weapons to us. All of you. When your meeting is through, we shall return them."

Zercien handed over his sword and watched as Euvard took his battle-axe from over his back, while Fynnian hesitated, but eventually surrendered the still-sheathed Sanctum Order armament.

Lloyd was the last person who would ever comply to such a thing. Or so Zercien thought. Instead, the swordsman passed his sword to another guard. He didn't even have his dagger attached to his belt.

Another guard bade them entry and led them inside the immense Castle Ciprius. The entryway was offset by two colossal stone pillars, holding the weight of the castle on their backs. Zercien's steps felt light, as if he walked on air, the muffles of everyone's boots faint in his eardrums. Upon entering the throne room, he and his companions walked on red fabric carpets, trimmed with gold, up a set of stairs leading to King Lennard's throne. The walls were decorated with paintings as large as humans, all portraits of Ariglioth's past kings.

The stairs ended, and the throne stood straight ahead with King Lennard sitting on it, wearing a majestic red robe.

He leaned back and to the right, with his elbow resting atop one of the throne's arms and his right hand clenched into a fist against his chin. His other hand drummed his fingers along the left arm. A long, golden lance with a bladed edge rested against the side.

King Lennard flared his nostrils as Zercien approached.

Zercien beckoned his companions to take a knee, and they all did— save Lloyd. Euvard tapped Lloyd on the shoulder as if to wake him up, but he didn't budge.

"Lloyd!" he whispered near-inaudibly, but to no avail.

His Majesty spoke, and a powerful, deep voice boomed and echoed throughout the throne room. "You must be Sir Zercien and company. You are seeking counsel, and I shall grant that favor."

Zercien cleared his throat. The soft and gentle King Lennard—he and the man sitting on the throne ahead could not have been the same. "Yes, Your Majesty."

King Lennard sat up. "And why does *he* not kneel before his superior?"

Lloyd's expression was unchanged. "None deserve the bend of the knee."

Zercien stuttered, but croaked out, "Your Majesty, I apologize—"

"Silence! Your apologies do nothing. Do not waste my time any further. Tell me why you are here before me today,"

Zercien fumbled with his words, mumbling out a slow, "Your Highness, today I—"

"Speak, now!"

"Your Majesty, we are here to request reinforcements. Entervia has been invaded by Ankarth, and we cannot survive alone. We require the assistance of Ariglioth's army."

The words leaving his mouth should have brought forth relief. Like a heavy burden set down onto the floor. But no such comfort awaited Zercien. The continued drumming of King Lennard's fingertips blasted like a hammer into his mind.

"If I see proof, I shall give consideration," the king said.

Zercien handed a nearby guard his letter, and with tepid steps, was brought to the throne.

"I see. King Durnan requests *my* aid," King Lennard said as he stared down at it for a few seconds. His expression remained stoic, unwavering.

And Zercien gasped as he watched the king rip the scroll horizontally, and then again vertically. Repeating his motions, slow and deliberate, until King Durnan's letter became shreds of parchment floating to the floor like raindrops.

Zercien's world stopped. His body ceased movement. No muscle would budge, no words could flow. He put a hand to his chest to ensure his heart still beat.

"Your Majesty! Why?" Euvard shouted, and Zercien shoved his hand in front of his friend's face. But far too late, as the enraged king took hold of his mighty golden lance.

"Silence, boy!" said King Lennard, straightening his back on his throne. "Why should I send my aid to *Entervia*?"

"We, Entervia and Ariglioth, are allies, Your Majesty," Fynnian said.

"I will grant you that, yes. And I am aware of the situation in Entervia."

How? Zercien's mind cried out before he blurted a response.

"Then why have you done nothing? And why do you deny us still?"

King Lennard stood up from his throne, and slammed the lance's gold sauroter onto the hard floor. The crash alerted all guards within earshot, and they flocked to the throne room in a furious stampede of footsteps.

"What has Entervia done for Ariglioth?" King Lennard said. "My people, they suffer in poverty. All while King Durnan sits atop his perch. I implore you to tell me one reason why I should send aid to a country so hellbent on ignoring its allies."

"Your reasons are well-founded, and yet, you force those same impoverished citizens to slave away for your ridiculous moat," Zercien said, a chill thundering up his spine at the words.

What am I doing? Arguing with a king? he thought, but then shook his head. *We've nothing more to lose.*

"I am protecting my people!" King Lennard boomed back, a fire rising to his cheeks that Zercien feared would spew from his mouth.

Pained gulps and mumbles bubbled from Zercien in return.

"Insolents, the lot of you," the king said. "Guards! To me! When I'm through, they are to be beheaded."

"*Beheaded*?" Euvard shouted. "Your Majesty—"

"Silence!"

King Lennard's guards gathered near the throne, and the king himself sauntered toward Zercien and company. His lance clanked about the floor, echoing with each step. His wrinkled face centered on Lloyd.

"You," came King Lennard's snarl as he neared the swordsman. "The one who would not bow to me."

Zercien watched as Lloyd's hand moved toward his sleeve.

King Lennard raised his lance and readied it to strike, the tip not five finger-lengths from Lloyd's face. "Perhaps I'll kill you myself."

Lloyd then reached into his sleeve and pulled forth his dagger. With one lunge, its serrated edge was buried deep into King Lennard's treacherous heart.

The king's eyes bulged as he fell backward, knife embedded into his chest. Blood pooled and dripped from around the edges of the dagger onto the floor, and his magnificent golden lance crashed and echoed throughout the silent hall.

Zercien stood mouth agape, his time slowing. The king of Ariglioth lay slain, his bloodied corpse upon the throne room's floor, and his guards stared with stupefied faces. But Lloyd's remained unwavering.

"After him!" yelled a guard.

Lloyd grabbed the approaching guard by his sword arm and yanked backward until it cracked. With a yell, the guard dropped his sword and Lloyd claimed it as his own.

"Leave," he said, and glanced back to Zercien. "You will certainly die in this place if you remain."

And the rest of the guards were on Lloyd, brandishing swords, lances, and halberds.

"*Fuck*," Zercien muttered. The clash of Lloyd's newfound sword clouded his thoughts. Screams of the slain guards pierced into his mind like one of his headaches.

All he could concentrate on was an unmanned staircase to the right, and he beckoned Euvard and Fynnian to follow. With the guards distracted, the three bolted toward the stairs and descended the dimly lit steps.

Rats scurried by as Zercien ran through cobwebs and other waste—he cared not to see what it was. Once he was sure they were not being followed, Zercien grabbed one of the standing candles from against the stone wall and slowed their pace to a walk. The only sounds were the faint echoes of clashing steel from above, seeping through the floor.

"A dungeon?" Euvard whispered as they passed a row of empty, dark jail cells. Zercien's heart thumped too loudly to articulate an answer, and his mind cursed over and over.

As far as he could tell, the dungeon was devoid of any guards or prisoners. From how dirty it was, it seemed scarcely used. Odd, considering how King Lennard behaved, he thought. But he found any sort of coherent reasoning difficult.

He wandered aimlessly through the halls, footsteps mixing with the clanging of swords.

"Zerc, what do we do?" Euvard asked, his voice hoarse and coated in tar.

"I—we can't leave Lloyd alone," Fynnian said with a gulp. "We find any sort of weaponry, and we help him escape."

I don't know. God, Zercien thought. *I don't know.*

He cursed at himself for making a deal with the bloodred-robed man. With Holunt at his side, he employed an extra guide. A master strategist and combatant. And he threw it away.

He shined his candle down a near-pitch black hallway, looking even less traveled than the other parts of the dungeon. "We hide here and formulate a plan."

To his surprise, the hall continued, and the cells dwindled until he was met with just a bare wall. But he cocked his head at a slightly ajar brick, noticeably out of place.

He reached a hand toward it but pulled away. Probably nothing. He shrugged.

I'll take anything right now, he thought.

As soon as Zercien touched the brick, it pushed into the wall and settled in with a satisfying *click* that echoed throughout. He jumped back with a gasp just as loud as the noise.

"What in—what was that?" Fynnian whispered.

The wall of bricks fell, revealing an entrance to another room. And from it came a stench reeking of blood.

"What the hell?" Euvard groaned and held his nose.

The light of Zercien's candle revealed a dark red puddle upon the floor, leading to a back wall. Leaning against the stone was the darkened outline of a corpse draped in a regal red robe.

"It can't be. That doesn't make sense," Euvard mumbled. "This doesn't make any damn sense."

Zercien's mouth dropped. "King Lennard?"

Impossible, he thought. King Lennard had died mere minutes ago. But the corpse's face resembled the man they had just spoken to—the late king of Ariglioth.

"No one could have moved his body down here. It's impossible," Euvard said. "Unless there's some other entrance."

Zercien tip-toed around the blood pool and bent down, holding his candle over the body.

"Stab wound right through the heart," he said. With his other hand, he pointed at the blood that still leaked. "The gash. It's fresh."

"Did either of you see his body when we ran?" Fynnian said as he knelt next to Zercien. Not that he was *looking* for it, but Zercien couldn't recall.

The omnipresent echo of steel above their heads then abruptly silenced, followed by a victorious shout. Zercien didn't think his stomach could drop any further, but he felt it in his legs. He wobbled his way back through the secret entrance, staring blankly into the black dungeon ceiling.

"I didn't think it was possible," Euvard said, and bowed his head.

"Wait! No." Fynnian's hair ruffled as he shook his head. A gentle tear dripped down his cheek. "We need to go back. We're not leaving him."

Zercien's head drooped, and he clenched his fist. "We can't waste Lloyd's sacrifice."

They came to another set of stairs leading up into a well-lit room— Zercien surmised it to be another exit. He looked around carefully as they ascended and saw no guards. To his left, the castle gate, also bereft of lookouts.

Zercien nodded and beckoned Euvard and Fynnian to follow. Once past the gate, they came across the pile of their missing weapons, including Lloyd's sword, lying in a mess where they had surrendered them.

He gestured Euvard and Fynnian to hurry ahead, through Castle Ciprius' front gates, his mind shouting incessantly.

We've failed. I've failed.

Chapter Fifty-Two
Grim Ingenuity

Ariglioth did not send aid.

The mighty swordsman Lloyd, dead at the hands of the Ciprius guards.

Ardian's whereabouts, still unknown.

The three dashed through Ciprius, and a few citizens shot them strange looks, but mostly were ignored. Zercien pushed through the gate guards, and upon leaving the city, found their steeds just outside. Without speaking, the three mounted the horses. Fynnian sat behind Zercien.

Zercien looked back one last time as his horse trotted, a gaping hole forming in the pit of his stomach.

"We're really leaving," Euvard said, as solemn as Zercien had ever heard him. He turned and faced the road.

"Unless one of you has a better plan," Zercien said, "we begin our journey back to Vellard." The words stung his tongue as they left his mouth, and his companions' silence spoke all he needed to know.

"How do we return?" Fynnian's voice carried over Zercien's back and to his ears. "The same route seems illogical."

"Shit," Zercien muttered under his breath. He hadn't quite thought it through. Under the assumption they'd have the Arigliothan army in tow and could travel wherever, he didn't plan a return route.

We could pass through the desert instead of the forest. But another trek underneath the Okoro, Zercien thought, ideas swirling about his head. *And even with the Matriarch dead, there were many halls and rooms we avoided. Could we risk losing our way?*

With the fearsome city of Ciprius all but a shadow in the midday sun, Zercien stopped and motioned for his companions to join him in dismounting. He unfurled his worn and tattered map of Dregnal over a nearby tree stump. While both Euvard and Fynnian looked over his shoulder, Zercien traced possible routes with his index finger, but continually coming to dead-ends with furious pokes.

He hovered over the Duspen border, and gasped.

Duspen, he thought. *That's it.*

"We will not risk the forest or the caves."

Euvard raised an eyebrow. "Do you plan on swimming?"

Zercien tapped the tattered map below Ferronwood Forest and the Okoro Mountains. "Here. The most efficient route is through the desert outskirts, avoiding the forest. And instead of passing through the Okoro, we continue south—"

"You do realize that's *the* South you're pointing at?" Euvard interrupted. "Might fare better with the forest folk than those barbarians. Then again, the Spiritual Leader all but said she'd have our heads if we came back. Why not go toward Reland?" Euvard pressed the town name with his finger.

Zercien shook his head. "We're fugitives. No town in Ariglioth is safe for us."

"Fine," Euvard said, accompanying a sigh. "But is going to Duspen—for a second time, I might add—still safer?"

A small smirk spread to Zercien's lips, but only for a moment. "Still have the placemat?"

"It's right here, but Zerc, are you feeling all right?" He took it from the rest of his belongings.

"Here." Zercien beckoned and yanked it from his friend's hands. Removing his still-sheathed sword from his belt, he wrapped the edges and tied the table mat tight around. Euvard and Fynnian furrowed their brows at each other, Euvard whispering that Zercien had lost his mind.

No. Maybe I've finally found it, Zercien thought.

He raised his creation into the air, the placemat catching the light breeze like a sail, waving Ariglioth's Coat of Arms high into the sky.

Two hard slaps fell onto his shoulder.

"You rigged us a makeshift banner," Euvard said.

"Duspen fears Ariglioth. If we wave this while in their lands, we'll have nothing to fear from Arvaros. They'll think we're part of the Arigliothan army or on patrol," Zercien said. "And this route is far shorter. If we ride into the night, and these horses are as strong as the forest folk claim, we'll be in Vellard in far less time than it took to reach here."

Zercien shuddered at his own mention of the Arigliothan army.

The feel-good breeze of positive news, for once, was short-lived and soon all their smiles faded. Zercien and his companions mounted once again, and he raised their "banner" high as he urged his horse South, toward Duspen.

And however confident he was in his plan, the fires of shame burned from within. How would he tell King Durnan? Saena?

He had fantasized of an extravagant return journey, him and his companions leading the charge back into Vellard, with the Arigliothan army at his back. But such a dream was now forever dead, slain amid the walls of Castle Ciprius.

CHAPTER FIFTY-THREE
A GOLDEN OPPORTUNITY

The boil-faced man groaned, rubbing his cold hand over the spot on his chest where he'd been stabbed by the miscreant. Another boil pushed itself through his pores, below his nose.

His lance lay beside him, alongside a dozen guard and soldier corpses, sprawled about in the dark, shadows of dim candlelight flickering about their pale faces.

By the state of the corpses, he surmised he'd been dead for one night, maybe two. He questioned why the bodies of those slain in the battle still lingered, having not been disposed of. Though he wasn't complaining about an easy recovery, he scoffed at the Arigliothan soldiers' reputation of fearlessness.

It made sense—train to never lose, and you shall never face the death you fear most.

The boil-faced man choked out a laugh and stood, reaching for his lance, but froze when voices echoed into the throne room. Instead, he threw one of the dead guards' cloaks over the lance.

He drew his knife from his dingy attire and stabbed through one of the dead Arigliothan guards' backs, releasing a slow drip of blood. Slurping, he lapped up his disgusting, unappetizing snack out of necessity.

Footsteps from the hall echoed. The boil-faced man looked back, the dead man's blood dripping from his lips. No time. This would have to do. He stood, imagining the attire of the Arigliothan guard, and snarled.

His face smoothed, hair turning a light blonde, color returning to his cheeks, and soon the garb of the Arigliothan guard replaced his drab robes. He admired his biceps as the muscle sculpted and stretched.

He licked his lips. A strong one, at last. Not like the weak, kingly body. He considered keeping this guise for quite some time.

The footsteps neared and he gasped and turned around to see two Arigliothan guards entering the throne room.

"I'm sorry," one of them said. "Didn't mean to startle you—wait!" The guard put a hand to his chin. "Tomas? Is it truly you?"

"Tomas" gulped. "Yes, it is I! Tomas." The boil-faced man smiled.

The other guard put her hand on his chest, feeling up and down, as if determining for herself he really lived. With each touch, Tomas shuddered.

"We were told you died in the attack," she said, and retracted her hand.

Tomas' hairs on the back of his neck stood on end. He shrugged it off and smiled, twirling around, arms out. "Seems you were misinformed."

When his twirl turned backwards, he saw the *real* Tomas' pale, drained face staring up at him. He spun back around and backed up a step to ensure none could see behind. "Though I did suffer a wound. I was incapacitated for a spell."

Silence. He stood a moment, smile still spread across his face, though sweat bubbled on his forehead.

"Well, we are glad you survived," said the male guard, returning his smile. Both gripped Tomas' hand in a firm shake. He tried to hide his cringe but failed.

"But what are you doing here?" the guard said. "His Majesty deemed this place off-limits, and sent us to aid in the disposal of the bodies—"

His voice trailed off as he looked around the room. "Including the late King Lennard's. Where is the body?"

A new king, crowned already? How curious this situation grew to be.

"Were you not aware?" Tomas said. "When I met with His Majesty myself, he requested me to do the same. Perhaps you were too slow."

The guards both blushed and winced, the woman running a hand through the strands of hair falling from her helmet. "Can you blame us? 'Tis a grisly task."

Tomas spat out a bit of his held breath. "Have no worry. As you can see, I have complied with His Majesty's task."

The male guard nodded, but still his gaze danced about the dim throne room. "Yes, but where did His Majesty request you to bring King Lennard's body, and that lance he possessed? I assume the proper royal funeral procession will be required."

"Ah, well, you see—" Tomas raised his index finger. "I was asked to dispose of the body unceremoniously. For the man he had become, His Majesty decreed that the late King Lennard is undeserving of our traditions. 'No festival for tyrants,' he said."

"I see," said the male guard, following a sigh. "While the reasoning makes sense, our new regent gives us all pause, too. We're now preparing for a trip to Entervia."

Tomas' ears perked. He knew nothing of this new king, but quite liked the idea of a spot of chaos.

"To Entervia, eh? What for?" he said.

"Those visitors spoke of requesting reinforcements, and His Majesty has obliged," said the female guard.

He snarled behind grit teeth. Annoying to have been jettisoned from his throne and replaced in such speed, but perhaps opportune. "When does the army mobilize?"

"Soon. Within the week."

"Would they accept a humble guard into their ranks?" Tomas hid his sly smile behind a closed fist. The two guards tilted their heads.

"Are you not hurt?" the female guard said.

"Fine as fine can be, I am!" Tomas smiled. "Now, move along. I've been tasked to complete the cleanup by morning."

Both guards bid their farewells and turned to leave, but the man said, "Will you tell His Majesty—"

Tomas winked. "I will say you aided me in the late hours."

The guard gripped Tomas' shoulder. "Always could count on you, Tomas."

When the excruciating pair's echoing footsteps grew light, Tomas let out a relieving groan. "Too close."

He stared down at the cloak covering his lance and put a hand to his chin. If he were to join the army, he wouldn't dare leave the lance here, and to take it with him unconcealed would rouse suspicion. Perhaps a bit of cloth wrapped about it would do the trick. He'd already masked its appearance once with the golden shine. What harm could come from a second disguise?

But the army, marching to Entervia. Oh, what a tantalizing thought. Though his ambitions of conquest were struck down quite early, perhaps following that little group of Entervians would prove fruitful. He smirked as he worked to pile the bodies and gather more of the real Tomas' blood.

Careful, now, he thought as he slipped more of the rotting blood into a jar. Always dangerous taking on the blood of the dead, but it was not yet the time to drink his own blood and revert to his normal self. Perhaps in secret, when the threat of being discovered passed by. For now, he'd take on the body of a dead man.

But if a sword were to find his neck in this form…

He shuddered at the thought of joining the pile of corpses—permanently.

CHAPTER FIFTY-FOUR
EVENTIDE

B lack smoke billowed from over the hill, the edge of its cloud lapping the top of the grass. A foul burning smell wafted into Zercien's nose while he eased his and Fynnian's steed to a steady trot. As they neared the top of the hill, the backs of a handful of people in torn clothing dotted the horizon, all facing the origination of the smoke and smell—a handmade pit.

"Don't like the looks of this, Zerc," Euvard said, low as he was able, bringing his horse alongside Zercien's.

Fynnian craned his neck over Zercien's head for a better vantage. "Just what are they doing, though?" He rubbed the spot on his chin where a bit of blonde stubble poked through.

"We're deep in bandit territory. Whatever it is, it won't be good." Euvard shook his head and pointed to the Arigliothan cloth hanging from a sword sheath. "No better time to use our improvised banner, I'd say."

Zercien motioned Euvard to retreat some paces down the hill, and eyed his ridiculous attempt at posing as Arigliothans. A placemat embroidered with the Ariglioth Coat of Arms, the edges of the emblem's fist tied to a sword sheath. Raising it high would prove their desired effect of scaring away anyone from Duspen, though the idea of tricking the uneducated folk seemed cruel. And while agreeing with Euvard appeared the logical solution, as of late, logic more often than not played the villain.

"Not a blade to be seen on any of them," Zercien said, pointing at each of the people's backs. "While they are of Duspen, perhaps they're not bandits. They may be in need of assistance."

Euvard raised both eyebrows. "Not sure if you've forgotten, but no one from the South has yet to show us, or anyone, any shred of mercy. Unarmed or not. And now you're wanting to *help* them?"

"After what's happened, I am in the business of helping *anyone*." Zercien slumped his shoulders. "And I would rather our return not be marred by bloodshed at every step."

Euvard clutched his axe with one hand; the other remaining on the horse's reins. "You're the leader." Zercien watched his friend's grip tighten so hard he feared the axe's handle would splinter.

"Thank you," Zercien said with a nod, and turned his neck to the side. "Fynnian?"

"Oh!" Fynnian gasped, as if not expecting a say in the matter. "Yes, I agree. If they can be helped, we should do so. Though to me, they don't appear to be in distress. Their posture suggests prayer."

"If that's what we're facing here, then I may take back my acceptance of your plan, Zerc," Euvard said, waving his hand. "I'm not about to interrupt a ceremony involving a fire pit."

Zercien watched as Fynnian's head drooped. Again, his hulking friend seemed to have the correct idea. But again, Zercien rejected it outright. With not a word, nor a shake of the head, he urged his horse to continue its trot.

Euvard's sigh flew into Zercien's ears, as did the casual walk of his horse's hooves. For the first time in long a while, a faint smile spread across Zercien's lips, though just for a moment.

A young girl in the center turned around at the horses' movement over the hill, and Zercien met her eyes. A deep, solemn brown. Her look suggested tears, but perhaps the heat of the flames in front dried them away.

Her clothes sat baggy over her tiny body, and the sides of her face held hardly more than cheekbones.

The rest of the Duspenese mimicked her movement, and blank stare. Their gazes held firm, causing Zercien's heartbeat to thump in unison with the crackling flames ahead. He moved a quivering hand to his makeshift banner, but stopped when the girl spoke. Her voice trembled, yet rose above the flame and smoke. "Arigliothans, we've no quarrel with you today."

At the mere mention of the country, the Duspenese surrounding her all gasped, looking as if they'd turn tail at any moment. Ardian proved correct—the people of Duspen truly did fear Ariglioth.

Zercien looked back at his companions. For what, he wasn't sure himself. He could grasp the banner and hold it high, command these destitute folk to bend the knee and obey his every command. And, to his confusion, a pang in his head told him to do so.

Instead, he answered the girl with his hand away from the banner. "And we have no quarrel with you, as well."

Zercien dismounted, and approached with hands raised. He craned his neck to the side and urged Euvard and Fynnian to follow.

The Duspenese released their tensed shoulders, but still looked upon the trio with fear.

Not bandits, Zercien thought. Just normal citizens of Duspen, of whom he had not met yet.

The girl went to move forward, but her crowd stood to block her path. With a nod, she convinced them to let her pass. "Then why has an Arigliothan patrol stopped to investigate us?"

"I apologize if that is what this seems," Zercien said. He winced at apologizing to this lot, a people that have caused so much heartache and suffering. "We are not here to investigate. We ask if you are in need of assistance."

The girl cracked a smile, and laughed out her words. "Assistance? Ariglioth will be providing us *assistance*? How rich."

Zercien looked back at his companions, and nodded. "Then we shall be on our way. Good day to you."

As he went to climb back onto his horse, a shaky "wait" forced him to stop. Turning around, the girl had closed the distance between them.

"It is my turn for apologies. We don't receive kindness from Arigliothan patrols. Normally, they wouldn't have approached us like you had. To Ariglioth, we are target practice." Her shudder, proceeded by a cold stare told Zercien this was no lie, and a bruise on her left arm showed a gory detail of Arigliothan ruthlessness.

"If you would like to learn of what we're doing here, then please, come with me," she said, and waved Zercien and his companions to follow.

Instead of moving, Zercien froze, his only movements hard gulps. The stench of flame, the ominous smoke. Everything before him looked to be an outright statement of danger, and any steps further could spell his end.

Euvard's giant hand clamped down on his arm, snapping him back to the present. "Zerc. My gut says she's telling the truth." A refreshing breeze, not hot nor cold, washed over his body, thawing his icy muscles. He thought so as well, but to hear Euvard say so was all he needed to push forward.

"This is how we honor the dead," the girl said as she led Zercien through the Duspenese circle. Their fearful stares continued to pierce him like javelins.

A funeral pyre, Zercien thought. A barbaric ritual, in his mind. Before stepping further, he cast his glance at the Duspenese, and none budged. While he did have a sword on his belt, Zercien knew if all these people swarmed him, he'd likely end up in the pit himself.

"You burn their bodies instead of burial," Zercien said.

"It's not quite so simple," said the girl, and motioned the three to look down into the pit. Its edges were rough, uneven, but perfect in its simplicity. Zercien flinched at the heat, at the smoke rising and drifting into his lungs. He hadn't a clue how this young girl, and the others, could stand here for so long. But perhaps such was commonplace.

Euvard joined him in peering over the ledge, but Fynnian's tepid steps kept him away far longer.

They saw nothing, save for flame. Whatever burned inside that pit was nothing more than ash and dust.

"We believe in the Eventide Progenitress," the girl said, her voice carrying over the crackling flames.

"Can't say I've heard of it," Euvard said, to which Zercien agreed. In his mind, it sounded akin to folklore.

"Neither have I," Fynnian said, gulping.

"They say your God is the father of the beginning," the girl said. "The Progenitress—she is the mother of the end. The creator of the final days."

Zercien couldn't face her. He focused on the flame. "And you worship such a deity?"

"Look around you," the girl said as she craned her neck, but each direction bore the same—ruined wooden homes, scattered debris, and barren plains. "We have nothing. And though Duspen has no churches or cathedrals, we believe in praying for the end, and for another chance after the last of all days."

"And hence is the reason for the fire," Zercien said. In a macabre sort of way, her line of reasoning made sense. "So your people may rise again from the ashes."

The girl chuckled. A scant few laughs from the other Duspenese as well. "No, not whatsoever. In death, the Progenitress' flames burn away all the deceased's demons, as well as ambitions. So they may carry no burden into the afterlife."

Despite the fire, Zercien shuddered. "When do you know to put out the flames?"

She shook her head. "We do not. We wait for the flames to fade, a rain to extinguish, or wind to blow them away. Signs from the Progenitress that the person's soul is cleansed, and free. Most are purified within hours."

Zercien said nothing, and stood mesmerized by the fire. The old stories spoke of fire as only destructive, an incantation cast by Pariah Arts masters to expel all who dare approach. Never as a means of restoring order, or to clean.

"What was their name?" Fynnian asked. "The person you honor today."

"Bold to ask the name of the deceased when you've not introduced yourselves," said the girl.

She's far too astute for her age, Zercien thought, but then nodded.

"I am Zercien of Ariglioth," Zercien said, ensuring to emphasize their Arigliothan guise, and pointed an open hand toward his allies. "These are my companions, Euvard and Fynnian."

"And you may call me Saoirse of Denon-Hein," the girl said with a bow. "The man you see below is Nolahn." She sniffled. "My father."

The fires below did nothing to quell the glacial spike throughout Zercien's spine. He glanced at Euvard and Fynnian, who too stood frozen.

"You have our condolences, Saoirse of Denon-Hein," Zercien said, though the words dripped with nerves.

"Thank you. Kindness was not something I expected when I saw your Coat of Arms." Her gaze fell back to the pyre. "Where is it you travel, Arigliothan?"

When Zercien said nothing, Euvard answered with "Entervia." Zercien stood to attention.

The girl huffed at the answer. "Filthy Entervians." She spat onto the barren ground. "No one can claim witness, but my father was found dead during one of his excursions. His body left to rot. Most assume he met an Entervian blade, but none know when."

All the blood drained from Zercien's face, and he grew pale. A screeching cold wind howled through his ears. "If I may ask, Saoirse, how long have his flames burned?"

She turned from the pyre, the red-orange glow illuminating her once dead and drained eyes. "Three days."

CHAPTER FIFTY-FIVE
CONFLAGRATION

Saena shoved her face against her bedroom window, the heat from the fires below carrying to its glass. In-between the hurried footsteps of both Entervian soldiers and citizens, shouts of "evacuate!" permeated through the crackling flame.

Only a scant few weeks had passed since King Durnan repelled the enemy commander's attack. But overnight, Ankarthan soldiers broke through the Entervian defense, overrunning the streets.

Saena dashed from her home with just the clothes she wore and a handful of throwing knives hidden on her person. An Entervian soldier waved and gestured her to run to his left.

"My lady! Make for the meeting house!" he shouted. "King Durnan is preparing the citizens for evacuation!"

The shadow of a jagged axe rose over the soldier's head from behind, and Saena shouted for his attention. But he was too slow in turning his lance. The axe came crashing down, hewing his head in two, sending severed flesh and chunks of his skull to scatter amid the flames.

A hand grabbed Saena's arm and tugged her away, into the cover of some shrubbery until the Ankarthan soldier escaped.

"Mayla!" Saena leaned her head against her friend's shoulder. Shaking, her breaths came in sporadic bursts.

"I'm with you, now. Okay?" Mayla grabbed Saena's hand again, peeked from their cover, and urged her to stand. "We'll reach the meeting house. Together."

Saena sniffled. "Where are they, Mayla? Where's Zercien and Euvard? Where's the army—"

"They'll be here soon. I know it. We have to hold on."

"I'm with you," Saena said, and breathed deep to suppress her fear.

The two leapt from the shrubs and ran into the heart of the city, that crawled with Ankarthan soldiers.

Saena followed Mayla's lead and pushed her back against a tree. Her throbbing heartbeat muffled the encroaching heavy footsteps of leather, battle worn boots. She pushed her arms against her ribcage as the footsteps stopped, breathing shaky spurts of air from her nose.

The steps began again, crushing the burnt grass, the sound lessening as the seconds crawled.

Saena looked to Mayla, who stood in a similar pose behind an adjacent tree. She peeked from behind the tree trunk, and nodded. Clear.

Into the once-beautiful Vellardian center they moved, the grass and rose gardens replaced with blazing fires and ash, and the central fountain smashed in two.

Saena couldn't fathom how her leader remained calm and composed. As arrows flung in the distance and the clash of swords echoed throughout her eardrums, Mayla's long and fearless strides flew across the burnt roads.

Skirmishes between roaming parties of Entervians and Ankarthans peppered the city streets, the two running lances and swords into one another. Mayla and Saena dove behind rubble to lay down and wait for the carnage to settle. Saena reached for a knife, but Mayla was quick to grab her arm and shake her head.

An arrow stuck into one Entervian soldier's back, and more Ankarthan fighters jumped from behind the flames of a burning house. The two forces merged as one, haphazard slashes and stabs tearing each other apart.

Mayla nodded to Saena, and the two were on their feet, running past amid the chaos, as the Vellardian soldiers were ripped apart by flurries of sword strikes. More guards valiantly charged to the slaughter, and civilians were cut down on their path to freedom. Both the corpses of common people and soldiers littered the city streets.

Saena followed Mayla around a corner, but stopped upon seeing her friend holding her hand up.

Two children, a boy and a girl who could not have been older than their fourth or fifth years, were backed against a stone wall with a raging fire above, stared down by a pair of Ankarthan soldiers. The children cried as the soldiers yelled in deep, guttural voices, "Tell us where your king is!"

Saena and Mayla watched in stupefied terror as the Ankarthans closed in on the children and unsheathed serrated swords.

"We should—" Saena whispered, but was interrupted by the *zip* of a throwing knife in the air. It found its way from Mayla's hand into the side of one of the Ankarthan soldiers. Mayla shouted and dashed ahead.

"What? Mayla!" Saena called after her.

She watched as her friend jumped between the two shivering children and the Ankarthans.

"Has the Ankarthan army stooped so low that they'll threaten children?" Mayla said.

A deep, echoing reply gurgled over the crackling flames.

"Then you show us to King Durnan," said the one with the knife sticking from his ribs. Without even a grimace, he yanked it free and tossed it aside. "We care not who does." Mayla reached under the hem of her skirt and drew forth another knife.

"Not on my life," Mayla said, and spun the throwing knife in her fingertips, catching the reflection of the blazing flames above.

One of the soldiers sauntered toward her and held his sword high. "If you show us to King Durnan, then—"

Mayla took the knife and shoved it deep into the soldier's jugular. Blood sprayed and stained the knife's handle as he choked and sputtered. When she ripped it out, the other soldier punched her hard on the side.

With a gasp, she fell to the dirt, clutching her hip. Now towering above her was his serrated sword.

Saena felt for one of her concealed knives, and wrapped her quivering fingertips about the handle. Envisioning the oak tree in front, she steadied her hand, rocked it to and fro, aiming as Mayla had taught her. With a shout, she flung the knife and watched it spin, the rotating sharp tip alternating with the handle.

It struck the Ankarthan soldier's helmet, bouncing off and clanking onto the ground. But the soldier stepped back, dazed, allowing Mayla the precious seconds she needed to leap to her feet and jab the knife into his chest. Black blood dribbled from the wound as she pulled it from the soldier's body, and the Ankarthan fell. Mayla stared at the pooling liquid, looking more like spilled ink than blood.

"Mayla! You okay?" Saena said, but too joined her friend in staring at the oozing blood. Too unnatural to be human blood, but Saena attributed it to a trick of the light. Mayla turned her head, her complexion a shade of white that reflected the shadows of bouncing flame. But she soon shook it off and winced in an attempt to hug Saena, holding her ailing side.

"You saved my life," Mayla said.

Saena's cheeks flushed red. "Only because you taught me well."

Saena cringed at her own words and repeated alternate ways of stating it over and over in her head.

The children's cries turned the two's attention. Mayla bent to one knee but groaned as she ran a hand through the little boy's hair. "It'll all be okay. We'll get you two out of here."

"I want Mother!" the little boy cried.

"Just come with us, all right? We'll take you back. Where do you think she is?"

"I don't know! Father tried to save us, but then he fell and couldn't move anymore. Then we ran away and lost Mother."

Saena's stomach dropped, and her head drooped with it.

Mayla picked up the little boy and held the brunt of his weight against her chest. She uttered a pained grunt as she stood. "We're taking them to the meeting house with us. Can you get his sister?"

Saena nodded and gestured the little girl to take her hands. With all her strength, she pulled the girl up, leaning her on her shoulder. Mayla grunted as she stepped forward, teeth grit.

"Are you sure you can carry him by yourself?" Saena said.

"I'm fine," Mayla said, accompanied by a wince. "The meeting house isn't far."

With the two siblings, Mayla and Saena sprinted through the streets and approached the meeting house. Ankarthan activity dwindled to nothing as masses of Entervian soldiers patrolled the road nearby. A sergeant of the Entervian army stood guard in front and waved them inside.

Thick planks of wood, hammered in with crude nails, blocked all windows. Only scant candlelight provided any sort of light and warmth. Vellardian survivors stood back-to-back, and those lying on the floor may as well have been on top of each other. Saena and Mayla stepped carefully to not crush a hand or foot.

They pushed through the crowds of panicked Vellardians, and through overturned chairs and tables. Small rugs and pillows were strewn about to add a tiny bit of comfort to the hardwood floor, but only enough for a handful of survivors.

A middle-aged woman burst through a wall of people, shoving them out of the way, her arms open and face filled with tears. The siblings jumped from Saena and Mayla's arms and met their mother in a long embrace.

"You found them, didn't you?" the mother said, tilting her head toward the two. "I'll repay you with all I have."

Saena's heart, for the first time in days, filled with warmth as she shook her head. "We couldn't take anything from you, especially right now."

"Worry about your children, not rewarding us," Mayla said.

"Bless you both." The mother stood, taking her children by the hands, and again pushed through the crowd.

Saena turned back and noticed Mayla hadn't joined her in walking further into the meeting house. "Mayla?"

Her friend just craned her neck, her lips a straight line. "I'm going back. More people need help."

With a grab on her strong shoulder, Saena forced Mayla to turn around, and she tilted her head up to meet her gaze. "Alone? I won't let you."

Mayla slapped Saena's hand away. "You're not stopping me." She shut her eyes. "I'm sorry. But I need to do my part."

"Then I'll be right there with you," Saena said, and nodded. Though she appeared strong, a crater of fear erupted in her stomach.

All Mayla could do was brush back her now-frizzy blonde locks. "No. You're staying here."

Saena sniffled. She knew she could never follow Mayla into the city streets. The run from her home to here was enough to make her want to sit in the corner for the rest of her days, lest the panic consume her. "Don't do this. You're hurt."

"Come off it," Mayla said, showing a brief smirk. "I'm fine. And, I won't be alone. Entervian soldiers are about as well."

Saena lunged at her friend and wrapped her arms in a tight embrace. "Promise me you'll be careful."

"Of course!" Mayla's words accompanied a pat on the back. Like she was an animal seeing off her owner. "I won't be long. Once I've scoured the area for survivors, I'll return."

And Mayla let go. With a nod, she stepped out into the streets of Vellard, and left Saena alone.

CHAPTER FIFTY-SIX
ICE AMID FLAME

Within Zercien's heart lay the fast-growing sorrow since leaving Ciprius, a feeling of hate, anger, and regret as he approached their beloved home with empty arms. But all dissipated when smoke marred the clear night sky. He spurred his horse forward, into a gallop, Euvard following in tow, the burning stench of flame wafting over the land and into Zercien's nostrils.

Any last shreds of hope dwindled as they approached Vellard's gate. Smoke rose from the tops of watchtowers, beds of fire occupying the roofs, and the clash of steel rang in the distance.

"We're too late," Zercien said as he dismounted. Euvard and Fynnian followed.

Almost immediately upon stepping away, their steeds turned and fled, dashing into the field. Zercien breathed deep as he watched the horses disappear over the hill. Not even the few "allies" they brought home would dare stay. Not that he blamed them.

In silence, Zercien led Euvard and Fynnian to tread the bloodied roads, with flames alight in the darkness. Neither Ankarthan nor Entervian soldiers barred their path, eerie and empty in the night, as dead as the corpses strewn about the streets. Zercien watched as Fynnian trembled while watching the flames, a shake in his step.

"We couldn't stop it," Zercien said as they walked by rubble and ruined homes. "But the enemy isn't here. All is not lost."

Euvard stared into the night sky, its stars hidden beneath a layer of smoke. "Zerc. We need to find Mayla and Saena."

He gulped to assuage his nerves, followed by a nod and a deep breath. Squinting, he saw a figure standing in front of the meeting house.

Is that a Vellardian soldier? Zercien thought and urged his companions to follow him. A familiar face, even.

Approaching the meeting house, a scant few guards and soldiers patrolled and remained on vigil. In front stood Sergeant Kanivar. He removed his helmet as Zercien came into sight.

"Sir Zercien! Our Star Recruit!" he said, his smile beaming. But Zercien only managed a wince.

In a few minutes, you'll wish I was never your Star Recruit, he thought.

"It's been a while, lad," the sergeant continued. "But now you've returned to us!" He craned his neck. "And left the Arigliothan reinforcements outside of the city so they'd not be noticed by the enemy. We can finally retaliate against these Northern monsters!"

Zercien, Euvard, and Fynnian just looked at their feet.

"Sir Zercien?" Sergeant Kanivar said, cocking his head.

Zercien cleared the hard lump clogging his throat. "Ariglioth refused to send aid."

The sergeant stood stunned, staring hard. "I see."

A subdued response. Not what Zercien expected.

"But…there are only three of you here," said Sergeant Kanivar. "Where is Captain Ardian?"

Euvard blurted out, "We don't know."

"We were attacked in Ferronwood Forest and separated. We never found Ardian again," Fynnian added.

"What are we to tell the troops in the field?" The sergeant breathed deep. "What message do you send to King Durnan?"

"The mission failed. Likely doomed from the start," Zercien said. "King Lennard rejected our claims outright with only but a second's worth of consideration. And now he is dead."

"Dead? What in the world happened?"

"King Lennard turned tyrannical, and was killed in his throne room. He declared Martial Law in Ariglioth, and we imagine the capital is in chaos. We fled soon after." Zercien paused, and the sergeant nodded. Another lackluster response, but perhaps he was just tired. Tired of fighting. Tired of failure.

Sergeant Kanivar turned and told another Entervian soldier to relay the message to King Durnan, but Zercien looked down and sighed.

King Durnan needs to know, he thought.

"Wait."

Both the soldier and Sergeant Kanivar snapped to attention.

"Sergeant Kanivar, there is one more item of import. We entered Ariglioth through the Okoro Mountains, and were forced to travel through its caverns. In the depths, we encountered and did battle with Helldregs."

The sergeant gasped, and fidgeted with his fingers, looking like he was trying to hide his fear. "Helldregs? You're certain?"

All Zercien could do was nod.

"I assure you, had King Durnan known of such things," said Sergeant Kanivar, shaking his head with rapid quivers. "Or of King Lennard's tyranny, you would not have been sent on such a... oh, I don't even know what to say to all you've endured—"

"Don't," Euvard said, and waved him off. "It's over now. Nothing we can do."

"Shall I send this information to King Durnan now?" the sergeant said, after a nod.

Heat. Whether it was from the flames scattered about or his own stomach, Zercien wasn't sure. "Yes. This is the extent of our tale. But what has become of Entervia's army?"

"Grandmaster General Urian is overseeing the forces, but with every day, our defenses shrink." The sergeant sighed again, and forced his eyes shut. Zercien caught a glimpse of a tear. "General Burgland fell in combat against the enemy commander."

Zercien put his hands against his cheeks, a pained groan coming through his lips. And a deep chill froze his spine. He'd only known General Burgland for a short time, but he was a mighty warrior, a brilliant leader.

What a waste, he thought, and watched as Euvard too slumped his shoulders and breathed deep.

"The army has taken heavy losses and every reserve soldier is on the field or defending the city's gates, but they still continue the struggle," said Sergeant Kanivar. "Enemy patrols slip past and cause damage to the city at random, but they've been unable to launch a full-scale attack. Though we cannot hold for long. Hope remains, but dwindles with each passing night."

Zercien nodded. The situation was better than he'd thought when they entered the city.

"Sergeant, how about the people?" Euvard said.

"We've scoured the streets for survivors. The ones found, or have escaped, are right behind me, in the meeting house, or in the schoolhouse." The sergeant pointed at the door. "They've received healing, prayer, and whatever nourishment we have left."

The schoolhouse. Zercien hadn't thought of it in so long, and now, he wanted nothing to do with it. The idea of walking through those doors, into a familiar classroom, only brought shame and embarrassment. His place was here now, he was sure of it.

"Father Sarentus still lives, then? What of my brothers?" Fynnian said, interrupting Zercien's thoughts.

"The priest has offered sermons and advice to calm the survivors down, and if your brothers live, then they are inside."

Fynnian sighed. "Oh, thank you, God."

Euvard nudged Zercien on the right shoulder. "Time to go."

With a nod, Zercien said, "Sergeant Kanivar, this is all we have to say. Thank you."

The sergeant placed a gentle hand on Zercien. "To even make it back here alive, you did well, lad. Remember that. We were right to call you our Star Recruit."

With a deep breath, Zercien broke free from the Sergeant's grasp and pushed the meeting house door open.

"Zercien, if you don't mind," Fynnian said, stepping away from him and Euvard, "I need to inform my brothers and Father Sarentus of what's happened. I'll meet you back here?"

"Of course," Zercien said. Though the meek Sanctum Order descendant already made quite the distance between them, stepping around the Vellardians scattered about the floor. For the first time since their arrival, he let a smile through, however short-lived.

At least one of us accomplished something, he thought.

A familiar woman's voice called his name, and soon, its bearer pushed through the crowd.

"Saena!" Zercien could barely let her name escape his lips before she shut him up with her own.

***

Like music, Father Sarentus' sermons always quelled Fynnian's ails. He overheard the old priest speaking to a group of Vellardians, and he gasped upon seeing Dyodore and Jyrren in attendance.

"They're alive," he whispered, clasping his hands. "Thank you, God." When his and Jyrren's gaze's met, his brother returned the gasp, leaping from his seat and grabbing Dyodore by the arm. Fynnian watched as Father Sarentus stopped mid-sermon to look in his direction and smiled.

The four met in the center and embraced. A comfort Fynnian hadn't known in a long while, however fleeting it may be.

"I knew you'd return to us, my son. I knew," said the priest. Was that a tear Fynnian saw, dripping down the stoic old man's cheek? He smiled, but huffed a long breath and, as much as it pained him, broke the embrace.

"I imagine news will travel fast. I may as well tell you now," Fynnian said and lowered his voice as he stared at Jyrren, Dyodore, and then the priest. "We have indeed returned from Ariglioth, but with no aid. Our allies have refused us."

Dejection couldn't hope to describe their faces. Broken, defeat, helplessness were the gazes now meeting Fynnian.

"What will happen to us now?" said Jyrren. Fynnian could only shake his head.

"I speak the truth when I say I've no idea. But please, keep this quiet until a formal announcement is made." With a deep breath, he continued. "However, I bear other news." The faces staring back turned to wonder and awe, with Dyodore's mouth forming an inaudible gulp.

"Dyodore, Jyrren." Fynnian breathed deep. "In the Darutan Dunes, I found him. I found Father."

His brothers, as if forgetting the news Fynnian had just relayed, near cheered in response. They stepped closer to Fynnian, floods of questions erupting from their mouths in both panic and awe.

"Why was he in the desert?" asked Jyrren. "Why isn't he with you?"

"Why did he leave us?" said Dyodore.

Though Fynnian found it odd to see the old priest stand silent. Perhaps he was fatigued.

His brothers' voices swirled about in his mind. All questions he knew he would have to answer, but he shrugged.

Father had his reasons, he thought.

"I learned a great deal from Father. I could not possibly say everything now." Fynnian beckoned Father Sarentus and his brothers to come closer, and whispered what his father had said, of the true nature of the war. He spoke low to ensure no others could listen—if the citizens caught even a word, turmoil would abound. Or so Fynnian thought.

"A knight in black and red armor is an envoy of the world below ours, or as it is also known, Efaltis," he said.

Dyodore and Jyrren's mouths hung agape, too stunned for words.

"I admit, this is the first I've heard of such a thing, but what are we to do?" Father Sarentus said. "To defeat one so powerful, we'd need—"

Fynnian blinked hard and drew his sword an inch out of its sheath, the faint golden light spilling free. "This."

"That sword—" Father Sarentus said.

"The Right Half of the Sanctus Dual Blades," Fynnian said, and pushed it back into its sheath to hide the light. "Father passed it down to me. The light is dim in my hands, but with this sword, I will be immune to the knight's Pariah Arts."

"Fynn," Jyrren said, his stare not wavering from the sword's sheath. "Are you saying you will face this knight?"

Fynnian nodded. "A dearly departed friend taught me swordsmanship. I don't know if I can win, but for the sake of our father, for the Sanctum Order, I will face the one who threatens all we hold dear."

CHAPTER FIFTY-SEVEN
FIRES OF RESISTANCE

Mayla motioned one of her throwing knives forward, aimed for an Ankarthan soldier's throat. She let the knife fly and it twirled through the dark sky, the sharp edges gleaming in the flame's reflection.

A direct shot, piercing the soldier's neck up to the handle. Blood, darkened by the night sky, gushed from the hole, covering the Ankarthan's hand as he clawed for the small blade. As he clasped a hand on the edge, slicing into his palm, his breathing stopped, and he fell to the dead grass.

Mayla nodded and slid down the side of the soot and ash-covered fountain she'd used for cover and nodded at the boy and older man sitting beside.

"It's safe now," she said. "I'm sure there's more hiding back there, though." She tilted her head opposite the direction of the soldier she'd just killed. "Hurry to the meeting house."

"Miss Forde," said the older man as he grabbed the boy by his arm. "Won't you join us? Now that the way is clear?"

She opened her mouth to reply but stopped. She stared out into the night, past two other bodies of Ankarthan soldiers that had fallen to her knives. Her side still ached from the earlier altercation, and the relentless throwing of knives rendered her arm sore. Fantasies of her beloved

Euvard returning filled her mind, and she wished to swap stories while draped in each other's arms, both heroes in their own right. And with two more lives saved, she'd done what she set out to do. Escaping now would be the safest option.

A soft cry, a deafened "help!" echoed across the darkness, and she gasped.

Peeking around the fountain, she saw no Ankarthans, but motioned for the boy and the older man to run. "Go. Now."

"Thank you, Miss Forde. We owe you our lives." The older man grabbed the boy's hand and hurried in the direction of the meeting house.

Mayla stared at their backs until they were consumed by the night, and the scream rang out again. She reached down and felt for another knife and peeked over the top of the fountain.

Faintly illuminated by the crackling flames, two Ankarthan soldiers stood over a young girl, perhaps just over her tenth year. The Ankarthans bore face-covering helmets, leaving nary an inch between their chain-link body armor and necks.

One brandished a jagged sword, and the other, a bent lance, aimed for the young girl's head.

"Your king. Show us to Durnan," their voices were deep, guttural. Like mud and rocks sliding down a mountainside.

Mayla raised a knife, tracing a throwing motion. She knew she'd strike the target from here, but with no clear shot at the neck.

Reaching back under her skirt, she felt for her last knife. Two more knives, two targets. But none she could dispatch from a distance.

"I could throw one as a distraction. Knock the one with the lance on the side of the head," she whispered, thinking of how she'd then force her way in between the soldier with the jagged sword and the girl. "Should allow enough time for her to flee."

Not the safest option, but as the two Ankarthans approached the shivering girl, Mayla ran out of time to plan.

She focused on the soldier wielding the bent lance, squaring her stare on his head, and flung her throwing knife in a perfect, twirling arc.

As it soared through the air, Mayla leapt from behind the fountain, drew her last knife, and charged ahead. Seconds passed between her projectile slamming into the lancer's helmet, and her lowering her shoulder at the swordfighter, pouring the full brunt of her strength and weight into the blow. Mayla fell to the ground with the sword-wielding Ankarthan, a mere foot from the panicking girl.

With a yelp, the child jumped to her feet, her quivering breaths all Mayla could hear.

"Go!" Mayla said, raising a finger in the direction of the meeting house. "Run!" Just as she said the words, the swordfighter elbowed her in the chest, knocking her off of him and onto the grass.

"Move!" Mayla shouted again, and the girl bolted from sight, the pitter-patter of her small feet bounding out of earshot.

Another guttural shout, and the swordfighter's armored face zoomed in front of her. A horrid stench of rotting food filled Mayla's nostrils, and she near-gagged as it wafted from his breath to her nose. The Ankarthan raised his sword over her head, but Mayla was quicker and shoved her throwing knife upward, the sharp tip jabbing through the chain armor. With a grunt and a gasp, the soldier dropped his sword harmlessly, and his dead weight grew heavy atop Mayla's knife.

Black blood oozed from the wound, dripping into dark splotches onto her midsection. Before she could even utter a word in confusion, footsteps of the dazed lance-wielder shuffled along the grass, drawing near. She pulled her knife from the body before tossing the dead Ankarthan to the side, and leapt to her feet just as the other swung his lance.

She fell back, the tip of the lance scraping skin from her forearm. Amid stinging pain, it dripped blood onto the grass. Mayla grit her teeth as the lance-wielder went to swing again.

A dive forward was all she needed, and she wrapped her arms around the Ankarthan's legs. She snarled and pushed, shoving the soldier to the ground. In surprise, he dropped his lance.

Mayla stood over him and delivered a swift kick to his side, though she winced from colliding with the metal armor. A low growl came in response.

"What are you..." she muttered. "No time for questions." She dropped down with her knife, and stabbed the blade into the lancer's chest, twisting and tearing in his flesh to dig deeper.

The groans stopped. Mayla breathed in quick bursts, leaning her arm on the grass and head on the slain soldier's chest, the cool steel of his chainmail a relief to her burning breaths.

Once her breathing normalized, she rolled over and tore a bit of cloth from the hem of her skirt to wrap the wound on her arm. She straightened her legs to stand, but she couldn't shake her gaze away from the slain Ankarthan. Her heart pounded like war drums in her chest as she inched her hand along the soldier's armor, reaching for his helmet.

No sooner did she pull it off was the helmet falling from her grasp and crashing onto the ground. White maggots where its eyes should have been stared back at her, crawling along flesh that took on the fiery shades of orange and red from Vellard's burning buildings.

Mayla gasped and walked back, hands shaking with each deliberate step. And, as if right on top of her, a deep growl crawled into her ear like a worm.

Chapter Fifty-Eight
The Flame Wanes

I'm so glad you're all right," Zercien said in a low breath, still holding his beloved just as tight as when they'd first seen each other again. "If anything had happened, I don't—"

"I've never seen such evil in my life," Saena said, and nuzzled her head on his chest. "It was all so sudden. The guards weren't even close to being prepared. So many died."

"We'll be all right," was what he said, though he didn't believe his words.

Euvard tapped Zercien on the shoulder, and he and Saena ended their embrace. "Not to ruin this moment or anything, but where's Mayla?"

Zercien cleared his throat as a bit of redness crept into his cheeks, and Saena gulped. "Mayla's the reason I'm here right now. She found me, and we ran here together."

"Okay. She *was* here," Euvard said. "Where is she now?"

"We saved two children on the way, and when we arrived…" Saena's voice trailed off, and she hid her mouth behind a closed fist.

Zercien furrowed his brow. "Saena?"

"Mayla left," Saena said with a stutter. "I tried to stop her." She blushed and backed away a step. "She said she wanted to look for more survivors."

Euvard rubbed his hand against his forehead. "When was this?"

"Perhaps an hour or two? Oh, no. I should have forced her to stay."

Euvard turned the other way and stepped back over the evacuees toward the door. "I'm off to find her."

Zercien stopped him with a gentle hand on his massive shoulder. "Not alone, you aren't."

He saw Saena about to speak in protest, but she just allowed a sigh to escape.

"Don't forget me!" Fynnian's voice came from the crowd as he stumbled through.

Euvard smiled. "You don't have to. I swear."

"Saena is here and safe, and my heart is better for it," Zercien said.

"My brothers are with Father Sarentus, and I've told them of my father," Fynnian said. "Euvard, it's your turn to be blessed."

Euvard put a hand on each of his friend's shoulders. "Enough with the dramatics. But thanks. I'm glad, through all this, I still have you two."

And back into the city streets they went, with Saena issuing a final "Be careful!" before Zercien shut the meeting house door behind.

They checked obvious locations first, near Euvard's home, around the general living areas, but to no avail. Remnants of weaponry, ashes, and corpses littered the streets. No signs of Mayla, though absent too were any Ankarthan soldiers.

Coming up to the once green and beautiful city center, Euvard muttered, though Zercien could still hear, "Come on, Mayla…"

From behind the charred fountain, a streak of golden hair in the darkness. Euvard gasped as Mayla appeared, his gaze unflinching, his feet rooted to the scorched earth.

But another figure too arose from behind, shrouded in black. He held a serrated longsword high above Mayla's head.

Euvard shook off his daze and yelled. "Mayla! Behind you!"

Zercien stretched his arm as far as he could reach, but it was too late.

Mayla's body lurched as the sword's tip stuck through her chest. She fell to the ground, atop a bed of dead and flame-scarred white roses. Frozen to his spot, Zercien couldn't move, let alone speak.

Euvard snatched his axe from over his back and leapt at the Ankarthan soldier, driving the bladed edge into his skull. The crushing of bone echoed into the night, blood splattering onto Euvard's face and clothes. He wrenched the axe from the soldier's head and hacked at the dead body with repeated blows, bone fragments and blood surging about the dead grass.

His arms slowed, and he let go; a low thud as his axe dropped to the ground.

Zercien and Fynnian stopped a few feet behind, watching as Euvard bent down on one knee to grab Mayla's bloody hand.

"Mayla." He breathed hard and fast quivering breaths, trying to resist tears. Blood oozed from the ripped skin on her chest. But Mayla's eyes slowly opened, and Euvard managed a smile. "Mayla! You're . . . you're alive!"

Mayla said nothing, and with her free hand, clutched one of the dead roses at her side. Euvard released his grip on her other hand, and she pressed his cheek with a waning warmth. She smiled wide. "You're home safe. I'm so glad. So, so glad."

Her eyes closed, her head drooped to the earth, and her hand fell limp.

Euvard's sporadic breaths came out in gasps, and he shook her lifeless body. "Mayla. Mayla? *Mayla!*"

When nothing came from her lips, he jumped to his feet, shoved his blood-soaked hands into his pocket and brought something small to his face. "No. No!" He threw it at the hard ground, and it bounced and rolled behind him.

Zercien's heart plummeted lower still as he stepped forward and picked up a small, gold ring with what was likely the world's tiniest gemstone on its band.

Without a weapon in hand, Euvard shouted and charged forward, running in the direction of the gate that would lead to the battlefield.

Zercien took off after him and grabbed his towering friend by the right arm. "Fynnian!"

At his words, Fynnian shook his head and followed, taking Euvard's left arm in an attempt to restrain him.

"Let me go!" Euvard shouted, writhing against his friends' grips. "I will kill every fucking one of those goddamn Northerners! Let me go!"

And finally, with a mighty heave, Zercien and Fynnian threw Euvard to the ground, and he fell with less force than a bump. Flinging the both of them off him, he clambered to his knees.

He crawled to Mayla's body, wrapped his arms about her coldness, and the hulking warrior openly wailed into the smoke-filled night.

"Mayla, please. Don't leave me all alone..."

Chapter Fifty-Nine
Cinders

Zercien entered the meeting house with his head down, meeting Saena's gaze, but not matching her smile. Saena's hands quivered, and her words came out in stutters. "What is it?"

His breaths were long and heavy, his eyes red and swollen. "Saena…" The words couldn't even flow. "I'm sorry. Mayla, she—"

Euvard slammed the door open, its wood crashing against the wall, and dragged his feet inside, Mayla's body draped across his arms. Fynnian winced as he gently closed the door behind. Gasps and shouts of nearby Vellardians clogged the air as they made room.

Saena ran to them and looked upon the unmoving body in Euvard's arms, and the frozen eyes of her dear friend stared back. All she could do was back away with shaking steps.

"Mayla? This can't—" she said. She cupped her hands in front of her face, muffling her rapid breaths. "This is some horrible jest. It must be."

"Why did you let her go?" Euvard looked upon Saena as if his puffy eyes were knives. "Why didn't you stop her?"

Saena shivered and backed up, but Euvard mimicked her every footstep until she neared the wall.

Zercien pushed past Saena, standing in between her and his fuming friend who looked every bit the part of a bloodthirsty bear. "Euvard! Enough!"

With one arm, Euvard turned Zercien to the side and pushed him away. He caught himself on the wall.

"Shut the hell up, Zerc!" Euvard yelled. A tear dropped from his chin, and he faced Saena. "If you didn't let her wander off, she wouldn't be dead in my goddamn arms right now."

Saena's lips opened and closed, but nothing save for short gulps escaped.

"You killed her."

She slid against the wall to a crouch, covering her head with her arms to avoid Euvard's fiery gaze. "It's all my fault." Tears rained down from her cheeks to the floor. She jumped to her feet, hands spread over her face, and bolted through the crowd, toward the back.

Zercien shot a glare at his friend. "Euvard. Listen." His words flowed in angered breaths. Only low snarls came in response from the blood-soaked warrior, face splotched with gore down to even his front teeth. A bestial, frightening gaze.

Before Zercien could speak, Fynnian placed a hand on Euvard, and the dull roar quieted.

"I don't mean to tell you how you should grieve, but Mayla needs to be honored in death," he said. "Do this for her, and for you. She'd want you to share one last moment together."

Euvard huffed and averted his gaze from Fynnian, not saying a word.

"Come find me later, please. I'll have Father Sarentus say a prayer for her," Fynnian said to Euvard's back. "Okay?"

Still no response. Fynnian took his hand off Euvard's shoulder and walked away, through the evacuees. Off to see his brothers and priest again, Zercien surmised.

With a gulp, he said, "Euvard, I—"

His friend turned to face the wall. "Go, Zerc."

Zercien thought of staying, to comfort Euvard in his most tragic hour. But then of Saena, whom Euvard had just accused of being responsible. He curled both hands into fists, tightening hard enough for the pressure to spark a flame, or so it felt.

With a breath, he turned his back to Euvard and walked past the curious, horrified onlookers, shaking as if preparing for an imminent brawl. And some of these people perhaps knew of him, even told of his looks. Now they watched as their supposed saviors stood embroiled in conflict among themselves.

If I hadn't been selfish, Zercien thought as the Vellardians made every effort to step out of his way. *Would Holunt have—*

He shuddered.

A muffled cry soon interrupted his thoughts. A fluffed, messy head of black hair leaned against the back wall.

Zercien ran his hand along her arm, and she turned. To an even lower pit than he thought possible went his heart. "Stop. You must not blame yourself."

"How can you say that? You heard him. If I had just forced her to stay, she'd be alive. Mayla would be alive—"

A tap on his shoulder. Startled, Zercien jumped and jerked his head around. A guard in the royal purple Entervian garb stood in front.

"Sir Zercien?"

"What?" he huffed. "Make it quick."

"I apologize, sir, but King Durnan has sent a response to your message."

All he could do was wince. King Durnan now officially knew the mission was a failure.

"Aside from some stragglers, the North is quiet," the guard said. "Our scouts say they may be planning a full-scale assault. His Majesty King Durnan has ordered the army to make one final stand. He wished to deliver this message in person, but due to circumstances, we've forbade him from leaving his quarters."

One last stand, Zercien thought.

"And if that fails?"

"If we are unsuccessful, Entervia will surrender to Ankarth before more civilian casualties mount."

A chill rushed down Zercien's spine. "Ma'am, His Majesty had no response to my news? Have he any new orders for me?"

The guard removed her helmet and rested it against her side. "To rest, sir."

Zercien looked to Saena and raised an eyebrow, then back to the guard.

I shouldn't have expected it to make sense, he thought.

"His Majesty has heard your tale." The guard drew a deep breath. "And is deeply sorry for sending you on such a reckless quest. 'Please, Sir Zercien, sleep away your worries for just one night, and tomorrow we shall live our final moments as Entervians.' Those are King Durnan's exact words."

Zercien shrugged and let out a long sigh. "Understood. Please relay this message to my companions."

"Yes, sir."

And the guard left, deftly maneuvering through the crowd. Saena's tears stopped flowing, and she looked into his eyes, the solemness chilling his body.

"We—I failed, Saena," Zercien said as tears brimmed. "King Durnan placed his trust in me, and I failed."

She said nothing and wrapped her arms around him. "It's not your fault. None of this was."

Zercien brushed her hair back, and let go. He reached for one of the sheets and pillows strewn about the floor, sat down, and motioned for her to join him. He threw the sheet over them both, pulling his beloved close.

Like a hammer to an anvil, his heart thumped. Saena put a finger to his chest, as if she could hear.

It's time, Zercien thought.

"I need to talk to you."

She rustled an inch closer. "I told you before. If it pains you, please—"

"I may never have another chance."

Saena nestled her head against his chest, and their gazes locked. "I'm listening."

"Do you remember those old stories I taught to the noble kids?"

"Of course."

One deep breath. One blink. He exhaled. "What would you say if that was me, in those stories?"

Chapter Sixty
The Hero's Speech

Saena was still lying on Zercien's chest as he awoke the next morning, the slow, light rising and falling of her breaths almost lulling him back into slumber. But against everything he wanted, he squeezed out and spread the sheet over her.

Most of the citizens, too, remained asleep, piled against one another on the hard wood floor. Zercien skulked through the crowd, and to the door, careful not to disturb what little rest they could muster.

Fynnian and Euvard already stood outside, speaking to a handful of soldiers and sergeants. Zercien watched as the royal guards formed up—about one hundred and fifty fully suited for battle, awaiting command. One of the sergeants informed them of the standing army just outside the city. The last one thousand soldiers.

Zercien tapped Euvard on the shoulder.

"What, Zerc?" Euvard said as he turned around, his voice soft and measured.

Zercien rubbed his temple, hoping to force something out that would comfort his friend. Anything to stave off his sorrow for just one day. But all he could muster was, "I'm sorry, Euvard."

"You didn't do anything." Euvard ran a hand through his hair and sighed. "It should be me apologizing."

"I don't want you to. Just know we're all with you. And we need you with us, too." Zercien thought he saw his friend crack a smile, but in a second, his lips flattened.

"Thanks."

The two turned back to join Fynnian and the royal guards and army sergeants.

"Do we know how many we're up against?" Fynnian said. Not a question Zercien expected from the soft-spoken and reserved man.

"The last scouting report estimates four thousand Ankarthan soldiers stationed a few hundred feet from the city gates," said Sergeant Kanivar.

"They'll march right through us." Euvard huffed, and all energy and confidence he once had drained from his voice. "Might as well surrender now and at least escape with our lives."

Zercien clenched his right fist and rubbed his arm with the other hand. "Just lay down and surrender? After all we've been through? I refuse."

"Huh," Euvard said and crossed his arms. "Never thought I'd see the day you wanted a fight, and I didn't. Must be the army training still clinging to you. Would've liked to have that too."

Unsure whether to laugh or not, Zercien just nodded.

"Morale is low," Sergeant Kanivar said. "And not just among the armed forces. The citizens are restless. We have told them to flee."

"Wait!" Zercien said. "We can't. Not yet!"

Without waiting for a response, he ran back into the meeting house, Fynnian's voice following. "Zercien! What are you doing?"

He didn't answer.

Inside, the surviving Vellardians stirred from their slumbers, gathering whatever belongings they could to prepare their exit. Darting his head around, Zercien racked his brain for an idea—and for some reason, that propelled him to find the highest possible point. A large, round table pushed against the east wall.

Am I really about to do this? he thought as he placed a hand atop the smooth wood. But he was, and climbed atop.

"Everyone!" he shouted and waved his arms about like a helpless baby bird. His antics drew wandering eyeballs and raised eyebrows from the common people, including his friends. Zercien's cheeks flushed red as everyone turned, drawn toward him.

It'll be just like your lectures, Zercien thought. He imagined each Vellardian sitting at a student's desk, inkwells and papers scattered about.

"You mustn't leave!" he said. "If you all escape, then the army will have nothing to fight for!"

"Aren't you Zercien?" a shout interrupted him, from a "student" in the back, face awash with a mix of anger and sadness.

"It was your duty to find reinforcements, wasn't it?" came another.

"How can someone who failed tell us about what we should fight for?"

That last one stung.

Zercien's mind raced. *What am I doing? This is*—he couldn't think. Insults flew from all corners of the room, interrupting even the slightest attempt at a coherent thought.

Maybe he was too literal in hoping it would be akin to one of his lectures.

"Everyone, forget what I've done! This is what—" Zercien tried to say, but couldn't raise his voice above the commotion.

"Will you stop this? You're embarrassing us. And yourself."

His cheeks flushed red, and he looked about the room for Saena. If anyone could help him turn this horrific situation around, she was it. He focused on the center of the crowd, spotting Saena standing in a group. Her arms moved about in wild fashion while she spoke, and though her speech was inaudible, Zercien knew she pleaded his case. He smiled when those she spoke to shrugged and remained in their positions.

However, Vellardians standing near the door turned to exit. But the front door came bursting open, two people on the other side—one older woman with white hair, and a younger and scruffy man, but bald.

"I'm gone for a little bit and you're already giving speeches?" said the bald man, and he winked. "What have I missed?"

It can't be, Zercien thought. Jumping from the table, he pushed through the whispering crowd, uncaring of the dirty looks. "Ardian?"

His old comrade smiled and crossed his arms. "Miss me?"

"Where in the world—" Zercien eyed the broad-shouldered older woman beside him. She wore light leather armor, and looked more muscular than he. "Who is this?"

Ardian smiled and pointed to his new companion. "Zercien, meet Aoife. She's from Reland, the Arigliothan town past Ferronwood I told you about. Their militia leader, as luck would have it."

"Militia leader?" Zercien said.

Aoife scowled at Ardian, and accepted Zercien's hand in a firm shake. "*Retired* militia leader." Enunciated loud and clear. "Your friend over here tends to forget that part."

"With that sword?" Ardian laughed. "You don't look retired."

How can he laugh right now? Zercien thought.

Though the large, impressive sword over Aoife's back would require even Euvard to wield it with both hands.

"I called out for you, you know," Ardian said, and Zercien's back shot up as if someone trickled cold water down his shirt.

"I'm sorry," Zercien said. "With the rain, and the arrows, it was just—"

Ardian waved the back of his hand. "Aoife told me about Ciprius, and King Lennard. Even knowing what was likely to befall you, I couldn't join you there." He stopped speaking to wink, as he was wont to do. "Let's say we're even."

With a sigh, Zercien lowered his shoulders. "Then you know why the Arigliothan army isn't here."

The guard captain nodded. "I'm just happy you made it out alive, lad. I half-expected my return to Vellard would be greeted with news of your death."

Zercien turned his gaze to Aoife, switching glances between her and Ardian. "King Lennard is dead. After an altercation in the throne room, Lloyd slew him where he stood. But we then found his body in the dungeon. I imagine the country's rule was under that of an imposter for some time, unbeknownst to the Arigliothans."

Aoife blinked, shaking her head like someone distraught at the news. Not many would mourn the death of a monarch with genuine sadness, but King Lennard seemed to inspire a certain confidence in his people.

A long breath sputtered from Ardian's lips. "A tragedy. But at least you lot escaped."

Zercien craned his neck toward the buildup of murmurs turning to shouts. The Vellardians grew more restless by the minute. How he wanted to tell Ardian every last detail but hadn't the time. Instead, all he could muster was pointing his gaze to the floor, fidgeting his right wrist. Ardian's slight eyebrow raise served as his reply.

"Lloyd sacrificed himself for our escape," Zercien said, met with an even longer, louder stream of noisy breath from the guard captain.

"I won't lie. I thought Lloyd nigh invincible. A goddamn shame." Ardian crossed his arms. "But we have a war to win, don't we?"

His optimism was refreshing, if not a bit tired.

"The Vellardians here are minutes away from evacuation," Zercien said. "And Ariglioth did not send aid—"

"Oh?" Aoife interrupted, and smiled. "Last I checked, the three hundred militia fighters I have stationed right outside Vellard are indeed Arigliothan."

Three hundred soldiers? Zercien thought. Still dwarfed by the opposition, but three hundred Arigliothan warriors could match the prowess of six hundred Entervians. the momentum of the room, the morale of the guards—everything changed when Aoife announced those words. Time stood still, as if waiting for someone to say something, or act.

Zercien thought back to the plains of Ariglioth, to the cloaked man's words.

"I need to accept it," he muttered under his breath. "Accept my true self." Whether the fog entering the room was a trick of his mind or not, despite his deal with the robed man, he wasn't sure. But instead of letting it devour him, he pushed and swatted it away as he ran back to his makeshift stage. He launched a booming voice into the crowd, above the noise.

"Citizens of Entervia! Though not her standing army, we are gifted armed forces from Ariglioth!"

He looked down and saw all eyeballs on him again. None shouted in his face nor protested his speech. A quick debate in his head of whether to turn them all into students again was swiftly ended when he cast any and all remaining doubts away, choosing to see them as they were.

"Even still, this battle before us will not be a sure victory. We should not expect to overcome such overwhelming odds. But we will not just roll over and admit defeat," he said. "We are Entervia! And this battle is for glory!"

He launched a battle-cry into the air and raised his fist high—and his audience returned the favor in cheers.

"After this war's end, no matter the outcome, we will be remembered as those who never surrendered. Songs will be written of our sacrifice, even when all seemed lost. And so, we will take the fight to Ankarth."

Amid more cheers and applause, Zercien took a deep breath. "That is why I now ask of you, my brethren, to stay with us. Do not abandon our country. And if any able-bodied fighters stand before me, I ask you to step forward and lend us your strength."

Zercien looked down and watched as Fynnian made his way to the table. His voice trembled over his loud gulps. "I'm with you."

Where this confidence came from, Zercien hadn't the foggiest. But from the crowd, he watched as Euvard followed, now standing behind Fynnian. Pain still shone through his tired, bloodshot eyes.

"I vowed I wouldn't leave your side. Some friend I'd be if I abandoned you when you really needed me."

"Euvard…" Zercien said, but his friend held out a hand to stop him.

"This is the moment I told Mayla I always wanted." A tear dropped from his right eye. "Let me have this."

A barrage of victorious shouts spouted from each corner of the room, multitudes of Vellardians retrieving old swords, pitchforks—anything sharp or heavy enough to resemble a weapon—from upon the floor or hanging on the walls. They charged outside and joined the ranks of the guards, awaiting orders. Fynnian rushed into the back to ensure his brothers did not take up arms, and insisted they stay with Father Sarentus.

When Zercien jumped from his stage, he found Ardian leaning against a wall, arms crossed, with a wide grin.

"Interesting speech," Ardian said. "A little over-dramatic for my tastes, but not bad for your first real one."

Zercien only remembered bits and pieces of what he said. Everything in his mind, fuzzy. He winced, hoping it didn't come off too strong, or worse, embarrassing.

"It wouldn't have happened if not for you," he said. "We owe you more than our lives, Ardian."

"Knock it off. You had plenty to do with it." Ardian nodded as he stood straight and looked Zercien square in the eye. "Don't tell me you forgot. I'm awaiting your orders, Captain!"

Zercien at last let a smile slip through. "You and Aoife will lead the militia. Euvard, Fynnian, and I will join combat with the main army. Bring the militia around and meet up with us."

"Yes, sir!" Ardian said and saluted, though Zercien couldn't tell if it was sarcastic.

With a nod to Euvard and Fynnian, Zercien pointed outside. But before joining them, he turned back.

Saena lunged at Zercien, pressing her face against his chest. "I don't care how well you spoke, or what words you spewed. I've already lost so much. I can't lose you, too. Promise me you'll come back."

He wanted to. He truly did. But their chance at victory, despite bolstered forces and morale, stayed slim. He wished nothing more than to forget everything and take her hand, and run away from it all. In that moment, he desired nothing but her.

"I can't."

She raised her head up from his chest, a narrowed, furious gaze replacing her solemness. "What? Zercien?"

"We are hopelessly outnumbered." He cleared his throat, struggling to maintain eye contact. "I need you to prepare for the worst."

Huffing, she shoved him hard, out of her face. "How can you be so heartless—"

Zercien gently took Saena by the shoulders and held her in place, despite her wriggling to spring free.

Wiping away the remaining tears from her cheek, he said, "Saena, I need you to promise me something."

"What?" Her writhing stopped.

"Should I not return, take all the time you need to mourn. But when those days pass, I want you to live your life."

She shook her head in rapid twists, as if she didn't believe it. Like this was all some fever dream. Though the past however many months could very well have been, or Zercien felt. He clasped her hands, covering hers with both of his.

"Don't waste more tears on this idiot schoolteacher who accepted some absurd quest." But it was Zercien's turn to sniffle, at last giving way to the sorrow he so desperately tried to stop.

She cupped his cheek in her hand.

"That's not you. Not anymore." Saena smiled through the tears. "Now, go. Go be the hero the stories say you are."

Zercien bent down and placed his hand on the back of her head, bringing her lips to his, and they kissed like they'd never meet again.

CHAPTER SIXTY-ONE
RESOLVE

Late afternoon. No clouds permeated the deep sky. The summer-turning-fall sun was warm on Zercien's back, and his memories, however short, of his brief military stint rushed into his mind.

This time, he would no longer be granted benevolent interference. Though, newfound strength from his supposed treaty coursed Zercien's veins. Energy pulsated within, beating, pounding, drumming. While not direct as he had been accustomed, Holunt would indeed still ride by Zercien's side this day.

In the center of the Entervian standing army, Grandmaster General Urian aided their new recruits and fashioned their armor, ensuring all swords and lances stayed sharp. And right behind Zercien and company were the citizens armed with farming tools and rusty blades.

Maybe asking them to join us was a poor idea, he thought.

"Sir Zercien. Or should I say, our Star Recruit," Grandmaster General Urian said, a smidge of a smile brimming to his chapped lips. "It is a pleasure to meet you, at last. Even in the darkest of hours."

"It's mutual, General," Zercien said as he shook his hand. "How go the preparations?"

A shrug met his question. Not the most confidence-inspiring of gestures the old general could have chosen. "We're as ready as we'll ever be. Once we've merged with the militia, we will lead our final charge." He looked out at the common folks joining his ranks. "And these people have volunteered?"

Despite the fumbling of weapons and wincing with every layer of armor, the citizens remained stalwart in their resolve.

"No talking them out of it now," Zercien said.

The general just stared down at the dirt. "Ordinarily, I wouldn't allow such things. But now, I won't deny them that right."

Euvard was the last to join their circle, and Zercien watched, heart beating with fury, as he and the Grandmaster General fixated their stares upon one another. Both men crossed their arms, flexing.

"General Urian," Euvard said.

"Euvard Girant," Grandmaster General Urian said.

Like two statues, they sat petrified and stoic in their stances. At last, Grandmaster General Urian relaxed his shoulders.

"I know we've an animosity between us, but this one time, I call a truce. Let us not be held down by our foolish emotions. Not today."

Euvard snarled under his breath. Zercien met Euvard's glance, and stared. After a sigh, Euvard let his arms down and held out his right hand.

"Then a truce we will have."

The two shook hands, and Zercien quelled his clanging heart.

From behind came the marching of footsteps, loud and confident, as if they weren't about to parade to their deaths. The Reland militia arrived and merged with the army, and Ardian wandered to the center, Aoife in tow.

"Grandmaster General Urian, it has been some time." Ardian gulped, but followed his greeting with a bow. "I am glad to see you alive and well."

"Aye, and you too, Captain Ardian."

He seemed relieved at the general's words, and then pointed his right index finger at Aoife.

"General, this is Aoife Dílis, leader—pardon me, *former* leader— of the Reland militia. And the reason I'm alive."

"Thank you, Madam Dílis," Grandmaster General Urian said as the two shook hands. "I'm sure you had no obligation, but here you stand."

"Ardian made quite the case." She smiled with her words. "Unlike our imposter king, I'm proud to support our allies in their time of need."

To Zercien's surprise, Aoife didn't retreat. He expected her to return to the meeting house. "Madam Dílis, do you—"

The former militia leader drew her dense steel claymore from over her back, resting its tip on the ground, hilt in hand.

"I don't carry this around for show," Aoife said. "Now, if the situation calls for it, I'll be retreating. I've a wife and daughter to think about. But for now, I'm with you." She nodded, and fell in with the militia.

I see why Ardian took a liking to her, Zercien thought, but too found it incredibly reckless for her to fight, given her family. He said nothing out of hypocrisy's sake, for he risked similar.

But Zercien's thoughts were cut short. Time came to take position.

The main army, militia, and volunteers gathered, placing the veterans and stronger soldiers in the front, scattering the less armed throughout. Grandmaster General Urian, Zercien, Euvard, and Fynnian each took to the front lines, while Ardian and Aoife stood with the militia.

Zercien toward to Fynnian. "If you're more comfortable, stay in the back."

"No." Fynnian let loose a stream of air. "I will not run again."

Zercien scanned the horizon a thousand times over, in every which way, hoping to spot even just a glimpse of the Ankarthan commander. An enemy he remembered in exact detail, and one he expected to face again. To his surprise, Fynnian too craned his neck.

In the distance, a group of Entervian scouts rushed toward the army in a full sprint. "General Urian, Sir!" one shouted. "The Northern army is on the move!"

"Thank you," Grandmaster General Urian said, calm as can be. He drew his longsword from its sheath and held his kite shield at chest-height. "Join whichever rank you see fit."

"Yes, sir."

Zercien took a deep breath and saw as the tiny specks marched where the sky met the earth.

"Here they come," Euvard said, and he took his axe from over his shoulder. "Zerc?"

With a slow, grating and satisfying slip of steel, Zercien's sword was in his hands, and his heartbeat mellowed. His head didn't ache. No fog clouded his mind. For the first time since leaving Vellard, Zercien's psyche was free of turmoil.

"This moment will be mine," he said.

Fynnian pulled the Sanctus from its sheath, the radiating light, however weak it was, still shining, even in these scant few hours of sunlight.

The specks grew in both number and speed. A furious charge, hellbent on destruction. With a shout, Grandmaster General Urian returned the favor, and spun his sword above his head.

Zercien leapt forward at the tip of the general's cry, just in front of Euvard and Fynnian. And in the glare of the waning sunlight, the two armies clashed in the middle.

Zercien noticed some Ankarthan soldiers moving at a speed near-inhuman, their serrated swords gutting through the commoners daring to stand at odds. Many breathed guttural, grunting noises as they swung. A pervading stench whisked across the battlefield. It all seemed familiar.

The forces mixed, and every soldier fended for themselves. The rush of the Ankarthan army pitted two or three of their soldiers to each Entervian, and commenced the slaughter. Zercien looked on with a pit in his stomach as the townspeople and civilians fell, skewered by lances, decapitated by serrated swords.

He watched as one stuck a pitchfork through an Ankarthan's chest, but could not pull the prongs out in time, and fell victim to a battle-axe over the skull, crushing the top of his head and splitting it open. But soon the enemy was upon Zercien, and he could no longer see the last of the civilians.

Ardian and Aoife stood near each other, not letting the enemy jump between. Ardian swung Arrowsbane out in front, knocked an enemy down, and finished it off with a downward stab by Spike. Yanking the bloodied tip out, he swept the metal pole across his body, bashing against an Ankarthan soldier's head.

The old veteran had lost speed, but with low grunts and heavy groans, Aoife swung her sweeping two-hander with might no woman her age should be capable of. She slammed another foe down its spine, ripping through the flesh and exposing its bony insides.

Ardian darted his head behind and nodded, and held out Arrowsbane to block an incoming lance, snapping its metal tip. He jabbed his own lance forward, gutting a helmet-bearing Ankarthan where it stood.

Black blood oozed from its wound, gurgling as the soldier hit the ground.

"Wait. Just like—" Ardian muttered, but had no time to examine the remains before more Ankarthans charged.

Euvard yelled with every massive swing of his battle-axe, shouting Mayla's name. He banged a fist upon his chest, purposely attracting attention. As soon as a new challenger approached, he left them without a head, or with a crushed and bloodied skull. Hosts of Ankarthan soldiers fell with their bodies ripped in two, their blood pouring onto the once-green field. They now surrounded him, but Euvard didn't care.

Taking one by the head, he launched the soldier into another, and landed a punch on one who thought he was open. His axe finished it, severing his opponent's head and leaving it in half.

Zercien was accosted by multiple foes, parrying strikes and waiting for a chance to retaliate. He spotted Euvard jumping into the air and cleaving downward, crushing the back of Zercien's enemy, snapping his spinal cord. But the Ankarthan army seemed to grow in size by the second, and there were far too many for both Zercien and Euvard to handle.

Zercien grunted as the metal side of a shield knocked him to the ground. Euvard's attempts to close distance were fruitless—every step forward he took was met with more opposition.

Not like this, Zercien thought, and raised his blade into the air, parrying sword strokes from his backside. Exhausted, the only action he could muster was rolling to the side, avoiding the enemy's sword strikes. He swept at one Ankarthan's legs and knocked it down, the body landing on top of his back. Using it as a shield, he crawled up to his knees and pushed it off, colliding with another soldier.

"Zerc!" Somehow, his friend's voice carried over the carnage. From his knees, he watched as Euvard lopped off an assailing Ankarthan's head.

"I'm with you," Euvard said quickly as he lashed his hand out to help Zercien to his feet. Though he didn't have time for more than a nod as enemy soldiers rushed them. Far outnumbered as they were, Zercien shoved his back against Euvard's and the two turned in circles.

Over the hills, Zercien caught multitudes of Ankarthan soldiers pouring through, slaughtering any poor Entervians who stood in their path. But a heavy clopping noise entered his ears. Thundering, quaking upon the earth.

He lifted his gaze and turned for only a moment to see a line of horses at his back, bathed in the breaching eventide, bearing a standard with a spiked fist. A mighty rumble accompanied the slamming of lance sauroters upon the hard ground.

It can't be, Zercien thought, but twirled on his feet and stuck his blade deep into the neck of an Ankarthan soldier, twisting and pushing it deep into his foe's flesh to ensure he was not dreaming. His sword broke through the skin. Warm blood oozed onto his hand.

The army Zercien promised to bring had arrived.

Rapid and strong rumbling continued to quake. As the shadows of horseback soldiers galloped into the battle, the enemy ceased their attack.

Arigliothan riders crashed into the side of the Ankarthan force. The man in the lead jumped from his mount and charged, cutting down enemies left and right with a blade. Ankarth soon abandoned the Entervian army to meet their new foe.

"Why? Why now?" Zercien's now-hoarse voice managed to croak.

"I don't understand," Euvard said between heavy breaths.

The two nodded at each other. The Arigliothan army had come, and Zercien no longer thought of glory. His mind screamed only for victory.

With a mighty shout, Zercien led his comrades straight into the fray, splitting the enemy's ranks. The aid of the Arigliothan horseback soldiers allowed them to cut a path right through the middle.

But their offensive came to a screeching halt when a sphere of black energy landed atop a squad of Entervian soldiers, burning their insides and roasting their skin to ash in a pile of cinders upon the field. A burning pain crawled through Zercien's arm, as if underneath his skin, and he stopped his advance. Through the hole they'd cut, he saw him, the knight in black and red armor.

The Ankarthan commander slew everything within a few feet, either by cold steel or black-coated magic. Four Arigliothan horsemen blitzed him with lances, but before they even came within striking distance, a black spear jetted from the sky, piercing through the horses. All fell to the ground, missing legs and heads, crushing the riders beneath their weight.

His voice boomed above the battlefield, a rallying cry for his forces. As if rejuvenated, the Ankarthan army regrouped and charged with renewed vigor.

"Fall back! To the gate!" Zercien heard Grandmaster General Urian's voice over the carnage. He turned tail and fled from the knight, the slow burn of fire leaving his body.

Both the Entervian and Arigliothan armies retreated to the gate of Vellard, chased by thrown spears, and arrows raining from the sky, interspersed by bolts of dark energy vaporizing all who were unfortunate to come in contact with the murderous, visceral storm.

CHAPTER SIXTY-TWO
RADIANCE FADES

Though large in number still, Fynnian's blade distracted those with the serrated swords. As soon as the strange, guttural and pungent foes neared him, they backed away, hands held over their helmeted faces. With a mighty cut, Fynnian burned the closest enemy's flesh as if the Sanctus' steel were alit with flame. Using everything Lloyd taught him, Fynnian stepped, swung, and slashed his way to victory over several foes, even though beset by many. Their fear beset hesitation, and Fynnian burned their mistakes with each slash.

A shadow formed above him, capturing his gaze. With a gasp he stepped back, for the oozing darkness flying over his head was not one created by the night sky, but of magic. Memories of his mother casting her Pariah Arts re-played in his mind, though her conjuring differed.

He shuddered, but plunged the Sanctus forward, into an oncoming enemy soldier. Over his fallen adversary, Fynnian saw him, encased in the black armor with red streaks. A shock sent his body into a tremble as he watched the Ankarthan commander slay all in his path, his blade slicing Entervians in two while his Pariah Arts burned Arigliothans to ashes.

Fynnian ground his teeth hard enough he felt they'd crack. "If I'm to do this, the time is now."

His deep breaths bumped through his throat, and he charged into the enemy ranks, holding his radiant sword high. He stopped once near the Ankarthan commander, and trembled. His dirty and bloody hands gripped the Sanctus until his knuckles turned white.

And he gasped when the enemy commander turned to meet his stare.

In cautious steps, his foe approached, his head angled to face the small light exuding from the Sanctus. Fynnian darted his head side to side at the growing crowd—he stood surrounded by Ankarthan soldiers, each bearing a jagged axe, sword, or lance.

The knight's eerie eyes twitched, and he spoke. "Who are you? How do you wield that sword?"

An inquisitive tone. Not one of malice.

"I am—" Fynnian managed to croak, and looked down. "My name is Fynnian Lovell, a descendant of the Sanctum Order. This sword was passed down to me by my father."

The knight's pupils enlarged, but not with rage. He raised his right hand and commanded all his soldiers to step away, and the crowd dispersed. "Lovell? Is your father Tyrrowan?"

When Fynnian raised his head to meet the Ankarthan commander's stare, he expected to feel the touch of dread and darkness upon his words. But the imposing man in heavy armor emanated no such aura. Instead, a feeling of familiarity.

"How is it you know my father's name?" Fynnian lowered his sword.

The knight stayed silent as Fynnian searched him up and down, from his black eyes to hair, though blonde at the roots. He couldn't stop his head from shaking, his heart from screaming louder than his own voice could, and breathed an exasperated gasp.

If his father wore similar garb, and were of darker hair and eyes, he would be near-indistinguishable from the man who stood before him.

"Why?" Fynnian shook his head. "Why do you resemble my father?"

The Ankarthan commander took one step forward, and held out a hand to signal peace.

"Fynnian. You were not meant to have that blade." His voice was powerful, yet calm. "Listen to me. You must tell me where your father is. Immediately. It is of utmost—"

"Do you take me for a fool?"

The knight's eerie dark pupils widened, and he craned his head in each direction. Fynnian looked on, brow furrowed. It was as if the knight were panicking. "No, Fynnian! The opposite. Take me to Tyrrowan, and this war shall end."

"You would have me trade my father for this country?" Fynnian scoffed. "What sort of sick demand is that?"

"One to ensure the good of the world."

Fynnian stared into his enemy once more. No longer eerie, the black pupils looked upon him with warmth. Like a parent welcoming a child home. Fynnian shook his head back and forth, eschewing whatever feeling burdened him.

"My father told me about you," he snarled. "About your kind. An envoy from Efaltis, seeking to eradicate the Sanctum Order. I would never trust you with anything."

The knight nodded. "Of this, Tyrrowan is correct. Though I was not born in Efaltis. But here, on Dregnal. Fynnian, I repeat, it is you who should not be here, and you should not have that sword."

His father hadn't mentioned this man's birthplace being on the continent he called home.

"What are you saying?" Fynnian said.

"The removal of the Sanctum Order was predestined in an age long ago," said the Ankarthan commander. "It states, when the Order is deemed beyond saving, twins will be born. One, the last Sanctum Knight, and the other, the bringer of their end. And thus, the Sanctum Order would be eradicated."

Fynnian's hold on the Sanctus loosened as he stared into the knight's facial features once more. One flinch, and his sword would fall to the hard ground.

Don't be fooled, he thought, but his words would not listen to his mind, and he spoke in gulps and nerves. "And these twins. They're—"

"Correct." The Ankarthan commander interrupted him with a nod. "Fynnian, my name is Tylsien Lovell. And I am your father's brother."

His words sunk into Fynnian's head like a slowly pushed dagger. Instead of a reply, he only mustered a gulp.

"When I showed signs of Pariah Arts knowledge in my teenage years, your father and I came to blows," the knight said and shook his head, directing his gaze to the dirt. "I made the mistake of assuming him the type to respect his ancestors, and allow the natural order to come to pass. But he fought back. He left me for dead. I imagine your father knew the repercussions of outright killing me, and thus never dealt the finishing blow. Now, he passes that dereliction of duty to his son."

Fynnian spat his reply. "No. How long have you rehearsed this story?"

"Fynnian, I'm—"

"A pact? Twin brothers? Which would make you—*you*—my *uncle*?" He almost laughed at the thought. "Ridiculous. My father never told me any of this, and he *would* have."

Fynnian glared, a fiery anger rising to his throat, speaking before the knight even had a chance. "You're lying. Your words are poison."

"I am not lying, Fynnian!" The knight held his hands in front, as if begging, his speech coated in honeyed exasperation. "My recovery took many years. When I could not locate Tyrrowan, Entervia became our target. Lead me to your father, and we can end this ludicrous war."

Fynnian put his hands over his ears, trying to block the filth pouring into his mind. "Stop. Stop talking!"

"Tyrrowan has sent you here to duel me in his stead, hoping to reverse the Sanctum Order's fated end once more. I'm sorry, Fynnian, but your father is using you."

Fynnian lowered his hands, tightening his grip upon the Sanctus. "I will have no more of your lies, or your nonsense!"

He watched as the Ankarthan commander's shoulders slumped, his lips in a straight line. But the knight unsheathed his long, steel sword. "It seems my brother's deception runs deep."

Fynnian's feet quivered in his boots. But staring down, he gazed into the circling silvers and golds underneath his wrist and stamped out his fear. He brandished the Sanctus. "Pound for pound, muscle for muscle, I've no chance. But for my father, for everyone counting on me…using this sacred blade, I will strike you down."

The knight sighed, and nodded. "Gallantly spoken. At your ready, then, Fynnian."

Fynnian stood in his stance, waiting for the knight to make the first move. At a surprising speed for someone in such heavy armor, the Ankarthan commander dashed ahead and swung down—Fynnian was barely able to parry it, the light of his sword holding strong. He blocked another, but knew the strength of his arm would wane.

In a mush of thoughts, all of Lloyd's teachings came raining down into his mind. Stepping lightly, he avoided the knight's next stroke instead of parrying. Fynnian jumped over a low blow, the soles of his boots not an inch away from the sword's edge. Landing hard, he stumbled a bit, parrying another strike while off-balance. The might of the blow sent him to the ground, and he rolled away to avoid a downward stab. He then unleashed the final technique Lloyd taught him.

Unperfected and clumsy in his hands, he had no other choice. Rushing to the knight, he slashed upward, the crash of the two blades generating a wave of steel sounding. His next strike nailed the knight's sword at the top of the hilt, just missing his hand. The enemy commander jumped back in surprise, but Fynnian attacked, unabated by fear. Letting loose everything he had, he slashed up, down, side to side, all in quick succession. Each slash of faint light met with its opposite of dark steel.

The two blades caught in the middle, and Fynnian forced both hands upon the Sanctus' hilt, pushing with his remaining strength. His dirt and sweat-covered face sat not an inch away from the Sanctus's light, and his screams grew ever-louder.

But his enemy's strength overpowered him. With a shove, Fynnian flew to the side and slammed onto the hard ground once more. Stunned, he saw the knight's charge just in time to repel his attack, but the force of the blow threw the Sanctus from his grasp.

Fynnian rolled and crawled, frantically reaching for his sword, but glimpsed the Ankarthan commander readying a spell. A black orb appeared overhead, taking in the dark red from the dusk's sunset. Climbing to his knees, Fynnian wrapped his bloody fingers around his left wrist, the silver and gold swirling veins radiating underneath.

He screamed as the light enveloped his arm and shot into the sky, forming a pillar of pure white stretching high above the battlefield. Throwing his arm forward, Fynnian launched his Seraph Arts like a spear, eradicating the dark orb and bathing the knight in virtuous light.

Panting, he coughed up blood in spurts upon the ground, and crawled to find his sword.

**

The Ankarthan soldiers closed in on Vellard. Zercien and Euvard, accompanied by many Arigliothans and Entervians, stood side by side in front of the gates, denying all those seeking passage. But in the distance, a flash of light occupied Zercien's gaze, with the enemy commander caught in its blast. Soldiers on both sides held shields and elbows in front of their faces as if a strong sunray burst from the dusk.

Fynn? Zercien thought.

"Euvard!" he called out. "We're moving out to Fynn's location!"

His friend felled an enemy soldier and replied hastily, surrounded by foes blocking his path. "I can't get through. Go without me." His axe found another, splattering blood over his coat.

Zercien nodded, and charged forward, shoving his way through the enemy lines, breaking an opening, and rushed toward his ally.

***

Fynnian stayed on his knees, grasping the Sanctus in both hands, rapid breaths escaping from his mouth. As he stood, the Ankarthan commander came running from his holy prison, his armor scraped and worn, red streaks cracked, his face scarred and bloodied.

It took all of Fynnian's strength to block the knight's forward slash. He grit his teeth, holding tight to the Sanctus' hilt.

"You surprise me, boy," the knight snarled. "But you are Unanointed. Your light is weak."

The two exchanged blows, Fynnian taking steps backward with each swing. The brush of bark and twigs rubbed against his back—a small tree, impeding his retreat. With the enemy commander closing in, he could move no further and awaited the onslaught with his raised sword.

Fynnian ducked out of the way of the knight's stab, the sword lodging in the tree. With the Sanctus poised and ready, Fynnian focused on the knight's chest, the center of his armor, and went to lunge.

But with a mighty heave, the enemy commander pulled his sword and uprooted the tree upon its tip. He swung across his body, and the tree's full force smashed into Fynnian's side, sending him rolling across the field. Fynnian pushed both hands against the ground in a vain attempt to rise, but fell right back to the dirt. Blinking hard, his eyesight blurred, revealing the fuzzy outline of the knight about to stab downward.

Fynnian held his sword out with a shaky grip, struggling to force his eyes open. But nothing happened, save an annoyed grunt from the knight.

Amid distorted vision, Fynnian saw the Ankarthan commander turn on his feet, facing another target. It was then he noticed Zercien launching himself at the knight, his sword scraping across the black armor, managing to topple the fearsome foe. The last thing Fynnian saw before at last reaching for the Sanctus at his side was the knight throwing Zercien off and tumbling over the grass. Fynnian clutched his side and hobbled forward but failed to muster the strength to meet Zercien before the knight could.

***

"I remember you," the Ankarthan commander said as Zercien leapt to his feet and took up his sword. Though he had no interference to aid him, he charged ahead, meeting the knight's strong, rapid sword swings. Their blades glanced off each other, and he met the Ankarthan commander's with a piercing glare. One more strong strike and Zercien launched his enemy's sword away, and it landed with a soft thud upon the dirt.

For the first time, the formidable foe and slayer of so many Entervians was open. Unprotected.

Zercien aimed a stab, but the knight shoved his powerful hand forward, grabbing his forearm mid-lunge. His sword harmlessly fell. Zercien grunted as a steel-coated fist bashed his stomach, and one after another, the knight rained punches into Zercien's midsection.

He raised one hand to soften an incoming blow, but the knight's arm proved stronger, and the steel glanced off Zercien's face. His vision grew hazy and dark. Blood seeped from his smashed lip.

Grabbing the enemy commander's gauntlet with his free hand, Zercien loosened his grip just enough to break free, and threw himself onto the ground.

As he tried to regain his footing, bloody coughs sputtered from his lips. But he could only summon the strength to rise on one knee. Looking up, he saw the knight didn't approach, and his shoulders slumped. His head bobbed up and down, as if he, too, were running low on breath.

Zercien snarled over grit teeth, goading the Ankarthan commander to move, hiding that he himself could not.

With a shout, the knight conjured a black orb over his head, and spoke. "You may have saved the Entervian general's life at my fortress, but you will not escape me again."

Zercien shook himself free of the dazzling white stars as the orb flew from the knight's hand. A burning, splitting pain ruptured through his chest, beating as if occupied by two hearts. The black orb enlarged as it neared his head, now encompassing the full scope of his vision. His veins throbbed with heat, blood bubbling underneath the skin.

And before the orb could collide, it dissipated into the air, as if sand in a windstorm.

Zercien's hands shook as he tried and failed to will his body to move. The spell's energy seeped into his skin, and he convulsed, absorbing its power.

"What's happening to me?" he grunted. This wasn't like the fortress. It wasn't fear. A ripping surge of power erupted in his veins, coming close to popping, to the sweet relief he sought.

From his fingertips sprouted black sparks. One from each finger, they arced forward and singed blades of grass, but faded upon contact.

His mind cried for more. More of this dark energy. He wanted to shout out to the knight, order him to fire another spell. But nothing came. No other spells, no other strength. Just a bubbling pain he so wished to rip free. He could do nothing, held down by the fire beneath his skin.

**

Fynnian grunted, sliding his feet over the grass, kicking up its dead and burnt strands. The knight stood frozen in time, at least to him, now within grasp.

Fynnian screamed. He took the Sanctus in both hands and lunged forward with all the strength remaining in his arms.

The sacred blade stabbed right through the black and red armor, its light-imbued tip marred in blood protruding from the knight's chest.

The Ankarthan commander's arms went limp, and he fell to his knees.

"You have no idea what you've just done," he said. "My brother's cowardice will be our undoing."

And the mighty knight in black and red armor fell, his blood coating the Entervian soil.

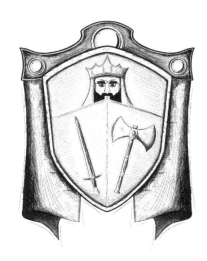

CHAPTER SIXTY-THREE
THE IMMORTAL

All around Zercien and across the battlefield, multitudes of Ankarthan soldiers collapsed and died with their commander. Others retreated and ran north, back to their country. The combined victorious shouts of Entervia and Ariglioth filled the air.

Zercien lent Fynnian his arm. "Fynnian, you—"

All Fynnian could do was breathe. No words flowed. But a smile did brim.

Euvard came into Zercien's line of sight. "Zercien?"

Zercien too ran short on breath, unable to formulate a reply, but stared down at Fynnian's drooping head. "Fynn. Talk to me."

"Fine. I'm fine," came the elongated, tired words from Fynnian's mouth.

"We're both a bit rough at the moment," Zercien said to the silent, staring Euvard. His eyes were glossy, like the adrenaline from battle had worn off and his thoughts commenced their invasion on his mind. Zercien knew the feeling. "But we're okay."

Zercien looked around the battlefield, watching as the remaining Entervian and Arigliothan soldiers stretched out along the grass, too stunned to celebrate. Many still clutched their weapons tight in fear of a ruse, but one that would never come.

"We need to find whoever it was leading the Arigliothan army," Zercien said, and leaned Fynnian's slumped body against Euvard. But through the corner of his eye, he caught a lone soldier in the distance, over a hill. However, too far to clearly see a face. Zercien craned his neck and within a blink, the soldier was gone.

"Zercien?" came Fynnian's weak voice, and he beckoned him to bend down close enough so that Euvard could not hear. "His Pariah Arts did nothing to you. Why?"

Zercien shuddered. "Perhaps your spell weakened him."

No answer. Hopefully a suitable response, and Zercien could stop sweating.

"Ah! There you lot are," a familiar voice called out. One that once made Zercien shudder, now very much welcomed.

Ardian, Spike and Arrowsbane both over his back, waved as he neared. "Been looking for you."

Already? Zercien thought, though he did smile.

"Happy to see you're all right, Ardian." The guard captain's cheeks sported spots of blood and dirt, and a bit of his armor ripped, but seemed healthy. More than Zercien. He could only imagine how disgusting he looked.

"I'll be honest, I wasn't confident in still being upright after so long. But Aoife fights like a soldier half her age." Ardian tipped his head in the other direction. "She's wrangling the surviving militia fighters now."

Zercien couldn't stop his smile. Not that he *assumed* Aoife would die, but someone her age had no place on a battlefield. Or he would have thought, had Ardian's words not convinced him otherwise. Even with his newfound strength, Aoife was not one he'd want to make an enemy of.

Ardian smirked, then turned and waved his hand, as if beckoning someone. "Look who else I found."

Zercien cocked his head to the side, and from behind Ardian stepped the same man who had led Ariglioth's charge, his black garb and hair hardly visible in the darkening sky.

"*Lloyd?*" Zercien almost shouted. Fynnian would have if he were able, and he just looked ahead with his wide-eyed blues.

"What the—how did you—" Zercien tried to spit out words, but nothing made sense.

"If you thought something as little as my actions in the Ciprius throne room would be my end, then you know nothing of my skill," Lloyd said.

An Arigliothan knight approached Lloyd. "Your Majesty, our orders?"

And the four of them sat in stunned silence.

"Remain here. Await further command," Lloyd said, and the knight saluted and jogged away. Zercien scratched his head and opened his mouth, but nothing came out.

"The Arigliothans realized the stupidity of slaying the one responsible for removing their dictator," Lloyd said. "They surrendered without much of a battle."

It sure sounded like a battle, Zercien thought, recalling the shouts and clashing of steel above their heads.

"They then crowned you as king?" Zercien couldn't fathom it at all. How could this emotionless swordsman even come across as kingly?

"We've a shared admiration for battle prowess, and I showed the strength to remove the one they could not," Lloyd said. "Do you wish I had declined?" At the end of those words, Zercien could have sworn a corner of the swordsman's lips curled up.

"We need to call you 'Your Majesty' now, don't we?" Fynnian said.

"Do not dare refer to me as royalty." Lloyd growled, and crossed his arms. "I acted out of necessity. Finding a new home is a nuisance."

An ulterior motive, as always, Zercien thought.

Euvard reached for the sheath on his belt that should have been there, but came up empty. Padding down his clothes, he couldn't find whatever he was looking for.

"Sorry, Lloyd, I had your sword but must've dropped—"

Euvard shut up when Lloyd sheathed his Arigliothan blade and revealed a second on his belt.

"You had my sword in plain sight," the swordsman said. "I retrieved it during the battle. If I were an enemy, you'd be piled among the dead. Your lack of attention to surroundings will one day be your undoing."

Zercien's wince stretched so long it almost turned into a smile. Becoming a ruler of a nation did nil to soften the blow of the swordsman's words. In typical Lloyd dramatics, he turned and began his slow walk back to the city. Zercien shrugged, and urged his companions to follow.

A Vellardian guard awaited their return upon reaching what remained of the gate.

"Sir Zercien! I am relieved you and your allies have survived. But now, please prepare to receive His Majesty, King Durnan."

"King Durnan is *here?*" Zercien rushed to flatten his crazed hair and dust off his armor, flinging dirt and dried blood, but in a moment, King Durnan stood in front of him.

He bent to one knee, but King Durnan waved his hand, and stared. Much like their first encounter, Zercien's cheeks grew red as he felt King Durnan's inquisitive gaze linger, the same heat from the Ankarthan commander's magic rising in his skin.

"I believe I should be bowing to you all instead," said King Durnan.

Zercien's mouth hung wide as he watched his king drop to one knee, albeit for just a moment, and rise to speak again.

"There is no reward great enough to offer you, but you have my eternal thanks. Sir Zercien, for your heroics, I award you with this."

King Durnan took a large key from his pocket, engraved with the letter *E*. As Zercien tilted his head, unimpressed by whatever it was this key signified, he saw Fynnian's eyes at last resume their normal, bright blues.

"An heirloom passed down to me by my father, and his father before him," King Durnan said, and placed the wrought iron key in Zercien's hand. A weighty thing, and cold to the touch. The engraving looked like it came from the ancient world.

"Admittedly, I am not sure what it is used for," King Durnan said. "But it is a cherished Entervian treasure. I give it to you as a symbol. Within our city's walls, you will always be held in the highest regard."

A rush of breath from Fynnian brushed Zercien's arm.

"Your Majesty," Zercien said, "I am unworthy of your generosity." Especially if he knew what in the world this thing was for. He looked down at Fynnian. "But there is one of us who is." Taking the key in his palm, Zercien placed it into Fynnian's hand. A gasp followed.

"Fynnian slew the Ankarthan commander, ending the war," Zercien said. "I believe this relic should be his."

"You would just give this to me for nothing?" Fynnian's excitement seemed to momentarily assuage his pain. Zercien nodded, and Fynnian clutched the key to his chest.

"This is one of the four keys to the World's Tower," Fynnian said. "My father spoke of these, and to hold one, it's—

"While I am not exactly sure what that means," King Durnan interrupted, "I am glad it is in your hands."

"It bears resemblance to the one I also possess," Lloyd said, holding out another iron key with an *A* etched into the tooth.

Fynnian breathed a pained gasp. "How did you—"

"Underneath the Okoro. It sat upon the rubble of the throne room."

"And you didn't say anything?"

"Correct."

Two keys to the World's Tower, Zercien thought, though it brought about a terrible tremble in his heart.

But his thoughts halted when he watched Fynnian's adrenaline wane and Euvard catch him before he landed on the dirt.

King Durnan addressed them all once more. "I loathe and hesitate to do this, but now, I've a subject of great importance. It is why I wished to speak with you all."

Zercien cocked his head. *Of all times, now?* King Durnan was well-intentioned, but his timing left much to be desired.

"Your reports from Duspen and Ariglioth have concerned me about Entervia's standing, not just within Dregnal, but throughout Oniro," King Durnan said. "If even an Arvaros leader has reason to critique our country, then I know we have erred. Entervia will no longer be neutral, and instead aid other nations across the world. Thus, our first order is Telurdia."

Zercien put a hand to his chin. Telurdia. The other continent on Oniro, to the southeast of Dregnal. He knew as much about it as anyone. Which was next to nothing. But the mere mention of the continent set his mind to churn. He'd not heard of anyone willing to make such a journey.

"Queen Kiara, ruler of Telurdia's capital city of Isyonesa, has sent repeated disturbing, cryptic messages for years. I am embarrassed to say, we have ignored each and every one," King Durnan said. "Guards sent to gruesome executions, increased need for basic goods, and civil war. Though not mentioned by name, it seems Queen Kiara has grown more concerned with the behavior of their emperor."

Zercien shrugged and held his hands palms-up.

We've hardly had a chance to rest, and King Durnan decides this is the best time to test our tired heads? he thought.

"I've heard of this emperor. Kandhiran, is it? Blessed with long life, they say he's ruled Telurdia for over one hundred years," Ardian said. "Always thought it was just a story, though."

No story the common people could read, for sure.

"Emperor Kandhiran's tale is as true as you and I," said King Durnan. "I've known of Emperor Kandhiran and his long reign, but Queen Kiara's messages state their emperor struck a deal with a man in dark red robes and conquered Telurdia many years before even I was born."

Zercien froze, his hair sticking up on the back of his neck. The words came in rough spurts. "I wonder why none have attempted regicide."

"All coups have failed. Emperor Kandhiran's defenses seemingly cannot be breached," King Durnan said. His gaze fell to Zercien, and then to each of his allies. "Which is where you all come in. I would task you, my—erm, Sir Zercien, and your comrades to set a course for Telurdia. You are to uncover the mysteries of Queen Kiara's messages."

What felt like burning coals assailed Zercien's feet, and he jumped back. But no matter where he stepped, he stamped upon flame. "We are to travel to Telurdia, Your Majesty? It seems abrupt—"

"Queen Kiara's messages tell me the situation in Telurdia worsens by the day," King Durnan interrupted. "The matter is urgent."

Because of how long you ignored them for, Zercien thought but didn't dare say.

Instead, he felt his allies' stares fall upon him, save for Lloyd. Even Fynnian's head popped up.

Again, a rush of heat washed over Zercien, almost forcing him to say yes. Much like the original message, he could not bring himself to decline anything from King Durnan, though Saena would be far more cross.

"Your Majesty, if my allies agree, we shall set a course for Telurdia," he said.

"I'm with you," Fynnian coughed up. "If I am to aid my father in his quest, I cannot sit idle once more."

Zercien darted his gaze to Euvard, who stood still. He slouched and averted Zercien's gaze.

"Sorry," Euvard said, and sighed. "I'm coming. I have nothing left here."

"I will join you as well," Lloyd said.

"Do you not have your duties as a monarch to attend to?" Zercien said.

"Before marching to Vellard, I appointed a council to assume the affairs of the city in my absence. I will inform them of this departure, and they shall continue until my return."

Wanting to speak, Zercien hung his mouth open, but couldn't find the words. What Lloyd had just said seemed all too reasonable and, dare he say, intelligent. Not something he expected this fearsome swordsman to do.

King Durnan raised his right hand, index finger in the air. He furrowed his brow and moved his mouth to try and find the words Zercien failed to. "Pardon?" were what came out. "Sir Lloyd?"

Zercien shook his head. "Your Majesty, Lloyd has been crowned as the next king of Ariglioth."

King Durnan's face contorted into—something. Horror? Surprise? Shock? A mix of all three? Whatever it was, it wasn't an expression Zercien would soon forget.

"Well, Your Majesty, I will not turn your aid away," King Durnan said. "Though we owe Ariglioth much—"

"Do not refer to me as royalty." A low growl accompanied Lloyd's interruption. Even King Durnan shuddered at his voice.

"Regardless, it seems the matter is settled—"

"Well, not quite, my king!" Ardian said. "Your Majesty, I also request to follow Zercien."

"Then consider your request accepted, Captain. You five shall embark to Telurdia in two weeks. Please understand that I cannot send more soldiers."

Ardian smacked Zercien on the shoulder, a beaming smile spread across his face. Zercien couldn't help but return it. As much as he'd improved as a leader, Ardian's company brought a sense of security he sorely missed.

"And what of Aoife?" Zercien asked.

"I requested Madam Dílis to remain here in Vellard to help with the reconstruction efforts, and allow her access to a room inside the castle," King Durnan said. "We will escort her family from Reland when able."

The retired militia leader was to be rewarded with a vacation inside a castle, likely with guards and servants waiting on her at all hours, bringing whatever manner of wine and cheese she desired.

And I get to visit fucking Telurdia, Zercien thought.

"She proved a great ally," he said to Ardian. "You were lucky to meet her."

"Aye, I was," Ardian stretched his arms high, letting loose a satisfying *crack* from his back. "But, I'm rightfully tired now, aren't you all? Especially of talking—no offense meant, Your Majesty."

"Mhm." Was Euvard's grunt in response. "And I think Fynn's hurting bad over here."

"It looks worse than it is. Really," Fynnian said. He let go of Euvard and walked on his own, holding his side to try and hide his painful wincing. "See? It's nothing. Once I see Father Sarentus, I will be ready to embark again."

With a smile, Fynnian continued his walk down the street, toward the meeting house.

"Thank you, gentlemen," King Durnan said. "I shall return to the castle. The Ruling Council and I must discuss our rebuild. I hope the future bears more tales of your heroism."

Zercien watched as retainers went to lead King Durnan back to the castle, but the king's gaze lingered upon him. Though only for a second, and the king forced his head in the other direction. Zercien's stare followed, but was interrupted by Euvard's heavy sigh.

"I should head home too," Euvard said.

The thought of no one being there to greet him sent Zercien's stomach into a tailspin. He placed a comforting hand atop his friend's strong shoulder, though a bit flimsier than usual. "You're more than welcome to stay with Saena and I."

"I need to be alone."

A frank response, unlike any Zercien had heard from him before. "I understand. Is it all right if I visit later?"

"I'd like that."

Ardian raised an eyebrow as Euvard began his slow, trudging walk home. "Not the reaction I expected from him after winning a war."

All Zercien could do was let air loose from the corner of his pursed lips. "Mayla was killed by an Ankarthan soldier."

Ardian lowered his head and breathed deep. "Ach, that's awful. From the way he spoke of her, she truly was a shining gem."

It was then Zercien noticed just he and Ardian remained. Lloyd, the swordsman-turned-king, must have crept away without a sound. Still as slippery as ever, despite the extra regalia.

An odd feeling, standing alone with Ardian. His presence at this moment twisted his stomach into knots.

"I believe that's our cue to—" but Zercien was interrupted by the all-too-familiar grab of Ardian's hand on his forearm.

"You saw it too, did you not?" His voice was almost a whisper, but drove a chill into Zercien's side all the same. "The Ankarthan soldiers. Something wasn't right."

The black blood. The armor covering all inches of their bodies. Their inhuman speed and fighting force. It could only have meant one thing.

"They were Helldregs, weren't they?" The words tasted of ash as they left Zercien's lips.

Ardian nodded. "I can think of no other option. The soldiers here are blaming it on the adrenaline. The black blood is just how it looked to them in the height of their panic. You know how superstitious soldiers can be. But me? I can't shake it."

Zercien, unfortunately, agreed—the beasts had a familiar air. One he could easily distinguish.

"Not much we can do about it now," he said. "But we should rest. The time will fly before we—" he groaned as another heavy hand fell on his shoulder.

"Just one last item," Ardian said, and, of course, winked. "I swear."

Zercien groaned. As was his typical response.

"Leading us to Ariglioth, giving those speeches, you've some aptitude for all of this," Ardian said. "Even in the beginning, when I stuck you with the leadership stick, you never complained."

Zercien's cheeks flushed red. "I did what was asked of me."

"That isn't the problem."

Pulling away from Ardian's grip, Zercien crossed his arms. "Out with it, then."

"I saw you run after the knight."

And there they were, the hairs on Zercien's neck, standing on end. *Shit*, he thought. The last person he wanted as a witness. "And?"

"I saw the black orb he conjured." Ardian stuck a finger into the air, and then tapped it on his chin. "Unless I need to brush up on my studies, that magic was Pariah. And, well…you came out unscathed. Much like the first time you faced the Ankarthan commander. Or so I was told."

"Pure luck, I'm sure." Zercien's stutter returned. "The knight was struck by Fynnian's Seraph Arts. Perhaps he was weakened—"

Ardian put a finger up to shush Zercien. "I'm not so sure about that, friend. Even if he *was* weakened, a spot of magic just up and disappearing?" He held his hands at the height of his shoulders, palms out. "Doesn't make sense."

"Coincidence, is all."

Ardian scratched at his cheek. "The Seven Legends' weapons protected them from Pariah Arts. As does the sword Fynnian holds. But you knew that already. And we both know Holunt was naturally immune."

The flush in Zercien's cheeks gave way to ghostly white.

His thoughts flashed to the townspeople all running up to him, asking for his time. A barrage of onlookers besetting his and Saena's home.

In no world did he believe Ardian to keep this quiet.

Sorry, friend. Not yet, Zercien thought, and shrugged.

"I charged in recklessly, and was lucky to survive. That is all."

"Still not budging? Well, it's no matter." Ardian backed away, hands still raised. "Now that we're off to unknown lands again, I'm quite relieved to have someone as *'lucky'* as you with us, my friend."

CHAPTER SIXTY-FOUR
THE PROMISE

Two weeks passed in a heartbeat. On his walks through the streets hand-in-hand with Saena, he saw Vellard wasted no time in beginning its rebuild.

Farmers and gardeners already took to the fields, planting vegetables and flowers. Other common people, who had either fled the city or remained in the meeting house, joined in to help whenever possible. The Entervian army, the Reland militia—everyone who joined in combat—received explicit orders from King Durnan to rest and heal their wounds. Which meant Zercien could do nothing to help, though Saena didn't mind him at last staying home for an extended time. Choosing to spend his days with Saena, he made no effort to visit the schoolhouse, nor did he send any notes or messages.

As for Ariglioth's soldiers, Lloyd sent half home with a detailed letter stating his departure but ordered the rest to remain in Vellard on a temporary basis, to act as guards during the reconstruction. Though with the Arvaros in check, such an occurrence was low.

Zercien and Saena now stood in front of the mess that was Euvard's home. It had survived the war, but their friend had done nothing to clear the debris from his grass.

"It's best for me to not speak to him right now," Saena said, looking down at her feet. "I still can't believe Mayla's gone."

Zercien reluctantly agreed with a nod. He hadn't the words to describe the feeling. While he was beyond happy to have his beloved to return to, a pang in his gut reminded him that not everyone could be so lucky.

"I'll be quick. I have doubts he'll allow me to linger," Zercien said, turning to face Euvard's front door. He ran his hand along a wooden practice sword on the ground, and picked it up. "Go on home without me."

Saena nodded, and after a quick peck on the cheek, turned and resumed her walk back home.

With three taps and a sigh, Zercien drummed on the wooden door. It was unlike him to wait this long for an answer, but eventually, the handle stirred and opened, albeit slow and steady.

Euvard stood on the other side with a bloodshot gaze. "Oh. What can I do for you?"

Somehow, Euvard's demeaner was worse than he'd imagined. The fearless warrior he'd trained with and fought beside in so many battles still stood in front of him, but now slouching and powerless.

"I thought we could take some time to spar before we leave tomorrow." Zercien waved the wooden practice sword like a toy.

A small smile emerged on his friend's face but faded as quick as it appeared. "Honestly, I just don't feel like it."

Damn it, Zercien thought, and then said, "You're certain?"

Euvard nodded. "I don't want company right now. But I'll see you tomorrow at the port, all right? And when we're there, I'd like to speak with Saena."

Curious, Zercien thought. Even at the service held for all the lives lost, Euvard never looked Saena's way. Ever since the war's end, he'd hardly seen his friend, let alone speak to him.

"Of course," Zercien said. "But if you need something, just come by, okay?"

"Thanks."

Zercien thrust his hands in his pockets and turned to leave.

"Before you go. One last thing," Euvard said.

"What is it?" Zercien's ears perked as he faced his friend again.

"Have you asked Saena to marry you yet?"

Zercien shrugged and relaxed his shoulders. "With us being pulled away on another mission, with what's happened to you, I just cannot—"

Euvard grabbed Zercien by the shoulders, but in a gentle hold. "Listen. If this Telurdia business is as dangerous as King Durnan says, we might not come back. And if I've learned anything from all this, our time's too precious to waste."

"Euvard—"

"I waited too long to ask Mayla to be my wife. I don't want to see what happened to me happen to you."

Zercien didn't have time to reply before the door shut in his face, and he heard the faint *creak* of a latch locking tight.

CHAPTER SIXTY-FIVE
TO FARAWAY LANDS

H
ave you told anyone else?" Saena asked. Zercien jumped and looked from side to side to ensure no one was within earshot. As the two walked through what was just a battlefield two weeks prior, it didn't look the part. The dead had been buried, and stray weapons and barricades either destroyed or moved.

"No," Zercien said. "But Ardian may have guessed."

"You need to be honest with them."

"I don't want anyone to think of me differently because of my...*u-nique* heritage."

"I think anyone would be delighted to hear of a shared ancestry with the great Seven Legends!"

Zercien stopped and lowered his hands, palms-down, repeating the motion to tell Saena to quiet her voice.

"Yes, but," he whispered, "It's not like I'm *just* a descendant."

They came upon the Port of Entervia. While not officially re-opened, King Durnan made special arrangements for a vessel to carry Zercien and his company. Under the guise of a trade ship, though Zercien wasn't sure of the difference. According to Queen Kiara's notes, only ships of imported goods were allowed into Isyonesa's port, and all others, turned away.

A few battered ships floated off the dock, but otherwise, everything seemed in order. Euvard stood next to the ship, and as soon as he looked in their direction, Saena hid behind Zercien, refusing to move.

"Please just talk to him," Zercien said.

"Will he just yell again?" Saena said, and crossed her arms.

"I promise he won't."

She huffed. *"Fine."*

Looking up, Zercien saw Fynnian and Ardian already on board, moving some supplies. He stared at Fynnian, watching as the Sanctum Order descendant lifted tools, wood, and other boxes, and walked about like he'd never been wounded.

How in the world? Zercien thought, but brushed it off as he approached Euvard. His friend picked at his fingernails and ran his hands through his hair that he hadn't bothered to cut.

"Zercien," he said. His nerves somehow made Zercien more nervous.

"Are you ready?" Zercien said, though Euvard's nerves were near-palpable. Saena appeared at Zercien's side, and Euvard averted his gaze.

"As much as I'll ever be," he said.

Zercien looked at both him and Saena. "I'll leave you two to talk."

He grabbed the handles of the ladder ahead, and climbed aboard their ship. The deck stretched far, and three masts jetted high into the cloudless sky. Far larger than he anticipated. Each sail bore the proud Entervian Coat of Arms, stretching to every corner. A bit comically large, Zercien thought. Next to the sword was the same signature he'd spotted on all the paintings in Castle Vellard.

He peeked through the door leading underneath the deck, following the descending stairs to two long benches, each seat occupied by a strong-looking rower. Except one. The rowers chatted among themselves, pointing to the empty spot, but Zercien paid it no mind. Perhaps one of the rowers ran late. He shrugged. Something he related to.

"How big of a ship do we need, though?" Zercien muttered to himself. The whole thing just seemed excessive. But knowing his country, he wasn't surprised.

***

Euvard gulped and tried to still his wavering voice. "Saena."

He saw she looked just as nervous, her voice too, shaking.

"Yes?" She stared at him a moment and turned her head when he didn't answer.

"I'm sorry," Euvard finally said, and let a rush of air through his nose. "I take back all those awful things I said. I don't know what I'm thinking half the time, and what I'm saying, even less. Can you forgive me?"

Saena exhaled. "Of course. I just—how can she be gone? It feels almost unnatural for her to not be here right now."

"She was my world. My everything." Euvard sniffled. "But it wasn't your fault, okay? It never was."

Tears formed in Saena's eyes in response. "But—"

"It was mine."

"What? Euvard!"

"If I were faster, stronger, if I'd gotten there sooner, she'd be here, standing next to you, seeing me off." Euvard's stare turned to the sky. "But I wasn't. I wasn't strong enough to save her. Because of me, she's buried in that goddamn hole behind the church."

Saena grabbed his arm, though the numbness throughout his body prevented any reaction. "No! There was nothing you could have done."

Euvard said nothing for some seconds. The silence felt like hours.

"Thanks for forgiving me." He held a finger up, as if he forgot something, and dug into his pocket. And from it, a pair of throwing knives. Tiny in his massive hands, but blood-stained and sharp. "I went back to where I found her. These were near her body, hidden in the grass."

Saena covered her mouth to conceal her gasp, but her gaze gave away all she knew. "Her knives."

Euvard's lips curled ever-so-slightly into a smile, but just for a moment. "I guessed you would know about them."

After a long breath, Saena spoke. "Mayla always kept a handful of throwing knives on her person."

He laughed, startling Saena into taking a step back.

"I should've known she'd try something like this," Euvard said. "Seems like she was more than willing to tell you, though."

"Only recently. She taught me how to defend myself," said Saena. "I owe her my life." A tear slipped from her eye onto her cheek.

"Was she good?" Euvard looked from the knives and back to Saena.

She smiled through a bunching of tears. "Could hit a target from anywhere."

Euvard sniffled and brought a finger to wipe his eye. "Of course she could." He gestured, waving her on with one hand. "Hold your hands out for me."

Though she tilted her head and raised an eyebrow, Saena obliged. She gulped as the warm knife handles fell from Euvard's hand into both of hers.

"I want you to have them," he said.

"Shouldn't you—"

"Don't need them where I'm going. Besides, you were her apprentice. The only one who knew her secret, too. They're rightfully yours."

Saena shut her eyes, and nodded once. "I'll cherish them."

Euvard nodded, but then turned around to face their ship. The sea breeze wafted through his hair, and he stared into the blue sky. "I'm going aboard. I'll send Zercien down, okay?"

"Euvard…" she whispered. Saena reached forward and put a hand on his back, near his shoulder. He stopped and turned his head, staring into Saena, but said nothing.

Once he moved, Saena's hand fell, and he climbed onto the ship without looking back.

"I'm done," Euvard said once he found Zercien. "You brought the ring, right?"

"I did, but—"

Euvard cocked his head and gave his friend a side-eye. "It doesn't matter what happened to me, all right? This is your life, not mine. You should be happy, no matter how I feel."

Zercien sighed, but smiled when Euvard at last put on his usual grin, if only for a moment.

"Thank you," Zercien said. "It's time, then."

Euvard nodded and blinked a tear away. "Good man." He choked on his words. "You both deserve it."

***

As Zercien descended the ladder, he saw Lloyd entering the port. It set his mind at ease, knowing he was their ally from the start. Lloyd didn't make eye contact as he passed Zercien and climbed the ladder aboard with little effort.

Zercien just chuckled to himself, and approached Saena. The two clasped both hands together.

"You're already leaving," she said. "And you've just returned. *Again*."

Zercien sighed. "King Durnan trusts me."

"Well, I'll wait for you to come back. For a *third* time."

Looking into her blue eyes, Zercien noticed they weren't watery, nor on the verge of tears. It was almost instinct to raise a finger to wipe them, but this time, he had nothing to clean.

"I told you, Zercien. I told you I wouldn't cry," she said as if she'd just read his mind, though he could see her fighting the tearful urge. Zercien smiled, took a deep breath and bent to one knee.

"What are you—" Saena began to say.

"Saena," Zercien said and cleared his throat. "When this mission is all over, when all that is wrong with the world has come to a close, I want to be with you. Forever."

Zercien reached his left hand into his coat pocket and took out a white-banded ring with a modest diamond in the center. "When I return, Saena, will you do me the honor of being my wife?"

She put both hands to her mouth. "Zercien. Yes, a thousand times, yes!"

He slipped the ring over her finger, rose to his feet, and they kissed, each feeling the other's warm smile. He heard Ardian let out a "whoop!" and tried to suppress his laughter.

"I will cherish it," Saena said, staring down at the ring on her finger.

"If I should not return, keep the ring as a memento to never forget me," Zercien said, and tapped her hand with one finger.

"Stop speaking in dramatics, will you?"

Zercien smiled. Too much time spent around his band of personalities, he wagered. "His Majesty couldn't give us a timeline. I may be gone for much longer than I was before. Will you wait for me?"

She shrugged. "Eh. I suppose."

The two shared an obnoxious and loud laugh together, and one last kiss.

With a final goodbye, Zercien turned and climbed the ladder, the steady breeze of Entervia's midsummer flowing through his hair. His companions—save Lloyd—swarmed him.

"Well, look at you. A soon-to-be married man," Ardian said, and a beaming smile spread across his face.

"Congratulations!" Fynnian said. "Father Sarentus officiants weddings, if you—"

"I'm happy for you both," Euvard said, accompanied by a nod. "Really."

For once, Zercien welcomed their stares. "Are we ready to depart?"

"The rowers are waiting below the deck," Ardian said. "As soon as you give the order, we move out."

"I admit, I'm nervous. I've never been on the ocean," Fynnian said. "It's magical, almost."

"Mhm," Euvard said.

They all looked at Lloyd, and he groaned. "Yes."

Making his way toward the prow, Zercien stood and looked over the edge, into the deep blues of the sea. The strong breeze flew into the sails, and the seabirds sang above.

"Ah, wait! Master Zercien!" A voice from below, accompanied by a rush of footsteps upon the port's wooden dock. Zercien turned just as a moderately-muscular young man with light auburn hair and brown skin climbed aboard their ship, using only one hand. The other gripped a long pole forming a thin, oval-shape at the top, the whole thing cloaked in a black cloth. To Zercien, it looked distinctly oar-shaped, whatever it was called. Though it did seem to bulge in the back.

The young man breathed heavy and fast, as if he'd sprinted the entire way. "I apologize, milord. I overslept."

"And who would you be?" Zercien said, crossing his arms and staring this newcomer up and down. Though he couldn't help but crack a light smile.

Can't say I don't sympathize, he thought.

The young man's face bore some light scratches, hands rough and calloused.

"My name is," he said and caught his breath, "Gilcrest, milord."

A light beige tunic with loose and baggy trousers covered his body, similar to the attire of the rowers from below. He wore a traveling coat on top, buttoned up to his chest.

Zercien raised his index finger and nodded, remembering the empty seat. "You must be the last rower. There's a space for you belowdecks."

Gilcrest bowed. "Yes, milord."

"We are about ready to depart. I shall escort you downstairs."

"Thank you, sir!" Another bow.

Zercien nodded to his companions as he led the new rower below, and asked him to sit on the empty spot at the end of the back-left bench. The others greeted Gilcrest by name.

When he was settled in, Zercien breathed deep, gave the order to prepare for departure, and marched upstairs.

"At your ready, crew," he called down to them.

"Aye!" came their uniform responses. And Zercien was gone, back above the deck.

Gilcrest darted his head about, releasing his held breath when he realized none of the other rowers looked upon him, and Zercien was nowhere in eyeshot. With a snide smile stretching across his face, he laid his covered oar onto the floor and unraveled its black wrapping. A hint of gold shimmered behind the wood.

He licked his lips, and from his coat, withdrew a vial of blood.

And they sailed on, floating among the dark waters and into a world few had traveled and even fewer had ever seen, carried by the waves of time and currents only felt in dreams.

THANK YOU FOR READING

Thank you for reading *Fogbound* by N.J. Alexander.

Reader feedback is always valued, and honest reviews help every indie author succeed. Leaving a review on Amazon and/or Goodreads is appreciated. Thank you for your support.

ACKNOWLEDGEMENTS

To someone unfamiliar with the process, writing a book seems a solitary task. While much of it may be so, it truly does take a community to actually *finish*!

I would be remiss to not first mention my incredible family and friend support group, whom all have put up with me disappearing for days on end to finish my drafts. First, to Mom, for sitting with me as we combed through every synonym known to humankind to help me title this book, and for the Writing Fuel in the form of Greek pastries. To Dad, who listened to me gush about whatever nonsensical writing related topic I felt like chatting about on that particular day, usually while attempting to make my thirteen year old car last another year. Thank you to my brother, Greg, for brainstorming potential pen names when I was struggling *hard*.

And of course, to Grace, my amazing girlfriend. Not only are you my rock and inspiration, but you're always there to pull my head out of the fog (not unlike our friend Zerc). The one who willingly listened to me read thoughtful comments from my beta readers and encouraged me to carry on when progress seemed impossible. Whenever I took a break from an hours-long writing or editing session, I would rush to my phone, knowing a message from you would be waiting for me. Thank you for being you.

A huge thank you to my incredible beta readers, and those who provided feedback on my first ever draft so many years ago: James, Robert, and Alex. Thank you to my proofreader, Scout, for wading through my egregious em-dash usage. You somehow turned my ramblings into something resembling sense. To finish the job, thank you to Kari for the wonderful interior formatting.

This book is better because of all your feedback, edits, and comments. You're all rockstars, and I would not have crossed this finish line without you.

Thank you to all the wonderful artists I commissioned. Firstly to Félix, for the breathtaking cover illustration, and to Fay for the incredible cover design. To Stephen, who created the first ever art for my characters. I won't lie, I teared up a bit seeing my characters come to life. That feeling is not so easily topped. And Dewi, for the incredible map and chapter headings. To this day, I have no idea how you created such a stunning map that was true to my vision based on the horrific sketch I sent!

Lastly (and certainly the most unexpected), thank you to all the incredible people I've met in the various online writing communities. I had no idea such a thing existed, and you've all made my writing adventure all the more palatable. Not only did I find friends, but beta readers, proofreaders, editors, and artists. If you're part of this community and had a hand in the creation of this book, then you can count this section as a double thank you!

To everyone: You have all been an integral part of my journey, and the reason I can write this line. Zerc's story exists because of you, and for that I will always be grateful.

Thank you.

About the Author

Tom Briere Photography

N.J. ALEXANDER is a writer with a business degree. When not writing, he enjoys reading, playing video games, recording podcasts, watching sports, and adventuring for new food. He is from Massachusetts, USA. *Fogbound* is his debut novel.

For book updates, social media, contact links, and bad jokes, check out: www.njalexander.com.

Printed in the USA
CPSIA information can be obtained
at www.ICGtesting.com
JSHW020059171023
50082JS00005B/3